Three Twins
at the
Crater School

Three Twins at the Crater School

Chaz Brenchley

WIZARD'S TOWER

Wizard's Tower Press

Trowbridge, England

Three Twins at the Crater School
A Crater School Novel

Text © 2021 by Chaz Brenchley
Cover art & design by Ben Baldwin
School badge designed by Elizabeth Leggett
Editing by Shannon Page
Book design by Cheryl Morgan

First published in Great Britain
by Wizard's Tower Press, May 2021

Paperback ISBN: 978-1-913892-10-4

http://wizardstowerpress.com/
http://www.chazbrenchley.co.uk/

Contents

CHAZ BRENCHLEY

Dedicated with the greatest respect and admiration
to the memory of Elinor M Brent-Dyer,
onlie begetter of the Chalet School,
from which all comforts flow.

Praise for the Crater School Series

"What a brilliant wheeze, to transplant a girls' school story to a steampunk Martian colony. Chaz Brenchley performs a pitch-perfect quantum shift that's full of plums. If you're a fan of Brent-Dyer or Brazil or Blyton, you will love Three Twins at the Crater School."

Val McDermid

"All the earnest charm of a British boarding school story, plus aliens! I wish I were a Crater School girl."

Marie Brennan

"Three Twins at the Crater School is splendidly full of peril and charm. It calls forth very particular memories of books and mountain schools and the adventures of teenage girls."

Gillian Polack

"In a past that isn't ours, in a world of aether ships and an Eternal Empress, the Crater School embodies all the values, passions, high jinks and adventures of the classic girl school stories of the first half of the twentieth century. For every fan of The Chalet School, Malory Towers, Dimsie or the Abbey Girls, this is a guiltless pleasure."

Farah Mendlesohn

"Who would have thought an English boarding school story and a science fiction adventure mashup would work so spectacularly? This is a one-sitting page-turner!"

Sherwood Smith

"The British Empire has met its match in Chaz Brenchley's Mars. Mysterious aquatic aliens have transported humans to the Red Planet by means unexplained, and the Brits, willingly taking on the colonizing of this new world, establish themselves well. The Crater School brings to mind the rigidity of Aubrey Upjohn's Malvern House, the rowdiness of Stalky's Coll, and the resourcefulness and sheer heart of St. Trinian's. Brenchley had me at 'British girls' school on Mars'."

Jennifer Stevenson

"If Angela Brazil and Edgar Rice Burroughs had decided to write a story together, Three Twins at the Crater School might have been the delightful result. Friendship, family ties—good and bad—and schoolgirl shenanigans set against the backdrop of a Mars straight out of early science fiction makes for exciting and yet cozy reading. I was especially intrigued by the hints of alternate history—the deathless Queen Victoria, a Great War fought between Britain and Czarist Russia—there's much to explore here, and I sincerely hope there will be further instalments."

Marissa Doyle

"In this inventive combination, Brenchley offers readers an entertaining opportunity to revisit the school stories and planetary romances of days gone by. Along the way, he interrogates the assumptions and attitudes of those books and their era with charming ruthlessness. Highly recommended."

Juliet E. McKenna

"A rollicking good read from start to finish! Move over, Enid Blyton, there are new girls at school—they fight monsters!"

Ellen Klages

"Twins we will never forget and cool Mars creatures."

Miranda and Talia, age 9

CHAPTER ONE

Two Red Heads and a Black One

"**Y**es, I thought I might find you two up here."

The voice was like a cold hand on the back of their necks, positively *pulling* them away from the battlements. They shared one swift anxious glance between them, then turned around guiltily to see the aweful figure of the Head Girl herself standing at the turret door.

Instinctively, both girls looked down. The flat roof of the castle was slabbed with the same red sandstone that made its walls; their feet shuffled forward almost of their own accord, until they met the mortared crack between one flagstone and its neighbour. Miscreants summoned to the headmistress's study "toed the line" on one particular floorboard to hear their fate, and the same habit had trickled down through the school to become an absolute tradition whenever sinners faced Authority.

These two would almost rather have faced a mistress, even the Head herself, than Rowany de Vere. Tall and stately and self-possessed, she had a way of merely looking at you that could make younger girls burst into tears without a word being said, and had been known to reduce even Seniors to spluttering incoherence. Tawney and Tasha were certainly too old for tears, being thoroughly mature Middles comfortably ensconced as leaders of the Lower Fourth, but even so: the dreadful quality of that silence had them folding their fingers together into intricate knots, staring at their shoes, breathlessly waiting for doom to be pronounced.

"And why, pray tell, should I expect to find you here?"

That was mean, putting it as a question. Scolds could be endured, but questions had to be answered. She would only wait now until one of them spoke, while that silence grew thicker and weightier with every passing moment.

"Um, because we come here often?" Tasha was always the bolder of the twins, first into the breach.

"Indeed. Despite—?"

"Despite it being against the rules." Wherever Tasha led, Tawney was safe to hurtle after.

"Despite *its* being against the rules; 'being' is a gerund. You should know that by now. But however pleasant it is to wander in a garden of bright grammar, let us not distract our minds from the greater issue. As you so rightly observe, Tatiana, coming onto the roof without a prefect or mistress is *strictly* against the rules, for reasons that would surely be obvious even if I hadn't caught you dangling out over the wall like a pair of hanging baskets."

The novelty of that comparison almost cracked both twins at once. Seeing how their faces contorted, Rowany herself let the hint of a smile show through her sternness. Tasha immediately tried to seize advantage: "Please, though, 'tisn't term yet. Miss Leven said that rules were, were, were in aboyance until tomorrow..."

"Abeyance, Natasha, not 'aboyance'—and *some* rules is what Miss Leven said. Do you really suppose she meant to include those rules set in place to protect little girls from the perils of their own idiocy?"

Neither twin liked to be addressed by her full name; which meant of course that they only heard them when they were in trouble, which of course made them like the names even less. And no girl in the history of three planets has ever liked to be called "little" when she has attained the fine age of fourteen; and furthermore, that was another of those unfair, resented questions. Tasha ground the toe of her shoe into the mortar, and muttered, "No, Rowany."

"No. Quite so. You really must stop cantering up here whenever the fancy grips you. And never, never let me catch you hanging out through the embrasures—wait a minute, though. What does that face mean, Tawney?"

"Please, I don't know that word," and a strange word was like a thorn in her foot, only to be drawn out by enquiry.

"Embrasure? All right. Turn around and look at the battlements. Try not to hurl yourselves through them," added dryly. "Now. The gaps between the teeth? Those are the embrasures. And the teeth themselves are not in fact teeth, but merlons. That's another new word for you, Tawney. Now face me again, please." She surveyed them once more; and sighed, and shook her head at two such sorry specimens of humanity, and said, "I ought properly to report you to the Head—but I think perhaps one of the rules currently in abeyance is the one that says I have to do everything properly and by the book. So—unless you'd rather toe the line in Miss Leven's study? No, I thought not—rather than risking your lives unsupervised on the roof, you can amuse yourselves for the next week or two by boning up on the history and architecture of castles, with examples drawn from our very own and beloved example. Work on it together; Tawney, your handwriting is at least legible, and I happen to know that Tasha can turn in a pretty map when she's a mind to do it. You can take a clean notebook from the stationery cupboard, and do your best to fill it before half-term. Understood?"

The twins' older brother Robbie had told them how more than once, he'd begged to be caned at school rather than gated. For the first time, they thought perhaps they could understand that. One swift punishment was surely better than a dreary task dragged out over half a term. Tragically, though, there was no caning at the Crater School. For a moment, they might have trembled on the verge of asking to be sent to the headmistress instead—but only for a moment. Then, as one, they nodded and said, "Yes, Rowany."

"Good. So tell me then, what was so entirely fascinating down in the courtyard that it was worth risking life and limb to see it?"

"Two red heads and a black one," irrepressible Tasha blurted.

Rowany raised an eyebrow; Tawney interpreted. "We think they must be the new girls. Miss Leven said at breakfast that she was expecting three to come today. They're in the courtyard now with Miss Harribeth, and we think she's giving them her famous tour of the castle."

"Perhaps you should hurry down to join them," Rowany suggested. "It'd give you a flying start for your new project; there's nothing Miss Harribeth doesn't know about this place." Then, suddenly relenting, "No, that wasn't fair. I won't tease. Though seriously, if you have any questions or find anything you don't understand, she's the person to go to. Meanwhile, what's so interesting about new girls? Apart from their sheer newness?"

"Two red heads," Tasha repeated. "They must be sisters, mustn't they? Red's such an unusual colour, you wouldn't get two at random coming at the same time. Especially such an unusual time, Trinity, the last term of the school year. But— oh, if they're sisters, d'you think they might be twins? They might, mightn't they?"

"Ah—now I understand. Well, I suppose they might. And they might even be the reason I was sent to find you. I'm afraid you have to go to the study after all, my children; but not as penitents, unless you choose to confess. Miss Leven wants to see the pair of you. You can't go like that, though, or she'll have you toeing the line before you can catch your breath. Run down to the San and tidy up first. Tawney, you'll need to change your tunic, you've ripped that seam right open wriggling about on the stonework. And Tasha, you have black lichen on both your knees. Better wash that off before it festers. Go on, scoot."

Ten minutes later, two hastily scrubbed, brushed and tidied schoolgirls knocked at their headmistress's door. They entered when bidden, bobbed the little curtsey that was a treasured inheritance from their sister foundation back on Earth, and chorused, "Good afternoon, Miss Leven."

"Good afternoon, girls. Come and sit, please." She gestured towards the cushioned window-seat beside her desk. That meant they really weren't in trouble; Rowany's reassurances had been almost enough, but not quite.

Of course, sitting with their backs to the window also meant that their gazes couldn't stray to the distractions of the view: the deep and mysterious lake, the crater walls, the wide and tawny sky. It was even possible—Tasha had been heard to allow, once—that Miss Leven sat them there deliberately and for precisely that reason, when she wanted to speak seriously on a matter.

Without the grim and foreboding desk between them, and with no shameful reason to duck their heads and glower at the floorboards, they could focus more readily than usual on Miss Leven herself: the steel-grey hair that she wore cropped uncommonly short, the tweed costume with just a touch of lace at wrists and neck, the grey-green eyes that were kinder than her stiff appearance might suggest.

"Well, girls, how has your holiday been?"

Not much of a holiday was the answer that their friends might have looked for, but their headmistress obviously could not receive. In any case it wasn't true, although it had been what they'd feared, what they'd anticipated, when Mother's letter told them they must stay at school over Easter, while she and Father made an urgent trip Home. Some trouble that Robbie was in at Westminster, that could only be settled by his parents in person. Of course there was no question of the twins going too; journeys by aethership were prohibitively expensive, when you lived on a government salary with no family money behind you. Besides, they couldn't hope to get there and back again during the holiday, and the parents were oddly keen on their not missing a day of school if they could help it. To be fair, so were the twins, mostly.

They had resigned themselves accordingly to three weeks in an empty school with resentful teachers watching over them, but it hadn't been like that at all. There were a dozen girls who stayed, because of illness at home or families gone back to Earth or—in Rowany's case—extra tuition for her Oxford entrance; and the staff who stayed with them—Miss Leven included, and none of them obviously resentful—had contrived to give everyone a jollier time than they could remember, in school or out of it. They'd had parties, games, unexpected challenges, expeditions all around. The solemnities of Easter had been duly marked and made a deeper impression than before, perhaps because they had been set about with such fun. Three weeks had flown by, and the twins were almost—almost!—sorry that this interlude must end tomorrow, when the rest of the school returned.

It was a hard thing to say, to the adult most responsible. They did their best, though, tripping over each other's broken sentences as they struggled to convince her that they weren't being merely mannerly, they really had enjoyed themselves thoroughly. At last she laughed aloud, clapped her hands to her ears and cried, "Enough, twins, enough! I don't quite think that 'splendacious' is a word within the meaning of the act, so I'll ask you not to use that again, please, but the meaning is clear and delightful to hear. I may also say on behalf of the staff and myself that it has been a pleasure to share our Easter with you, and I will be writing to your mother to say so.

"But now," she went on, abruptly solemn, "I have something to ask of you, Tasha, Tawney. I know you have a double-score of friends here, in your own house and others, in your own year and others; and I know that even so, you are much inclined to keep your own company when it matters, that you two are all in all to each other. That is inevitable; it must always be 'two against the world' to some degree, for twins. But this term I'd like to see you make a special effort to let a third in, if you will.

"Of course I can't oblige you to make friends, let alone to share your private times and special places"—oh glory, did she know about the roof? She seemed to know everything else—"but you may be the only ones here who can truly help this girl. She's a twin, you see, and only you two can really know what that means, deep inside. But Rachel is here without her other half, she's a twin alone. I think particularly that only a twin can understand that especial sorrow. I was afraid a little that seeing you two together would only exacerbate her trouble, but in fact I am in hopes that you can comfort her, in ways that we singletons would never conceive."

They had been apart, of course: on separate trips with one parent or the other, and once for a cruel, eternal month when Tawney took the mumps and Tasha didn't, the only thing they'd never thought to share. They gazed at each other now, reliving that time, that sense of loss; and then

Tasha—of course Tasha!—asked, "Please, Miss Leven—how did she come to lose her twin?" It was their worst nightmare, the impossible fancy; they were holding hands tightly on the window-seat now, struggling not to imagine it.

"Oh—heavens, child, the girl's not dead! Don't be so morbid! Their parents have simply decided the girls will be better apart for a while." Something in Miss Leven's face suggested that she didn't agree, but she was certainly not going to say so. "Rachel's your age and will be coming into your form, and I'm putting her in your house and your dormitory too, so she'd be around you all day in any case. Please, girls, will you take her under your wing? This term is going to be difficult for her, and I do believe that you two are her best chance to see it through."

"Of course we will, Miss Leven!" Sometimes one twin spoke for both, sometimes the other. Sometimes they were never quite certain afterwards which had done so, or if they'd both solemnly chanted together in some spooky lights-out ghost story kind of way.

"Bless you, girls. I never had a doubt, of course; a Crater School girl will always step up at need, and you two are Cratereans through and through. Now," with a quick glance at her wristwatch, "if you hurry, you should catch them up in the library, where Miss Harribeth likes to close her tour. Tell her you are sent to steal Rachel away; you can show her the rest of the school yourselves. What you think to show her—and to tell her—might be less instructive, but perhaps more practical. And nutritious. Miss Harribeth would never think of including the kitchens in her tour; whereas I happen to know that Mrs Bailey is baking honey cakes this afternoon, and those are always best straight out of the oven.

"Rachel very much needs the company of her own kind just now. Don't just talk at her, girls, talk with her; listen to her; don't let her button up her feelings. A stiff upper lip is all very well, but only for public display. You girls are better

17

than that. Take her into your hearts, show her the true heart of the Crater School, and you will have done all that I could hope or ask of you."

Dismissed, encouraged, they bobbed their curtsey and went to the door; and as they left she said, "Oh, and don't take her onto the roof without a prefect in attendance. Ask Rowany."

CHAPTER TWO

New Beginnings

"To a historian's eye, of course, it's really not a castle at all. It's a mockery. You can't even call it pastiche; it's sheer trumpery. A layman's notion of what a castle ought to look like, with the double burden of being designed as a hotel, by a man who had no more notion of the hotel trade than he did of Norman architecture."

Miss Harribeth was short and stocky, forthright and ruthlessly dismissive. Even so, Levity thought she loved this place, however determined she might be to disparage it. *Methinks the lady doth protest too much.* She glanced at her sister, to try if she could express that with a grimace. They were used to sharing everything out loud and immediately, and this notion of public manners was a trial. Mamma had pleaded with them not to blurt, and not to whisper confidences unless they were properly alone; they had promised, and they really were trying.

So far, Miss Harribeth's tour of the school had shown them the Great Courtyard and the Divided Stairs—"girls on the eastward branch, always; prefects, staff and visitors to the west"—with a detour through the dining hall so that they could see the glories of the little private chapel beyond, with its high arched roof and vivid stained glass depicting St Francis with the animals, including sandcats and other denizens of Mars. Merlins too, in all their forms, nymph and naiad and imago. Levity had challenged any suggestion that merlins should be counted among the animals; Miss Harribeth allowed that there was some doubt about it, but said it was a matter of theology or areology or both, and she was a mere historian.

Now they were in a corridor of stone and dark timber, with windowed doorways on either side offering glimpses of blackboards and desks in neat rows, long tables with stools set around, other rooms whose purpose was harder to guess.

Levity's two companions on the tour were her sister Charm, younger by a mere fifteen months, and a dark sullen girl named Rachel. *She* wasn't going to speak at all if she could help it, and Charm was tongue-tied by the effort not to babble sixteen to the dozen in her sister's accustomed ear; which meant that all the burden of conversation fell on Levity. No Buchanan has ever been shy, and she and her sister both were well accustomed to adult company, and even so. She'd never had much to do—had never had anything, indeed, to do—with schoolteachers in all her fourteen years, and she wasn't quite sure where to begin.

It was rude to question grown-ups, but she'd been doing it all her life. How else was she supposed to learn, except by asking questions? Still, she'd learned sometimes to frame them another way. She gazed around at the bare walls hung with noticeboards and prints in frames, the floor with its stones rubbed worn beneath coarse rush matting, and said, "It's hard to picture this as a hotel."

Miss Harribeth snorted. "It barely was one, for a season or two, no more; and that more than seventy years ago. There may be no one alive now who remembers it. The man was either a fool or else fifty years ahead of his time, which may amount to the same thing. He thought the lake here would draw people from all over, and so it does: holidaymakers, sportsmen and women, the sick and the frail, all sorts. Now, it does. But he thought they would come as soon as the district was opened up. He paid to install the funicular and started building up here on the rim when the Queen Empress was still new to her throne, sure that by the time the castle was ready, guests would be lining up at the door. That was plain foolishness. We'd been on Mars for two generations, no more; we were still building a country, still struggling with the land and the creatures, still learning to navigate the seasons here. No one had time for leisure, however much they needed it. He was a wealthy man, but he broke himself trying to build his paradise in our sweet air. He built it, and nobody came.

"He tried to sell out, but who would buy a hotel with no trade? Authority leased it for a time and found it impractical as a focus for local government, hard to reach, inconvenient for everybody. The Army tried it as a training base, and again found that the disadvantages outweighed the gains. So then it stood empty, except for occasional field trips from universities back Home, coming to study the naiad in the lake and develop our understanding of bubbletalk. Miss Tolchard came, as a student from Oxford. Twenty years later, when it was quite decided what she would do, she remembered the great forlorn castle she'd camped at in her youth, and knew where she wanted to establish her school.

"It had served as a hospital during the war, but fell empty again after, when the Sanatorium went up across the water. The lake and the air and the views were drawing hikers and families and visitors from all across Charter territory and further yet. Tour companies from Earth were starting to add this region to their itineraries. If Miss Tolchard had been five years later, who can say but that the castle might not have been a hotel again? Certainly the opportunity was there.

"But the girls of Mars needed schooling, and Miss Tolchard came to an agreement with the owner, and the Crater School has been here ever since. We've put up new buildings, of course, as the school expanded, but all our classrooms are here in the castle; and the dining room you've seen, and the chapel too. The turrets are reserved for staff bedrooms and studies. And here, now: here is the library."

A high Gothic door set in a carved stone arch closed off the corridor. Miss Harribeth flung it open and stepped inside, giving them just a moment to peer into a gloom pierced by slanted beams of vivid colour, where the sun struck down through more stained glass. Then she swept her hand down across a bank of electric switches, and many lights blazed out at once.

"Oh!"

Even the scowling Rachel couldn't bite back her cry of delight. Before them stretched a book-lover's paradise indeed. Desks stood in alcoves, tables stretched down the middle of the long, long room—and every wall, every alcove was shelved with dark oak, and every shelf was tight with books, from old worn leather bindings to bright modern paper jackets. Levity was content merely to stand and look, to take in the glory of the tall windows, the high beamed ceiling, the spiral staircase that wound up to an ironwork gallery and yet more shelving, yet more books. Charm, she knew, would ache to bury herself in the fiction section, seeking out the school stories she loved so much. Levity preferred to read history, and especially the history of the British Empire on Mars, the great men—yes, and women too—who had founded the colony and built an abiding presence here over a century and a half; but she had their mother's eye for colour and design, and for now, it was enough to look.

Miss Harribeth was beaming at her side. "It is impressive, girls, is it not? For once, this isn't down to our adapting the original building to the needs of a school; this was always intended for a library. What sort of visitors he thought it might draw, I cannot say. What kind of man he was, I think his own house tells us. Visionary, romantic, extravagant, capricious, all of those; and engaged, resolute, hopeful, those too. A man of parts. He achieved a great thing here, though he personally never found success with it. Everything we have made ourselves, from Miss Tolchard's original vision to our realisation of it, this school as it stands now, everything has its foundation in his work. He didn't know that we were coming, or that we should be so grateful—but he knew that he built for the ages, and however much I want to deprecate the artificiality of his castle, I find that in honesty I cannot. We are grateful, and with cause—and more than that, I think I should have liked him, had we only had the chance to meet."

Just then there came the patter of urgent feet behind them, in the corridor. Levity glanced around to see two girls about her own age, leggy and blonde and stunningly alike. For a moment she thought it was only the uniforms they wore—a deep forest-green gym tunic beneath a blazer with gold piping, smart and striking both at once—and the long straight ponytails in which they wore their hair. A second look told her she was wrong, though. Everything about them was identical, from the slight snub of their noses to the cool misty blue of their eyes. Even their stances, as they stood side by side and put their hands politely behind their backs and lifted their eyes to the mistress.

"Please, Miss Harribeth"—did they decide beforehand which one would speak, or did it happen by instinct?—"Miss Leven sent us to collect Rachel, if you've finished with her."

"Thank you, girls. Tasha, is it?"

"Tawney, Miss Harribeth."

"Tawney, I do beg your pardon. I still say we should try colour-coding: a thread of blue or red in your lapel, like the ribbon of the *Légion d'Honneur*—discreet and telling. Though I suppose you might swap blazers, and then we'd never be sure."

The other girl smiled, with a glimmer of wickedness. "Miss Leven can always tell. So can Rowany."

"Miss Leven is wise in her generation, as Rowany in hers. Those of us with less wisdom must get by with asking, and trust you to be honest. As we do. Very well, girls: you may take Rachel now. Levity and Charm"—the twins' eyes bugged suddenly at the sound of their names, and Levity felt her sister's hand nudge hers, *See? Told you!*—"find a book each and sit quietly, till someone comes for you. Remember this is a library, please, so no talking."

Neither needed telling twice. Charm made a predictable beeline for the novels; Levity was happy simply to browse the nearest shelf. She was half tempted to watch the other girls depart, partly for the fascination of twins and partly just to see Rachel's demeanour, if she were as sulky in the company of schoolgirls as she was with a grown-up.

They were still very much on their best behaviour, though, she and Charm both, and Mamma always told them not to stare. To look, yes, and to see clearly, to consider what they saw; but staring was unmannerly. "New girls need to tread lightly," Mamma had said. "It's going to be a big change for both of you, I know, but first impressions matter at school almost more than anywhere else. Don't gabble, don't yell, and don't stare."

So she focused on the faded leather bindings on the shelf closest at hand, and found that this was the Geography section—or Areography, rather, books about the lands and waters of Mars. *Cassini, the Crater City*—but Cassini was far from here, and Levity had read that already, when they spent a winter living there. *The Peaks and Canyons of Tharsis*—but the book had no pictures and no maps, and what was the use of a book about Tharsis without a picture of Olympus Mons to dream over, and a map with contour-lines to show how high it stood, and how deep the Mariner Valley?

Our Martian Canals and the Ships We Sail There was a better book, richly illustrated. Again, though, she had read it before, that time they had spent on a steam-liner cruising back and forth between Marsport and New Victoria while Mamma filled sketchbook after sketchbook. And besides, it was shockingly out of date. Of course there were still sailcraft on the canals, and many of them; but the Age of Steam had dawned in the last century, and that book took no account of it at all. Which was just silly.

Ooh now, this was better: *The History of Lowell Lake, from the Charter to the Great War's End.* She'd only need to walk outside to see the landscape it described; the Crater School stood on the very margin of Lowell Lake, looking out across its dark waters. And better yet, the book was only a few years old; the school itself might even be mentioned in its pages!

Levity perched on the nearest chair, opened the book—and found a sheet-map glued inside the back cover, folded tight to fit. That was best of all. She laid the book flat on the table and spread the map out to its fullest extent. She barely noticed when her younger sister came to sit beside her. By then Levity was kneeling on her chair and stretched on her elbows across the table, utterly absorbed, poring over the map's every detail with her nose just an inch above the paper.

"Careful, kid. You'll do yourself a mischief."

The voice was warm and gurgling with laughter, and it came with two firm hands attached. Which was just as well, for Levity startled and tried to twist her head to see who had come at the same time as trying to slide back into her chair like a civilised human being. She failed at both. The tabletop was polished to the slipperiness of ice; she lost all balance as her elbow slipped, and her jerking legs sent the chair skidding away across the equally well-polished floor.

"Whoops! Who knew I was going in for a prophetess?"

Those welcome hands caught Levity with a grip like iron springs as she squawked, as she flailed, as she felt herself about to fall awkwardly between table and chair. Charm gasped, but there was no need; the dark stranger took her weight easily, set her lightly on her feet, held her until she was steady and then released her with a nod.

"You'll do. But for the love of Michael and all his saints, don't treat the furniture hereabouts as a climbing-frame. Old Mr Felton loves his polish-can, and he gives everything a special rub-up for the start of term. Treat all the woodwork like glass for a week or two, I should. And don't ever let him catch you deliberately sliding on it, for there's nothing he hates more and he's a tongue like one of his own rasps. Now, stand there and let me look at you. You too, girlie. And don't look so scared, your sister's not hurt. Are you?"

Levity shook her head stoutly, though in fact the sudden fall and equally sudden rescue had set all her body atremble.

"No, I thought not. Just shaken up. A slip like that can rattle your brains entirely. Believe me, I know. My name's Melanie Fitzwalter; I'm Games pree, and head of Stokes House for my sins. Which must have been greater than I knew, because I appear to have been landed with both you babes at once. Come along with me now, and I'll show you the house and your dorms and so forth. Levity—you're Levity, the elder, yes?—you're in Herschel, and Charm's in Cavendish. And of course I shan't ask, I *can't* ask, because manners are important here, you'll learn that if you learn nothing else in all your days as Cratereans—but if you chose to tell me how you came by those names, I can guarantee that I'd be interested."

"Oh, that's simple." Apparently the shock of seeing her sister fall had driven all promises of discretion out of Charm's scatterbrained head. "We're both redheads, you see," which was possibly the most redundant statement ever uttered aloud by a girl with blazing ginger curls in the company of her copper-topped sister, "and Mamma doesn't believe at all in old wives' tales about bad temper going with red hair, but she does believe in sympathetic magic and the power of names. She says she named us after light-hearted virtues so that we'd grow up cheerful and contented, in defiance of society's expectations. She thinks too many people provoking us in hopes of a temper-tantrum could push us over the edge and prove the rumours true; and she thinks our names help us to push back against it. But please"—and now that she wasn't quoting their mother she sounded like herself again, young and uncertain and slipping a cool slim hand into Levity's for the comfort of her sister's grip—"can't we be in the same dormitory? We haven't ever been apart, we've always shared a room together, and..."

"Sorry, girlie, can't be done. You're going into Lower Third, which is firmly Junior territory; your sister's in Lower Fourth, which is Middles through and through. Can't have Juniors and Middles in the same dorm. You'll have different bedtimes, for one thing. Don't worry, though, there'll be plenty of chances to see each other; that's why you've been put in the same house, I expect. Family is important to us, here at the Crater School. Well, it has to be, when so many of our girls have relatives in the Sanatorium across the water. But at the same time you'll need to make friends in your own crowd. If we do our jobs right, you'll want to. The Juniors are a happy crew, by and large—and if you don't find them welcoming, I'll be asking the reason why. Has either of you been in school before?"

"No, we never have." Levity fielded that question, to give her sister a chance to catch her breath and possibly bite her tongue. "Nor had a governess, either. Mamma's always moved around so much, and always wanted to keep us with her; she says there's more than one road to an education, and it doesn't always mean sitting in a classroom reciting multiplication tables and Latin declensions."

"Well, she's quite right, as far as that goes—but on the other hand, multiplication tables and Latin declensions are both of them quite handy if you want to make your way in the world, and reciting them in class with your friends is a neat way to swallow them down."

She was walking as she talked; they followed her perforce, to a corner of the library where three stone steps led down to a shadowed doorway.

"This is the back way in; we use this more often than the front door. It's a short dash from here to Stokes, or any of the other houses. Just don't let anyone catch you treating the library as a shortcut through to your classrooms; that's frowned on. Same rule for chapel, of course. That has a back door too, just the other side of the arch here, but you don't ever use it for access to the dining hall or the rest of the school."

She held the door open and ushered them through. They came out at the back of the castle; it rose behind and above them, solid and timeless, a high red wall. On their left, an archway led back to the courtyard they had already admired. Beyond the arch, as Melanie had said, the tall stained glass of the chapel made a pair with the library's own.

Here there was no moat to bridge, as there was at the front. The rear of the castle was paved rather than defended, presumably to make it easier for supply-wagons and steamtrucks to come and go, for deliverymen and kitchen staff to fetch and carry in and out. Beyond the paving stood a line of stables, apparently empty now. Melanie turned to walk them briskly past the run of open stable doors, past the tack-room and the muck-heap and the gardeners' sheds.

"We do keep half a dozen ponies, but they're all down below for the holidays. Some of the staff will ride them up tomorrow, rather than take the funicular. If you're keen on horses, you'll have your chance to try that ride sooner or later. It takes half a day, but the views are spectacular as you rise up from the plain. The track zigzags back and forth, all the way up the crater wall. Only you have to earn the opportunity, by mucking out and cleaning tack and so forth for a term or two. Ponies take a lot of looking after, and there's no stable lad to do the work. Just us."

Charm was mad on horses, happy to let herself get filthy and ravenous and exhausted in the process of seeing them clean and fed and content. Levity left her to say so, at length, since the older girl seemed just as keen as she was. For Levity herself, it was enough just to walk along quietly and look at their new home. She couldn't hope to take in everything at first glance, but at least she was paying attention and learning what she could. Charm would be seeing nothing, she knew, except a delightful dream of ponies. At least one sister should be able to find her way around.

Past the stables lay tennis courts, original to the hotel to judge by the handsome palisade that surrounded them. Beyond were four large houses spaced apart, each with their own gardens round about. Built of the same red sandstone as the castle but to a much more modern design, roofed with grey tiles and with their feet rooted in spring-green growth, they looked cosy and welcoming.

"Butler, Jopling, Greenaway and Stokes," Melanie recited, counting them off one by one with a pointing finger. "That last, of course, being our own home from home. Come along, and we'll see if your trunks have been put where they should be. If so, we'll get you both unpacked tonight; tomorrow will be the most dreadful scrum. Such a good idea, sending new girls up a day early. Gives you the chance to get your feet under the table before the mob descends."

29

Levity was still chanting under her breath, *Butler, Jopling, Greenaway, Stokes...* "They're all artists," she announced abruptly.

Charm stared at her. "Who are, loopy?"

"Butler, Jopling, Greenaway and Stokes. Famous artists, from the last century."

"Famous *women* artists," Melanie amplified. "Of course they are. Just as the dormitories are all named after women scientists. Didn't you read the prospectus?"

"We haven't even seen the prospectus," Charm said. "Mamma left us here in a bit of a rush, you might say." She was glancing sideways at her sister, biting back a giggle; Levity glowered crushingly. The last thing she wanted was for that story to become common gossip.

"Oh." Melanie looked a little blank for a moment. "Hope it wasn't a family emergency or anything like that?"

"No, not really. Just Mamma." At least Charm had the sense to leave it at that. For now. Levity resolved to have a quiet but firm word with her, as soon as they could contrive to be alone.

"Well, then. Yes, Levity, all artists: Elizabeth, Lady Butler; Louise Jopling; Kate Greenaway; Marianne Stokes. Each house has at least one original work by their namesake, and plenty of prints. You must be keen on art, to know them from their surnames if you really hadn't a clue before."

"Not a hint of a clue, no. But—well, we get it from Mamma. She practically raised us in galleries." Now suddenly it was Charm's turn to glower, hers to wish she might have bitten her tongue.

"Did she? Oh—wait a minute. Your surname's Buchanan, isn't it? You're not by any remote chance talking about Isobel Buchanan, the sculptress?"

Levity and Charm glanced at each other, two sisters with but a single thought: *We told her so, we said we should register under another name but no, "Hide in plain sight," she said, as if that could ever hope to work...*

CHAPTER THREE

The Lady in the Lake

"I hate this place!"

The words were so sudden, and the sentiment so shocking, for a moment neither twin knew quite how she felt, never mind how to answer. They turned to each other, as they always did in a crisis—and Tawney the peacemaker saw her sister flush with fury, and dived in headlong to avert the storm.

"I'm sure you mean you hate it that your twin's not here with you."

There: she had said it. By unspoken agreement, she and Tasha had been tiptoeing around the subject of the missing twin, not wanting to raise it until Rachel did; and Rachel had said almost literally nothing, until now. Her outburst would surely have provoked Tasha into a response even more undiplomatic, if Tawney hadn't intervened. Like every right-thinking girl, they both loved the Crater School uncritically, but Tasha was always more fiery in defence of her passions.

Just now, Tawney was wishing for a little of that fire in her own more thoughtful soul, as Rachel turned a smoke-grey glare upon her.

"Don't tell me what I mean! I mean just exactly what I say!"

"Well, but you can't." What Tawney lacked in heat, she could make up for in simple stubbornness. Standing by her guns was a natural state. "You haven't been here above an hour. That's not long enough to work up a proper hate."

"Even if the Crater School was the most hateful place on Mars," put in Tasha. "Which it's not. Just the opposite," she added hastily, feeling that perhaps she was damning with faint praise where she had in fact meant just the opposite, so she said so.

"So," Tawney continued, recognising the mulish look on Rachel's face from many a glance in the mirror, and trusting that it would be backed by the same innate honesty that plagued her own bouts of the sullens, "you must have come here intending to hate us all; which means it's not really us, it's just baggage you brought along. Which means it's having to come without your twin. Am I right?"

Rachel glowered for one little moment longer; then her mouth twitched in a reluctant smile. "Are you setting up for a psychologist? Because you could out-Freud the master, if you keep this up. Of course it's being here without Jessica that I hate. School's school, it doesn't matter one way or the other; but splitting us up is the most hateful act on three planets. Which I suppose means I ought to hate my parents, who decided to do this to us; but I can't do that—or at least, I can't admit to it—so..."

"So you decided to hate us instead. It all makes perfect sense—except of course that you're wrong about school. All schools aren't the same, and it does make a difference where you go. There's nowhere better than the Crater School. Your sister—Jessica?—is the one who landed unlucky."

"Well, that's true enough. Oh, not because your school's so grand, however much you and your teachers want to puff it up; I still say a school's a school, and you won't change my mind on that. I hate being stuffed up indoors at the best of times, and classrooms and teachers are never ever that. But poor Jess got sent to some dreary academy down on the plains. She's a lot brighter than I am, you see. We may look alike, but we're really not. Our parents think she has at least the makings of a brain, where I'm just a distraction to her. So she's condemned to some awful crammer to make her fit for Oxbridge and a career after, while I'm sent out of the way so she can concentrate."

The saddest thing about that little speech was how weary and defeated Rachel sounded, as though even her anger had been worn out of her.

"Aren't you a bit young to be thinking about universities and careers and all that?"

"Tell that to our people. They say it's never too early to start swotting. For Jess, that is. For me, apparently it's already too late."

"Well, if they really sent you here to put you out of the way," inconceivable as that sounded to either twin, "they chose the wrong school to do it. Nobody here is going to treat you like a discard, Rachel." Tawney tucked her arm through the other girl's to prove it, ignored the scowl that she won in response, and towed her determinedly down the corridor. "Come on; we're on a mission from the Head."

"What mission?" Even Tasha sounded bewildered now, hurrying to catch up.

"Honey cakes!"

The head of the main staircase to and from the subterranean kitchens lay behind a serving-hatch in the dining hall. Girls were never supposed to use it, unaccompanied. Indeed, they were not properly supposed to go downstairs at all, without a mistress or a prefect in tow. Just as they weren't supposed to go out on the roof.

But the twins had an official warrant today, from Miss Leven herself; and besides, they had their own ways up and down. Catch them tripping over a maid with an armful of dishes, or worse, Mrs Bailey herself, the tyrant of all that lay below! No, they knew better. They had learned better, their first term here; all the girls did. All the wily ones, at least.

The castle might be a mere Victorian folly, but it sprawled over as much acreage as any proud mediaeval foundation. And built deliberately as a hotel, of course it had a system to bring food and water to every room while they were still hot; no paying guest would have been content with less. Every corner turret had its own dumb waiter, reaching down into its own corner of the kitchens. Maids and pages could hustle trays up to any floor, as soon as they were called for.

Only one of the four survived now, to ferry dishes up to the dining hall and down. The wise heads of authority had seen the others screwed shut, to prevent wicked girls from ferrying each other likewise up and down. However, each dumb waiter had a staircase winding up around its shaft, to allow servants quick and private access to every floor of every turret without disturbing guests. Those turrets housed staff quarters now—and no teacher at the Crater School was above an occasional private trip down to the kitchens to beg a tray of tea and biscuits, to carry back to study or bedroom.

Nor was any girl above a clandestine sidle into one of these off-limits stairs, if the prize below was a honey cake and the only risk an unforeseen encounter with one of those occasional staff. The boot-boy used the same stairs, but he was their willing slave already, no risk at all.

Besides, the twins today were clad in the Head's own authority. She had positively told them so.

Here was the nearest turret, with the wide worn steps of its staircase winding up, meant to give privileged guests access to the desirable tower rooms. Those guests had never come. In their place, mistresses occupied those rooms, coming down to classroom and library and chapel, to dining hall and beyond. Schoolgirls trotted up and down these same stairs daily, reporting to one study or another with textbooks to work through, essays to defend, sins to confess.

Beside the open staircase, though, stood a green baize door. A small brass sign above the handle was engraved, No Admittance. A handwritten paper notice had been pinned to the centre of the door, just at eye-height to a tall four-teen-year-old; that was new since last term, possibly new since yesterday. It read: "If girls persist in sneaking down to trouble the kitchen staff below, this door will be kept locked, to the great inconvenience of everyone ENTITLED to use it. (signed) M E Leven, Headmistress."

That was all right; they weren't sneaking anywhere. And they wouldn't be any trouble down below. There weren't enough girls about to constitute trouble, not to Mrs Bailey. Not till tomorrow. Tasha heaved the door open, Tawney ush-ered Rachel through without a second thought.

Here was the dim square servants' staircase, ascending and descending about its blocked-off lift shaft, lit only at every landing. The twins skipped down merrily, with Rachel following; they turned four corners, and here closing off the stairwell was the door into the kitchen.

Tasha applied an insouciant shoulder, in a way guaran-teed to have brought calamitous justice down upon her head if anyone in authority had seen her. There was only one way for a decent young lady to open a door, and that was emphatically not it. But no one saw, no doom descended; the door swung wide, and they stepped through into light and noise and bustle.

Tomorrow, the kitchen would be ten times as busy, with ten times as many mouths in school to feed. Tomorrow, any girl venturing down here would be a hundred times less likely to find a welcome, let alone to wheedle a treat. Oh, it could be done; it would certainly be tried, again and again throughout the term; but the school's domestic tyrant was always more tyrannical in term-time.

Today, on this last easy afternoon, even Anneke the harassed little scullery-maid was sitting in comfort at the long deal table that dominated this end of the kitchen. She and all the downstairs staff were enjoying a cup of tea and a rest, while their domineering mistress herself sweated red-faced at the great range that lined the far wall.

The twins looked to Anneke first, by instinct and long training. Overworked as she always was, she was still the girls' best friend herebelow, closest to their own age and so more easily drawn into their plots and stratagems. She winked at them now and beckoned hastily; she had a plate right there that still held a handful of cooling honey cakes...

"Oh, and what do you think you're doing, you three? Sneaking around behind my back, snatching cakes from the servants' tea..."

It was the voice of doom, echoing across the kitchen. Even Rachel froze in place, who had never heard it before. Guiltily, all three girls turned around to find Mrs Bailey advancing upon them, with a steaming tray in her hands.

"And you, Anneke: I made those for you to eat, not to give away to importunate children. If you don't want them, pass them up the table to those that do."

She slammed her tray down—and this close, even through that wreath of steam they could see that she was unexpectedly smiling even as she scolded.

"Here," she went on, using a corner of her apron to slide six sizzling-hot honey cakes into a clean napkin, "take these, and take yourselves off out of my kitchen. I don't have time nor space for you down here, today or any day. If I don't see you again before half-term, it'll be too soon."

Mrs Bailey's bark was notoriously worse than her bite, or no girl would ever dare venture down here; but school legend held that she never ever smiled, and sharp experience said she was more likely to offer the blunt end of a ladle than a sweetmeat.

Still: no girl ever flinched away from fortune. They took the napkin, with cries of gratitude interspersed with yelps of pain as the cakes scorched their fingers even through the linen; they grinned at Anneke, who was emboldened enough to take two more cakes for herself before sending the plate up the table; then they fled, before the dread Mrs Bailey could change her mind.

Back through the door, back up the stairs—and then Tawney and Tasha snatched one each of Rachel's hands and towed her without a word down a passage, through a high narrow doorway and so out of the castle.

Three stone steps led down into the great courtyard, where cobbled paths divided stone-flagged quarters. In term-time, the rule was that girls kept to the paths, however silly it might be to march solemnly two sides of a square when you could just dash across on the angle. But this was still holidays, and rules—some rules!—were in abeyance yet; and the twins tugged Rachel joyously across the flags to the gatehouse.

She had come into the castle this way, they knew. Miss Harribeth's tours always started beyond the moat. Nevertheless: once was never enough, to experience the slightly chilly thrill of the almost-tunnel between the sunny courtyard and the world beyond. In a real castle, if you'd crossed the drawbridge and broken down the gates, here was the killing-ground where defenders would be pouring boiling oil down on your heads, and poking spears at you through narrow window-slits. The black-painted doors on either side could look awfully sinister in that shadowy light, even when you knew that they only led into Mr Felton's janitorial preserves: his living quarters one side, his cubby the other.

And no girl could help glancing upward just before she reached the sun again, to see the heavy spikes of the portcullis jutting down above her head. Of course it never would come crashing down without warning—but it did always look as though it might.

And here were the gates proper, standing wide as they always did; and here the drawbridge that was never raised, though the chains and windlasses were there to suggest that it could be at need. Miss Harribeth said that drawbridge and portcullis both were jokes to amuse the absent hotel guests, but you could see they were real enough. And there was certainly a naiad in the lake and always had been, with a squadron of nymphs to attend her. Year after year, the junior dormitories had thrilled to tales of the night the naiad rose in anger from her deep cold bed, and only the castle's traditional defences could prevent a massacre.

There might be no truth in the tales, but who cared about that? The naiad was real enough, and so the danger too. There was some reassurance in a bridge that could be pulled up, a portcullis that could slam down. Even if the moat didn't go all the way around, so that the rear of the castle lay open to any scuttling horror that might come. Even if a shallow moat was nothing in any case, nothing at all to any merlin, naiad or nymph or flighty imago; and wooden gates nothing too, an iron portcullis still nothing much, nothing to write home about. Nothing to trust your life to.

They were there, and they looked imposing enough, as the whole castle did, standing proud on its bank above the lake; and the gardens that lay between stone and water were lovely at this time of year, with the thaw behind them and spring stretching its legs and settling in, not a thought yet of turning towards slow summer. And when Rachel said, "I was told this was the Mistresses' Garden, no girls allowed," it was a simple matter to shrug two pairs of heedless shoulders, to chant in unison that school rules were in abeyance until tomorrow so they could if they wanted and in any case it was always okay to cut directly through, and so to steer her between the roses and down to the lakeside path.

Here was something to trust to, better than barred gates and unfinished ditches. What kept the girls of the Crater School safe, what their parents trusted more than walls and rules and governance, was the bold nature of the girls themselves, the pioneer spirit of Mars Britannicus. So there were merlins in the lake. So what? They weren't Earth girls, to cower indoors and never venture forth for fear of being eaten. If trouble came, then they would meet it: intrepid, indomitable, unafraid.

And sensible, of course, that too. Tawney did at least think to ask, "Do you have the fingertalk?" before they reached the water.

"I do," Rachel confirmed, with a glance at the dark still lake. Of course she did. It wasn't a formal requirement for entry, and any junior girl who arrived without even basic signs at her fingertips was swiftly paired with an elder to tutor her, and not allowed anywhere near the water until she had them down pat; but no parent would send a girl in her teens to a lakeside school without ensuring that she had the minimum means of survival.

Confident, then, in their own preparedness, they strolled along the path that circled all the rim, a bare dash above the lapping water's edge.

"Good thing there are three of us," Tasha said indistinctly, still munching on her second cake. "Rules may be in abeyance—but not that one. We don't need Rowany to tell us that."

Tawney spelled it out for Rachel: "We're never allowed on the path or anywhere outside school grounds unless there are at least three of us. It's the old Pioneer rule: one to be hurt, one to stay with her, one to run for help."

Rachel nodded. No girl of Mars would ever need such a rule explaining, and it would take a reckless girl indeed to defy it. She might be miserable without her twin, she might still be determined to hate this school and everything about it—despite any friendly overtures, with or without sweet hot crumbly honey cakes to help them down—but she wasn't *foolish*.

Aloud, she only said, "Who's Rowany?"

The twins stared at her, bug-eyed. "Only the Head Girl," Tasha said, gasping. Didn't this new kid know *anything* that mattered?

"Only the one who caught us on the roof earlier," Tawney added mournfully, "and gave us the worst punishment ever thought of in the history of meanness."

"What's that, then?"

The twins took their time explaining to her the absolute horror of half a term's work, which would have to be done in their very limited free time: maps and writing and drudging all over the castle, and even—horror of horrors!—maybe having to take questions to Miss Harribeth, because Rowany would never accept a slapdash job, so...

Rachel listened, more and more slack-jawed as they went on; and when they were finally done, she said, "Oh, you—you

41

pink-footed pelicans! That's not a punishment, it's an open invitation!"

Their turn to be slack-jawed in amazement. Had she not understood, did they have to explain it all again...?

"Don't you see?" Rachel went on. "Whatever she meant, your precious Rowany has given you *carte blanche* to go anywhere, in bounds or out. And to record it, to map it... This place is a castle, built by an eccentric; it must have secret passages, tunnels, hidden chambers, even beyond the servants' ways in and out. And you have permission to hunt them all down. Don't you *see* what an opportunity this is?"

The twins stared at her, and then turned slowly to stare at each other instead. Neither one could see any obvious signs of decrepitude in the other, but how else to explain it, how else could they need a new girl to point out what should have been so very, very obvious...?

CHAPTER FOUR

Nymphs and Shepherds, Come Away

Nobody could seriously suppose that Melanie Fitzwalter—the Head of Games, no less, the very definition of sportsmanship and fair play!—would ever spread gossip around the school. Oh, she would share news with her particular set, of course, but only in confidence; and they were as discreet as a face of rock, the prefects and the Sixth together. A sad disappointment to anyone trying to mine information from her seniors.

Nevertheless. Before they could contrive to join forces again, both Levity and Charm had been brought to realise that their not-so-secret identities were already common knowledge.

Perhaps that was only to be expected, in a school so proud of its arts education, on a planet so fierce in defence of its own. Surely Melanie was not the only one who'd paid attention to modern and Martian artists, or remembered that the renowned Isobel Buchanan was known to be mother to two likely daughters.

Even so: when the truth was borne in upon Levity—it took no more than two staring schoolgirls, nudging each other and whispering not softly enough, on a bench in the garden as she passed by—her first reaction was shockingly close to heresy.

"Oh, *perish* that Melanie!"

Her companion gaped at her, bereft of speech, almost of air itself. Lise Harper was a Crater School girl through and through, to the very bone of her; and more than that, she was a Stokes girl too. The best house in the best school on three planets: who wouldn't cherish that? And the house drew its spirit from its captain, as any team always does; and Lise was a sportsman before everything, living for cricket and boating in the summer, hockey and lacrosse in spring and autumn, skiing and skating through the winter and indoor games all year long. She worshipped Melanie quietly, uncritically, from afar: followed her deeds on and off the sports field, feared her wrath, lived for her good word and her smile.

"We're not allowed to say that. And honestly, why would you want to? What's Melanie ever done to you?" Lise would be Levity's classmate, as well as occupying the next cubey in their dorm. It made perfect sense that she should act as sherpa, to help the new girl negotiate the steep and slippery slope of her first weeks at school. At least, it had made sense until now, when the new girl revealed herself to be utterly loopy.

"Didn't you hear those two on the bench there, as we passed? All *That must be one of them now, she's famously a redhead* and *This one doesn't look too brilliant, anyway, perhaps you don't inherit genius*?"

"I did, yes; and I was going to tell you to ignore them, because Hilda Rathe and Christine Elphinstone are famously idiots, whoever they inherited it from. And of course I wasn't going to ask you what they meant, but now I have to. And again, what in three worlds does Melanie have to do with two third-formers having horrible manners towards a new girl?"

44

"Two new girls," Levity said flatly. "This affects Charm as much as me. And Melanie's the only one who's worked it out, who our mother is. So it must have been her, spreading the news all over."

"New girls should probably think twice, before accusing their own head of house on evidence that wouldn't hang a curtain." Perhaps it was only the scorn in Lise's voice that made Levity flush crimson; she wanted to think so, at least. "So your mother's somebody, is she? She'd be in *Who's Who*, then?"

It went without saying that she meant *Who's Who on the Red Planet*. It was vaguely understood all across the province that another edition appeared at Home, but no one would ever see the point of consulting it.

"Well, yes..."

"Under the same name?"

"Buchanan, yes." And then, defiantly, because the cat was out of the bag already, all but the tip of its red-sandy tail, "Isobel Buchanan."

"Blimey." Just for a moment, Lise showed all the coarse amazement of her grandfather, at the world she inhabited these days. Then she shook herself and said, "We're not allowed to say that either, in case you were wondering. Still. Even I know who she is, and I'm the despair of Miss Calomy's whole art class, never mind Miss Calomy herself. Anyone here could have heard your name, checked the book—there's a copy in the library, on a lectern by itself, for easy reference; Miss Leven is always saying that we should know the powers that be, the great figures of our land and the stories behind them—and put two and two together. Anyone. You've no call to be blaming Melanie," stoutly, returning to the issue at hand.

"No-o. I see that. I'm sorry, then." *It might have been anybody else* was no great defence of the school Lise claimed to love, because it surely had to have been somebody, but even so. "I suppose it was almost sure to come out, one way or another. Charm and I had already decided we weren't going to lie about it, if anyone asked. We just hoped that nobody would ask, and it would somehow not come up."

Lise laughed briefly. "That by itself would be enough to tell me that you've never been to school before, either of you. Parents always come up, one way or another. I don't really see why you'd want to hide it, though. Given who your mother is, what you'd be hiding. Idiots will always be idiots," with a dismissive nod of her head back towards the bench, where the two girls were still staring after them, "but most of us know how to behave. And it's *int'resting*, having a famous artist in your family. My people are farmers, nothing more."

"Mamma says that farmers are the heart of Mars, the bedrock of our life here."

This time, Lise's laugh had an edge to it. "The heart and the bedrock? Miss Peters would call that a mixed metaphor, I think. But yes, everyone says that, or something like it. I think they're trying to make us feel better about getting up before dawn and working till sundown, day in and day out. Though I have seen some of your mother's work—that piece she called *The Pioneers*, we had a school trip to Cassini last year and it was on show at the Art Museum there—and I may not know much about art, but I do know truth when it hits me in the face. She's caught them absolutely, the husband and wife towing their own barge down the canal because no one was breeding horses yet on Mars and they couldn't afford steam. I couldn't look away. Those could have been my own people, my great-grandparents: not quite first-comers, but almost, the second wave of immigrants that no one troubles to remember. We don't have any pictures, they weren't the sort to sit for portraits—but now whenever I think of them, it's your mother's sculpture that I see. She gave me faces for them, and I'm truly grateful. I think she's wonderful. For my post-card home I sent a photograph of that sculpture, when I might have sent a view of Thunder Fall, or the great houses along the waterfront, or the lake itself, or anything. But that's what I mean, I don't see why you wouldn't want everyone to know. I think I'd want to tell the world, if she was my mother."

"She says we should seek our own fame," Levity said slowly, "not try to rise on hers." It was hard, feeling her way through layers of truth that only served to hide other, deeper truths she could never tell. Telling the truth and feeling all the time that she was lying, to someone whom she'd like to make a friend. "She says it's a kind of stealing, to use her reputation to boost our own. And honestly—I love it that you love her work, and I'll tell her what you said in my first letter home because she'll be thrilled, but I really don't want to spend the next year talking about my mother."

"Oh. No, I can see that. You may be doomed to do it any-way, whenever idiots like Hilda and Christine corner you—but come on, then." Here was a rose arbour, with a bench delightfully set beneath it, and a long view over the lake. Lise tugged Levity down beside her and went on, "Tell me about yourself instead. Are you really only here for a year, or was that a figure of speech?"

"No, just the one year. Or that's the plan, at least. At pres-ent. Mamma's a nomad, she follows her inspiration, a year here and a year there, wherever the Muse leads her. Before this, she's always taken us along with her—but people keep telling her it's no way to raise girls, and, well. This year she decided to listen. She says we'll all be glad to have a break from each other," and never mind what else she'd said, that was really not for sharing. Even with a friend, or so Levity supposed. She wasn't sure. She didn't think she'd ever had a friend, as such. Her sister of course had been ever-present all her life; and there had been other children here and there, but rarely for longer than a few weeks. There and gone. She hadn't ever been lonely, exactly, but...

Layers within layers, truth within truth. It wasn't ultimately the reason they were here, but *These children need schooling,* Mamma had written to Miss Leven, *in more ways than the obvious. They need the company of their own kind; they need to make mischief, and to make friends, and to make mistakes. As much as you can teach them, in what time I can spare them to you. They've spent too much of their lives with adults.*

Looking at Lise now, Levity wondered if perhaps the same wasn't true of her too, in a different way. Mamma had talked a lot about the lives of pioneer children, in the time she'd been making that sculpture and others in the series. How they were barely given the chance to be children, with all the work that needed doing just to stay alive in the colony's early days on Mars; and how the same was still true on the border farms, in the most distant outposts of Charter territory.

Perhaps that was why Lise was here. Her parents could be making a deliberate sacrifice, giving up a needed pair of hands on the farm to open doors for their daughter that had always stayed closed for them. And paying for the chance, of course, finding school fees somehow...

"Why are you looking at me all asquint?" Lise demanded suddenly. "Have I come out in marsles? Can't feel any bumps," making great play of checking for the ugly spots of Martian measles, fingers pinching at her own brow and cheeks.

Levity flushed, even as she giggled. "No, of course not. I'm sorry. I...was just wondering what your plans were, for after you leave school?" There, that was close enough to the truth.

"Well—that's a way off yet, I hope. But easily answered, actually. I mean to go to college, to study modern agricultural techniques and how we can apply them here. There's a school newly opened outside Marsport, on the site of one of the earliest settler farms, where we can see the results of a century and a half of careful cultivation. I'll take my degree there, and then go home with everything I've learned, to help my parents and all our neighbours. I hate being away so long," she went on, staring out across the garden to the lake and the jagged rim, the wide sky beyond. "Do you know the plains country at all?"

"We spent time there, yes." They'd spent time everywhere, it seemed sometimes. Everywhere on Mars, at least. Mamma had always refused to take them offworld; indeed, she never went herself, despite all the offers and invitations.

"It's beautiful, isn't it? Don't you think?"

Levity preferred mountains and wild rugged scenery, land where something different happened every time you turned a corner. The endless plains seemed staid and dull to her, with crops stretching to the far flat horizon on every hand, interrupted only by roadways and waterways and railways, by windmills and cottages and villages that all looked alike, and then abruptly by one of the great slow canals so broad you could never see the other bank.

But beauty was a thing you learned early, Mamma said, which made it a prejudice, not a truth. And if you were born to it, she could understand how—no matter how hard the work—you might find loveliness in that rich green landscape that turned so gold in the summer, in the dark damp red soil, in the running water and the still water and the quiet country lives. It would never be her life, or she hoped not; but she was unexpectedly moved at how very much Lise wanted it, where Levity had supposed that she would only ever want to move away.

She said, "Tell me about it. Where you're from, I mean. Mamma wanted to show us the history; we spent most of our time in museums, when we weren't searching for the sites of the great disasters." Or when they weren't posing as the starving children of the first pioneers, for Mamma to sketch in charcoal and in clay as models for her pictures and prints and her later lifesize bronzes. Levity and Charm had sworn never to mention that some of their mother's most famous works were portraits of themselves when they were younger. "Tell me what you love, what you miss so much."

"Oh, I miss it all, from first to last. Being woken by the rooster, before the sun is up. Fetching a basket of eggs, still warm from the straw. Herding ducks to the water—because we have to shut them up at night, along with the chickens, or the sandcats would hold festival—and squabbling with the geese. We don't need to guard the geese, they guard themselves; no sensible sandcat is willing to challenge a flock of Plains geese on the warpath. I wouldn't do it myself, if they didn't know me. I'm always careful with them, the first days I go back after term; they do remember, but it takes a little time.

"And there are the cows to be milked and the fields to walk, looking for any signs of trouble, sand-rats or sandcats, they both do their own kind of damage, though we mostly put up with the cats because they keep the rats under control. So long as they don't get in among the poultry. And of course there's hoeing and weeding and fertilising, even when there's nothing to plant or harvest. There's always work, on a farm. A lot of it is dreary, some of it is backbreaking, but there's always compensations. Looking up to see an imago fly over, or sunset in the shadow of a sandstorm, that's majestic.

"And then there's a dance at the parish hall and everybody comes, or the apple festival that migrates from farm to farm as the different varieties ripen, or a puntnic on the canal, or—"

"Or a *what*?"

Lise giggled. "That's a picnic, when everybody comes down the water in their own big punt, and we make a fleet and share food and play games from boat to boat, and half the kids fall in before the end of the day and the rest of us jump in deliberately. Everyone has towels and a change of clothes, because we all know it's going to happen and of course we can all swim anyway, we grew up in and out of the water. It's the best fun."

"Sounds it." Levity felt a pang of envy, for the kind of life she'd never had the chance to live. She looked out over the lake—and suddenly cried aloud, "Oh, look! Look there—!"

She was pointing and calling and running all at once, because that was what you did, what you were trained to do. All your life, from the days you could first remember: boy or girl, farm-raised or city-raised, on the water or far off in the dry, parents and teachers and adults of all kinds taught the same truth. *If you see a merlin come to ground, from water or from the air, point it out and cry the alarm and run. Run towards it if it's a nymph, if you have the fingertalk; if not, run away. If it's a naiad or an imago, always run away. But always, always run. Never dawdle, never stand and stare.*

"Levity, Levity, stop!" That was Lise, running at her side, as she should be; but laughing too, grabbing her arm and holding on, dragging her to a halt.

"Don't you *see*?" Levity demanded. "There, those ripples, there's a merlin rising...!"

"There is, yes. It'll be one of the nymphs, they come up often. And see there, on the path? Three girls? Two of those are ours. I expect the third is a new girl, like you, I don't know her—but I do know the twins. They'll be fine. We can go down anyway, if it'll make you feel more comfortable, but truly. There isn't a nymph alive that would dare to eat those two. Besides, every nymph in this lake is practically a friend. The school raised them, more or less. I'm not saying they know us individually by sight, but they must recognise the uniform."

Levity was somewhat reassured by the other girl's calm, but wanted to keep moving none the less. Lise shrugged, and fell amiably into step beside her.

"Here it comes, then. Up and out. Probably looking for a snack; we're not supposed to feed them, but there's always a cabbage-stalk or a basket of corn-cobs going begging in the bin by the kitchen door. You just have to know who to ask. And if anyone's safe to know that, it's the twins."

Levity's mind boggled a little, at the thought of feeding a nymph the way she used to feed ducks in the park. Still: Lise seemed so confident, she let her feet dawdle while she kept her eyes riveted on the water. At first there had been ripples swelling out in a circle, as the creature swam up from deep waters. Then there was a wake, as it angled in towards the bank. Now it broke the surface, and water spilled off all around as it rose like a rock, like a legend, like an elephant in a lobster's shell, like...

"That's no nymph!" The girls cried it out both together.

"That's the naiad." Lise said it, because one of them had to. "We never, it never... Oh, come on!"

And now they were running again at full pelt, snatching each other's hands for greater speed, for comfort, as they ran towards the peril hauling itself bodily out of the lake, between the three girls on the path and the spurious safety of castle walls.

CHAPTER FIVE

Over the Hills and Far Away

When a naiad rises, all the village does well to run.

It was a saying that dated back to the earliest years of settlement, when whole townships had been destroyed in a night by a naiad disturbed from her lake. In those days few had the fingertalk, no one the bubbletalk; there was little communication and less understanding.

Things were different now—but not that different. A naiad out of the water couldn't be reasoned with; she couldn't be spoken with at all. Bubbletalk only worked underwater, and in the shift from nymph to naiad, it seemed that she forgot her fingertalk. No one could explain why that should be; the changes in her body or her brain between one state and the next might account for it, but you couldn't cut her open to find out. It might be mere etiquette, like a girl leaving her country dialect behind when she married a duke. No amount of cutting would teach you that.

For the moment it was simply a known fact, that you couldn't talk to a naiad on land. People had tried, and died. It was better to run away. She might not come after you. Might not.

It was hard, though. Hard to run. When she was so big, and so thunderously demanding of your attention; when she filled your view and your brain together, so that you couldn't really remember how to move at all.

The three twins stood where they were and stared, as the creature hauled herself out of the water. They held hands and stared more, as she dragged her cumbersome body up the bank and onto the path, no more than a dozen yards away. In the water—they'd been told—she could be monumentally graceful, almost elegant. Out of her natural habitat, she was merely monumental. She had nothing of a nymph's razor fluidity, only bulk and determination. And too many legs, and claws in all directions, and a carapace with so many encrustations and so much weed hanging from it she might have been a unique environment all by herself, if you could only find a jar big enough to bottle her.

Perhaps they backed up slowly, unthinkingly, one step at a time. Not far, not far enough. Half the width of the lake might not be far enough. She might seem awkward on land, but that didn't mean she wasn't quick. And she certainly knew they were there; they could see her antennae twitching, reaching towards them, sniffing the wind.

Her teachers might have been surprised—or they might not—that it was Tawney the quiet twin who tugged her hand free of their new friend's and started signing in fluent fingertalk. Asked afterwards why she'd ever bothered, she could only say, "If she was going to eat us anyway, I wanted her to know that we weren't sheep. I wanted her to *remember* us..."

At the time, as far as she or her sister could remember, what she actually signed was the phrase that everyone always started with, which was supposed to be a greeting but everyone just called it the *please-don't-eat-us*; and then the *how-can-I-help-you?* which literally translated somewhat closer to *if you are lost in darkness, let me guide you to the light.* Except that this was a naiad, not a nymph, and just in time Tawney remembered to turn that around. *If you are lost in light, let this little fish guide you to the darkness*: she knew how to blow the bubbles for that one, if only the naiad had stayed where she should, down in the deep waters of the lake.

How they might actually help, the girls had no idea. They could do no more than point at the water, and surely the naiad knew where that was. Why she might have come up at all, they couldn't begin to guess. Naiads never left their depths, unless something drastic happened to disturb them. Nothing had happened on the lake here since the two major construction projects, the castle and the Sanatorium. Those were both in the previous century, so long ago that they were lost in history, and were said to have brought up no more than a couple of nymphs curious to see what was afoot and whether there was anything worth eating.

The naiad made no reply to Tawney's careful fingertalk. Several of her secondary eyestalks did seem to turn in the girls' direction, even while her head with its compound primary eyes was scanning the crater rim and turning towards the school. Did she hesitate? Perhaps. Perhaps she did still understand the sign language so carefully developed over time; perhaps she might even have replied, if her antennae hadn't lost their suppleness or her mind its subtlety.

Or she might have eaten them, just as a snack on her way to the summit.

They never had the chance to learn.

Two things happened.

Two girls came plunging down onto the path beyond the naiad, both of them gesturing frantically, half fingertalk and half just wild waving. They shouted as they waved, but between their breathlessness and the distance and the shocking creaks and groans and snaps that emerged from the naiad's shell as she moved, it was hard for any of the twins to hear. Or to listen, through the simple mind-numbing impact of having a naiad between them, and almost close enough to touch.

One word they did pick up, though. Not by hearing, but by sight. "Why does Lise's friend keep signing 'nymph'?" Tasha demanded. "She must be a new girl, and I don't know where she's from, maybe she's never seen a merlin of any sort before—but this close, no one could think this one's a nymph."

"It's not 'nymph' she's signing," Rachel said. "It's 'nymphs'. Plural. And the other girl's pointing to the lake."

It was hard, so hard to turn their heads away from the naiad in her presence, in her potency. But they looked, all three of them, one by one, towards the water the naiad had renounced—and yes, it was turbulent with more creatures rising up, a squadron, almost a swarm of them.

Every naiad has her own attendant nymphs, schooled to feed and tend her. Any others she would eat, but these she kept for their service, for their loyalty. There was another saying, all through the colony: *never come between a naiad and a nymph*. It was truly not a place you'd want to be. If the nymph was a stranger, you were standing between a naiad and her lunch; if not, between a servant and its mistress. Either way would not end well for you.

The first nymph to break the surface pulled itself onto the bank behind the three schoolgirls, so that they found themselves willy-nilly standing between it and the naiad. On the narrow pathway, the only strip of level ground. One creature must cross it to reach the other, whichever way that went.

The lake offered no escape. There was another nymph just at the water's edge, stretching out its first long spindly legs to come ashore. And more beyond it, seemingly all the nymphs the lake contained, the naiad's entire entourage.

There were four, five, six that the girls could see; the water seethed with them.

"Oh, help..."

There was no one to help them, though, except themselves. Tasha was fingertalking frantically to the nymph, and winning no response. Tawney had given up on the naiad and was signing past her to the other girls, too pale and breathless to shout across the distance. It needed Rachel to seize each twin by an elbow, interrupting whatever they were trying to say, and drag them across the path.

They had left the Mistresses' Garden some way behind them, and the fenced walkway that would have led them through to the playing fields. That walk marked the end of school grounds, and the end of man's work to tame the crater wall. Here it rose up, high and stark, bare red rock in jagged crags.

"Climb," Rachel said shortly. "We have to. I'm tallest, I'll give you a boost."

"No need," Tasha said, after one swift glance at the rock face. "Dad says we're half monkey. We can climb this, if you can."

With a nymph on one side and a naiad on the other, Rachel thought she could levitate if need be. But the rock was rough, offering handholds to nimble fingers and ledges for feet. She took the twins at their word, trusting them to follow as she stretched up to the first hold and began to climb.

She and Jessica had been climbing with their parents on the lower slopes below Cassini. Their father had promised them a holiday in the mountains and proper coaching from a member of the Olympian Club, someone who had stood on the highest point known to humankind, the summit of Mount Olympus itself. There was nothing daunting about this solid slab. *Don't look down* was always good advice, though; so was *don't look back* when you knew there was a merlin behind you. She set her mind to the task and scrambled quickly upwards.

Fifteen feet or so above the path, she found a ledge wide enough to squat on. Was that higher than a nymph could reach? Perhaps; but she wasn't sure about the naiad. Even so, she deliberately paused there and went against all that good advice. She looked down to see where the twins were, and found them both hot on her heels, racing up to the same ledge. It was broad enough to hold all three of them—but there were two nymphs now unnervingly close below. Could nymphs climb? Possibly not, but she didn't know for sure. And naiads certainly climbed at least once in their lives, when they forsook the water to hang from the branch of a high pine in their chrysalis, before hatching out as an imago. Maybe nymphs could chase up a rock wall as readily as sand-roaches scuttled up brick and plaster.

"We need to keep going," she gasped, bending to offer Tawney a helping hand.

"Yes, but wait..." Tawney helped her sister in her turn, then gestured largely to the Crater School girls still lingering on the path beyond the agitated merlins. They exchanged fingertalk; Rachel couldn't see what Tawney was signing, with her so close and the merlins so distracting, but she saw what one girl below signed back.

High in the tree, the chrysalis holds three nymphs safe till the imago comes.

The girl was clearly batty. That made no sense at all.

"Come on, Rachel. While they're still fussing with the naiad, we need to get higher up."

Tasha suited her actions to her words, leading up the next pitch with no more delay. Her sister followed; Rachel brought up the rear, after just one last glance down to see how the nymphs had massed about the naiad, while more figures came running down the path from the school.

Another ten-foot climb brought them to level footing, a sudden unexpected plateau among the rocks. The drop lay behind them, another rock wall ahead. On their right, towards the school, the ledge dwindled to nothing. Underfoot was a scrape of soil and a desperate cling of grass. Against the wall stood a boulder, worn smooth by time and rain, that seemed almost designed to be sat on; and to the left lay what looked quite a lot like a goat-path. It was narrow and steep, squeezing between crags and twisting out of sight behind a boulder.

"Do you think we can stop here?" Rachel asked, peering down once more at the swirling chaos of merlins below. "They don't seem to be chasing us, whatever it is they're doing; so eventually I suppose they have to stop, and go back into the water, and leave the path clear."

"That might not be till after dark," Tawney said. "And we're too high for a ladder now, and no one would let us climb down the way we came up, even in daylight. Going down's always harder. If we stay here, the best that might happen would be Miss Whitworth climbing up with a rope, and lowering us down like baggage."

"Besides," said Tasha eagerly, "you saw what Lise said. They won't be looking to find us here."

"The girl on the path?" Rachel queried. "I thought she'd forgotten all her fingertalk and was making signs at random. Or talking in code. Or else she'd gone lulu, quite honestly."

Tasha giggled. "Not Lise, she's a solid soul. But she was trying to say something that fingertalk really doesn't have the words for, and she didn't dare try anything complicated that we might not have seen clearly, especially with that great naiad in the way; so she just fell back on the simple signs that everyone can read, and trusted us to work it out." And then, seeing how both the others were staring at her, "Tawney, don't you realise where we are? This must be Sister Anthony's Step!"

Her sister smacked her own forehead in self-disgust. "Of course it is! Which means that path must lead up to the Eyrie!"

"If it still is a path," Tasha said, a little darkly. "If there hasn't been a rockfall to block it, in all the years from then till now."

"Lise knew it was here, the Step. She must have been here; you couldn't see it from below, she'd have no idea if she hadn't come up this far. Like we didn't. We'll have to have a talk with her about that. But someone's sure to have walked the path. You couldn't know this was here and hold the secret—even from us—and never try to go all the way, could you?"

"Well, we couldn't, no..."

The twins snatched at each other's hands in excitement, their eyes glued to the path. Rachel almost thought they'd forgotten about the merlins down below. She said, "What under the two cursed moons are you two talking about?"

"Oh—sorry, Rachel. Forgot you wouldn't know. Well, you've met Sister Anthony, the school matron?"

"I've seen her, yes." A tall woman even by Martian standards, and gaunt by any standards, almost spectral in her black habit and stark white coif. "She said she'd have time for me later," though of course Rachel had wanted to say not to bother, she didn't want to unpack anything, she really didn't want to stay.

"We would have taken you, after tea," Tawney said. "Unpacking is a sacred ritual at the Crater School; you'll learn. But terrible things happened to Sister Anthony during the war—nobody knows what, so there's no point asking—and she came to the crater here to be alone. She built herself a hermitage, right up high on a crag somewhere, and lived on berries and moss."

"And milk and cheese," the more practical Tasha added, "from the shepherds who graze their flocks on the slopes outside the crater. There's a whole village of Basques, who came here to escape persecution back home."

"They thought she was a saint," Tawney went on, scowling at her twin. "And perhaps she is; we can't say. But everyone knows that she made a pathway down from the Eyrie, to a place where she could sit and look out over the lake and pray. Every day she came down here, whatever the weather, for years on end. Before the school found her, and offered her another mission."

"And you think this is the place?"

"We think it must be." It was hauntingly familiar to Rachel, how one twin could so easily speak for both. Now it was Tasha's turn. "And what comes down must go up. At least, if it's a path. That's what Lise meant, don't you see? High in the tree, the chrysalis holds three nymphs safe till the imago comes. Obviously we must be the three nymphs, and the chrysalis high in the tree has to be the Eyrie."

"Does it? There's a perfectly good sign for nest," Rachel said. "She could have used that, if she wanted to say eyrie."

"I expect she forgot it. Or more likely forgot that 'eyrie' means 'nest' in the first place. Whatever was going on in her head, I think her fingers were clear. We should make our way up to Sister Anthony's old hermitage, and wait for someone to come from the school to find us. They'll have to come the long way, around the outside of the crater; there are sheep-paths all the way to the crest, and shepherds who know them all, but it'll take time. We may be in for a long wait. And a hard scramble first," Tasha added, eyeing that steep and narrow path. "Anyone got any chocolate?"

CHAPTER SIX

The Head Girl Pushes In

Rowany raced along the path, seized the two Middles by a shoulder each and positively dragged them away. Only just in time: here came another nymph, pulling itself from the water right where they'd been standing.

She said, "Have you two lost what little sense God gave you? Coming between a naiad and her nymphs..."

But there wasn't time to lecture them as they deserved. She'd been walking in the Mistresses' Garden, a privilege granted to the Head Girl and school prefects, when she saw the two youngsters racing by. Instinct had drawn her after; when girls of that age were in that much hurry, trouble was sure to lie ahead.

She hadn't anticipated this. Nobody could. Who ever heard of nymphs swarming about their naiad, out of the water? Since its foundation, the school had kept careful records of every merlin sighting, and there was never a mention of this or anything like it.

There still might not be, if she didn't get these two to safety. None of them might survive to record it. How far away they'd need to be, she couldn't guess. Further than this, though. She could see every drop of water streaming from the nymph's carapace. If it only turned its head, it would have an equally clear view of them.

Happily, it and all its cohort seemed intent on their naiad mistress. That might not last, though. One hand firmly on the collar of each girl, Rowany went to tug them away—and was astonished to feel them tug back.

"Rowany, wait. The twins are trapped, the other side of— of that..."

"That" meant the mêlée just ahead. Tall as she was, Rowany couldn't see over the heaving mass of merlins to whatever might lie on the path beyond, whoever might be caught there.

"Both the twins?" she snapped.

"Yes, and a new girl too."

"Well, at least if they're together there's a chance they'll act like a rational being, not the halfwits they are on their own. There's nothing we can do from this side anyway," though she understood better now about the girls' hurtling rush. At least they hadn't just been coming down to gawp. "They'll likely run halfway around the lake, and we'll hear from the Sanatorium that they've shown up safe."

"No, they're not on the path. They got cut off, and had to climb." Lise was pointing at the cliff-face, where it sprang suddenly skyward, lifting the crater rim high and high above the school's grounds.

That made a difference. There was no easy way down on this side; Rowany knew.

"Very well. We still can't help from here, though." She scanned the rock as best she could and saw nothing moving, no glimpse of jewel-green uniforms against the red Martian sandstone. "And we can't linger anyway," as there was a great stir of movement in the mass of merlins: a surge away down

63

the path, a pause, a surge back towards them. "Best foot forward, kids. Run!"

Her own long legs could have carried her swiftly away, but
she kept to her juniors' pace, hurrying them along as best she
could. Keeping them moving too fast to look behind, and not
so much as glancing back herself.

Blessedly, they hadn't far to run before there were other
figures suddenly on the path ahead of her, members
of staff, adults she could hand over to. Hand over the kids,
responsibility, herself included...

"Oh, Miss Leven! I'm so glad you're here! I don't know
what's happening, but—"

"Don't you, dear? Stay, then. Stay and watch. We'll be
quite safe."

Would they really? It still felt dangerously close to Rowany. But six years at school had trained her in trust, as well
as obedience. She relinquished her two excited charges to
the headmistress's companions—handing them over phys-
ically, one to Miss Whitworth the games mistress, one to
Miss Hendy who taught Natural and Martian Sciences—and
turned to stand beside Miss Leven.

Looking back at last, to see that no, the nymphs hadn't
chased after them. Instead they were still clustered about the
naiad, still on the path there, just where the school grounds
ended.

Should she feel insulted at being judged so negligible,
dismissed so casually? It was the way of the merlin race, most
of the time. They brought humans here and then ignored
them, living quite separately, rarely interacting. Barely able
to communicate: even fingertalk was largely a mix of weird
metaphor and hopeful guesswork. According to Miss Hendy,
the one sure thing was that no one actually said what they

thought they were saying, when they spoke in sign language to a nymph. And bubbletalk with a naiad was worse.

She decided to feel grateful, rather than insulted. It was better to be ignored than eaten. Once she'd settled that in her own mind, she said, "Miss Hendy? What are they *doing*?"

"Well, what do you think they're doing, Rowany? Watch and report."

That was the theme of all her lessons. *Use your eyes, then use your words,* she said that often. *It would help to use your brain between,* that too. Rowany watched, as she was trained to do; but it was one of the youngsters—not Lise, the new girl whose name she hadn't had the chance to hear yet—who spoke first.

"They look almost like they're herding the naiad. Trying to," as the great creature blundered away from its smaller attendants one more time.

Blundered, yes. "If I didn't know better," Rowany said carefully, "I'd think the naiad was blind." Blind, or stupid. But naiads were the deep thinkers, the plotters, the great minds of the merlin triad. When the first colonists negotiated the Charter, it was naiads they had to deal with. Nymphs were too vicious and unpredictable, imagos—*no, Rowany, the plural is imagines,* Miss Hardy's remembered voice again, *four syllables, from the Latin*—too flighty and skittish and simply unreachable. Everyone agreed, naiads were in charge.

Except it didn't seem so, just here just now. The new girl was right: the nymphs were like a pack of collies around a single straying sheep, trying everything they could to usher it back towards the water. Force wouldn't do it even if they could have brought themselves to try, even if they would have dared. They weren't built to push. But they massed themselves ahead of the naiad, whichever way she tried to turn. They built walls of their own bodies and left her only one route open, to the lake. They tried to chivvy her, they

65

tried to nudge her massive bulk in that direction; and at the same time their antennae were always talking when they weren't touching, when they weren't stroking hers. Rowany had never seen that behaviour either. It reminded her of trying to calm a frustrated baby, soothing with voice and hands together. But the naiad must be generations older than the nymphs. Perhaps they were more like nursemaids dancing attendance on a wilful, demented old lady...

"Not blind, Rowany, no," Miss Hendy said, "but she is near her time. Her body is ancient, and perhaps starting to fail; she is restless and uncomfortable within it. She feels the need for renewal. Whether she knows it or not—because her mind may be failing too, we cannot tell—she has left the water looking for a tree to climb."

"Please, Miss Hendy?" It was Lise who asked what all three girls were wondering. "Why won't the nymphs let her go?"

"She is their charge; they were laid as eggs for this duty and none other, born to it and raised to it. They know no other life. They have been the best servants imaginable; now they are the worst, because they cannot conceive of any change, and they will not allow it."

"Then how—?"

"How will she ever reach her tree, Levity?" Miss Leven answered this time, seeing how Miss Hendy had grown distracted by the activity on the path. "In time her own needs will drive her, beyond argument and beyond persuasion. She will kill them all, when they try to prevent her once too often. Yes, and eat them too; their flesh makes her last meal, which she will need to see her through her final change. Not this day, though, I think. She may rise half a dozen times, before the last. Watch, girls, watch. You may never have another chance to see this."

So they stood and watched, until at last the naiad abandoned her struggle against the pack of nymphs, allowing them to steer her back into the water. She slid below the surface after one last yearning look back up at the crater rim, where it was fringed with high pines in their majesty. One by one the nymphs followed, until the path stood clear and nothing but puddles and churned mud remained to speak of what had happened here.

Then, only then did Rowany remember what the younger girls had told her. "Miss Leven, Lise and, and—Levity? Really? That's charming—but Lise and Levity told me they'd seen some of our girls chased up the cliff when the nymphs swarmed the path."

"The twins, and another new girl," Lise confirmed. "The nymphs were all around them, Miss Leven, they didn't have anywhere else to go..."

The headmistress fixed her with a famously gimlet eye. "As opposed to you two, Lise, Levity, who seem to have distinguished yourselves by running recklessly *towards* an emerging naiad, where two seconds' thought might have had you running for a mistress, or running to sound the bell, or running anywhere except into the naiad's mouth. But we will discuss that later," she went on, turning away from the shuffling, blushing pair. "Miss Hendy, Miss Whitworth—your eyes are sharper than mine. Do you see any sign of our girls up there?"

"I don't, Headmistress."

"Nor I." Miss Whitworth shaded her eyes with her hand and scanned the rock for some time before going on, "There is a path up, though—or at least a hard scramble. I've considered taking senior classes by that route, all the way up to the rim. You'd see very little of it from down here. It starts from a shelf, thirty foot or so up the face, and even that's not visible from below."

"Sister Anthony's Step," Rowany said quickly. A little too quickly: the staff turned as one to look at her, and she could feel herself blushing. Nothing for it now, but to confess. "Uh, most of the seniors have been up already, Miss Whitworth. It's become a sort of rite of passage, or a welcome to the Fifth form says it better, perhaps." And then, defensively, "No one does it unless they want to, and we always take them up with people who've been before." And at last, almost desperately, "It's never been forbidden...!"

"Perhaps that's because we never knew you were doing it," Miss Leven said, at her chilliest. "You know that's no excuse, Rowany."

"Yes, Miss Leven. But it does mean that we know the path's in tolerably good condition. We helped a little, perhaps, just by using it as we have..." That was no excuse either; she heard her own voice die away, and had to make a conscious effort to rally. "They'll find their way to the Eyrie, if they just follow the path. And with any luck they'll settle there, they must know someone will come for them—"

"That's what I told them to do," Lise interrupted.

"You told them, Lise?" Miss Leven repeated. "How was that?"

"Well, sort of. With fingertalk; only I thought of it very suddenly, and I couldn't remember the best signs, so I just had to be mysterious and, and hinty, like the merlins are. But I think the twins will've understood me."

"Indeed? Well, we must hope so. And how did you know about the path, Lise, and where it leads? I hardly think you're old enough to have been included in one of Rowany's guided climbs."

"Oh. No, Miss Leven. Only, well, the whole school knows that Sister Anthony's Step exists, somewhere; and I, well. I just found it, one day. I didn't have time to climb the path, but I knew where it had to lead. So I told them."

"Hmm. Miss Whitworth, I think you and I need to sit down and draw up some rules about who may go climbing on the ridge, where and when, and under what supervision. But meantime, we have three girls on their own and far from home. You did well, Lise, to send them up to safety; now we need to recover them. And not by that same route, I think. The Eyrie is accessible from beyond the rim, Miss Whitworth, yes?"

"Oh yes, Miss Leven. By a much easier route, if you only don't get lost among the sheep-tracks."

"I know the way, Miss Leven." Rowany still felt a need to redeem herself. Her expeditions to the Eyrie suddenly all seemed a little underhand.

"I've no doubt of it," Miss Leven said. "Can you get there before dark?"

She glanced at the sun, and then at her wristwatch. "Yes, I'm sure—but not there and back. And I shouldn't like to chance those paths at night."

"No. It seems extreme, for an adventure that began so close to home—but I think those girls must weather the night in Sister Anthony's old hermitage, and come back to school in the morning. Which is why we need a party to reach them before dark, to be sure they do nothing foolish like trying to find their own way home. It's easy to put yourself in trouble on those slopes, if you don't know the paths and can't see the dangers. Very well: Miss Whitworth, will you lead the party?"

"Of course, Headmistress."

"Thank you. Rowany, then, for native guide; and—"

"And I will go too." Miss Hendy, firmly.

"Good. No one knows the perils and possibilities of these lands better than you, Miss Hendy. Very well; you should set out as soon as possible, please. Take blankets and lamps, and whatever Mrs Bailey can rustle up by way of a cold collation. You'll not be comfortable, if all's true that I've heard of Sister

Anthony's former residence, but at least you can be warm and fed, albeit nightbound on the rim. I'd say to take ponies, if they weren't all at the bottom of the hill. As it is, you must carry for yourselves and for the girls too. Off you go, now, and fetch them home as soon as may be in the morning. Now, you two." The headmistress turned resolutely towards her two younger pupils. "I mislike to scold so early in the term, but for shame: two Mars-raised girls, and you have no better sense than to pitch yourselves headlong at a naiad...?"

Out of sheer kindness, Rowany turned away. Flanked by a mistress on either hand, she headed up towards the castle, facing a night of unexpected adventure even before school proper started in the morning.

CHAPTER SEVEN

The Shadow in the Darkness

Just ahead, one great slab of the crater wall had split vertically in two, and the rough path thrust into the gap. Tawney paused for breath, peering uncertainly into deep shadow.

"I suppose it must go on," she muttered. "All the way through. There wouldn't be a path else, would there? And there definitely is a path. So. On we go, then."

Even so: she stood where she was, waiting for the others to catch up. The way was reasonably flat just here, just briefly; this was a good place to rest for a moment. They might not see the sun again today. It was reaching down already to touch the far side of the crater; by the time they emerged from the crevice ahead, it might be gone altogether. She thought about clambering on in the dark, and shivered abruptly. If she'd known how hard this climb would be, or how long it would take them—well, she never would have left Sister Anthony's Step. Nor let the others leave. Even at the price of waiting to be rescued, like stupid stranded kittens in a tree.

Even at the price of her twin's contempt. Tasha would have been furious. She would have blustered, she would have threatened to go on alone if need be—but she wouldn't really have gone. Not once she knew that Tawney meant it. That was what twinship meant, that you stuck together and never left the other in the lurch. That was why it had to be so hard for Rachel, almost unimaginably hard, being forcibly separated from her sister...

As though the thought had summoned her, Rachel loomed up at Tawney's back, with Tasha following after. The new girl was breathing hard, but no more so than either of the twins, despite the steep scramble that had brought them up this high. She leaned a friendly hand on Tawney's shoulder, but there was no weight behind it; if she was conspicuously quiet, it was because the view and not the climb had stolen her breath away.

So Tawney hoped, at any rate. Otherwise, Rachel might be brooding still over her twin's absence. Tasha always did something mad when she brooded, and got them both into trouble as often as not.

"Magnificent, isn't it?" Tawney said. *Testing the water*, she thought, and wanted to giggle, wanted to nudge Tasha and whisper it to her, make sure she got the joke.

"It's amazing." Rachel took a step forward, to stand right on the edge of the path, closer even than Tawney had dared to come. Directly in front of her—directly below—was a long, long fall to the waiting lake. And then a deep, deep plunge to the waiting naiad and her nymphs. If anyone had ever measured the crater's depth, they hadn't told Tawney. Mostly, people left the dark secrets of the water to the merlins who inhabited it. They rowed about on the surface—and skated, of course, through the winter months when the whole lake froze over—but no one even fished these waters seriously. People dangled the odd rod, just to show that they could, and left most of the sturgeon and trout and stranger native fishes to the appetites of the ever-hungry dwellers down below.

Those waters might sparkle in sunlight, but they lay as dark as their secrets now, already in the long shadow of the crater wall. That held the lake in an almost perfect circle, the smooth ring of water making a sharp contrast to the jagged broken rock of the wall rearing above it. Standing this high, on this open viewpoint, they could see it all. There were only two gaps, where the wall dipped down almost to the level of the water. One held the great square blocks of the Sanatorium; the other was just a little way behind them now and a long way below, the buildings of the school looking shockingly small from up here, as if to stress how far the three twins had come from safety.

"The merlins have gone back into the water," Tawney said, staring down at the path that looped like a crimson thread all the way around the lake. "And we were so close, before. Perhaps we should just have stayed where we were. It seems crazy now, to have climbed up all this way."

"Lise told us to," Tasha reminded her virtuously. "Up here is where they'll be looking for us. We're just doing what we're told."

"And we'd better get on with it," Rachel added, "if we don't want to be feeling our way in the dark. How much further is this blessed Eyrie, anyway?"

"We don't know. This is as new to us as it is to you. All we know is what all the school knows, that it lies up on the crater rim, in a gap between two of the teeth. Can't be far now," Tasha added, with a shudder at the outline of blood-red rocks against the ochre sky. "Don't they look like giant monstrous teeth to you?"

"Always," Tawney said. "Which makes us the spinach caught in the gaps, I suppose." She glanced down at her dark green uniform, then up at the literal gap that awaited them, the split in the crag. Something in her really didn't want to tackle that. She'd rather turn around and go back down, even after all this climb. But Tasha was already plunging ahead, crying, "Come on, then! Last one through's a Russkie!"

Just for a moment, Rachel hesitated. "My surname's Abramoff," she said bluntly.

Tawney flashed a smile at her. "That must be why Miss Leven asked us to sherpa you." *One reason why.* "Though I don't suppose she meant it this literally, hauling you up mountain slopes."

"I don't understand?"

"Oh—didn't we say? *Sherpa* is what we call it, when we're told to help a new girl settle in."

"Not that. I don't understand why my name would lead Miss Leven to hand me over to you two, particularly."

"Oh. Didn't we say? We're Russian too. Tatiana and Natasha Mishkin: our full names give us away completely. Tasha meant me, not you. She knows I'm a slowcoach." In truth, it was a private signal between the twins, telling Tawney to bring up the rearguard, to keep Rachel sandwiched between them. The honour of the school was at stake; it was up to them to deliver her back safe and sound. "Go on, you catch her if you can. Stop her doing anything too crazy..."

Tawney hurried Rachel into the crack ahead of her, and followed swiftly after. It might as well have been full night already, as soon as they stepped out of the sunlight; the dark closed in around them like a damp and musty blanket. She was almost grateful that this crevice was so narrow, she could put her hands out and touch both walls at once. She could use that to guide herself in the blackness, while her feet felt cautiously forward over the rocky, unreliable slope up.

Tasha, she knew, would be dashing heedlessly ahead. Rachel was between them in more ways than one. Tawney could hear her making brisk headway, brisk but sensible:

in no danger of treading on Tasha's heels, in no danger of having Tawney tread on hers. Indeed, her speed was more of a challenge than Tasha's recklessness. If a new girl who didn't know the country could get along so quickly, then surely an old hand shouldn't be lagging this far behind.

Tawney picked up her pace as best she could, considering her wary nature. The way grew even darker, if that were possible, and the thin crack of sky overhead seemed to grow further away, as though the walls rose more swiftly and more steeply than the path. Still: she pressed ahead, and stayed close enough to hear the footsteps of the girls in front of her, the sounds of their breathing echoing strangely like a breeze in the still air, the occasional mutter or yelp as one or the other stumbled on the uneven ground.

Then she heard her sister's voice calling back, strangely uncertain: "Tawney?"

"No, this is Rachel. Tawney's behind me. What's up?"

"A wall is up," Tasha said, on a choking little laugh. "A wall of rocks. It's blocking the path completely, one side to the other."

"Landslide, I suppose," Rachel replied. "Yes; if you look above, where the crag ends, see? You can see where one side collapsed. Hope nobody was underneath when it came down."

Tawney wasn't interested in what had happened, only what would happen now. She cried out, "Tasha, don't do anything mad!"

Too late. She knew it was too late, even before she'd finished yelling. She could hear her twin's determined scrambling, the patter of disturbed pebbles falling further, Rachel's sudden, "Hey, you shouldn't—!"

Of course Tasha would want to climb, if the rockfall was remotely climbable. Tawney would have caught hold of her before she could start. Rachel had no idea, and was still standing at the foot of the slope staring uselessly upwards when Tawney joined her.

"I'm sorry, she just..."

"Just went? Of course she did. Nothing you could do, you weren't to know." Tawney found the new girl's elbow in the dark, and squeezed it reassuringly; then she called upward. "Tash? How is it?"

"Simple. Not too steep, and there's lots of holds. Some of them are a bit loose, but if you're careful—"

That was as far as she got. She must have been almost at the top of the slide; Tawney could see her silhouette against the darkening sky. Only then there was suddenly another shadow rearing up above her. Rachel yelled, "Look out!" while Tawney just stared, bewildered.

Tasha shrieked, and fell. There was a chaos of tumbling rocks and dust and Tasha in the midst of it all, coming down on top of them—and something else, something stronger and stranger by far. A heavy body that was somehow sure-footed even in its hectic descent, more leaping than falling, coming to land close beside Tawney. Even as her sister cascaded to ground among the rubble, Tawney was aware of a sleek grace and a fierce purpose, a rumbling threat in the air, a smell of musk and the touch of rough fur brushing her leg.

In a moment it was gone, bounding away down the narrow cleft as though the path had been made for it and it alone. Tawney shivered at that brief contact with something purely wild, purely Mars. Then Tasha moaned in the darkness at her feet, and suddenly nothing else mattered.

Tawney crouched and felt for her, and found Rachel there ahead of her.

"Where does it hurt, Tasha?"

"...Everywhere?"

"Do you think you can stand?"

"I, I think so. Yes. If you help me up. Tawney...?"

"I'm right here. Take my arm, you can lean on me."

All the way back to school, if necessary. It wouldn't be the first time one twin had acted as the other's crutch at need.

But she and Rachel lifted Tasha between them, and stepped back to let her try to stand alone—and she screamed, and almost fell again, except that Tawney was right there to grab her.

"What is it?"

"My, my ankle, I can't..."

"Can you hold her, Tawney?"

"Always."

"Let me see, then. Or feel, rather, for I can't see a thing. Don't worry, Tasha, I'll be gentle."

Rachel squatted down beside them, and reached to touch the ankle that Tasha couldn't stand on. Light-fingered as she was, Tasha still cried out again, clinging to her twin.

"Well, the good news is I don't think it's broken," Rachel said, rising to her feet once more. "Jess broke hers one time, when she took a toss from a colt. We were supposed to be breaking him, but he had other ideas. This doesn't feel that bad—but I don't think you'll want to put any weight on it for a while. It's swelling already, so I'd guess you've wrenched it pretty badly. Here, put an arm round each of our shoulders; it'll be easier for Tawney then, as well as for you, while we work out what to do."

"We could carry her in a queen's chair," Tawney suggested.

"Well, we could—but carry her where? Not up this slope, not three of us together. And if we go back, we could get as far as what did you call it, Sister Anthony's Step? And then what? We couldn't get down from there; and no one from the school will be looking for us there, and—"

"I don't think I could bear it," Tasha said faintly. "Not all that way. But I saw the Eyrie. Just for a moment, at the top there. It's just the other side of this, out in the open. We're so nearly there..."

Tawney looked up and realised that it was true, the crack did open out just beyond the rockfall. She saw first stars appear, and Deimos start to slide between them. Her fingers shaped themselves automatically into the sign for watchfulness, for guard; but even with their clever telescopes her Russian kin on the moon, her own country's enemies couldn't hope to see down into this shadow, even if they had any interest in schoolgirl misadventures.

If Imperial troops had still held the moon, perhaps they could have signalled somehow, and the duty officer could have sent a message to the school. But if ifs and ands were pots and pans, there'd be no need for all Mrs Bailey's kitchenware.

Instead of wishing for the moon, Tawney said, "Well, then. We'd better get you over this ridge and into shelter. Quick, before someone comes from the school to rescue us. We've never needed rescue yet, and we're not starting tonight. You know how far we have to go, Tash; one step at a time, do you think you can make it?"

Tasha whimpered a little, but nodded determinedly. "Yes, I think so. I hope so. I think I have to. If I can hold on to you..."

"Of course. We'll do it three-legged: two of mine and one of yours."

"I'll go on ahead," Rachel said, "to make sure the slope will hold. And I'll wait at the top, to help any way I can."

"Be ready to fight off monsters," Tasha said thinly. "What was that, anyway? I just, I felt the heat of its breath, and then it was there, all over me. I couldn't help falling."

"We know," Tawney said comfortingly. "We saw. And it was a sandcat, I think."

"Definitely," Rachel confirmed. "Big male, by the smell of it. We see them on our land all the time. Our tenant farmers are glad of them, because they keep the sand-rats down; and they're welcome as far as we're concerned, as long as they don't trouble the horses."

"They're not welcome hereabouts," Tawney said. "This is sheep country. Maybe it's superstition, but the shepherds say they take lambs in season and worry the sheep all year. There are boys guarding every flock, and they'll band together to hunt and kill a sandcat. I hope this one has the sense to stay inside the crater wall."

"It's not superstition," Tasha said. "I've seen the mother sheep, bleating for their lost lambs. Our friend Paco the shepherd-boy showed me one day when Tawney was in bed with a cold, and there was nothing left but a bloodstain on the grass and the mark of a sandcat's pug. He said one cat can devastate a flock—and this is springtime, when all the sheep have lambs and the cats have kits to feed. But please, if we're going to go over this slide, can we go now? I don't think I can stand up much longer."

Rachel needed no more prompting. She scrambled cautiously up the slope, testing every handhold and every foothold, knocking down anything that felt too loose to trust. "I think it'll take the two of you," she called down from above. "If anything, that last fall made it easier. Just come slow and steady—and you yell out if it's too much, Tasha. We can always stop and set you down and think again."

That was the one sure way to make Tasha set her jaw and say nothing, however bad it got. Tawney knew that, and wondered if Rachel had guessed it too, because there really wasn't any other choice for them now. The way back was too far and too uncertain; one way or another, they had to get

Tasha over this rockfall; and she would have to do a lot of the work herself.

Slow and steady was the only way. Tawney tried to be a prop for her sister, but it was hard when she needed both hands for herself. It worked better when she climbed up ahead a couple of feet and then just set herself, to give Tasha a living rope to hang on to as she hauled herself up, two hands and one foot, dot and carry one. Then Tasha would just hold on while Tawney climbed ahead again.

That way, little by little, they won the summit. There was Rachel, reaching down to heave with a will, to help them up the last of the slope and steady them at the top. Then she said, "That's the worst of it behind us, and we can see where we're going now. And I can see the pair of you, and you both look beat. Climb on my back, Tasha; I can carry you this last stretch. I haven't done my fair share yet."

Both twins protested, but neither with much conviction. Tasha was in tears from the pain, however hard she tried to swallow them down, and between effort and anxiety, Tawney wasn't much better. Rachel refused to listen to either one of them. Up onto her willing back the injured girl must go; and then it was nothing but a careful march down the gentler slope of fallen rock and back onto the revealed path, which brought them swiftly up by starlight to the doorway of a rough stone shelter.

Tawney peered uncertainly into the dark interior. "Hullo? Is anybody here...?"

No answer came; but Tasha said, "Wait; there's a light down on the slope there, coming up."

The shelter—which must be Sister Anthony's Eyrie, it couldn't be anything else—stood between two of the daunting Teeth, on the very rim of the crater, with the ground falling away on either hand. To the one side the path led precipitously down, as they knew, almost to the lake itself;

to the other, gentler slopes offered rough pasture all the way to the valley bottom. There was where the Basque shepherds guarded their flocks, against sandcats and other perils of the night; sheep-paths cut the turf in all directions.

And along one of those narrow paths, indeed, a light was coming. Rachel let Tasha slip down from her back, with Tawney there to catch and hold her; and then the three girls stood outside the doorway and only waited, until the light came close enough to show who carried it—"Oh look, that's Miss Hendy! And Miss Whitworth too, and isn't that Rowany leading them...?"—and what they brought besides, baskets and blankets and packs.

Then Tasha made an odd noise in her throat and collapsed all at once, before her sister could catch her.

CHAPTER EIGHT

Neck and Halter

"**C**heer up, Levity."

Levity startled a little, as Lise slipped a warm arm through hers. Nevertheless, she was grateful to be shaken out of the megrims.

"Sorry, I was just—"

"I know exactly what you were just. Everybody does just the same, after their first scolding from Miss Leven. That one was a scorcher. It should go down in legend. And on your first day, too, before school proper even begins! But there's no point dwelling on it. What's done is done, you'll find, at the Crater School. Miss Leven won't mention it again, and neither should we. Besides, they don't ever give us time to brood. The whole staff is devoted to keeping us busy as waterbees, every blessed waking hour. And the prees are worse."

As if to prove her true, Melanie Fitzwalter caught them in the cloakroom of Stokes House, before Lise had even had the chance to change outdoor shoes for house slippers.

"Where on Mars have you two been? — No, never mind. I've no time for excuses. Sister Anthony's here, and she wants me to oversee Levity's unpacking. I know you're all sorted already, Lise, but you can come too. It'll save time if you show Levity the one true way to stow all her things, while I mark them off on the list. Come along now."

Levity's heart sank into the shoes she couldn't change yet. Of course she had known this moment was coming; but there'd been so much else going on since they arrived, she'd almost managed to forget it. And compared to all those merlins erupting from the lake—and compared to Miss Leven's withering comments about her common sense!—a simple everyday awkwardness should just fade into nothing, shouldn't it...?

And yet it didn't. Her heart pounded while her breath came short, while her feet felt incredibly heavy as she dragged herself every reluctant step through the corridors of the house to the stairs up to the bright attractive Herschel dormitory, with its half-dozen curtained cubicles. Here was her own, with its bed made up and its neat empty locker on one side, its chest of drawers on the other; here was her trunk at the foot. Here were its keys in her hand. There was the official list in Melanie's hand, of everything that the trunk ought to contain.

"I don't have all day." There was Melanie's impatience, spurring her to fit the key to the lock, to throw back the latches, to show...

"Is this even the right trunk?" Melanie asked, after a long and dreadful pause.

"It's the only one I've got," Levity said. In her head, she hoped to sound defiant; to her own ears, she only sounded sullen.

"Well, I'm sure these clothes are serviceable—heavens, some of them are delightful!"—and the older girl held up

Levity's favourite, a frock that had been embroidered for her
by a fellow of the Royal Martian School of Needlework last
Christmas, by happy coincidence in the school's own colours
of green and gold—"but honestly, Levity, I can't think what
your mother was thinking. Do you have no uniform at all?"

Levity bit her lip and shook her head.

"Whyever—? No, never mind. This is out of my stars; you
need to explain to Sister Anthony, not to me. Wait here."

With that, Melanie left them alone: which only meant
that Lise could ask the questions that Melanie had swallowed
down.

"Didn't your mum go to Aspell's for your uniforms?"

"That's in Marsport, isn't it? We were never within five
hundred miles of Marsport."

"No, but you can send them your measurements and
they'll make up everything you need and ship it back to you,
or else ship it here to wait for you. We're all supposed to get
everything from Aspell's except our evening frocks. I know it
says that in the prospectus, quite firmly."

"We never saw the prospectus." Levity dropped the lid
of her trunk, to hide its disreputable contents. Then she
plonked herself down miserably upon it, and sank her head
into her hands. "Mamma sent us here in a terrible hurry, and
there was no time to do anything about uniforms. She said
she'd write ahead to explain, but I don't expect there was any
time to do that either. There often isn't."

Lise sat down beside her, and put a chummy arm about
her shoulders. "Tell me more. And sit up straight, or Sister
Anthony will make you wear a back-board for a month. I'm
not joking, either. I've seen her do it."

Levity peeped sideways between her fingers, then sighed
and straightened. She tugged her dress into some kind of
order with fingers that couldn't help but be neat, and said,
"When Mamma has a new project in her head, everything

84

else goes by the board. This time, 'everything else' includes us too, my sister and me. It never did before, she always hauled us along—but not this time. She says we need schooling or we'll grow up wild, and she doesn't have time to teach us herself any more. So she asked the bishop and the doctor's wife, and they both said to send us here. Then she more or less pushed us onto the next boat headed this way. Of course there wasn't a direct steamer, so we've been days and days on the water, on our own. The crews were kind, and Mamma had given me plenty of money to pay our way, but even so..."

Even so, it had been a long hard journey with a younger sister in tow, and an overmastering sense of responsibility weighing on her with a great many worries beside, and the great mystery that was school life ahead. Levity had been exhausted before they arrived, and needing finally to explain about their trunks and absent uniforms was all suddenly a step too far. She sniffed and scrubbed her eyes, and still felt tears threatening.

Lise must have known. She sat quiet for a moment, then asked a question that should have been innocuous. "What is your mother's new project, then, that meant she had to send you and your sister away? If she always took you with her before?"

Levity shook her head hard, trying to shake the tears away. "We don't know. She didn't tell us. Only that it meant a lot of travel, and that we couldn't, we couldn't go..."

There. Nothing about that was a lie. And if it hid the greater truth, the real reason they had been sent here—well, Levity had promised to do that. They both had. No growing friendship could be great enough to break that oath. Not when you thought about the terrible truths that it concealed.

And there it was at last, the final straw. She was sobbing now, uncontrollably. And Lise's closeness helped not at all, any more than her murmuring voice in Levity's ear, "It's all right, Levity, don't cry. You're here now, and you got your sister here safely, and we'll look after you till you have somewhere else to go. Look, don't worry about the uniform. I'll lend you one of my own spare tunics—"

"That you will not." Another voice, a new voice, crisp as the footfalls that carried it. Both girls startled, and leaped to their feet. Levity struggled to lift her gaze above the black floor-length skirts of the newcomer. Briefly she found an excuse in her handkerchief, but once she'd wiped her wet eyes and blown her nose, there was nothing for it but to look up. Up and up, to where a gaunt thin-lipped face was frowning down at them from what seemed an unreasonable height even for a grown-up, even for a Martian.

That face was framed by the white coif and black veil of a nun. Levity would have known who this must be, even if she hadn't been forewarned. Even so, Lise stepped in urgently to make everything clear: "Oh, Sister Anthony, this is Levity Buchanan, she's new, and she was sent here in a hurry and her mother didn't have the time to order uniforms, and—"

"Yes, so I assumed from Melanie's report. Nevertheless: girls sharing their clothes? I never heard such a thing, and I will not abide it. The offer does you credit, Lise, but the results would be entirely undesirable. How would I ever keep track at laundry-time? Besides, it isn't necessary. Levity is hardly the first girl to arrive at school without a proper uniform. We keep a stock of tunics and blazers and so forth that older girls have outgrown, precisely for these occasions. That is, if Levity thinks her mother won't mind our dressing her in cast-offs, until such time as new clothes can be ordered for her?"

The sudden relief was too much for Levity. Her mouth twitched, and she couldn't hold the laughter back; it broke out of her, as uncontrolled as her sobbing a minute earlier.

"I fail to see what's so funny, child."

Sister Anthony's brief, biting comment was as effective as a five-minute scold. Levity sobered abruptly, and said, "I, I beg your pardon, Sister. It's only—well, no, Mamma won't mind if we wear cast-offs. Half our lives, she's dressed us from jumble sales and gleanings." The other half, she and Charm wore handmade gowns, gifts from Mamma's artist friends, as often as not sewn from fabrics that they'd woven and dyed themselves. Sometimes, they were delightful. Sometimes. Jumble sales were more reliable, on the whole.

"Is that so? Very good, then. It won't hurt you to wear your own clothes for the rest of today. Bring your sister to me after breakfast tomorrow—I assume Charm is in the same case, yes?—and I'll see you kitted out with everything you need *pro tem*. And take your measurements, so that as soon as your mother approves it we can send to Aspell's for your proper uniform. They're usually very swift, and this won't be a busy time of the year for them; I doubt you'll have to wait too long. Meanwhile, take a minute to wash your face, now that you've stopped that ridiculous howling, and let's see what you *have* brought with you..."

A brisk half-hour later, Levity's trunk had been emptied, repacked with various items Sister Anthony deemed either unnecessary or unsuitable, and consigned to storage. There was no time to dwell over it, but Levity was almost skipping as Lise hurried her back towards the castle for tea.

"What are you so cheerful about?" her new friend queried. "That was bad enough, just standing there and listening to it. If she'd aimed all that at me, I'd have been crushed. Crrr-rushed," again, for emphasis.

"Oh—I'm just glad to have it all behind me. I'd been dreading that, and it wasn't so bad, really." If Lise hadn't noticed that Sister Anthony's idea of "unsuitable" covered all the worst of the embarrassing frocks that Mamma's friends had foisted upon her, Levity wasn't about to draw her attention to it. Privately, Levity was delighted, and hopeful that Sister Anthony could do as much for Charm, before any other Junior caught sight of the contents of her trunk. She might not know much about school, but she knew girls well enough to guess how much teasing might lie in store. Mamma had always said that was the worst of uniforms, that they opened the door to bullying for anyone who dressed differently.

Still, she and Charm should be reasonably safe now—and safer still, once they had uniforms of their own. Two simple schoolgirls, invisible among two hundred more all dressed alike: she knew absolutely why Mamma had made this sudden decision, to send them both away to a school far off. Far from anyone they knew, and—more importantly!—far from anywhere they were known, where no one had heard the names or seen the faces of Isobel Buchanan's two hopeful daughters.

Levity still thought they should have changed their names regardless, but Mamma said that it was harder than you'd guess, to operate under *noms de guerre*. And she should know, if anyone did. Better to be who you were, she said; better to let the name possess you, to become who the name declared you to be, with all that that implied. Here and now, that meant to become two more girls on the school roll, with nothing to single them out for notice beyond the school grounds. *I'm sending you into shelter*, Mamma had said. *I want you to relax and enjoy it, and grow into what it means. Be schoolgirls together, and let's see where that leads.*

Where it led just now was through the archway between library and chapel, a right turn in the courtyard beyond, and up the steps into the dining hall. This was high and broad, with great beams across the ceiling; it was lit by electric lanterns in sconces on every wall, and more hanging in chandeliers above the long tables. Three of those were given over to each house normally—for Juniors, Middles, and Seniors, Lise explained, with a prefect at the head of each—while staff occupied one table on a dais at the head of the hall.

"It's lifted up so's they can see who's misbehaving," Lise whispered on a giggle, "not so's we can admire them in their finery. Though some staff do have lovely frocks, and grab every chance to wear them. Nobody'll be dressed up today, though. We're still under holiday rules: only a couple of tables laid, see, as there's so few of us have come yet, and the mistresses who are here will sit with us and share. They have chairs at top table, of course, but here they'll join us on the benches; only the people at the ends get chairs. and that'll be Rowany and Melanie today, Head Girl and Head of Games. They're splendid"—she spoke with all the awe of a worshipper whose gods trod the very ground that she did—"well, you've met Melanie, so you know—but some of the staff are quite fun too, when they let their hair down. Let's try to sit with Miss Hendy, if we can; she's always int'resting. And she's our housemistress besides, so it's only manners, really. Maybe we can get her to talk about the merlins."

"Miss Leven said we weren't to." The headmistress had been forcefully clear on that point; they were not to discuss what had happened on the lake path with anyone, until the missing girls were safely back.

"Oh, but she didn't mean Miss Hendy. She can't have done, Miss Hendy's *staff*. She can talk about what she wants. But I meant in a general way. She's Natural Sciences, so she knows everything there is to know about merlins..."

But Lise's favourite wasn't present, to judge by her frowning scowl as she gazed about. Before she could hatch another plan, Levity felt a hand on her arm and looked down to find her young sister at her elbow, with an unusually pleading look on her face.

"Sit with me, Liv? Please?"

"Aren't your own crowd looking after you?"

"Yes, of course," and Charm gave a half-guilty glance over her shoulder, to where a couple of girls her own age were already lined up at a bench, clearly keeping space enough between for a third to join them. "Marigold and Andi are in my dormy, and I think we're going to be pals—but please, Liv? They say we'll hardly get a chance to be together once school starts properly. I don't want to take you away from your new friend," she went on, turning tragic eyes on Lise, "but—"

"But something in you is going to break, if you don't have a minute to talk to your sister before bed, right, kid?" Lise was laughing at her, but kindly. "I know how that feels; my own big sister was already a prefect, and hugely important, before I came to the Crater School. She's five years older than me, you see; Mumsie had a string of boys in between. I was shy as a bean and only wanted to be her mute little shadow, and she never had time for me. But look, benches make this easy. Marigold, never mind saving a space between you two; you budge up with Andi, then Charm can go in on this side, with Levity next to her and me next to Levity. And everybody's happy."

Levity guessed that "happy" might not be quite the word, for Charm would obviously have liked to talk privately. Privacy would be in short supply here, though, that was already clear, and they might as well get used to it first as last.

No one was sitting down yet, only claiming a place and standing there. Charm's shoulder pressed against Levity's arm, and apparently that was enough contact for now; her bright red head was turned away, to listen to the animated chatter on her other side.

"Your sister calls you 'Liv', does she? I like that," Lise said, while they waited.

"She always has. Mamma did it when we were small, because my whole name was a bit much for either of us; and Charm latched on to that and never let it go." There. Not a word of a lie. It was deceptive none the less; that was something else to get used to. "Honestly, though? I'd prefer to be Levity here." Mamma had been almost urgent about that. *Use your full names, darlings. All the time. Be Levity and Charm and no one other.*

"Of course, if you want it. Hush now, here comes Miss Leven..."

The headmistress came in with Melanie Fitzwalter. Levity heard Lise suck air between her teeth and didn't quite understand why, even after Melanie went directly to the head of the other table. Miss Leven smiled around at the gathered girls as she took the head of this one; she nodded to Melanie and the tall athletic prefect immediately began a Latin grace.

After the communal Amen, the girls at the benches' ends drew them out, and everyone slid around or else stepped over into their places. Lise was the last to sit down, after staring distractedly the full length of both the occupied tables.

"It's not just Miss Hendy who's missing," she hissed to Levity. "Miss Whitworth isn't here either—she's Games, you know, and awfully trig—but more than that, where's Rowany? She should be at the head of this table. Miss Leven's taken her place. That's not proper. It's a prefect's right to take the table, always..."

She sounded really indignant, as though a fundamental rule of nature were being breached.

"Well, someone had to stand in, I suppose," Levity said soothingly.

"Yes, but why aren't they here? Two staff and a prefect: something's going on, I tell you, and—oh, wait. I bet I know what it is..."

So too did Levity know, or she thought so. It wasn't that hard to guess—no, to *extrapolate*, from what they were already certain of. What they absolutely couldn't talk about, of course, with Miss Leven herself right there to oversee them.

Which was going to be really hard, because of course Lise wasn't the only one to notice missing faces. Already, a girl across the table was saying, "And it's not just staffs, the twins aren't here either. Nor that new girl we saw them sherpa-ing. Can you imagine, having Tasha and Tawney in charge of you? They've probably got her into desperate trouble already. I mean, it has to be their fault, doesn't it? There's obviously trouble afoot, at any rate; and you mark my words, those two will be in it, neck and halter..."

CHAPTER NINE

Rowany Comes Through

The longest night comes at last to an end, and the sun's rise makes everything seem better.

So Rowany had always found, at least. She was an early riser by training and inclination both, and it always gave her heart a lift in the long winter months, to see the first stains of light touch the eastern sky. She was familiar with dawns in England too, and had welcomed them as warmly, but it was still Martian dawns that held her true devotion. *Like milk spilling into a sand-pit*, she had said once, in an English essay. Miss Peters called that the worst analogy of the week, and even Rowany felt obliged to admit that it ran a little contrary to current notions of gravity—"but no one understands Martian gravity, Miss Peters, so who can say...?"

Miss Peters had felt herself able to say more, and at some length. But Rowany still clung to her original image in the privacy of her head, even if sand-pits tended not to overhang the land in an inverted way, nor milk to spill upwards, even here. All the colours of sand were there in the sky, to be discovered every morning by the slow leak of light. She loved to watch it happen, for its own sake; she loved it better when she had been waiting for the day to come.

Waiting and waiting, sometimes. Like this night just gone. She supposed she might have been less comfortable, at some time in her life—there had been nights out camping with the Pioneers, and with her family of brothers, when it seemed that tree-roots and pebbles were actually worming up from the soil below, to dig at her through the groundsheet and all the padding of her sleeping bag—but she really couldn't swear to it. Sister Anthony's old hermitage had never been meant to sleep two people, let alone six. Or five, at any rate: whenever Rowany woke and turned over, which was often, either Miss Hendy or Miss Whitworth could be seen standing watch in the doorway, a silhouette against the stars.

This time it was Miss Hendy, now a silhouette against the brightening sky. Thank goodness for that; Rowany took the rising sun as licence to rise herself. Slowly, carefully, painfully aware both of the kinks in her own body and the still-slumbering bodies packed close about her.

Miss Hendy saw her move, and touched finger to lips in silent warning. Rowany nodded, and wrapped the blanket she'd slept in around her shoulders for extra warmth. She knew from many an early outing just how cold it was likely to be, out there on the crater's crest. High-stepping with exaggerated caution, she picked her way over Rachel's sleeping form and around Miss Whitworth, to join the other mistress in the open air.

Miss Hendy beckoned her away from the doorway. "I don't want to risk waking the younger girls unnecessarily," she said in a soft murmur. "The twins especially have had a very disturbed night of it, and Tasha needs all the rest we can allow her, if we're to take her down to Sister Anthony today without a crisis."

Rowany nodded. In her own wakefulness, she'd been very aware of Tasha's tossing and moaning. Tawney had made every effort to calm and comfort her sister, but Tasha's ankle was very badly wrenched. It was strapped up as tightly as she could bear, and the mistresses had been giving her aspirin at intervals throughout the night, and even so: little cries of pain had punctuated the dark, and if she slept now it was only because she had at last sobbed herself into exhaustion.

"She was trying to be brave," Rowany said.

"Oh, I know it. Just as I know how hard that is, when you're this far from your own bed and any real care. Miss Whitworth knows more than I do, but that ankle needs better treatment than either one of us is qualified or equipped to give."

Without discussion, they had moved towards the eastern edge of the rim, where they could watch the sun as she came up. On this side lay the sheep pastures, cropped turf falling away into the valley, interrupted by many an outcrop of boulders. Waiting for the first rays of light to touch them, Rowany said, "How are we ever to get Tasha back to school, though? She can't possibly walk. Tawney will hold her hand all the way, that's understood; between the four of us remaining, it's a long way to carry the girl. There's not a wasted ounce on her, but even so, she's a solid, springy thing..."

"Miss Whitworth and I will manage that. We can carry her in a queen's chair, if we take our time about it. I won't have you two girls trying to share the work. That would only be asking for more trouble than we face already."

Rowany took a breath to dispute this, then reconsidered it; then said, consideringly, "Well, perhaps not Rachel. She's no more robust than Tawney, and those two have done enough, getting Tasha this far by themselves. I think they may have had enough, after that effort and the night we've just endured. But honestly, Miss Hendy, at least I can spell the two of you now and then, let you each have a break without needing everyone to stop still." She was taller than either, and surely just as fit—and just wise enough not to say so.

"No. I appreciate the offer, Rowany, but it won't do. What would we ever tell your parents, if we allowed you to overstrain yourself, perhaps doing some permanent damage? Young bones need as careful a nurture as young minds, if they're not to grow awry. No, don't argue with me. Take a breath now, and take a moment to watch. Here comes the sun."

Theirs weren't the only eyes turned that way, as a brisk moon heralded the arrival of the languid sun, like a page boy bustling before his master. Somewhere on the slope below, a ram bleated a respectful welcome to the day. Miss Hendy laughed aloud; out of nowhere, Rowany said, "I know another way to manage."

"I beg your pardon?"

"The sheep, Miss Hendy—I mean, the shepherds. I know all the boys who watch the local flocks"—they had been her fascination when she was a Junior, her cronies when she was a wicked Middle; they were her willing slaves now, and she knew it—"and I know they've taken to keeping a mule up here, to help carry the milk down to the village."

"Have they, indeed? Do you suppose they would lend it? I didn't think to bring money. I don't know if Miss Whitworth has any, but—"

"Oh, they'll lend it, Miss Hendy. If I ask."

Miss Hendy laughed again. "Like that, is it? Very well, dear. I'd best not ask, I suppose—but I'd best not let you go alone, either. I'd come with you, but then there would be no one to tell the others what we hope; and I don't want to wake Miss Whitworth. She had the worst of the night, I know, and she's only just gone over now. Still—"

She looked back towards the dark doorway of the hermitage, and fell quiet suddenly. Following her gaze, Rowany saw what she'd seen, movement in the shadows. A moment later, Rachel stepped out, pushing long dark tangled hair back from her face and blinking sleepily.

"I knew I should have made you plait that before bed," Rowany murmured. "If bed is what you want to call it, when it's nothing but a blanket on a floor of beaten earth."

"If earth is what you want to call it," Rachel said, scowling as she tried to work out a knot with her fingers, "when it's mostly stones."

"Hush, girls." Miss Hendy was almost laughing at them, which hardly seemed fair. "Rachel, leave your hair alone until you can come at it properly with a comb and brush; you'll only make it worse, fiddling about like that. Tie it back and forget about it for now. You've woken at just the right time, you're the very person we want; will you go with Rowany, on a mission to see if you can come back with a mule? I'll start the primus stove in the meantime, so there'll be a cup of hot chocolate awaiting your return, as well as those sweet rolls we brought up last night..."

"I'll tell you something," Rowany said musingly, as they tramped together across a high pasture. "Yours may be the strangest beginning any girl's ever had to her career here. Chased up a cliff by alien creatures, climbing a landslide in the dark, spending the night in an old abandoned hermitage..."

"...And now hunting sheep in the dawn," Rachel finished for her. "Well, the twins did say this school was different."

"They were not wrong about that. Though technically I suppose we're hunting shepherd boys; the sheep are just a clue, where we might find them. Like footprints in the mud. First thing in the morning, they might be anywhere; sheep and boys are both inclined to stray, and they both have favourite places to pass the night. Like sandcats," she added, with a sidelong smile. "Hold on to that memory, Rachel; you'll probably never be as close again to anything so wild. Or so bone-deep Martian. Miss Hendy could tell you more, but I know current theory holds that merlins came from elsewhere, as we did. Sandcats are truly native." Rachel nodded, unnervingly solemn in one so young. Rowany grinned down at her and went on, "Which means they should probably be entitled to the occasional lamb, as, as rent owed, if you like; but I'm afraid the shepherds don't agree with me. Run up onto that outcrop, will you, and say what you see?"

Rachel scampered obligingly to the top of an upthrust seam of stone that broke through the turf like the prow of a sinking ship. She peered this way and that through the broadening day, then called down, "Nothing. Just the bare slope, I mean—no sheep."

"'And I awoke and found me here,'" Rowany murmured, "'on the cold hill's side.'"

"I'm sorry, what did you say?"

"Never mind. Stay there, I'm coming up."

She scrambled up behind her junior. Added inches and years of experience helped not at all; the hillside seemed empty, scan as she would.

"At a guess," she said, "they know there's a sandcat about and they're being extra-cautious, to keep the young lambs safe. These great steep rocks that line the rim, they call them the Devil's Teeth. There are all sorts of caves and crevices where they can pen a flock up at night; they may not let them out until full day. They know that sandcats hate the sun. Let's try what a call will do."

With that, she raised her head and let out a full-throated yodel.

Rachel's eyes widened, into something approaching awe.

"How do you do that?"

"Oh, years of practice. My parents have a place in the mountains, and it's really the only way to get someone's attention, across the breadth of the valley. Besides which," she admitted, "the echoes are fantastic. Sometimes I'll call just for the sake of it, to hear the mountains calling back."

"Can you teach me?"

"Yes, of course—if you promise not to try it out on school grounds, because that way lies nothing but trouble for the pair of us. Hush now, and watch... See there?"

A small figure had emerged from a cleft at the slope's height, where the crater's exposed rock thrust upward to the sky. Rowany called again, and waved mightily; after a moment, the distant figure waved back, and began to run towards them.

"Perfect," Rowany breathed. "I was beginning to worry that we'd have to search half the hill before we found anyone. He'll be here in a minute, these lads are amazingly fast, barefoot over stony ground. I think this is the boy I was hoping for, too."

"How can you tell?"

"Oh, it's mostly guesswork; they do all look alike at a distance, black curly hair and a sheepskin coat. But Zeru's family usually graze their sheep hereabouts at this time of year, and they can get positively territorial about it, even though the pasture's supposed to be open to all. I had to stop him and his brother fighting a rival one time, over the right to water their flock at one particular spring. Besides, I've known him since he was a bratling in his brother's shadow. That's Zeru, I'm sure of it."

Zeru it was, trotting to the foot of the rock they stood on, gazing up at Rowany with an expression that made Rachel giggle aloud.

Rowany gestured impatiently for her to be quiet. Then she smiled down at the boy and asked after his health, and his mother's, his father's, his brother's, all in order; and then the sheep, all-important, and his pet birds, and various other aspects of his life that had to be negotiated before she could even enquire about the mule, let alone suggest that she might have need of it.

When she could at last get there, when he allowed that the mule was indeed in its crude little shelter down the way, of course she offered a fee for its hire, although she had no money. And of course he refused, indignantly, tempestuously: was she not an old friend of his family, known to his brother even before him? Friends did not speak of money. She would take the mule as a favour to Zeru; and more, he would come too, to lead the creature every step of the way, so that she wouldn't be at all inconvenienced by having to return it. The sheep could tend to themselves, penned as they were; and more, he had milked those ewes whose lambs were weaned already, and he had a canful the young ladies could share for their breakfast, along with some cheese he had made yesterday. No, indeed, he insisted, absolutely...

"Always start by insulting them," Rowany said to Rachel, as they stepped down from the rock with negotiations satisfactorily concluded. "When they're offended—especially by money—they have to offer twice as much in return... Why are you staring at me that way? His family won't lose out. He'll give us a morning of his time, a drink of milk and a handful of cheese, and we'll pay his mother down in the village. The women are always more practical."

Rachel shook her head slowly. "I'm sure they are. They wouldn't worship you, the way that boy does. When he looks at you, he sees an angel stepped down from heaven; it's written all over him. I'm sorry I laughed, only he looked so gormless! But—what language was that you were speaking?

I've never heard anything like it, even with all the people my father deals with."

"He's Basque, like all the shepherd folk around here. There's a whole community of them; driven out of their own land by persecution, they were allowed to settle here, and they've never left. I picked the language up when I was your age," *mostly by being wicked, though she wasn't about to tell a Middle that. New girl or not, wickedness was endemic at that age, and didn't need encouragement.*

"Can you teach me?"

Rowany laughed. "Is that your answer to everything new, that you want to learn it for yourself?"

"Yes, of course. Isn't it everybody's?"

"Sadly, no. You hold on to that, Rachel, and it'll see you far. I don't think I have time to teach you Basque, it's a difficult language and I have my own work to do; but ask the twins, they'll help you pick it up." *They're as wicked as I ever was.* "Come on, now. We don't have time to waste."

"Where are we going?"

"Oh—of course, you didn't follow any of that, did you?"

"Not a word."

"I'll explain as we go, then. I know your people have horses; do you have any experience with mules...?"

They returned to the hermitage in triumph, with a mule, a guide, and provisions, to find everyone in the party awake and sipping warm chocolate from tin mugs. Zeru shook his head shyly when they offered him a share of their meal. In a quick burst of Basque he assured Rowany that he had eaten already, and he'd just wait over there with the mule, where it could graze its own breakfast from the fresh spring turf...

The sheep's milk was still warm, and as deliciously creamy as the cheese; Mrs Bailey's sweet rolls still tasted fresh; the view was remarkable as dawn stole across the plain, revealing the vivid reds and greens of desert and farmland below. Still, no one lingered. Not with Tasha looking so pale, and in such obvious pain. As soon as could be, they made ready for their hike. The pots and dishes were wiped clean and packed away with the primus stove; when Miss Whitworth went to shoulder that pack, Zeru quietly but firmly took it from her.

"Oh, nonsense, child, I'm perfectly capable of carrying this...! —For heaven's sake, Rowany, translate for me, will you?"

Smiling, Rowany held a rapid conversation with the boy, then turned back to the mistress.

"I'm so sorry, Miss Whitworth, but he won't allow it. He says that, that no man of his village could ever live with the shame. He'd be obliged to throw himself into the lake and feed himself to the naiad. Besides which, his mother would beat him," she added.

"Did that postscript come from him, or from you?" Miss Hendy enquired curiously.

"Oh, from him; he's very matter-of-fact about it. Let him carry the bag, Miss Whitworth. He'll be terribly upset if you don't."

"Very well—but I shall insist on paying him porterage. He can give it to his mother, if he's too proud to take it for himself."

"I can promise you, he won't take it at all. It's not all pride, either. Money's no good to him. He lives his life out on the hills here, hunting and gathering and bartering with the other boys for anything he lacks. I don't suppose he's been down to the town once in his life, and there are no shops anywhere closer. None in his village. Of course his mother would be glad of the money, but you'll have to take it to her directly. Or I can do that for you; I do know where she lives."

"You know a good deal about their lives, don't you, Rowany?" Miss Hendy said thoughtfully.

"Oh—well, when you've been at school as long as I have..." Rowany blushed, and lost her way a little in her sentence, and let it slip into silence.

"Many girls spend as long with us, and learn far less. You're a credit to the Crater School, my dear. But come along now, we'd best be moving. Miss Whitworth, will you help me see Tasha settled aboard that beast...?"

Together, the two mistresses lifted the injured girl onto the mule's narrow back. There was no saddle, only a belly-band of rope for her to cling to. She took that in a fierce one-handed grip, while her twin stood alongside holding tight to the other.

"Quite steady, Tasha? You're sure? Very well, then. Off we go. You keep with your sister, Tawney, and the rest of us will follow on. Mind you stay clear of that creature's rear end, girls—the most equable mule may still kick out, if it feels crowded. Perhaps I'd better walk immediately behind, then Rowany and Rachel can follow me and Miss Whitworth bring up the rear..."

Sheep-paths ran this way and that, all across the great ridged and broken slopes of the pastureland. Seams of rock erupted from the ground, forcing wide detours; streams from the high springs cut across paths, too wide to leap and too deep to wade.

Nevertheless, Zeru never hesitated in his choices. Rowany had thought she knew this side of the crater as well as anyone could, but he proved her swiftly wrong. Time and again he surprised her with a shortcut she would never have guessed at, leading them over bare rock outcrops and through tangles of gorse, taking paths that were somehow always wide enough that Tawney never had to leave Tasha's side. Rowany was always willing to offer Rachel a helping hand when the way turned steep or slippery, but the younger girl seldom needed it. Where a boy could go with a mule in tow, she seemed to feel, a girl unhampered could certainly follow.

Miss Hendy was in seventh heaven, constantly darting to one side or the other, picking a leaf or pointing out an insect, finding life that was native to Mars thriving none the less in the rough scrub that had been grown from English seed.

"This is the great experiment in progress, girls—and this far neglected corner of Charter lands is living proof of its success."

"So are we," Rowany said consideringly, "if you choose to look at it that way. Aren't we? Native to England, thriving none the less in this far foreign country."

"Indeed. The very bones of Empire, secure in another generation. And here's the school, do you see? Or at least the far neglected corner of our grounds. The boy has brought us here a full hour quicker than I thought possible. We really must pay him for his trouble."

"We really can't do that, Miss Hendy," Rowany repeated, with an inward sigh. "Let me take him to the kitchens; we'll send him off with a satchel full of Mrs Bailey's baking, and he'll think he's woken in the Garden of Eden. I've tasted the bread these boys live on, and it's...well, you have to soak it before it's even chewable. Then we can go down to the village first chance and give some money to his mother. She's much less romantic."

Behind them, Miss Whitworth laughed. "Isn't that always the way? Very good, Rowany. If you'll take that on, I'll give you the money this evening. No, be quiet—we won't let you give up your own pocket-money, don't be ridiculous. I know how you girls have to husband your pennies, to see you through the term. Just mind you don't let the boy slip away before he's seen the inside of Mrs Bailey's domain. She'll take one look and start feeding him up, I know. And not let any of you girls out on the mountain after this without a bag of buns, as like as not."

"Don't worry, Miss Whitworth. He'll need to feed and water his mule; I'll feed and water him. However he tries to wriggle out of it."

"And when you're done with that, I want you to report to Sister Anthony, please. Yes, indeed—all you girls are bound for a hot bath, a bowl of porridge and a morning in bed. You need proper rest, if you're to be fresh when the rest of the school arrives this afternoon. No, I'll hear no arguments. Head of School you may be, but you'll still do as you're told."

CHAPTER TEN

A Short Journey on a Slow Train

The hubbub was indescribable.

Miss Peters stood at one end of the platform, gazing at a seething sea of green and gold—or no, long and narrow as it was, bordered on both sides, it was more appropriately a canal, she supposed. If canals were ever this busy, this hectic, this *loud*.

It was like this at the start of every term, of course. Two hundred girls, broken down into gangs and sisterhoods and coteries who hadn't seen each other all the length of the holiday: naturally they would need to find their special friends, and cluster inconveniently, and grab hold of each other, and *shriek...*

Still, long years of experience had produced a remedy fit for the cause. Miss Peters looked about her, and yes: there was Brigitta, looking her way, ready for the signal. Standing a head—and a vivid flaxen head at that—above any of her fellows, she was easy to spot in any crowd; which meant of course that others too could spot her, and worm their way through to her side. Specifically, predictably, there was Izzy's dark head, not even reaching Brigitta's shoulder. They were the most unlikely of pairs, the tall Dutch girl and the diminutive Basque. But they had found each other and attached themselves as girls will, and become an inseparable whole.

Miss Peters lifted one arm and made a pumping gesture, as though she pulled a cord above her head, twice, firmly downward. Brigitta waved an acknowledgement; then she turned and ploughed her way towards the puffing, steaming locomotive. Miss Peters almost had to stand on tiptoe to see Izzy following in her friend's wake. She could certainly have taken that on trust, but watched nevertheless. And so saw them reach the cab, and step up onto the footplate in tandem. Here it was Izzy's turn to shine, for the engine driver's family was beholden to hers in some complicated clannish way that no one outside that bloodline had ever yet contrived to understand. She peered up at him and her rapid hands flew with her words, as she'd never learned to hold them still in conversation.

Even from distance, Miss Peters could see his nod of acquiescence—but then, this was long-established ritual, and he had likely been ready and waiting for it, much as the girls had. He lifted and lowered his arm, as if in deliberate echo of her own signal, drawing down on the cable that ran above his head.

Once, twice: two long strong blasts of the train's steam-whistle silenced every girl on the platform. Again, most of them must have been waiting for this. They turned as one, to find her; she stepped up onto a luggage-cart, the better to hold their attention now that she had it.

"Girls! I know you're excited to be back together, and back at school—but do show a little courtesy to our neighbours herebelow. Half the town must know by now that the Crater School is back"—or more likely more than half, for girls had been arriving all day by train and boat, some with long hours to kill before this last leg up to the crater rim; every café, every shop, every street corner must have been seeing green and gold today—"so please let's not leave them with a poor impression. Talk to your friends by all means, but softly, softly..."

Her words had their effect, as they always did. To be sure, the volume would build again, as the more heedless girls forgot her strictures; but the prefects were alerted now, moving through the crowd, shushing each individual throng as it threatened to grow rowdy. And there was the stationmaster blowing his whistle and opening carriage doors to say that the train was ready and the girls could begin to board.

At last! Excitement might rise to fever pitch, but at least each gaggle of girls could only riot now in their own compartment. And once the train drew free of the town, they could only disturb the sheep and the eagles, who were tolerably used to this.

Miss Peters left it to prefects to usher the girls aboard, to settle any disputes about who was sitting with whom, and finally to distribute themselves amongst the rowdiest. It was odd but abidingly true that one of their own could quell a riot in the making, more readily than any mistress. It had been true in her own schooldays—at this very school, no less!—and it remained true to this day. It was how they could let the whole excitable mob ride up on the train together with only a single mistress to supervise. The girls themselves were generally reliable in public, but the start of a new term was enough to shatter any resolve. Conversely, nothing could shift the prefects' sense of responsibility, especially at the start of term, when they were all too conscious of the honour of the school lying on their smartly uniformed shoulders. They took their duties so seriously, it made life easy for the staff; it meant that this particular member of staff could choose her own seat without regard to the needs of discipline or good order. She would be aboard if needed, and the prefects knew it, and would do their very best to ensure that she was not needed at all.

Accordingly, she glanced up and down the platform as the girls filed into their separate compartments. Making a swift decision, she stepped up to one open door just as a leggy bespectacled brunette reached out to close it.

"Room for one more in there, Arie?"

"Yes, I'm sure so, Miss Peters—if you don't mind sitting with us," she added, a little doubtfully. "I've mostly got Juniors in here, and—"

"—and you'll all make splendid company for the run up to school," Miss Peters said briskly, overriding whatever closing argument that sentence might have reached. She stepped up into the compartment and pulled the door firmly closed behind her. That should bring a halt to any further suggestions that she might be better suited elsewhere, with older girls, Sixth-formers, where a mistress properly belonged...

Besides, Arie Bunker was a Sixth-former herself: just not a prefect yet, and not given to spending time exclusively with her own tribe. Which—taken together with her innate kindness, which was something of a legend throughout the school—made her a magnet for younger girls, especially those who were feeling lonely or homesick or at a loss. The staff was aware, and keeping a mindful eye on developments; Miss Peters had made a sudden decision to observe at closer quarters.

A quick scan revealed four Juniors and one shy Middle in the compartment with Arie. All their eyes were on herself now, with a mixture of trepidation, disappointment and frank horror: how terrible to find themselves trapped with a mistress, where they had reckoned to take shelter with a reliable friend-in-need!

"Well now," she said, firmly suppressing her first wild impulse to giggle at their appalled faces, "I don't teach you all yet, so let me test myself: Janice, Sarah, Harriet, Margaret—oh, but you prefer Daisy, don't you? This school has far

109

too many Margarets, so you're doing us a kindness, actually—and Patience, yes? Splendid. Daisy, if you wouldn't mind scooting over and sitting next to Patience, while you others squash up a little—and I know you're best friends, so you won't mind sharing two seats between the three of you— then I can squeeze in here in the corner, and everybody's happy."

That was something of an exaggeration, but she wouldn't chide herself for it. Nor give in to the temptation to make mischief. Her own schooldays were ten years behind her now, but she still remembered how small and unimportant she had felt in the first days of term, and how much she'd missed the securities of home. These girls eyeing her sidelong must be feeling much the same; girlhood and school life didn't change much with the passing generations. They didn't need teasing, they needed reassurance. And had looked to find it with Arie, and were feeling desolate now, seeing the moment snatched away by her own untimely incursion.

She smiled brightly at them and rummaged in her bag. "You've all made this journey before, I know," though only once or twice for most of them, "so you know how slow the climb is. Plenty of time to suck a toffee before we reach the top."

The journeys behind them might more readily be measured in days than in miles; they were safe to have eaten their own sweets long since. Miss Peters handed around the promised bag of toffees—not neglecting Arie, not neglecting herself: schooldays were not so far behind her that a sweet was no longer a treat—and then settled quietly back in her corner, with a book in her lap that she had no intention of reading. The crushing impact of a teacher in the compartment would last perhaps five minutes. Perhaps not so long, if Arie stepped up to the mark. That should leave plenty of time to see the older girl at work.

The stationmaster blew his whistle, three peremptory times. The engine-driver replied with a single louder longer blast; the carriages jerked and shuddered, the linkages moaned strangely, and the whole train began to move. They were off!

The town was formally called Terminus, though few people used the name. It was just "town" to the locals, and to the school too. Two canals and a railway met and ended here. Those three between them reached far and far into Charter territory, and brought Craftereans from all corners of the colony. The town had grown up almost incidentally from small beginnings—a boatyard and a few workers' cottages, a military outpost, a scatter of traders fetching in necessities for the first bold colonists to venture this far, to stake a claim and settle down to farm—but there was nothing incidental about this last spur on the railway. From this point on, everything had been meticulously planned, one man's obsessive vision.

The train ran for several miles along the valley floor, flat farmland on either side, really nothing much to look at. The girls with window seats looked anyway, waiting perhaps for their first sight of the crater wall looming impossibly steep ahead. Or perhaps they were only looking out to avoid looking inward at their company, not to catch each other's or—worse!—Miss Peters' eye. The girls in the middle seats were resolutely sucking toffees and staring at their shoes, until Arie said, "New game, people. Tell us about your holidays, the best and the worst together—but you have to do it in one sentence. I have chocolate for the shortest, and for the longest, and for the funniest. Miss Peters, will you judge that the sentences are fair and legal?"

"I will. I'll choose the winners too," because that was the only safe way to ensure that Arie didn't draw her into the game—and besides, it gave her the chance to go on, "because of course you'll participate, Arie. Why don't you go first, to show the way?"

"I'll be glad to." The Sixth-former thought for a moment, then smiled and said, "'My family and I spent Easter all together in the deanery, which was quite lovely—except that my being the incumbent's daughter obliged me to go to every one of my father's services, which meant sitting through the same sermon no fewer than five times.' How did I do, Miss Peters?"

"Forty-five words, by my count. Room for improvement, in both length and quality."

"Ah, well. It's always difficult, going first; you can't help setting a target. Still, at least it made someone giggle."

Arie glanced at Harriet, who smiled back shyly and said, "No, but is it true, Arie? Really? My dad's a vicar too, and he'd never get away with giving the same sermon twice, let alone five times..."

"Alas, it's all too true. Mine is a rural dean, which gives him obligations in a whole string of parishes, especially at busy times like Easter. One of his vicars was down with canal fever, so Dad had to step in there; and another parish is vacant at present, so again, send for Dad. And then he's on the Board of Governors at the school my brothers go to, which didn't break up for the holidays until Spy Wednesday, so of course he took me along for their last day of term, and of course the school chaplain asked him to take a service. And he was invited to preach at the cathedral on Good Friday, which is a tremendous honour even if the building is hideous, and besides, you don't say no to the Bishop of Marsport; and finally he led our own Evensong on Easter Sunday. He said no one could reasonably expect a fresh sermon on each occasion, so he didn't even try, he just gave us the same one over and over again. And I'm sorry, Miss Peters, but I really don't see how I could have got all that detail into a single sentence."

"And if you had, I'd have lost count halfway through. Besides which, you can't reasonably expect to win your own chocolate. As you say, all you've done is set a benchmark. I daresay someone can pitch shorter than that, and someone else longer. And you win no points for funny either, I'm afraid; supplementary details don't count."

"Harriet laughed," Arie objected.

"She did—though I think it mostly came from fellow-feeling. Very well: one point. Who's next? Patience, will you play?"

Bashful Patience would have declined, surely, if she'd had a true opportunity. But seniority put her next, and so did seating-order, and for the honour of the Middles she had to take a turn. Even she couldn't yield the game to a gaggle of Juniors without at least a token effort. She said, "I don't mind. I don't think I can manage forty-six words, though, so I'll try to be brief. 'Auntie took me to Cassini, which was delightful; sadly, it never stopped raining.' There. That's the best I can do."

"And it'll be very hard to beat, within the rules," Miss Peters said. "Thirteen words, Patience—well done! I'm sorry you didn't see Cassini at its best, but it very often does rain there in the spring. For weeks on end, if you're unlucky. Ask your aunt if you can go again next Easter; that should fall in the autumn, unless it's very late, and autumn is the best time of year to see the Crater City, when the sun's low enough to lay its shadow across the lake."

"I'll do that, Miss Peters. Thank you. And we did have a lovely time, actually," in a sudden confiding burst. "I think I could live in the Museum of Mars, if they'd let me. We went to lots of other places when the weather allowed, but I did keep dragging poor Auntie back there. I'm afraid she was terribly bored," but clearly the pangs of a nice conscience weren't enough to overcome the girl's fascination.

"What was it that drew you?" Arie asked. "I've been there myself, and I love those bizarre fossils they have in the entrance hall, all the early Martian animals that had thankfully died out long before ever we came here, but—"

"Oh, but those are just the eyecatching headlines, like, like the illuminated capitals on a mediaeval manuscript. They're exciting to look at, but they don't really mean much. You have to look beyond them, to find the real story."

"All those dusty dry cases of exhibits, do you mean, Patience? Ugh!" That was Janice, who would cheerfully own in any company to being no kind of scholar.

Patience blushed, but struggled on regardless. "They're not dusty *or* dry, if you only look for what they mean. All the story of Mars is there—and that's our story too, in among all the native creatures and the merlins. And the plants, and the rocks, and the maps, and..."

She ran down at last, blushing furiously, feeling everyone's eyes on her.

"My dear, I'd no idea you were this passionate." *About anything*, but that was a thought to be saved for the staffroom. "If that's how you feel, you must certainly speak to Miss Hendy. I know she has friends at the Museum of Mars, and I'm sure they could arrange a tour behind the scenes, if you can ever persuade your aunt to take you there again. And if not," *if your enthusiasm has soured her against the very notion*, for Miss Peters had met the woman once and retained no fond impression, "well, there will certainly be a school trip to Cassini sometime in the next year or so. Miss Hendy would be only too delighted, I expect, to peel you away on a side-visit."

"Really, Miss Peters? That would be...marvellous." Her tongue stumbled over a different and forbidden adjective, before landing somewhere safe and legal; they both pretended that no such thing had happened. "It's what I want to do, you see, after school: I want to be a, a curator. At the Museum of Mars if that's remotely possible, but anywhere would do."

"After school and university," Miss Peters corrected gently. "A degree would be a prerequisite, for such a career. Besides being the opportunity of a lifetime."

"Oh—really? Because I'm not sure my aunt..."

Being entirely sure that she was right, that her aunt would move to crush any such ambition, Miss Peters said nothing more just now, but resolved to speak to Miss Hendy as soon as might be. Meanwhile, she turned to the girl in the corner beside Patience: "Daisy? It's your turn."

She knew. No longer staring out of the window, no longer feeling trapped between a Middle and a mistress, she seemed quite prepared; but then she only said, "All my brothers were home."

"Were they? Oh, but surely you can find something to say about that, the good and the bad...?"

"No, you don't understand, Miss Peters. That *is* the good and the bad. That's my entry. 'All my brothers were home.' Five words! That's one word each, because I have five brothers. And I love them all, of course, and it was lovely to have them all home at once, because they never are—but can you imagine? Five boys, and just me to deal with them? They know, you see," nodding her head at the other Juniors, who were convulsed with laughter. "And Arie, she's laughing too, she's heard all about my brothers..."

She was indeed. Miss Peters acknowledged the point with a laugh of her own. "Very well, Daisy. That's a five-word winner, I think, and funny too."

Harriet went to the other extreme, scoring for a deliberately tedious narrative that involved stringing together the names of every one of her own long family and the cousins they had gone to visit up at Tharsis. By the time she was done, her friends were in stitches, and the game was clearly over; nobody could compete on length, one way or the other. "Funniest" might still have been arguable, but it didn't really matter. Whoever won the chocolate, they were going to divide it equally around the compartment in any case.

Miss Peters duly awarded the prizes—"with a bonus for Patience, for correct use of a semi-colon; for yes, I hear them, even off the page"—and then nodded out of the disregarded window. "In case you haven't noticed, girls, we're coming up to the crater wall. I've been making this trip for years uncounted—at least, uncounted by anyone with manners, which I hope includes all of you—but I still like to watch. It always looks so impossible, that the train could actually climb that slope."

"I was frightened, the first time," little Janice confessed. "What if the train fell off the rails?"

"It can't," Arie assured her. "The cog mechanism locks us into place, so that even if the engine lost steam, we'd just stay exactly where we were."

"I know that now." Indeed, Janice was pressing to the window, as eager as any of them to watch the steep ascent. "Miss Lowe gave us a science lesson on the funick, funic—"

"Funicular," Miss Peters supplied. "Though it's not really a funicular, we only call it that from courtesy."

"Miss Lowe said that too," Harriet confirmed, "but I really didn't understand why? If it's not a, a funicular, why say it is?"

Miss Peters sighed inwardly, bracing herself for a conversation with a colleague about the desirability of including a little history in with the science, where relevant. Then she said, "The castle's founder, who built it as a hotel, was a very forward-looking man. He made mistakes, and lost a lot of money, but he did have good ideas along with the bad. He always wanted the very latest developments, and he was willing to pay for them. When he first settled on building here, he fetched in engineers to advise him. They built a true funicular, to raise workers and building materials to the rim of the crater; as I'm sure Miss Lowe explained, that's two carriages linked by a cable the height of the climb, so that one goes down as the other is going up. The weight of the descending car helps to counterbalance the weight of the rising car, so that you need less fuel to lift it. It's a practical method, but it is limited, and it wouldn't satisfy him in the long run. He was always going to want something better.

"So he asked his engineers to design and build him a solution, and never mind the cost. This is what they came up with." She patted the wall of the compartment, to symbolise the entire train: *synecdoche*, her brain noted automatically, *but let's not frighten the children*. "It's a rack-and-pinion system, that the locomotive engages with and every separate carriage locks into place, just about—now," as the carriage resounded to a heavy mechanical thudding from below. "It can't miss, and as Arie says, it can't fail. Safety has been designed into the very heart of the system. Our original founder meant that to reassure anxious guests; we find that it works as well to reassure anxious schoolgirls. And their parents. Especially when we point out that the same men went on to build the great funicular at Cassini, to the same design. And everyone still calls that a funicular too, though most of them have no idea why. That's when they're not calling it a wonder of the modern world, for it's that too. You must have ridden the funicular, Patience, up beside Thunder Fall?"

"Yes, of course. Despite the rain. Actually, perhaps because of the rain; Auntie tempted me out of the museum with the promise that the falls would be spectacular. I spoke to a man at the top who said they'd never measured so much water going over the edge, in all the years they'd been there."

"Oooh—did you take any photographs?" Sarah asked.

"I did, actually: from the top and from the carriage on the way down. Not at the bottom. I didn't like it very much where all that water drops into the pool. It's too noisy and too swirly, it made me dizzy. And you couldn't see much anyway, with all the spray. But I had my new kodak that Auntie had given me, and I used up a whole film on the fall. I'll show you the pictures later, if you like. I need to stick them in an album anyway."

"That would be wonderful! Thanks so much, Patience!"

That brief conversation had distracted the younger girls, during the possibly alarming moments when the pinions on the rolling stock engaged one by one with the rack between the rails, and the whole train tilted upward. By the time they turned back to the windows, that transition was behind them and they were climbing steadily, albeit at a sharp and unlikely angle. The gears were ticking below them with a regular *chunk-chunk!* and Arie smiled across the carriage at Miss Peters. Janice's anxiety was lost in the past, a neglected ghost. Their slow and solid rate of climb produced only questions of science, the kind that often troubled growing girls: just how fast were they going; and how long was the track, how steep the climb; and would they arrive at school in time for tea...?

CHAPTER ELEVEN

Hair Today

"**P**atricia Oren Cadigan! *What* have you *done* to your *hair*?"

The question was not asked so much as bellowed, halfway across the castle courtyard, stopping its target mid-staircase. She paused, turned, touched a hand self-consciously to her crown of short dark curls.

"Oh, Lise! I'm so glad to see you—and for you to see me, let's be honest. Do you like it? It's called a Martian bob, and it's quite the thing in New Victoria."

"Never mind what it's called, my lamb. You've got *curls*, and I want to know what you mean by it?"

"I know, isn't it mad? Thing is, when I was so sick last term—well, you know all about that..."

"I do, my love, I was there. Oh, but Levity wasn't. Pat, this is Levity. She's new, obviously, and she's in our dormy, so I'm sherping her. Is that a word? Anyway, Levity, this is Pat Cadigan, and you should really bring her all your problems, because she's much nicer than I am. She has patience, which I really don't. We're by way of being friends, she and I. But she used to have hair so long she could sit on it, and it was dead straight; only then she was grievously ill one night, and I had to go running for Sister Anthony, and we had such excitement. A doctor came over the lake from the San—the other San, I mean, the big one, not ours—and he rowed all the way back an hour later, with Pat swaddled in blankets and Miss Leven going along for the ride. They wouldn't let me go with her. I was a bit upset about that; but once I'd said goodbye Sister Anthony locked me up in quarantine for ten days and I couldn't see anyone at all. But the best thing about San, our San I mean, is that you can sit out on the gatehouse roof and watch life happen all across the lake. You get into trouble if you sit staring out of windows during class or prep or almost anything really, but if you're sick it's positively encouraged. And I wasn't even sick, not really, they were just afraid that I might have caught the same thing; so I was out in the sun next day with my Jane Austen, and I saw a zeppelin come in. That happens sometimes, but it's rare enough that it's always quite exciting; and I'd never seen an ambulance airship before. They're painted all white, with a great red cross on the balloon, both sides; and it was ambiguous, ambidextrous, what do I mean?"

"Amphibious, perhaps?" Levity said, with a giggle. Mamma would say she was learning her way around Lise, and so far she liked everything she'd learned.

"Yes, that, thanks, Levity: it was amphibious, and it landed on the lake and then motored over to the San. So I saw you go, my love," to her friend Pat, "and I know they took you to the Royal Victoria in Marsport, because I asked where I could send letters and Miss Leven told me; but you never wrote back so I had no idea what was happening. Or what was happening to your *hair*," coming back at last to the real point at issue.

Pat rolled her eyes at Levity, making her giggle again; then she said, "No, I'm sorry about that. I did get your letters, and thank you for those; but Mum had to read them to me,

I couldn't even manage that much myself, and I was far too sick to think about writing back. And then when I got out of hospital Mum took me away to convalesce, and of course my address book was still here at school, and I knew term would be over before a letter could reach you here. So I couldn't tell you the most dramatic thing ever, which was when the doctors decided to shave my head. It's old-fashioned, I know, but they do still like to do it with cases of lake malaria. They said I had enough to do getting well, without having to worry about a great heavy head of hair on top when I was still feverish. I must say it did feel easier once it was all gone, very freeing, though I wept buckets at the time—but then I was weeping at everything just then, so I don't know how much that means.

"Anyway," she went on, "that's what happened—and then it grew back curly. I don't know if that's just because it's short, or because I was ill, or what; but I think I rather like it, don't you?"

"Precious, it's adorable. You know that. And you absolutely have to keep it, at least till after Christmas. Just in case someone comes up with a pantomime: you'd be a sure bet for Prince Charming, or whoever. It may not happen, but it might; and Miss Peters will break her heart if you grow it out before then. You know she will. Have you unpacked yet?"

"I have! I'm just done, so I was coming to see who's here and who's available for mischief. We don't have much time," with a regretful glance at her wristwatch, "but—"

"—But there's time enough for a sick-room visit," Lise said firmly. "It's our Christian duty. If we're late down for supper, we'll be forgiven."

"Wait, who's sick? Already?"

"Tasha Mishkin. The twins had an adventure—of course!—last night, not even real term yet. They had to be rescued this morning, and Tasha came in with a wrenched ankle and got herself laid up in San. And Sister Anthony's far too busy to take care of her"—Levity was wise enough already in school ways to understand this to mean *far too busy to chase us off if we fall to plotting wickedness*—"so we owe it to her, to the school, to go up and learn the true story of what happened to them. Liv and I saw the beginning of it, and we'll tell you all about that, because that was exciting enough, in all conscience; but the rest of the tale is a mystery, even to us. There are all kinds of rumours, but I don't believe one of them. Go to the horse's mouth, say I, and cheer up an invalid while we're about it..."

Of course there was more of the castle yet to be discovered. Levity had never expected anything else. She thought she'd still be learning her way around its secrets at the end of the year, when Mamma came to take her and Charm away again. But she expected them to be dull secrets, mundane rooms and cupboards, nooks and crannies. If there were more glories to be revealed, why wouldn't they be included in Miss Harribeth's tour?

This, though: she had entirely not expected this. The school's sanatorium stretched across the front of the castle, high wide windows affording magnificent views of the lake from every bed. Every unoccupied bed, at this stage of term—except that one had its covers tossed back and a pile of books on the locker beside.

"Tasha," the all-knowing Lise said, nodding. "You wouldn't think it, but she reads more than anyone I know."

"Well, she's reading for two," Pat said. "Tawney never picks up a book outside of school. Or inside, when she can avoid it."

Quite sure of their welcome—or better, their being entirely overlooked by any semblance of authority—Levity's two dormitory-mates steered her between the beds to where two tall french windows stood open wide.

Beyond was a broad flat roof, surrounded by a balustrade of the castle's familiar red stone. From this height, with the wind in her hair and the lake spread out below in its rough round rocky wall, so very much like a mouthful of broken jagged teeth, Levity was so enchanted that she noticed nothing else until Lise nudged her quite forcefully in the ribs.

"Liv! Stop daydreaming and say hullo to Tasha like a decent civilised human being!"

"Oh! I'm terribly sorry, it's just so lovely here..." Levity blinked about in blushing confusion, finding three sets of eyes laughing at her: Pat and Lise, one either side, and one more girl below, lying on a deck chair with her bare and bandaged foot propped up on a stool and a book abandoned at her side.

"Don't worry, every new girl feels the same, her first few days. I know we did, Tawney and me. Our sherpa threatened to put us on leashes, we were so prone to wandering off whenever we saw something interesting."

"Not much changed there, then," Pat said crisply. "Levity, Lise, drag some of those deck chairs over here and let's get settled. We need to hear everything, Tasha, so don't think you can trim the tale by a single word."

"Oh, I'm just glad to have company," Tasha said. "We're sherping ourselves now, and Tawney's had to take Rachel off to the chemmy lab for a science test. And my ankle's throbbing like fury, and of course Sister Anthony's up to her ears in everything so I can't ask her for so much as an aspirin. Talking is the best distraction I know when you hurt too much to read. If someone would just fetch me a glass of water, I will tell all."

A nd all indeed she told. Even to Levity, who knew almost none of the actors and no more of the setting than Tasha could point to from the gatehouse roof, it was clear that the tale had lost nothing in the telling. Even so, it was clear too that Tasha wasn't making anything up out of whole cloth. Levity was used to judging truth from invention—some of Mamma's friends were prone to the wildest flights of fancy— and this story felt solidly true all the way, despite Tasha's investing it with as much drama as she could manage. And besides, there was her absent twin to consider, and Rachel too, never mind the Head Girl herself, whom Tasha all too obviously held in awe. With so many witnesses to check her, she wouldn't step far off the path of strict truthfulness.

And besides again, she didn't need to exaggerate anything. The tale was thrilling enough, in all conscience: merlins and a desperate climb and a sandcat—a sandcat!—at the top, all hot breath and savage eyes and the touch of rough fur against her skin... Levity tried to stay cynical and couldn't manage it. Tasha had a real storyteller's gift, and her audience was with her every step.

Every agonised step, by the end: soft cries of sympathy and applause as she described her struggle up the last slope with only her sister to hold on to amid the savage flood of pain from her ankle.

"...Then Rowany found us, and the staff, and they made us as comfortable as we could be for the night. That's all," meaning *that's all I want to say about that*. Levity understood her instantly, and so did her friends. "Let's talk about something else, before someone comes to chase you away and make me rest again." She had the pinched, weary look of one who would benefit from resting, even Levity could see that; but they were fourteen and not one of them could say so. "Levity, did you come here with a sister?"

Startled, Levity could do nothing but nod.

"Two red heads and a black one," Tasha said, nodding in her turn. "We saw you from up there," with a casual wave of her hand at the battlements above, "and there couldn't be even more new girls who are redheads. Miss Tattersall would say that was stretching the law of probability beyond all limits; so you had to be one of the two, and we were sure you must be sisters. Actually we were hoping you were twins, only that turned out to be Rachel."

Rachel: the sour, silent girl who had shared Miss Harribeth's tour with them. And Tasha was one of the twins who had turned up to take her away. Levity had known that all this while, but struggled none the less to marry the bright, vibrant girl from that memory with the wan and sorry creature stretched out here, her pale face tight with pain.

Wanting to distract her, now that she seemed to have lost the exuberant thread of her narrative, Levity said, "Sorry, no, we're not twins. Though people used to think we were, before I shot up all in a rush two years ago. Poor Charm still hasn't forgiven me for that. There's hardly more than a year between us, so we're as close as two sisters can be, who weren't actually born together. But—Rachel is? But there's only one of her."

"That's right. Her twin was sent to another school, and she's really cut up about it."

"Ohhh—that would explain why she was so..." Levity ran suddenly dry, seeing no way to finish that sentence that would be fair to the absent Rachel, but Tasha grinned anyway, understanding her exactly.

"Grouchy? Yes, indeed. She came here with a hate for school and all things schoolish. I think we broke that down, at least a little—but she is still missing her sister desperately, so I wouldn't be surprised if it all came out again. And now I'm not there to keep an eye on her..."

"Don't you worry about that," Pat said. "Tawney's got more sense on her own than the two of you have together—and we'll all help to keep an eye on her, as needed. You just focus on getting fit," with a fearsome scowl at the bandaged foot, as though her disapproval could hurry its healing. "Remember it's not just hockey and lax this term. The early thaw means tennis too, and maybe even cricket."

"Oh, don't I know it? I could curse that sandcat—except, you know, I can't really. I've never been that close, never ever. It was...otherworldly."

Lise snorted. "If there's one thing we're sure of on this crazy planet, it's that sandcats are native here. We're the otherworldly ones."

"Yes, but you know what I mean. A meeting of two worlds. Right there, right on top of me."

"In which case our world came off worse, is what I'm saying." Pat returned to her theme. "You should be ashamed. Especially as we had a really good chance of beating the Seniors this year. Levity, do you play?"

"Do I play what?"

"Anything, really. This is the term of all the sports when the weather works out handily, as it looks like doing this year; and we don't get many chances to play other schools, we're so remote out here, so the Middles versus Seniors is always hard-fought. And we're always expected to lose, so it would be fabulous if you turned out to be a hidden prodigy."

"I'm sorry, I don't think I am one. Though I don't know for sure, because we've never played team games. We never had the chance, Charm and I. We have played a lot of tennis, but I don't know if we'd be any good by your standards."

"We'll find out," Pat said, a little grimly, Levity thought. "And we'll test you for prodigy-ness, too."

"Prodigality," Lise said helpfully.

"I'm not sure that's what that means. Like the Prodigal Son, you think it's going to be the same thing and it just isn't. But I'm happy to try out for any teams you think I'm worth a shot at," Levity said. "Charm will, too. I don't suppose you have gymkhanas?"

Pat laughed. "We don't, no. If you'd seen our fat little ponies, you wouldn't have asked. They get a lot more grooming than exercise, and a lot more carrots than either. Why, are you a dedicated horsewoman?"

"Not me, no, but Charm is. She'd have liked the chance to compete," but it didn't matter anyway. A year wasn't really time enough to win a place on any team, they both understood that; and they'd have a year at most, Mamma had been clear about that. Likely not so long.

It wasn't time enough to learn much, either. They had both been quite clear about that, when they were arguing for some other choice, any other choice than school. It might be time enough to make some friends—like these girls here, now, who seemed quite disposed to be friendly—but for how long? There were friendly girls, and then there were friends of the heart who would keep in touch over time and distance, through change and sorrow. Even through shock and revelation. Levity had hoped perhaps to make such friends here—indeed, there seemed small point in this whole school adventure if she didn't—but would a year be long enough? Would they even be granted a year, before Mamma whisked them away again?

The others were still talking about horses: specifically, about whether Tasha would be allowed to ride with a dicky ankle. "It's the perfect solution," she asserted half-seriously. "I could get anywhere, on Old Tom Hopkins. From the house to the castle and back, I wouldn't need to stay in San at all; Sister Anthony would be delighted to see the back of me, I'm sure. I'm nothing but a nuisance here, she told me so herself. It's not as if I'm sick, because I'm not. I could park him in the courtyard, and hop to classes. Or ride him in up the stairs and right along the corridors, he wouldn't mind, he's the placidest beast imaginable—"

"He may be," Pat said drily, "but the staff are not. Can you imagine? 'Don't mind Old Tom, Miss Tattersall, he'll stand quiet at the back of the classroom and be no trouble at all...'"

"He'd probably be better at sums than I am," Lise said, trying to sound mournful but losing it in a giggle.

"He'd be like one of those fairground horses who are trained to count," said Tasha, not to be outdone. "She'd end up teaching him more than she could us, and he'd win all the prizes at Speech Day, and we'd be in such disgrace our parents would disown us. Speaking of parents—Levity, I know it's rude, but I do have to ask. Do your people have the same flaming red hair they gave you and your sister? I know it runs in families, and Miss Hendy gave us a whole lesson about that last term. I used to wish for red hair when I was a kid, though I think that was just to look different from Tawney. Yours is lovely, though."

"Tell me that again at the end of the summer," Levity muttered regretfully, "when my skin is just one giant freckle. But yes, our mother has the same hair. Except that hers has white streaks in it now. She tells us they're distinguished."

Lise nodded. "Miss Hendy said that redheads often go white prematurely. What about your father, though? Is he a redhead too? She said you need to have the history of it on both sides of the family."

"I don't know," Levity said. "We, we lost him in the war, when we were very little. Charm was still a baby, and I wasn't more than two. We don't remember him at all."

"No photographs, no portraits?" Tasha's face said *surely you must know the colour of your father's hair?*

"No. Mamma doesn't keep things like that. She's never talked about him much to us, and of course we can't ask."

And then, in a desperate attempt to steer the conversation away from the one thing she really didn't want to talk about, Levity said, "She's the artist, you know, Isobel Buchanan. We came to Mars back then, when we were tinies, and of course we couldn't bring anything with us, hardly. And we've lived on the road ever since, all our lives, following her instincts or else her commissions, all over Charter lands. We've never owned anything more than we could carry." *Only our secrets,* and sometimes in honesty those were heavy enough.

CHAPTER TWELVE

Back in the Swing of It

Every new term was like a new girl, always needing a week or two to settle in. Tawney had noticed it, time and time again.

Of course it wasn't really the term, that was just dates in a calendar. Perhaps she should say the school needed time to settle down—only there was no actual single entity that you could call the school, however much everyone pretended there was. Even Miss Leven did that, at the end of every assembly—"School! Stand! March!"—but that was, what had Miss Peters called it, something pathetic, making out that animals or trees had human emotions. Or schools. The Crater School was more than the sum of all its parts, she was certain of that: more than the buildings and the playing fields, more than the history and the reputation, more than Miss Tolchard and Miss Leven and all the staff who had ever worked here and all the pupils they had ever taught. It was something powerful and nebulous both at once, that she could never quite catch hold of however hard she tried to think about it, never put into words however long she and Tasha talked it through. Nevertheless: if the school was like a rosary, then each new term was a separate bead; and if it was really just two hundred girls and two dozen mistresses bumping each other into place and into order, it still felt as though every term was a thing in itself, its own coherent space.

And its own slightly awkward, stumbling start, while everybody caught their balance and their breath. There was all the giddy excitement of the first days, catching up with friends after weeks or months apart. There was the busyness of new classes and new books, helping new girls find their feet, feeling old habits reassert themselves, school discipline after the relaxation of the holidays. Everything just so, their cubicles kept as neat as their hair, uniforms tidy and every button in place, every ladder darned. A clean hanky and a brisk step, a steady sense of purpose, always somewhere to be and something to do.

It took a week or two. Even when you were fourteen, and you'd been at school for ever. For Rachel, to whom everything was new and strange anyway but the newest and strangest of all must be that terrible absence at her side where her sister belonged and was suddenly missing—well, it was no surprise that Rachel was still stumbling, still awkward and angry and not settled down at all.

They were both having to get along without their twins just now. Tasha's ankle had kept her in San for a week, despite all her pleading, despite Tawney's promises to help, to carry all her sister's books and other belongings, to be a spare set of legs whenever needed. Sister Anthony was unmoved, immovable; they might have saved their breath. And then just when Tasha was finally on the verge of freedom, some never-to-be-sufficiently-cursed Junior had spread a feverish cold among her cohort. Half a dozen of them filled one end of the long San ward—and next morning, when Tawney had skipped up to retrieve her twin, Sister Anthony stopped her at the door. Tasha had woken up with a temperature and a nasty ticklish cough, and under no circumstances was Sister Anthony about to risk an epidemic through the Middle School.

So Tasha was back in bed again, in isolation, headachey and sour; and Tawney had another week to face alone. Which should really help build her friendship with Rachel, because they were both like Peter Pan without his shadow, cut off from an essential part of themselves. Somehow, though, it wasn't working out that way. Maybe they were like wounded warriors, twitchy together because it was like looking in a mirror: you couldn't see the other one without being reminded of what you'd lost. Only of course it was worse for Rachel, because Tawney and Tasha would be reunited soon, and in the meantime they could at least wave at each other through the San's great windows.

All Rachel had to look forward to was years of separation, seeing her twin only in the holidays. After ten days of keeping close company with her, Tawney still thought it was cruel of her parents to do that. She could see how miserable Rachel was, and understood entirely why that inner sorrow showed itself as moodiness and temper. Understanding didn't make her any easier to live with, though. It was one more reason to want Tasha back in school; sherping Rachel would be so much easier with two of them to keep an eye on her.

She shouldn't really need a sherpa still. Indeed, she kept saying she didn't; but Tawney felt obliged to stay close, if only to keep her out of as much trouble as she could manage.

However much she did that, though, Rachel could always manage more. Today she wasn't just being difficult, she was being impossible; and if she didn't come to her senses soon, it wouldn't just be difficult to save her from the consequences. It would be impossible.

CHAZ BRENCHLEY

Tawney made up her mind at lunchtime, she would make one final effort before giving up. Tasha would expect it of her. That would have been reason enough, even if she hadn't felt responsible for seeing that Rachel made it at least to half-term without getting herself expelled or setting the school on fire. Or both.

"Actually it probably would be both," she thought, giggling to herself. "If she did set the school on fire, it would. She'd be safe to be expelled for that. Sometimes I think that's what she wants, the great idiot. It wouldn't change her parents' minds, I'm sure of that. They'd only be the more sure they were right, and send her to a worse school than this. I really ought to save her from that, if I can. Besides, I kind of like the girl. I think we could be real friends, if she wasn't so set on hating everything around her, including me."

With her mind made up, it was only a matter of opportunity. Talking seriously or privately was impossible over the meal table, with friends and classmates packed close on either side and the volume in the dining hall so loud you had to bellow to make yourself heard. After lunch, though, they always had half an hour to themselves: one of the rare periods in the Crater School day when nothing was timetabled and there was no need to be rushing from one end to the other. Indeed, rushing was forbidden. They were supposed to rest, reading or talking quietly, but no one policed them unless they grew uncommonly raucous. Which they never did, or almost never: going unsupervised was too uncommon a luxury to be wasted. No girl wanted to be guilty of bringing staff or prefects down in their wrath, and ruining this precious time for everyone.

Accordingly, as soon as grace was said at the end of the meal, Tawney rolled her napkin and cleared her place like everyone else, made sure that Rachel did the same—and then seized her victim's arm and said, "Come for a walk with me. We're not allowed down by the lake at the moment," not without a staff, not since the merlins erupted from the water so unexpectedly, "but there are still places I haven't shown you. We've just time to see the sculpture garden, if we hurry. Which we're totally not supposed to do, but no one's going to be watching, so..." This time was an opportunity for staff and prefects too to relax, if nothing too outrageous forced itself on their attention—a fact which was not, of course, lost on wicked Middles.

Rachel tried to shrug her off ill-temperedly, but Tawney was persistent. *Stubborn*, her teachers were inclined to say. Her friends and family both would probably nod in rueful agreement, but she preferred *persistent*. She thought that had to be a virtue, didn't it?

"Please, Rachel, do come? I need to talk to you."

"I don't need to listen."

"Yes, you do. Truly. It's important."

Rachel gave way with a bad grace, and they walked in silence through the courtyard and out into the bright sunlight beyond the castle. Tawney had to shake her head at half a dozen calls from friends, to spend the time with them. Any one of those invitations offered more fun than this, and she wavered between resenting Rachel's attitude and her own sense of unwilling duty—until she caught herself at it, and chuckled ruefully.

"What's funny?" Rachel demanded.

"Oh—nothing, really. Only that I can't decide who to hold a grudge against, you or me, so I might as well not bother."

"Oh, pick me. Why not? It's not going to make any difference to me. Besides, I keep telling you I don't need you tagging after me all the time, now I know my way around."

"If that's what you think, you don't know anything. Don't you realise I'm the only one who saved you from a Head's report this morning? Cheeking the prees is one thing, and that'll only cost you a lot of grief and a lot of fun you'll miss out on; but you can't cheek the staff, you just *can't*."

Rachel shrugged sourly. "I didn't see what cause Miss Tattersall had, to be so down on me. I'd done all the prep she gave us."

"Yes, and got all the sums wrong. And you're usually so good at maths, of course she was upset with you. You either did it deliberately, or else you just didn't try, and either one will bring trouble down on your head here. And then you were plain rude to her, in front of the whole class."

"Well, she'd been rude to me. In front of the whole class. And I didn't ask you to interfere."

"No, but someone had to, or she was fit to slaughter you. One more word out of you, and I swear you'd have been up before the Head if she had to drag you there herself." Tawney shuddered at the awfulness of that image, and then went on quickly, "What's wrong, Rachel? I know you're not happy here, but it's more than that. I thought you were too proud to do bad work, however much you loathe the school."

That stung, as it was meant to. Rachel flushed, and said, "What does it matter, anyway?"

"It matters to you," Tawney said. Persisting, or being stubborn. "You might as well tell me what's up, because I'll keep asking until you do. And you know you can't shake me off. We're in the same form, the same house, the same dormy; I'll be right here at your side, still asking, until you come through."

"Pest," Rachel growled—but her lip twitched, as if even she couldn't quite suppress a smile, even in the depths of whatever had embittered her so. And then, at last, "All right," she muttered. "I will tell you. Just you, though. You're not to tell anyone else."

"I'll have to tell Tasha," Tawney said bluntly. "We don't have secrets, she and I."

"No, of course not; I understand that." Who better? Telling one twin was the same as telling the other; that must be true all over the three planets. And the moons. "But nobody else," Rachel insisted, while Tawney was still glancing up and shivering, hoping to spot neither moon.

"Pioneer's honour," Tawney said immediately, crossing her fingers over her heart in the little gesture that would bind her for life if necessary. The Pioneer movement was that important here; if Rachel had learned one thing about the Crater School, it must be that. Besides, she was a Pioneer herself, with a sleeveful of badges from her former troop. She knew all about honour.

"Thanks." Rachel took it as the absolute promise that it was; but still hesitated, glanced about, put off the moment. "Where's this garden of yours, then?"

"Down past the houses and the sports fields. Come on, we'd best step on it if we're to get there and back before class. Mlle Latour does *not* love latecomers, and she'd make us write fulsome apologies. In French."

They could have talked as they went, but Tawney was merciful: let Rachel have a breather, gather her thoughts, take this last little time to work up to spelling out what was troubling her. Confession had always come easily to the twins, but she knew other families weren't raised as they had been. From earliest days they'd been given time with their parents at the end of every day to admit all their baby sins and indiscretions, even before they were old enough to take confirmation classes and make their first proper confession to a priest. Clearing her conscience before she went to sleep was second nature to Tawney. Other girls, she knew, sometimes needed help.

At school, there was nowhere better than the sculpture garden to give that process a push. She gave Rachel a literal push, down onto the bench beside the pond, where water bubbled constantly from the mouth of a surprised-looking mermaid.

Rachel looked around the little grove of very English trees clustered above the water, spotting elves and animals in stone and wood and iron, peeping out from the undergrowth or clinging to a branch. "Oh, this place is lovely!"

"Yes, it is, and I promise we'll come back to explore—but we haven't time just now. Come on, Rachel. Tell me."

Rachel rubbed at an imaginary stain on her skirt, then blurted, "My sister Jessica isn't happy at all, at the school they sent her to. Well, you know that, I've read you bits of her letters. So I went to see Miss Leven yesterday evening, to ask if I could telephone."

"Oh, Rachel, you didn't! I said not to do that...!" It was quite the worst plan Tawney could imagine, and she had told Rachel so at length, the first time the idea came up.

"I know, and you were right, of course. She said absolutely not. Which is stupid, because if she could just talk to me, Jess might calm down and sit it out. But Miss Leven wouldn't hear of it. She said that girls are never allowed to use the telephone, except in family emergencies—which this is, only she just won't see it!—and in any case, in our particular case, our parents were quite clear to her that they wanted a clean break between us. We won't even get to see each other at half-term, they're keeping us both in school."

"A lot of families do that," Tawney said, trying to be encouraging. "It's just too far for most people, to go home for a few days. We didn't even get home for Easter, Tasha and I. Our stupid brother was in a row at Westminster, and Mum and Dad had to go back to England to sort things out. It was fine, though, we had a lovely time here. The staff made sure of that. It'll be the same at half-term, you'll see."

"That's the point," Rachel said harshly. "It'll be just the same. We'll still be apart, and Jess will be climbing the walls by then, and hating everybody even more than she is already. Only it's worse than that, even, because now we're not even allowed to write to each other."

"Not allowed...?" The parted twins wrote to each other every single day, she knew that. Everyone knew that. You could hardly avoid knowing it: letters for posting had to be laid out on the hall stand in Jopling House—where everyone could see them—before bedtime, and Rachel's were there every night, a mute declaration and a passionate protest both at once. "They can't stop you writing, surely? It's the, the Royal Mail; it belongs to the Queen," as if that made any difference, as if it meant that any of Her Majesty's subjects must be free to use it. Tawney was rather muddled in her mind about that, but she was absolutely certain that interfering with the mails was a crime. Surely preventing someone from writing a letter counted as interfering? Besides, they were so keen here on being a good correspondent; weekly letters home were compulsory, and pen pals across the Empire deeply encouraged. Why, Tawney and Tasha even wrote to their abominable brother every week or so, even though he rarely wrote back, the louse...

"Miss Leven says that writing every day is *excessive*, and against the spirit of our parents' instructions." Rachel's voice was bitter and hard-edged, biting off every savage word. "She allows that sisters ought to stay in touch, but feels that one letter a week would be more reasonable. And not a multi-page budget, she says, not a letter that's written in pages every day and then folded together to be posted once a week. Just a regular weekly sisterly note. And she's writing to Jess's headmistress to suggest that she enforce the same rule. And she won't listen to me, and she won't let me talk to Jess, and she can't see what trouble's going to come of this..."

Tawney could see already what trouble was going to come to Rachel. They'd had a bare taste of it this morning. She said, "Is that why you didn't do your maths prep properly?"

"Miss Leven said I could write a quick note, to explain. A quick note! How do you tell your sister, your twin, that you're not even allowed to write to her any more? I wasn't thinking about anything else last night. Least of all Miss Tattersall's grisly sums."

"I did notice you'd gone awfully quiet. You should have said something, Rachel." *Then I could have saved you from a row this morning, maybe.*

"I, I talk to Jess, when something's bothering me. Nobody else." Rachel shook her head in frustration. "I don't know how to deal with things, without her. And she's worse, she won't tell anyone anything except me. We've always been that way. There's just us at home, no brothers or sisters; it's always been enough, but we do need each other."

Tawney could see why their parents might think the twins needed more than each other. At the same time, she thought tearing them asunder was the worst possible way to achieve that. She and Tasha had been all-in-all to each other, before they came to school. Now that she was fourteen and so much wiser than before—practically finished growing up, if only other people would see it!—she could see quite clearly how the staff here had eased them apart, pointing them at other friends and other interests, expanding their horizons without ever damaging that core of faith and family that linked them closer than any sisters ever were. They would die for each other, of course, that went without saying; they still turned to each other as a matter of habit, finished each other's sentences, shared each other's thoughts in class and dreams at night. But they each had their own independent friends too, and hobbies that left the other cold; and that only seemed to bring them closer, in some strange way she couldn't quite understand yet.

"Well, now that you've told me this," she said practically, "then you can tell me anything else, can't you? Tell us both, me and Tasha together, once she's out of quod. There's no need to hold back, the next time something's bothering you; we're your official Jessica substitutes. What we're going to do about Jessica—well, I need to think about that. And talk it over with Tash. I think your parents are just mean to treat you this way. They're neither of them twins themselves, are they? I know it runs in families, but they can't be, or they'd see how wrong this is. And I'm surprised at Miss Leven for going along with it; it's unkind, and she's not usually like that. Don't worry, Rachel, we'll think of something. We'll make them change their minds. It's, it's unnatural, that's what it is. It can't be allowed to stand." She made the declaration firmly, in words she'd found in a history book, from a parliamentary speech; then she glanced at her wristwatch and gasped. "We'd better run, or Mlle Latour will absolutely slay us. Come on!"

And she grabbed Rachel's hand and dragged her after by main force, as fast as two leggy girls could run.

CHAPTER THIRTEEN

A Chapter of Accidents

"Well, you're looking like a proper little schoolgirl these days."

Charm scowled up at her big sister as though that were the worst thing she might have said, but Levity still thought it was true. Indeed, the scowl proved her point. If you were a proud member of the Juniors, then patronising older girls were totally to be scowled at. Unless they were prefects, of course. If they were mere Middles themselves, and mere sisters to boot, then scowling was absolutely the order of the day.

It couldn't last, though. Charm glanced down at her neat appearance, then back up at Levity. "I suppose I do, really, don't I? Not that we get much chance to look like anything else, with the staff *and* the prees *and* Sister Anthony on our backs all day."

Levity smiled in sympathy. It was hard for them both to keep as tidy as the school insisted. She herself was managing, when she remembered; but Charm could have featured in a photograph for the Crater School prospectus, she was so spruce in her uniform blazer and tunic, with her long bright

141

hair hanging down in two careful plaits tied off with matching green ribbons.

"I do like the bows," Levity said. "They're definitely an improvement on Mamma's old paint-rags."

"Ooh, I'd forgotten that! Wasn't it awful? And we tried to wash the oil paint out, and only made it worse whatever we tried, and in the end Mamma just fetched her pinking shears and shingled us both, there and then..."

Now they were laughing together, as only sisters can; and Charm picked up the end of one plait and looked at the pretty bow a little ruefully and said, "Marigold still has to tie these for me, though. I can't seem to—"

Levity interrupted her, with what would have been a shriek if they hadn't been standing on the drawbridge over the moat, where she wasn't entirely sure they were allowed, in clear sight from Miss Leven's open study window. "Charm Buchanan! What do you call those?"

"Um, my fingers...?"

"They look more like Mamma's Chinese ink-sticks! Have you been *dabbling* them in the ink-pot? No wonder you were standing so modestly with your hands behind your back, I should have known something was up! You cut along to the bathroom quick and get them clean before anyone sees."

"I've been trying, but I can't seem to shift it, no matter how much soap I use."

"No, soap won't shift that. It's the pumice stone for you, my girl. Yes, I know you hate that, but there's nothing else for it. Except turpentine, I suppose, that's what Mamma would use—but we can't very well break into the art room to look for it. And there's only five minutes before classes start again. What were you doing, anyway, to get into such a state?"

Charm giggled briefly. "Marigold came up with such a good game. It's like netball, only you play it on a desk, flicking balls of blotting-paper with rulers and trying to get them into the inkwell. Only—well, I was trying to block Andi's shot, but I kind of knocked into the inkwell and spilled it over, and it just went everywhere..."

"And you didn't think of using an empty inkwell, of course? No, of course not. Come on, let's see what we can achieve before the bell."

Privately, she thought it would take a miracle to have her sister looking halfway presentable in the time. She did have to try, though. Little sisters were a perishing nuisance some-times, but you couldn't just let them walk into trouble.

Sometimes you had to risk worse trouble, hold your breath and hope. "We're not supposed to cut through the gatehouse—but there's no one around, and we don't have time to circumnavigate the whole castle just to reach a bath-room. Come on. If anyone catches us, we're just new girls and a little bit lost."

Charm snorted. "We might have got away with that the first week. Not now."

"I know, but never mind. Let's say it anyway, if we need to. We're not used to following rules, and there are so many, it's no wonder if we get a little confused. I'm honestly not sure whether we're allowed to be on the drawbridge, even though we came here legally along that footpath. We're not allowed in the Mistresses' Garden, and we're not allowed through the gatehouse; who knows if we're allowed to stand on the bridge between the two?"

She was moving as she spoke, steering her sister off the uncertain territory of the drawbridge, into the forbidden ground. Now that term had started, girls were supposed to come and go through the back of the castle, leaving this front way for visitors and staff. As Lise had pointed out, two hundred girls heading both ways in one narrow passage was a recipe for chaos, besides blocking the path for adults, "and looking awful, an absolute scrum, which would be the worst kind of advertisement for the school; and it's not like we have any particular reason to come this way, unless we're going down to the lake, and that's off-limits now thanks to the merlins dancing about. Everything that matters is behind the castle, our houses and the playing fields and so on."

Except that two sisters had found a legitimate reason to make their way to the front of the castle, where they could be alone for ten precious minutes; and now perforce they had to risk the passageway, with its doors to either side. Levity's eyes were on the arch beyond, that would release them into the safety of the courtyard. All her purpose was bent towards that sunlight; it was Charm who dragged on her arm, who hauled her to a halt. "Liv, wait, wait up a minute..."

"What is it? We haven't got a minute, we'll be late as it is, and I don't know who you have next period but we've got botany with Miss Hendy and she would not love me if I was late."

"You mean you don't want to risk a row with your favourite teacher," said shrewd Miss Charm. "*We've* got Miss Tattersall, which is ever so much worse. But look, Liv—!"

She pointed, to where a door in the passage wall stood open, with light leaking out.

"That's Mr Fulton's cubby," and the old janitor was notorious: sour-tempered at the best of times, which no time ever was as far as he was concerned. At least, that was his reputation. Levity had seen him round and about the castle, busy with a mop or a broom or a bucket of wet tea-leaves to settle the dust, but only ever at a distance. She'd been given good reason not to get closer. He was said to despise all girls indiscriminately, and to resent their every footstep on his immaculately polished floors.

"I know, that's the point. He's safe to have turps, isn't he?"

"I suppose so. But, Charm, you can't—"

144

But, being Charm, she already had. She'd knocked firmly on the open door; and hearing no answer, she had stepped inside. Really, Levity had no choice but to follow.

"Mr Fulton's cubby" was the phrase that everyone used, the school's particular name for where the janitor kept all his things, his mops and buckets and—hopefully—a bottle of turpentine on a handy shelf. Somehow that name had persuaded Levity to expect something small, not so much larger than the household cupboards she was used to. Which was ridiculous, of course, when the castle was—well, the size of a castle. And she knew the size of the gatehouse, square and imposing and bigger itself than any house she'd ever lived in, and even so. She stepped through that door expecting near walls and narrow shelves and shadow, and was stunned for a moment by the sheer impact of space and light.

The passageway behind them cut the gatehouse neatly in two; Mr Fulton's cubby occupied one entire side. Two walls—one they had just stepped through from the passageway, and one that backed onto the castle proper—held no windows, and those indeed were shelved from floor to ceiling. The other two, though...

Of course she had known that the gatehouse had windows, higher and wider than any true castle would ever have allowed. She had seen them, often and often. She just hadn't *thought*. Apparently she'd held two pictures in her head at once, the bright sunlit outside that she saw daily and the gloomy grim inside of her imagination, and never tried to match one to the other. Mamma would have been disgusted with her.

Those high wide windows in the other two walls looked out over the lake and the moat, affording views that she could have gazed at all afternoon, if she'd been free, if she'd been allowed, if Charm hadn't been urgent at her elbow and both of them trespassing here. But those same windows flooded the room with unlooked-for light, and it was so much more than any caretaker's cubby that her head could paint. She wanted to paint this, in vivid colour: the white walls and the high beamed ceiling, those majestic visions of Mars—the native crater and the human-built castle walls, like an expression of the Red Raj in two contrasting views—and the domestic comforts of the room itself, with its old worn armchairs around the fireplace, a teapot on the hearth, a book laid down as though its reader had only just stepped out...

She almost wanted to touch the pot, to see if it were still warm. Instead she remembered that door left ajar, and clutched at Charm's arm almost in a panic, determined simply to drag her sister out of there and pretend they'd never crossed the threshold.

Just at that moment, though, Charm pointed up high and cried, "There! There it is, see, Liv? On the top shelf there..."

At first, Levity could see nothing but the ink-stained paw Charm pointed with, a vivid reminder of why they'd dared to venture in here. But then she followed the stabbing finger, and saw a large jar of clear liquid set on a high shelf.

"Well," she said uncertainly, "it does look like it might be..."

"It is, it is! It's just like Mamma's!"

That was true, Mamma's studio always held the same giant glass bottle, where she kept her turps supply and regularly topped up half a dozen jugs.

"I can't see a label," Levity said cautiously. Mamma was scrupulous about that. With two curious girls about, she always said she had to be.

"Well, of course not. Mr Fulton knows what's in his own jars." *And girls are positively not allowed in here unsupervised,* but there was no need to say that; they both knew it. "Besides, we'll know it from the smell, won't we? Only I don't think I can lift that great heavy thing down, so..."

146

"I should think not. You leave it to me, and hold the ladder."

Blessedly, Mr Fulton was not a tall man, and the shelf stood very high. He had a ladder just to hand, against the wall beside the door. Levity would have felt more secure on a set of steps, but beggars can't be choosers and she did at least have Charm there to anchor the foot. They'd done this a hundred times or more, from kitten-rescuing to apple-scrumping missions all across Charter lands. Now she was committed—she'd followed Charm through the door, so of course she was committed; sisterly solidarity was the unwritten law that bound them close as twins—Levity lugged the ladder over without a second thought.

And set it firmly against the shelves, and tested it, and found it solid; and trotted briskly up while Charm set her own foot firmly on the bottom rung and held tight to both the risers.

The ladder didn't reach all the way to the top shelf. Levity still had to stretch up above her head to grip the bottle. And she needed both hands to hold it, which was sure to make life difficult, going down. She thought she'd be better off facing into the room and using her heels on the rungs, so she could lean backwards against the weight of it. So she was just inching her way around, feeling the rung suddenly narrow and awkward beneath her feet where it had felt so secure before, when—

"What in the world do you two think you're doing?"

The voice came from the doorway, where they'd left the door ajar. Levity startled, and twisted her head around to see who spoke. And almost lost her balance, almost fell—and in the effort of recovery, jerking back, she totally lost her grip on the great glass jar.

Which tipped as it fell, and she could watch it all the way, like a film in slow-motion, as the lid dropped away and the liquid gushed from the wide open mouth and it all seemed inevitable really. Charm let go of the ladder to catch the jar, to save it smashing on the hard stone floor; and in the process, she caught the full flood of the spilling liquid. It couldn't have hit her more squarely if she'd been standing in a shower-bath. It poured down over her face and hair, it soaked her uniform and puddled about her feet.

For a second, she only stood there, gaping up at her sister, sodden and shocked. Then her face twisted in that way Levity knew of old, that meant tears were coming.

A second later Levity was on the ground somehow, with no awareness of having moved at all. She was already reaching for her little sister when strong hands seized her wrists and a voice said, "No, don't touch her. You don't know what that is. Or do you?"

Levity struggled a little, because Charm was sobbing now, and looking scared as she stood there dripping, unconsoled. But the voice was kindly, if firm; and a glance over her shoulder showed her black tresses and vivid green eyes, unmistakable. "Oh—Lois! We, we thought it was turps..."

Lois Shannon looked blank for a moment, as if she couldn't understand why two new girls would be hunting for turpentine in Mr Felton's cubby. Her grip didn't slacken, though. She was a Senior, two forms above Levity; there was no point trying to fight her. She sniffed, and shook her head. "Doesn't smell like turps. Doesn't smell like anything much. Is it stinging or burning, little 'un? In your eyes or anywhere?"

Charm shook her head stoutly, though her tears kept coming. "It doesn't sting. But it, it's all over me..."

"I know. It'll be all right. I'll take you to Sister Anthony, and she'll pop you into a hot bath, and you'll be fine in a little while. Here, don't rub your eyes! Just let me put this old blanket around you, that'll soak up the worst of it, and then we'll be off. You stand still, Levity, no point both of us getting greasy..."

Levity did as she was told, ceding her sister's care to the indomitable older girl—and noticing how Lois actually still took care not to get any of the spilt stuff on her skin, even as she wrapped Charm up in a tartan rug and steered her towards the door.

"Wait, no, what about Liv? I want Liv!"

Charm sounded panicky, halfway to a full-throated tantrum. Lois was inexorable, though. "I'm sorry—Charm, isn't it?—but you can't have her. Someone's got to stay here and explain to Mr Felton what the two of you were up to. He'll know how to clean it up, Levity, and you'd best expect to spend the rest of the afternoon doing that," with a frowning eye cast on how far the liquid had splashed and oozed across the floor.

"Um, I'm supposed to be in classes," she muttered, flushing hotly as the bell sounded through the school.

"Well, yes; and so am I, and so's your sister. Who's your next period—Miss Hendy? Very well, I'll make your apologies there, once I've delivered Charm to Sister Anthony. I daresay the prefects may want a word with you too, after lessons. Whatever this is about, it's a confounded nuisance for everybody else. And just what Mr Felton's going to say, I can't imagine..."

"What Mr Felton's going to say about what?" Another voice, coming from the passageway, masculine and elderly and somehow irate and patient both at once, as though he had seen and endured—and commented on—everything, every possible result of every bad choice every schoolgirl had ever made.

Lois met Levity's gaze, and rolled her eyes expressively; then she said, "I'm afraid Levity and Charm have had an accident, Mr Felton. No one's been hurt, though, which is a blessing."

"Is it, indeed?" The janitor stepped through the door, a short grey-haired man in a brown dust coat, with a louring expression on his face. "I should feel blessed, should I? What happened here?"

"I, I'm afraid we spilt your—um, your bottle," Levity said. Mamma had always taught them to own up, and not let anyone else share the blame for their own misdeeds. "From the top shelf there. We don't know what it is, but it went all over my sister..."

"From that jar there, aye?" with a nod to where Charm had set the bottle down carefully, just before she'd started crying. "Well, nothing to worry about for the little girl, soap and water'll clean her up, and her clothes too. That's my mineral oil. Which I keep out of reach, exactly to stop it getting knocked over and running into everything," with a bleak, telling look around.

"I'm really terribly sorry," Levity muttered. "I'll stay and clean everything, of course," and never mind what trouble that brought down on her head from the mistresses.

"Oh—no, wait, you can't," Lois said suddenly. "I totally forgot in all the excitement, but I was actually looking for you two. Miss Leven sent me to fetch the pair of you. She wants you in her study, instanter. She knew just where you were, and it's been too long already, you'd better run. And explain that Charm's had an accident and can't come."

Levity hesitated, glancing from her to the silent caretaker; then she said, "I'm sorry, Mr Felton, truly. And I will come back, as soon as Miss Leven lets me."

"Aye," he said. "You will that. The work'll be done by then, mind, I can't leave it like this. But do you come back, and tell me what-all you were thinking. You knew you weren't allowed here, new girl or no."

"Yes, Mr Felton. I promise..." *I only wanted to clean my sister's hands* sounded suddenly pathetic to her own mind, hopelessly inadequate in the face of the devastation before her eyes. Then she turned and ran.

Up the steps and through the hallway, to Miss Leven's study door. A quick breath there, a moment to tidy herself as best she could—and bless the mind that had thought to put a mirror here, for anxious schoolgirls to check that their hair was tolerably tidy and their uniform tolerably clean—and then a tap on the door, a pause, and trying to turn the knob with nerveless fingers as the headmistress called her in.

Miss Leven was sitting behind her desk, very formal today. With her were two men in dark suits, the younger one standing behind his senior's chair. The elder was burly, bearded, looking at her with a cold kind of interest. Levity felt her heart sink, even before Miss Leven said,

"Levity dear, do come in at last. We've been waiting. No Charm? ... Very well, we'll go into that later. These gentlemen are from the Russian Interest section in the Swiss embassy, and they want to talk to you about your father."

CHAPTER FOURTEEN

Letters Home

*D**ear Mother and Father,***

Have you heard from Jessica since last week? How is she? I hope she doesn't develop canal fever. I know that's a common disease in the Plains. Dusty-lung is a threat too, I believe, though one of the girls here says it's easily mistaken for the duffus. Betty Waterhouse comes from that region herself—her parents sent her here for her health, to get her away from the dreadful summer heat, which Sister Anthony agrees is never any good for a growing girl—and Betty says that if there's ever a question, it's always the duffus...

It was the best revenge that Rachel could think of, her only way of hitting back. Every letter home—and letters home were an obligation, one to be written every week—would be about nothing and nobody but her separated twin. She wanted every word to bite, to remind her parents just how cruel they were being, and to make it clear that there could be no forgiveness this side of a reunion. If that only made them stretch out the separation longer—which was all too likely, she knew—that was the price she'd have to pay. But so would her parents pay it, with ever more recrimination from their suffering daughters. She was sure she could rely on Jessica to play the same game, even if they were forbidden to discuss the rules.

It was a short, bitter note she wrote, trying to play on every nerve in her parents' bodies, every anxiety in their guilty minds. Even as she sealed it up, she felt guilty herself; she knew it was a mean act. But they'd been meaner, and they deserved no better. Not until Jess and she were together again. She felt as though she'd lost the better half of herself. No, worse: she'd seen it stolen, by the very people who should be taking care of her, of them both.

She licked her envelope and sealed it firmly, licked a tuppeny red—wondering as she always did just what the ancient undead queen looked like now, in the dark of her cocoon, and how long they would go on using this old Jubilee portrait on her stamps, for want of any other—and thumped it into place with her fist. Then she carried it up to the desk where Arie Bunker was collecting home letters and ticking them off on a list.

"Yours done, Rachel? That was quick. Hmm," feeling the thickness of the envelope deliberately with her fingers, "it's a bit skimpy, isn't it?"

Rachel flushed, and shrugged. "Not much to say. School's just school."

"Ah, that's right. I remember, you're the one who really doesn't like it here, aren't you? So who was that I saw having a whale of a time out on the lax field last night? I thought it was you, but obviously not."

Was it even possible to blush any redder? She couldn't believe so, by the way her cheeks were burning. "That was me," she muttered, which Arie knew perfectly well; the older girl had joined in for the last half-hour, coaching Rachel in attack and defence. "We never had the chance to play lacrosse, where we lived before. It's okay."

"Well, I hope you go on thinking it's 'okay', because you'll be a sharp young player if you practice; and perhaps we can persuade you that other aspects of the Crater School are 'okay', too. And then you'll have more to write home about, won't you? Seriously, Rachel. Try to do better than this, next week. You don't have to write a budget, but your parents are entitled to a fair share of your school life."

Rachel opened her mouth to deny that, to claim that they weren't entitled to anything so long as they kept her apart from her twin—but Arie was a house prefect, and she was known to have a steely core beneath her kindness. There was no point getting into a row with a girl Rachel actually rather liked. So she closed her mouth again, and nodded neutrally, and turned away.

Sundays were a calming time at the Crater School. Rachel had learned already that there was no prospect of another raucous game of lax on the playing-fields. Mornings were taken up with chapel and mending, letters home and quiet walks, where Seniors could go in groups by themselves, Juniors went with mistresses, and Middles had to bargain with prefects for an escort. Ordinarily, she'd been told, walks tended to go one way or the other along the lakeside, or else scrambling up on the crater ridge. With the prospect of the merlins erupting again from the water at any moment, Miss Leven had totally forbidden that. This morning the Juniors had been restricted to the school grounds, while most of the Seniors were given consent to follow the coach road all the way around to the Sanatorium. Those with relatives there would welcome the chance to visit, while the rest could be trusted to entertain the patients at large, and a bus would bring them all home this evening.

Consciously or not, deliberately or not, that had deprived the Middles of their usual chaperones, as the school pre-fects had all opted to go with the Sanatorium party. Arie had stayed, though, with a handful of other Sixth-formers; they had banded together to co-opt Miss Hendy, and the Middles had ended up with a walk more organised than usual, a guided nature-ramble across the pastures to the railhead.

It was hard, Rachel found, to remember how much she hated being here, when they made it all so interesting. Like it had been hard to remember yesterday, when she was having so much fun pelting up and down the line, hurling the lacrosse ball with all her might and seeing it fly true towards her target. Lax was a revelation, a balm to her restless soul, as Miss Hendy's lessons were a balm to her enquiring mind—or they would be, if only Jess were here to partner her through all these new discoveries.

Without her twin, she kept running suddenly aground. As now, with that nasty little letter written and handed in, and all the rest of the afternoon ahead of her. Sunday afternoons were given to letter-writing, or else to quiet reading; schoolbooks were forbidden. But she had written the duty-note to her parents already, and the brief line she was allowed to write to Jess. She was too proud to send a letter to any other of their friends, in case the authorities suspected she was enclosing a further note to her sister, to be sent on. She'd sooner write to no one, and maintain a stiff and highly visible isolation. They were studying martyrs in Religious Knowledge; very well, she'd learn from that.

But she wasn't much of a reader at the best of times, and she wasn't allowed the one book she was most interested in, one that Miss Hendy had recommended, about the native fauna of Mars. She wanted to read about sandcats, but that counted as schoolwork, even when they weren't studying them in class and wouldn't until the Fifth form. Or else she wouldn't mind teaching herself a little Basque—Rowany might have awed and impressed her just a little bit more than she quite liked to admit to herself; she wasn't used to finding a role-model in a girl not so much older, someone to aspire to—but again, that wasn't permitted on a Sunday. Her friends were nose-deep in novels or school stories, but those really held no interest for Rachel.

So she felt very much at a loose end, stranded and alone and missing her twin desperately. She left the common room and mooched aimlessly across the hallway. She had to go somewhere and do something, or it was certain sure that a prefect or a staff would descend on her with an errand or a chore. They had an instinct for sniffing out idle hands and putting them to work. Even on a Sunday.

She could go to the hobbies room and look busy, claim to be working on a collection of something-or-other, that was allowed; but she didn't like lying or faking an interest she didn't truly feel. Really she just wanted to wallow in her solitude, if only to remind herself how miserable she was here—but this was the worst possible place for doing that. It wasn't only the mistresses and the prees; if her own cohort spotted her on her own, they were safe to seize hold and drag her off into their company. It was getting harder and harder to resist them, she found. Right now, though, she really didn't want to be drawn into fun, even the quiet kind of fun they had on Sundays. Her letter home had set the mood, and she meant to sharpen it, like a cook sharpening her knife to a razor's edge. Which meant being alone and staying that way somehow, because how else could she feel satisfactorily lonely and abandoned and misused...?

Just like up at the castle, girls weren't really meant to use the front door of their house—but it was right here to hand, and for this precious moment there was nobody else to see, so she worked the handle quickly and slipped outside. Bright flowers drew her eye from either side; there was a bent back among them, though, one of the Seniors trowelling weeds out of a bed, while a small knot of Juniors had gathered on a bench the other side, reading one book between the three of them. Hurriedly Rachel set her face forward as though she had a mission, and stepped out smartly before she could be waylaid.

She looked like she was going somewhere; she probably better had go somewhere, then. And this way, between the houses and past the playing fields lay the sculpture garden; that would be a place to be alone, if she was lucky. If no one else had had the same thought, if no pack of other girls had decided to infest the place.

Now that she'd thought of it, she was suddenly urgent to be there. It had seemed to offer a solution of sorts the last time, if getting things off her chest could ever count as a solution. This time she wouldn't have Tawney to rant at, but that was all right; she didn't want to rant. She wanted to sulk and be unhappy, and reassure herself that nobody else was suffering as she herself suffered, except for her mirror-image, her twin, who must surely be feeling exactly the same.

By the time she reached the grove that encompassed the sculpture garden, she was absolutely depending on having that space to herself. It was a bitter blow to her heart, then, when she heard voices coming through the screen of trees. Some other girl—two other girls at least—had got there ahead of her, and there was no hope now of being private; the garden simply wasn't big enough.

Which meant that there was no point going on, only to disturb the lucky ones when they'd clearly come all this way in search of privacy themselves. Rachel checked her speed before she broke out of the trees into the garden beyond. She stood still for a moment, hoping they hadn't heard her coming; and she would have turned to head back to the school buildings, if their voices hadn't carried so bright and clear on the breeze, if what they said hadn't first intrigued and then enraged her.

"How can they possibly have found us, though, Liv? When we've come all this way, to where nobody knows us?"

"Nobody knows us, maybe, but by now everybody knows who our mother is. And there are those Russian girls here, any one of them might've written to give us away..."

That was enough, after a lifetime of being pushed to the limit by sidelong glances and muttered asides and sometimes direct questions about their history or their loyalty or their name. After a lifetime of living under the baleful glare of the occupied moons, aware of that inimical relentless presence every time they glanced up into the sky. Rachel stormed out of cover, so angry she didn't even pause to realise how she was putting herself in the wrong.

"You take that back, whoever you are! Just because we have Russian blood doesn't make us disloyal, we're as true-red British as you are—and what mighty secrets do you have to give away in any case, who are you to interest the Russians?"

By then of course she knew just who they were, because they were face to face and equally furious. Well, Levity was furious, jumping up and meeting Rachel eye to eye, somehow pale and flushed both at once, while Charm cowered back on the bench, looking suddenly a lot younger than her sister.

"Never you mind, it's none of your business—and what are you doing anyway, sneaking about, spying on us? Listening in to our conversation?"

"I couldn't help that, you were talking so loudly—and I wasn't sneaking about, I was just coming to the garden to be by myself. I didn't mean to eavesdrop, I do know that's wrong and I'm sorry for it, but it was just an accident that I overheard you. Only then I heard what you said, and, and..."

And she was blushing again herself now, because she knew just how much she was at fault here. Her sudden temper riding on top of her bad mood had brought her blundering into something deeply private to these girls, all but proving Levity's original allegation. At least it must seem so, to this glowering, distrustful pair of red-headed sisters. All Rachel's fury disappeared in a moment, like a bubble burst. She sank onto the bench and buried her head in her hands, letting her long hair fall like a curtain between her and the world; and then she went on, "I am sorry, truly. I wouldn't have listened if I'd had any choice, and I wouldn't have said a word anyway if it hadn't been for what you said, about Russians giving you away. I've heard it all my life, that Russians can't be trusted, that we're not truly British, that we must have relatives and sympathy with the other side. None of that's true, we're not traitors, I swear we're not..."

She peeped up then, into the oppressive silence, and saw Levity oddly flushed again. Wondering, Rachel went on, talking almost at random now: "It's why we've never been to school before, one of the reasons why. Our parents were afraid we'd be bullied just because of our name. Of course they were too proud to change it, either for themselves or for us." And now both sisters were blushing, their cheeks in vibrant disagreement with their hair; and Rachel suddenly couldn't help herself. "I know it's rotten manners, and you can wish me to the bottom of the lake if you like, but honestly, I do just have to ask: what is it that you're hiding, that you think we might have given away? I promise you we haven't, neither me nor the Mishkin twins, and we're the only Russians that I know of here—but what's your big story? I mean, we all know you're Isobel Buchanan's daughters, with all that that implies; but you've never really tried to make any great secret of that, even if you don't much want to talk about it, and there's nothing in that to interest the Russians or lead any of us to betray you. Or is there? Why do you keep firing up that way, every time I talk about betrayal, or traitors? You act like I'm accusing you of something now. Something worse than jumping to conclusions about a person, just on account of her name. And there you go again. Come on, Levity, you might as well tell me the truth."

"We can't," Charm gasped, at Rachel's side. "We promised, long ago."

"Well, but I think I've worked out most of it, haven't I? If I go to the library and look your mother up in *Who's Who*, what's the book going to tell me about your father?"

"Nothing at all," Levity said fiercely—and then, losing all her defiance in a rush, "Mamma made sure of that, before ever she let her name go into it. It lists us, but it doesn't men-tion...him."

"So who's he, then? Someone who really would interest the Russians?"

"Oh, the Russians know all about him already. It really is us they want." And then, all in a hurry as though it were the only way she could ever say it, on a single giveaway breath, "His name's Peregrine Murray."

"What, *the* Peregrine Murray?" That was forced out of her, by the sheer shock of it, the brutal weight of that name. A moment later, she went on, "Oh, I'm sorry. Of course you mean the Peregrine Murray," they couldn't possibly mean anyone else. "But—oh, if that's true, if he's your father, why in the world did you think he wouldn't find you?"

"He's not even supposed to know that we're on Mars," Levity said. "Mamma came here quietly, secretly, when we were babies; and she took her grandmother's name, and she changed ours. Not altogether, because we were too young to understand but old enough that we already knew our names and answered to them, it was too late to change them com-pletely; but as far as he was concerned his daughters were Olivia and Charlotte, and since we came here we've always been Levity and Charm, so... So, well, we hoped. And time went by, and I think even Mamma had given up expect-ing trouble, which is why she decided to send us here. One reason why. She—she said she couldn't have us with her, for this year. And somehow now is when he tracks us down, when we don't have her to turn to. And of course I don't really think it was you or the twins who gave us away, unless it was by accident and I don't see how—but something has, or someone. Men came from the Russian embassy. Well, there isn't an embassy, of course, but there are Russians in the Swiss legation just so that our Viceroy can talk to them directly. Miss Harribeth mentioned that, remember, when we had that lesson about the results of the war? They have diplomatic immunity, and they can go anywhere, they're the real spies; and they found out about us somehow, and came here to tell us so. Our father's on Phobos, of course, making those awful broadcasts—and he wants to see us, and Mamma's not here, and, and we don't know what to *do*..."

It was the better part of an hour later that Rachel came back into Jopling House, once again by the forbidden front door because a little casual sinning was easy when you had far greater matters on your mind. As she passed the hall table she checked suddenly, seeing two letters laid out side by side, neatly centred. That wasn't really so unusual; girls wrote to family and pen friends all the time. Usually, though, Sunday letters would be passed to the prefect on duty along with the required letter home. It was odd to see them arrayed instead in the hallway, as they might be any weekday. It looked like a deliberate statement, as though they were there expressly to be noticed; and so of course Rachel was reminded of her own stubborn insistent letters to Jessica, that she used to lay out exactly there, exactly like that, for exactly that reason.

She was drawn inexorably over. Reading other people's letters was dishonourable, unthinkable, of course—but reading the envelopes was fine, surely? Envelopes weren't private, they were the opposite of that; that was the point of them, to be exposed and legible and read...

She still wasn't quite convinced, but nothing now could have kept her from checking the names and addresses. Or the name and address, rather, because each envelope bore the same direction:

Miss Jessica Abramoff

Low Bridge School

Low Bridge Junction

Hesperia Planum

Mars

It was lucky there were two of them, because she did have to read it twice. Even then, she struggled to believe her eyes. Could she be dreaming, or hallucinating?

But no: that one was Tawney's handwriting, definitely. She'd seen enough of it in recent days, as they ruefully compared marked tests and essays. And the other was so similar, it must surely be Tasha's. And there was a sudden bright giggle behind her, swiftly hushed; and when she swivelled around, there were the twins, hugging each other and struggling to stay silent, delighted with themselves. Tasha was thoroughly bundled up in coat and scarf, with the look of someone released on licence from the san, sent forth to walk for an hour in the air and not at all to conspire with her twin. Here she was, though, regardless; of course she was. Rachel only hoped that she wasn't still infectious. There'd be the devil to pay if that cold ran amok through the Middle School, after all Sister Anthony's precautions.

When they saw her looking, the twins made exaggerated shushing motions, fingers to lips—because the housemistress's rooms opened directly onto the hallway there, and the last thing anyone wanted was to call down her attention now—and then beckoned her away, down the passage to the back door and so legitimately out into the garden where they could finally feel free to talk.

"...I don't understand," Rachel said, though she rather thought she did. "Why are you two writing to Jessica? You don't know her."

"No, but we know you. And we know about being twins; and we know that being cut off from each other is the worst thing in the world," Tasha said fervently.

"And if you put all that together," Tawney went on without a breath, without a hesitation, "then we know what to do about it. You can't write to Jessica, and you can't ask us to write for you—but we can write on our own behalf."

"Behalfs."

"Behalves?"

For a moment the twins looked at each other, unsure if they were arguing or bargaining. Then they giggled, and nodded, and agreed on "behalves"; and turned back to Rachel and went on—Tasha now speaking for the two of them—"So we thought we'd do that, each of us, without telling you so that no one can accuse us of passing on messages—"

"—and we thought we'd put our letters out every day, just the way you did, to make it clear that we're not hiding what we're doing, and we think it's absolutely shocking what they've done to you—"

"—and let them just try to forbid us to write to her, the way they've forbidden you, because they wouldn't have a leg to stand on, they're always encouraging us to swap letters with girls in other parts of the province—"

"—and if they do think we're just acting as go-betweens, that's fine, they can open our letters and read them and see that's not true—"

"—and apologise to us after, and to you too, because they'd have to, they'd owe us that much—"

"—and, you know what? If two of us can make a difference, or at least make a point, then what's the odds of twenty...?"

"**I**t's open defiance."

Thus Miss Tattersall, a few days later, in the face of two dozen collected letters all addressed to Jessica Abramoff, all from Middles who could never have met her, but who packed close about the Mishkin twins' leadership.

"Of course it is," said Miss Leven judiciously, "but it's rather *nice* defiance, don't you think?"

"I don't, no. I don't call this anything but a slap in the face to due authority."

"Sometimes authority can use a slap. It's a reminder to those of us with power over others' lives that we need to exercise the greatest care, not to misuse that power."

"I don't understand you, Peggy. All we've done is follow her parents' instructions. Surely you won't deny that parents have a right to discipline their own children?"

"I won't, no—but nor would I ever claim that parents are always in the right. Especially when they seek to use us as the instrument of their discipline. In this instance, I think the parents have been wrong-headed from the start, and so I told them. They wouldn't listen, and they chose to exacerbate the situation, and—well, I'm half minded to ask them to take Rachel away at the end of term. Or sooner, if it can be arranged."

That brought a gasp, from all around the room.

"Margaret Evadne Leven! We have never expelled a pupil from the Crater School, in all its years; would you start now, when the poor girl's done nothing at all to deserve it?"

"I would not, no—but I'd willingly expel the parents. It's an unfortunate circumstance that that irretrievably means removing the child too."

"Yes, and it would lie on the child's record hereafter. You'd be tainting her entire future."

"Oh, I know it—which is why I only said 'half minded'. I don't expect to follow through. But I do most earnestly wish we'd never agreed to take her without her twin. We could have handled the two of them. The good Lord knows, we have experience! You all remember how the Mishkins were when they first came here, so utterly turned inward to each other. And now they lead the whole Middle School by the nose, and they're happy to do it individually if they must. Oh, I know they're little miseries when they're forced apart, but nevertheless. I take a shameful degree of pride in watching how they've grown into independently wicked creatures, each with their own coterie."

"And behold the fruits of that accomplishment," Miss Peters said. "This would have the twins' stamp all over it, even if we didn't know that the first letters had been theirs. What do you propose to do about it, though, Peggy, tell us that? We can't ban the whole school from writing to a girl; but we can't let it go on, either."

"Ah. As to that, I have an idea. These letters must go in the post, of course, as the twins' already have, and I hope they may have some effect. In the meantime, between lacrosse and the start of cricket and the last of hockey, not to mention the perennial netball and tennis and our half-term adventures coming soon, I think we can keep the girls too busy to write more this week. For the longer term—well, girls this age have no concept of the long term, so we needn't worry about that, but I believe I have the perfect solution to drive this idea thoroughly out of their mischievous little heads."

So saying, she walked to the door of the mistresses' common room, wherein she had been invited to discuss this latest outbreak of mischief, and put her head out. "Ah—Izzy, dear, would you have a minute to run an errand for me?—Oh, excellent. Thank you so much. Just dash up to the prefects' room and ask for Rowany, would you? I'd like to see her here as soon as possible, with any other prefects who are free..."

"So essentially the staff has a problem and they've dumped it off onto us?"

"That would be one way of saying it, yes." The prefects were gathered in cohort in their room, gazing with various degrees of scepticism at Rowany where she was perched at the head of the table. On the head of the table, indeed, disdaining her proper chair in order to let her long legs swing free, to flag this up as something more casual than a formal prefects' meeting that would need minuting and so forth. "Alternatively, we could say that they've handed this on as a challenge. It's actually a challenge to their authority rather than ours, but if they tackle it directly they're always going to look heavy-handed and unfair. Whereas we can be more subtle, and make the little dears wish they'd never been born without ever actually linking cause and effect. They'll know, if we do it right—but they won't be able to say so."

"I'm sorry, but I don't see it," said stolid Mary Holmes, beloved head of Greenaway House and library prefect and possibly the least imaginative girl that had ever graced the corridors of the Crater School. "What can we do, that the staff can't?"

"As to that," Rowany said, beaming around at them all, "I do actually have an idea. We'll need to *enlist* the staff, but it won't be *coming* from them, we can make that abundantly clear. We'll be the ones the girls hate, and deservedly so..."

CHAPTER FIFTEEN

Consequences to Explore

Free of crutches and free of cold, Tasha was joyfully reunited at last with her twin, her friends, her class, her life. She was a little surprised though to find that life now including Rachel, to the point where the twins had almost become a threesome. That seemed to have happened in her absence, when her back was turned. She'd known of course that Tawney was chumming up with the new girl, and she entirely understood why—heavens, she'd written letters herself to the unknown Jessica, from her bed in San; it was something she could do, at least, not to feel that she was missing out altogether on everything—but she hadn't expected to find them grown this close. She wasn't quite sure how she felt about that. School had taught the twins to forge and keep separate friendships, and not to be jealous of each other's company, but this was something new. This was almost like having a second sister thrust upon her. From first thing in the morning to last thing at night, Rachel seemed always to be there. Not coming between them, exactly—except at night, when she literally was, her cubicle lying between theirs like a buffer—but a constant third to be considered, included, consulted.

It wasn't a problem, exactly. Just odd. If Tawney wanted this, then Tasha was willing to play along, for now. At least Rachel had emerged from her sullens at last. She was still bitterly unhappy without her twin and furiously angry at her parents, both at once, but it showed now in a bright sharp temper and a fierce energy that was honestly much easier to live with.

Right now they were in the dining hall, Tawney on her one hand and Rachel on the other. Tasha often seemed to end up in the middle. Whether the other two were doing that deliberately to make sure she didn't feel left out after her long absence, replaced by this new friendship, Tasha wasn't sure. She did know that Tawney could be that thoughtful, and she suspected it of Rachel too. That was one of the reasons that this wasn't really a problem: Tasha liked Rachel rather a lot already, and thought there was probably further to go in that direction. Tawney would probably like her to go faster. Which was an odd position for headlong Tasha to find herself in, being nudged along by cautious Tawney; but it seemed as though all three of them had agreed, without actually talking about it, that she'd catch up sooner or later.

In the meantime, Rachel made a long arm for the lemonade-jug, hoisted it up and gazed at it critically. "Tasha? There's still an inch left in the bottom. Want to share it with me?"

Tasha glanced automatically the other way to check her sister's glass. Tawney still had an inch of her own, so she nodded easily. "Thanks, Rachel. Slosh it out quickly, before those greedy Uppers at the other end of the table catch wind of it."

"There's another jug on the counter, if they want it."

"Ah, but they'd have to fetch that. Or inveigle one of us into fetching it for them." A state of permanent war existed as by nature between Lower and Upper Fourth. Hostilities were passed down from one generation to the next; girls promoted from one form to the other changed sides and loyalties in a moment. For the most part it was a war of words, usually downright slanders that entertained their victims as much as their perpetrators. Occasionally it broke out into tricks and stratagems that could escalate to the point of attracting notice from the staff or even the prefects. At the moment, though, an undeclared truce was in place, and even the sniping was minor and perfunctory. They were all Middles together, after all, and there were greater issues at hand. The Uppers had joined in the letter-writing with glee, delighted to make war for once with the mistresses instead.

So too had the Upper Thirds, always game for mis-chief even if they couldn't match the genuine indignation that possessed the Fourths. Even Lower Third had offered. They'd been turned down, of course—"You're *Juniors*, and this is a matter for the Middle School," with never a word about how it was sure to bring trouble one way or another, and nobody wanted to involve the kids with whatever fate was looming—but not without a sense of gratitude, and something owed. In coming days, the denizens of Lower Third would find their seniors more generous with sweets and favours, more inclined to offer help with prep or coach-ing, just generally nicer than normal. If it didn't last beyond half-term, no matter. In the mind and heart of a Junior, half a term was akin to half a lifetime.

Rachel poured lemonade with tolerable equality between the two glasses, tipping the jug vertical to be sure of the very last drops. "What makes this so delicious? I've been drinking lemonade all my life, but it was never this good."

"Well, the lemons come from our own groves, on the southern crater wall," Tawney said. "They're a special variety too, developed locally to suit local conditions. Miss Hendy says that's what makes the difference. But *we* think Mrs

Bailey adds some secret ingredient in the kitchen, more than sugar. It's like nectar, isn't it?"

"Well, it is; but—"

Whatever Rachel had meant to say, she had to bite it back, as a bell chimed imperatively from the top table. All the girls might be drinking Mrs Bailey's fabled lemonade, but this was the meal known none the less as "afternoon tea", which was taken and supervised by the prefects alone. It was Rowany who had struck the bell, and Rowany who stood now, smiling civilly as silence fell across the hall.

"Girls, I know you're all eager to be about your business, because there's a lot to squeeze in between tea and supper—including schoolwork, I might remind you, which is *not* the least important of your daily activities—but I do actually have an important announcement to make, so possess your souls in patience, please, for a minute longer.

"It's come to our attention"—and when the Head Girl said "our" in that particular way, from that particular place at High Table, it was clear that she was graciously including the absent staff in her collective, as well as the gathered prefects—"that a great number of girls in the Middle School have been seeking pen pals in the Plains. The Crater School has always encouraged pupils here to learn about other girls' lives elsewhere, how very different they can be, while we yet remain all of one blood underneath.

"It's just unfortunate that so many of you picked the same poor girl to write to. She can't possibly answer you all, try though she might; so we've decided to step in to help. With the enthusiastic cooperation of everyone concerned at Low Bridge School down on Hesperia Planum, we have arranged to pair every girl who wrote a letter with a pupil there, so that you can write back and forth to your heart's content. They're eager to hear from you, girls, so don't let us down; school life on the Plains can be much less exciting than we have it here.

There's no horizon, to start with, never mind a view: just flat cropland for miles in every direction, with an occasional windmill for interest. No native wildlife: anything that might harm the crops or the workers was poisoned or trapped or driven off long since. Send them post-cards, or kodaks if you have them; tell them about the merlins in our lake, the sandcats in our hills. Try not to sound smug, but do what you can to lift their spirits.

"And furthermore," Rowany went on, before more than the gist of that could begin to sink in, "the staff are thrilled that you're all showing such an interest in the Plains area, where our colony began. They see this as an excellent opportunity to help you understand just how hard life was in the early days, and how tough our forebears must have been to have endured it.

"Therefore," and she was smiling now in a way that made the Middles shudder, "it's been decided that for the next while, as near as we can manage, the Middle School will live as girls from those early days had to live. We don't have time to card and spin enough wool to weave broadcloth, but you will have lessons in those skills, and you will sew your own clothes from stuff the school can buy locally from our Basque neighbours, who have of course done all of that themselves.

"Girls of that time would work in the fields, before and after lessons in the schoolroom. The early colonists survived because everybody worked, more or less from the time that they could walk. We can't really replicate that, because it wouldn't be fair to your parents to cut back on the education that they're paying for, and besides, we don't have the fields or the crops; but it won't do you any harm to get up an hour earlier to work in the gardens before breakfast, and again for an hour in the evening. We'll arrange that.

"And food, of course, lay at the heart of it all. The first colony nearly starved, because the merlins hadn't understood how little we could eat of what was native here. Some people did starve, before the second run of ships with stores and seeds, just enough to keep them going just long enough for the land to prove fertile. Our first generations lived a simple life on a plain and simple diet. We have good records of that time, so it's something we can share. Sister Anthony assures us it's nutritious, so you'll eat mostly vegetables, and lots of gruel. No more of Mrs Bailey's miraculous lemonade, I'm afraid," pouring herself another glass, sipping it ostentatiously, smiling directly at the horrified faces of the Upper Third and the two Fourths, "it took another generation and decades of work to establish citrus groves, but gruel-water at teatime will fortify you for your extra labours.

"And meanwhile your lessons will focus on the Plains, and those early days. History and areography, obviously; and botany, how they induced Earth plants and trees to grow here; and physical science, practical lessons in what they had to work with by way of engines and power, heat and light. We can't teach you how the aetherships work, I'm afraid; we still don't know.

"Every mistress is keen, I'm sure, to find a way to relate her subject to your new project. Exciting days ahead, girls; and it all starts in the morning. At six o'clock in the morning..."

The rest of the school filed out, table by table, talking merrily and laughing. Laughing at the Middles, mostly. Of course everyone knew about the letter-writing campaign, and the wise among them had only been waiting for Nemesis to strike.

The Middles sat quiet, mostly, still trying to absorb the horror of it. Gruel-water! Six o'clock in the morning!

Gradually, the level of muttering began to build. Tasha saw glares being aimed from all four tables, in one common direction: towards them as a threesome, but Tawney in particular. Tawney whose idea the letters had been, who had written the first and enrolled so many of her friends to do the same. Tawney who would certainly be blaming herself already, and would just accept the blame from everybody else and do nothing to defend herself. Which was, of course, why Tasha had to do it for her.

"You, Isidora Dolores Ibárruri Gómez," picking on one girl out of sixty because she was closest and even Tasha in a temper was wise enough not to invite trouble by yelling at everybody all at once; and because picking on Izzy meant bringing Brigitta in too, and Tasha was itching for a proper fight; and because she had carefully learned Izzy's full name last term, with all the proper r-r-rolling of the r's, and it seemed a shame to waste the opportunity. "Why are you glowering that way at my sister?"

"Because this is a punishment, and it will be terrible, and she brought us all into this."

"What, she herded you like sheep, did she? Are you as dim and, and *vacuum* as that yearling ram that follows your brother around all day like a pup, with never a thought to call your own?"

She couldn't have come up with anything better calculated to enrage the fiercely independent little Izzy if she'd puzzled over it for a fortnight. Without even waiting to watch it sink home, Tasha forged on: "It was Tawney's idea, certainly—but you chose to join in. You all did," glancing around, aware that she had a broader audience that was seething and uncertain and could still be swayed. "And of course this is a punishment, and a really mean one—which means Rowany thought of it, I'd bet anything; it's too, too *thinky* for the staff—but that doesn't mean you all get to pile onto Tawney like some mad rugger scrum. Every one of you made the same choice, and you were calling my sister brilliant for thinking of it while you were writing those letters to Jessica; you can't all turn on her now, just because we're getting punished for it. You didn't imagine the staff would just let it pass, did you? We hit them hard, to show them just how unfair they were being; of course they were going to hit back."

Big blonde Brigitta was sitting next to tiny dark Izzy Gómez. Of course she was; that was as inevitable as Tawney and Tasha sitting together. Or, now, Tawney and Tasha and Rachel too. Oddly, that was almost a comfort just now, to have someone on either side of her who was irrevocably on her side. She could warm to this whole idea of a threesome, Tasha thought. Especially if they were going to find themselves at war with their own tribe, as well as the school at large. She didn't want to fight either Izzy or Brigitta, let alone both of them together, though that was the only way they came; but Tasha would always fight the world if that was what it took to keep her sister safe. The same she thought was true of Rachel too, which must be why the girl seemed so baffled sometimes, finding herself so far away from Jessica and not at all knowing what to do.

Well, they'd tried one thing, and this was the result. But they'd get through this, and think of something else. They were a team now, apparently. And so should all the Middles be, but they were fractured at the moment and it was her twin who was the natural peacemaker, but she couldn't let Tawney talk just now. Tawney would just swallow down everyone's anger and take it all on herself and that was no good at all. Tasha knew that she'd likely only make things worse by kicking back, but it was all she knew how to do; and Brigitta had taken a breath and was all set to pitch in on Izzy's behalf, and for sure there'd be a dozen, two dozen voices to back her up, and oh, this was going to get messy...

Except that Brigitta's angry response seemed to die between her heart and her throat, and never escaped her mouth. Instead, her brilliant blue eyes seemed to widen even further than Nature had made them as she stared beyond Tasha's shoulder. Beyond and above...

Her own heart sinking, Tasha glanced behind her.

Sure enough, there loomed Rowany herself. With a bright smile on her face. A bright *listening* smile.

"Sorry," she said, transparently not sorry at all. "Didn't mean to eavesdrop, but honestly, Tasha, you were talking rather loudly. I was coming over to hurry you up, because you shouldn't be lingering in here, any of you," with a glance around at the four awestruck attentive tables. "But as I obviously did overhear you—and I think you meant 'vacuous', by the way, not 'vacuum'—let me just say that we don't want you to think of it as a punishment. It's...a discouragement, certainly; as Tasha says, you can't expect to rebel against a commandment without some repercussions, and we really don't want you doing this on a regular basis. Life's easier for everybody if you live within the law, even when you think it's unjust to one of your own. It always will be; no system can ever be fair to everyone. But try to look on this as an adventure. It won't do you any harm, to live for a while in the shadow of your great-grandmothers. They had to do this every day, and all their lives; for you it's just a short time, and barely a flavour of their actual reality. Like lemonade, against sucking lemons. You'll learn to be better Martians, for understanding a little of how the pioneers lived before us."

"Does that mean you'll be eating gruel, Rowany, and gardening at six o'clock like the rest of us?" That was Izzy, of course, ready to fight anybody at the drop of a handkerchief. Really, she and Tasha should be natural allies; perhaps they would have been, constantly at war with the whole school else, if it weren't for Tawney and Brigitta.

Rowany just laughed at her. "Not I, child. I learned this lesson long ago, without its having to be forced into me like corn into a goose. Now go on, all of you, run along outside.

Get some sunshine on your skin, and work your tempers
out in a game of lax or hockey. You won't have the energy to
spare tomorrow, or for a while after."

Under Rowany's eye, they streamed obediently out into
the courtyard, and thence into the yard behind the castle. Most did head off a little grimly towards the sports fields;
there was barely an hour before prep, and no free time after.
Running around and yelling a lot sounded attractive suddenly. Besides, Rowany was probably watching.

Not the new threesome, though. Tasha still wasn't allowed
to run around. Sanctioned or organised or otherwise, she
was off all games until half-term at least, at best. If she were
honest, her ankle was always twingeing sharply by this end of
the day, and she was just as glad not to put too much strain
on it; but even so, a token protest was essential. Honour
demanded that. And she could always dress it up as self-sac-
rifice, "You two go on without me, I'll just sit in the library or
something."

"As if we would. If you can't, we won't, and that's flat."

Strange, to hear that not from her own twin but from
Rachel. Tawney just rolled her eyes at Tasha, seeing the arti-
fice and no doubt the pain as well.

Tasha pulled a face at her sister, and said, "It isn't fair,
though. If I were a boy, they'd just tell me to run it off. That's
what his games master tells Robbie, every time he gets hurt
in rugby."

"Ah, but Robbie's such a tough, rugged fellow. It's different for us frail vulnerable girls."

The twins cracked up suddenly, irrevocably, both of them
having to grab hold of Rachel to hold themselves erect.
Tasha still found one corner of her mind to wonder at that,
how strange it was, because ordinarily they grabbed hold
of each other at times like this. But meantime Rachel was

staggering a little under her double burden and eyeing them dubiously. "Have you two gone bonkers, or what?"

"Sorry, sorry... You just, you just need to see Robs. He's taller than we are, taller than Rowany, even, and thinner than any of us. Thinner than all of us put together. Taken apart. Whatever. He'd be the world's worst rugby player anyway, but back Home, on Earth? In that gravity? Hopeless. But it's compulsory. So he's always getting hurt. Especially his ankles."

"We knit him socks, like Mum used to do for the troops in the war, only we're not allowed to send them because you can't export wool, not even a pair of socks..."

For a moment they seemed likely to break again. But Tawney at least held herself together, at least enough to say, "You drew him a picture of his socks, didn't you, Tash?"

She nodded. "Sent it with my last letter. Same time I asked him to write to Jessica. I thought he might as well do something useful. I bet they won't make him do stupid projects on the Plains and the first colonists."

"No—but then, he's in a lot more trouble than we are. We don't know if he'll still have the parents there, pleading for him. Actually, as far as we know he may already be on his way back with them, if their mission-of-mercy hasn't melted his headmaster's heart."

"What was his sin?" Rachel asked.

"We can't tell you, because we don't know."

"We're not allowed to know, it's that indecent. Something that we'd take for granted here on Mars, at a guess, that's absolutely forbidden down below. He's not a *bad* boy. Just, well, high-spirited."

"Like us."

Rachel shuddered theatrically, at the very thought of another just like them only taller and leaner and a boy. Then

177

she shook them off as they threatened to pinch her "like poor Caliban: as thick as honeycomb, each pinch more stinging than the bees that made 'em."

"If you two can behave," she said with great and crushing dignity, "why don't we carry on with the Grand Map? Because I'm absolutely certain that Rowany won't let us off that, and we're hardly going to have any spare time ahead, with all this other stuff they're going to heap on top of us."

Of course it wasn't Rachel's punishment—she hadn't even met the twins, at the time they were caught on the roof and condemned—but this was just one more way that she was becoming one of them, making two into three. She had assumed her place beside them as of right, as they tentatively tackled the task that Rowany had set them, to learn and record as much as they could about the castle's history and structure before half-term. Indeed, she'd become their scribe by common acclamation, her handwriting being unequivocally prettier than either of the twins'. They had half an exercise-book filled already, with her text and Tasha's careful maps. Between themselves they called the whole project the Grand Map, though it was so much more than lines-on-paper. It felt as though they were building a model in their heads, a model that reached back through time as well as occupying all the space they lived in, a model that was the same size as the original and overlay it so that sometimes they seemed to walk through both at once, the actual building and their own pencil-and-ink version.

"Cellars," Tasha said with satisfaction. Tawney pulled a face. She liked wind in her hair and the high places, roofs and towers and views. Tasha liked the roof well enough, and she could climb just as well as her sister, but it was the low dark hidden places that sang to her soul. After school, after university, when they headed out to conquer Mars entirely, it was understood that Tawney would be an Olympian, while

Tasha would dive underground and be a caver, finding all the hidden channels and buried spaces where ancient secrets lurked.

In this and other ways, Rachel was showing herself or learning to be a middle way. Tawney might be the peacemaker of record, but Rachel could be a bridge between the twins themselves, when they pulled in different directions. She said, "Down by the Secret Stair, then, and back up through the kitchens," because that was something to hold out for Tawney's comfort. A trip through the kitchens before supper was always fraught, but sometimes—often—rewarding.

And meanwhile, there was the Secret Stair...

Secret and unknown and undiscussed are different conditions, of course, as are secret and forbidden. The Secret Stair was, in honesty, anything but secret. That name sounded better, though, than the stairs-we-just-don't-talk-about, that lay behind the door-we're-not-allowed-to-open.

The sign on the door must have been there since the castle's earliest days: "before the Flood," as Tawney liked to say, meaning back when it was still the hotel that its owner had intended. The sign simply said *Private*, which would have been enough to discourage hotel guests. Whether it hid the owner's business-office or the kitchenmaids' stillroom or the laundry or the boot-boy's den, it would surely be no place for gentlefolk.

Which only added, of course, to its allure for schoolgirls. Anywhere prohibited, anything seedy: the countless pinholes in the woodwork bore testimony to many a notice from many a figure of authority, all no doubt variations on *Keep Out*. Scratches on the brass escutcheon bore testimony to years of determined rules, *This Door Must Be Kept Locked At All Times*, dull signs of wear on the fingerplate to the constant polishing-off of smudgy marks where girls had tried it just in case.

And yet, at last, it had become a school tradition not to try the door, not to ask what lay behind it, not to speculate. It was like a game, that the girls could win by being better than their elders thought they were. That was better than the alternative, having the staff declare it a matter of honour. If it became official again, then nobody could win. As things stood, the school had been winning for years. Mr Felton no longer bothered to lock the door. The twins—*the Three Twins,* Tasha thought, with a wry and private smile—only knew that because they had indeed tried it, because they had licence, nay, orders from Rowany to go everywhere and try everything.

They had tried it and ventured through, to find that it opened onto an unexpected staircase, leading down. Down and down: past the kitchens—with a door through into Mrs Bailey's domain, which they meant to take on the way back up, to see if their licence ran as far as a honey cake or two, or whatever else might be fresh out of the oven—to another level of cellars which the school as a whole had no idea of. Even the twins had never heard so much as a rumour. Nor had they spread a rumour, yet. Their first time down here, they'd had to scuttle back up pronto, not to be late for choir practice. Determined to be first to explore, and first to bear the news back to the world, they had kept determinedly mum for days now, worried that whispers of a whole new subterranean level would break the will of any girl. If there was anything worse than being pre-empted, they couldn't imagine it. If there was anything better than telling their friends about what they'd found, while knowing that those friends would feel honour-bound not to follow them down, they couldn't imagine that either.

So they dubbed it the Secret Stair and didn't discuss it even among themselves, for fear of being overheard; and now, at last, this was the time. Down and down, excited and anticipatory—and a little cautious with it, despite that much-flourished licence. Listening out ahead, ready to turn back if they heard voices coming up the stairs to greet them, really not wanting to meet anyone else herebelow. Explaining could be so difficult, when people just assumed you were in the wrong. Which grown-ups always did, in the twins' long experience.

Besides, adventuring was only fun when you were unwatched, unsupervised. So they all but tiptoed down, alert for the slightest sound below—and never thought that sound, discovery, capture might equally well come from above. Not till they heard the door open behind them, voices on the stairs.

CHAPTER SIXTEEN

A Voice in the Aether

All our roads are built on water.

It was something that Mamma said, often and often. Mostly as they travelled, be that by canal boat or airship or camelback or train. Of course it made best sense on the canals, because of course the colony survived and spread and thrived by virtue of that network. When they were little, she and Charm, they thought that was all that Mamma meant. On far distant mythical unreachable Earth, they knew, the Empire pushed inland from its coastal territories by means of roads and railways. Here they had found so many water-ways waiting, and land enough for many, many more that only needed digging. Of course they had built their communities canal-side and travelled by boat, between them and beyond. The British were a nation of boat-builders and navigators in any case; the great canals were narrow linear oceans, with steady currents and few storms. They took to this life as ducks to water. Mamma liked to say that too, just to hear her girls giggle.

As they grew, though, the girls understood her a little better. As their lives changed under them, changed and changed; as they moved from city to village to town, from canal to crater lake to desert height, following her inspiration or her patronage or whim. Never settling, always looking to the next horizon, never knowing which direction that might lie. Change, they understood, was the path life takes. *All our roads are built on water.*

Nevertheless. Accustomed as she was to unpredictable, unguessable shifts, Levity had never guessed at this, at any of this. Not school, and not of course the Russians—the Russians!—coming to see them with news of their father. Their father! Wanting to be in touch! While their mother was unreachable, and for the first time in their lives couldn't be depended on to appear without warning and whisk them away to safety...

On a closer, quieter level, she would never have guessed this either, that she would come back to Mr Felton's room to seek him out, for company, for comfort. He was old, even for a grown-up: older than anyone else in the school, she thought. White-haired. And grouchy, so grouchy. He was a legend all through the school, and none of the tales they told of him were good.

And yet, and yet. She had come back to his cubby after her interview with the Russians, because she had promised to do so and keeping her word was something to hold on to, when her life's road had suddenly turned to water beneath her and she felt as though she were sinking fast. As he'd promised in his turn, he had already cleaned up all that spilled mineral oil; but perhaps he had seen how she was white and shaking, because he sat her down with a brass candlestick and some polish, and instructed her sternly in the only approved method of raising a shine. Work had steadied her hands, focus had steadied her mind. And he had sat beside her with another candlestick and another cloth, and they had rubbed and buffed for a while in quiet concord until he asked her casually about Miss Leven's visitors, who had driven up in such a grand motor with the double-headed eagle flying on the bonnet.

And then somehow she had told him everything, though he seemed not at all disturbed by any of it, even the news of who her father was. She wondered if he had quite understood, he was apparently so unconcerned. In the end, though—when the bell rang for tea and she had to go, though eating was the last thing on her mind—he had said, "Remember that you have a choice, lass, who you grow to be. You don't have to carry your father's character, any more than you do his name. You can stand in contrast to him, if you choose not to stand at his side, and let that choice speak for you." And then he'd gone on, with a wry little smile, "And remember that there's always work for you, here in my cubby. Should you want it. The school has a mighty number of candlesticks, for all that we draw our lights from the electric these modern days."

She had thanked him prettily, as Mamma taught her, and had gone her way to find Charm, with the thought of returning absolutely nowhere in her head. And yet, she had returned. Once and twice and again, when she had the time and the need to be quiet, to be out of the hurly-burly of her school life. Once he'd not been here, but the door was unlocked and she'd come in regardless. And taken down a candlestick from the shelf, routed out the polish, buffed it to a high shine and left it on his worktable like a calling-card, like a statement.

That could only ever be funny once. Today she had come to find him, and there he was; but when she turned towards the shelf he said, "No, lassie, not this time. I've other work for you. Come along."

She had wanted to sit and tell him her news, because he was a calm and calming listener, seemingly unshakable. It quickly became apparent, though, that he knew it all already. Not that he said so directly; but as he led her through the castle he talked—as he had never done before with her, or as far as she knew with anyone—about the war.

"This was more than a hospital, it was a listening station too. There was a terrible fear, once the Tsar had taken the moons, that he would launch an attack on the planet proper. Surely, that was what he meant to do; what good are the moons else? Too small to colonise, they're just lumps of rock, barely enough air to breathe and nothing to do when you've breathed it. Except crouch up there and watch us, year in and year out. They do that, all right. Since the invasion never came, since they gave up so much ground on Earth they never thought they could pull it off up here. But anyway: we had watchers of our own up in the turrets, in case they came down hereabouts. And the wireless to listen for them talking, and to call the warning in, did they ever come. And all that apparatus is still here, stowed below; and I need a hand now to bring it out and put it all together, see what's what, what's working and what's not..."

She didn't ask why he'd need the set brought out. She knew. It lay unspoken between them, something heavier than the weight of an old wireless, and it was she who needed help to carry it. *Charm should be here too, by rights—but no, not her. I won't let her be involved with this, until she has to be. Later...*

He brought her to a door she'd never noticed—*Private*, it said, but nothing was private from the janitor, that was inherent—which opened onto a staircase leading down.

He gestured her to go ahead of him. Meanwhile he went on talking, though he'd already said more than she'd ever heard from taciturn Mr Felton. "Never you mind about your schoolwork for once, you can help me wire everything together. Crank it up. It's a science lesson for you, lassie. You ought to understand the way things work, that'll do you more good than any amount of book-learning."

Anyone would think he'd never read a book in his life. As it happened, she knew that wasn't true. She'd seen the books he kept in his cubby—and they weren't just decoration, there was always one by his chair, with an old leather bookmark to keep his place.

She opened her mouth to say something that would agree with him, while disputing his every assumption— Mamma had always taught them about real life and never from books, until this sudden late decision to send them off to school—only then she stopped, dead on the stair there. Stopped talking, stopped breathing, almost stopped thinking.

Said, "There's someone. I heard someone. Down below."

In honesty it was not so much a someone, except that her mind made a someone out of what she had heard: little more than a breath stopped short, a voice cut off before she'd really heard it, the scuff of a shoe on stone. Pieces of someone, that all added up to a whole person if she was doing her sums right. Or more than one person, because people don't often talk to themselves, and she was sure she'd picked up that silence that comes of someone abruptly not talking, when they had been talking before.

"No one comes down here." It wasn't that he disbelieved her, she could hear that in his voice behind her shoulder. He said it as though it were absolute, a rule of nature rather than a rule of school. But still: she was sure of herself, when she really didn't want to be.

The staircase plunged into shadow below her, even before it met a landing and turned a corner out of sight. She called down, "Who's there, please?"—and was startled but really not surprised to hear a soft voice calling back, "Um, we are. Who's that?"

There was half a giggle in the voice, challenge without threat, almost an unconcern. As though they didn't think

186

they could be in trouble. Perhaps they didn't realise she had an adult with her. Mr Felton spoke softly; they might only have heard a girl's voice, another schoolgirl like themselves. Not old enough to be a prefect.

She almost thought she knew the voice. At her back, Mr Felton was in no doubt at all. He snorted, "That Mishkin pair, of course. Who else?" He hit a switch, and the stairwell flooded with light. "Come up, you two. Come up now."

He was right, of course. It was the twins who showed themselves on the landing, Tasha and Tawney, looking only a little sheepish. Perhaps being caught by Mr Felton was not so bad as being caught by staff, or by a prefect. But he was wrong too, there weren't two of them; the new girl Rachel came with them, as she always seemed to do these days.

"It's all right, Mr Felton." That was one of the twins: Tasha, Levity thought, just from her manner. *Insouciant* was a word she'd learned from Mamma, but she thought it might have been invented just for Tasha. "We do have permission to be here."

"It is not all right," Mr Felton said heavily, "and you do not."

"Rowany said—"

"Rowany has no say here. The cellars lie under my purview. Miss Leven perhaps could override me here— perhaps—but no other staff member, and certainly no schoolchild, be she Head Girl or otherwise. Why did Rowany send you down here?"

"Um, she sent us everywhere." That was Rachel, stepping forward to support Tasha when Levity expected Tawney to do it. "It's a project, to chart the whole school and its history." No suggestion of *it's a punishment*, which all the Middles knew, of course—though Levity also knew that it wasn't Rachel's punishment at all, which only made it stranger to find her here making common cause with the evildoers, taking their burdens on her own back.

"Hmmph. And do you mean to chart me too? For I am a part of that history; and when you come down into my territory—where Rowany has no right to send you, no right at all—then it's me and not the school that you are measuring."

"We're terribly sorry, Mr Felton." Tawney, stepping up, stepping in at last. "Are they your things, down here? If we'd known that, we'd never have come down. Not without asking," added hastily because they were nothing if not honest, the twins, and of course they would have wanted to, as soon as he had banned it.

"Well, they're certainly not the school's things," he growled in response. "What's down here predates the school's time here. As do I. Did you know that?"

Blank looks; it had never occurred to them to wonder. He was the janitor; of course he came with the school. Where else did janitors come from?

He read their faces, and snorted. "Well, as you're here, you may as well make yourselves useful. We've a lot to shift, and if you've time to wander out of bounds, you've time to help me carry. Me and Levity," including her as by right. Which was, surely, right. It was his job; it was her father. Hers and Charm's, of course, but she still thought it better to let her sister run with her little friends and pretend that nothing was looming, at least till after supper.

At the foot of the stairs, a long passageway opened onto half a dozen separate storage rooms. The walls were whitewashed; Levity sniffed suspiciously, but she could smell no trace of damp. Nor see any flaking on the walls, or any mould.

Mr Felton quirked a narrow little smile at her. "Driest cellars you'll ever find, lass. Dug into the solid rock, and even two floors down, we're still above the level of the lake. You could store your grandmother's lace down here for a hundred years, and it would take no harm."

If Levity's grandmother—either of her grandmothers—had owned any lace, it was still on Planet Earth. Levity and Charm had no inheritance, no family history; it was safer that way. *We're starting fresh,* Mamma said, often and often. *We'll be our own family and make our own traditions: a new start for a new world. What could be nicer?*

Sometimes Levity thought that the opposite would actually be nicer. She'd like a grandmother or two. A big house to visit, all full of family at Christmas.

But she couldn't have it, and wishing for the impossible was foolish. It was better to fish your own canal, and take what came. Always looking forward, never back.

Mr Felton knew just where to find what he was looking for. He opened one door out of six, and here was more whitewash and shelves from floor to ceiling, all stacked with boxes, chests, coiled cables, odder shapes wrapped in oiled canvas.

A wooden box with brass hinges, padlocked shut; he passed that to Levity. "Can you manage this, lass?"

"Yes, of course."

"Good, then. Twins, this'll take the two of you…"

That was a metal trunk painted gunmetal grey. It had handles at either end, and they could lift it between them, huffing a little. Levity thought that was mostly for show. Mostly.

"Say if it gets too much, and I'll spell you. We've a long climb ahead."

As he spoke, he was festooning Rachel with cables. Then he hefted another wooden box himself, and said, "Onwards and upwards, girls. All the way up."

He wasn't joking. From the cellars, he led them up and up. Past the kitchen, with its alluring aromas; through the hallway on the ground floor to a turret stair, and so on up. Past the first floor, with its classrooms; past mistresses' studies and bedrooms; past even the access to the main castle roof. By then the twins were struggling, but they shook their heads at Mr Felton when he asked if they wanted to rest or swap.

"Very well, then. Not far now in any case," he said, vanishing still further up.

"Well, it couldn't be," Tasha gasped, panting in earnest now as the girls followed on. "One thing about towers, you know they can't go on for ever. And they can't have secret passageways. Not like cellars. Underground, you never know how far a way will lead you. It could tunnel halfway around the planet, if it's deep enough to run under the canals. There aren't any tunnels in mid-air."

"There's always the dumb waiter," Tawney called back from the other end of their trunk. "Fair enough, it's a shaft, not a tunnel, and it only goes back down—but it's almost a secret passageway, right at the heart of the tower. Maybe we should pry open one of these hatches and have a look inside, just so we can tell Rowany we were thorough."

"Maybe you shouldn't," Mr Felton growled above them all. "Maybe I screwed all those hatches shut for a reason. For two hundred reasons, and every one of them a nuisance."

Tawney chuckled breathlessly, and subsided. They turned one more corner around that hollow square shaft, climbed one more flight of stairs and were at the top at last. The staircase ended at a low, narrow doorway. Mr Felton fiddled with keys, while the girls rested their burdens on the steps; once the door was unlocked, he opened it and gestured them through with a warning. "No clowning around, now. It's a long way to fall."

It was. The turrets stood twice as high as the castle proper. Like the broad flat roof below them, the turret-tops were rimmed with battlements—"merlons and embrasures," murmured the twins dutifully—but while the view from the roof was dramatic, up here it was sensational.

They could see the whole of the lake, and the crater wall that ringed it, and distantly the long hairgrip-shape of the two canals that met at Terminus, diverging as they ran to the far horizon, shining like steel in the lowering sun.

"No time to stand and gawp," Mr Felton said gruffly. "Not if we're to be set up and working before we lose the light. You, girlie, you know how to raise a flag?"

Rachel had probably never been called "girlie" in her life before. She only bridled a little, though, and mostly at the question. "Yes, of course! We've been in the Pioneers since we were seven years old." Her voice faltered a little at the end there, as she felt the absence of her twin one more time; but she set her chin and glowered at him as though she were mortally offended.

"Aye, good, then. Run that aerial up the flagpole, will you? The toggle goes through the loop on the halyard, same as if it were a flag; then haul away. You others, help me with all this."

The twins' steel trunk proved to contain lead-acid batteries. No wonder it had seemed so heavy! The twins squared their shoulders and tried to look impressive, until Tasha flinched too noticeably and Tawney made her sit in an embrasure out of the way, to rest her ankle. Interestingly—to Levity, at least—it was Rachel who scolded her. "You should have said it was troubling you! I could have taken your end, while you brought the cables. They're awkward, but there's no weight to them. And all those stairs—honestly, Tash! I can't think what Sister Anthony's going to say, when she looks at your ankle in the morning."

"Can't you?" Tasha all too clearly had a very good idea what Sister Anthony would say. "But look, never mind me. You help Mr Felton get everything plugged in. I'll just sit here and watch. Right as rain, after a minute's rest."

Levity's box held a shortwave radio. For half an hour Mr Felton gave them a practical physical science lesson, connecting batteries and aerial to the radio, testing every wire and every connection individually. "None of this has been used since the war. It was in perfect working order when it was put away, I made sure of that, so there's no reason for it to fail now, so long as the dust hasn't got to it, or the dry rust; but Mars is full of little sins we have no name for, so—ah!" as a little light gleamed green on his control board.

The girls all looked at each other; by common unspoken consent, it was Levity who asked the inevitable question. "Mr Felton, were you actually here yourself in the war?"

"And where else would I be? They said I was too old to fight—even then, they did, and I am older now—but I was fit to man a listening-post. Many's the night I've sat right here on an old canvas camping-stool, with this selfsame rig, listening to the skies as much as watching them. Of course, it was mostly Morse that we listened for back then, not so much voices yet, but—well, let's see now. Mostly those nights what I heard was nothing at all, which was all I wanted to hear. Tonight we'll hope for something more."

So saying, he turned the tuning dial slowly with fastidious fingers. The little speaker he had set in an embrasure crackled and hissed—and suddenly broke into intelligible speech. Clear, seductive speech, in a crisp English accent.

"Phobos calling, this is Phobos calling: speaking to all of you down there on Mars, in your doomed little colony—"

Mr Felton cursed, in a manner that would have curled the hair of any staff who overheard him, though it didn't ruffle a single feather among these four girls. Levity for one had heard far worse, from some of her mother's artistic friends— but Levity wasn't listening to him. She barely noticed when his hand reached out to snap a switch and condemn the radio to silence. Levity was still listening to that voice as it echoed around and around in her head. It was the voice of a stranger, though she could have named him immediately; but then, so could any of her companions here, and any girl in the school, just from his call-sign. That was famous. Notorious. You didn't need to listen.

She didn't need to listen. Indeed, she never had. And nevertheless, she knew him and all his history, far more intimately than anyone here.

Phobos calling, this is Phobos calling...

CHAPTER SEVENTEEN

Treachery Loves the Darkness

"I'm really terribly sorry, Miss Leven. I never thought it could happen. With the sun still in the sky and Phobos falling away to the horizon, the odds against picking up...that man, that broadcast...so clearly were astronomical. If you'll pardon the pun."

"Never mind, Mr Felton. I could wish it hadn't happened, just for her own peace of mind, because Levity must be dwelling on it now; but she'll be speaking to the man directly soon enough, as soon as the moon comes around again. It'll likely do her no lasting harm, to be reminded of who he truly is. Who else he is, I should say, because he is still their father, despite all else. I shouldn't allow this otherwise. Perhaps I ought not to allow it in any case, but I cannot stand between a man and his children. I will not. If their mother could be contacted—but without her firm word, no. It is not my place."

"Aye. You won't give them over to him, though?"

"That I will not. Their mother brought them to me; I will let him speak with them, because I must—a father's place is sacred and I have a duty not to intervene—but she entrusted

194

them to me, and I will return them to her and to no one else. I have said this already, to his...representatives."

"You should have had me in here with you. You'd no call to be facing them alone."

"Oh, and what should I have said to them, about you? How could I have justified your presence?"

The old man had no answer to that. He only shrugged, and scowled. "I would not have had them in my house."

"I would not have had them in my school," Miss Leven said, "but that I saw no way to deny them. They have a *laissez-passer* from the Viceroy, and full diplomatic accreditation. And we are not at war now."

"An armistice is not a peace. We can never have peace so long as they are up there, on our moons, and staining the aether with their putrid broadcasts."

"I'm afraid you may be right, Mr Felton—but for our girls' sake, we must at least try for civility. And, for Levity and Charm, we must allow some measure of contact. Supervised contact, that is. I take it that everything is ready and in working order?"

"It is. At least we know that we can receive clearly, as soon as Phobos is above the horizon; and reception should be better at night. Not long now."

"No. And their housemistress is keeping an eye on the girls, for this little while..."

That was not entirely true. Certainly Miss Hendy, housemistress of Stokes, had both girls on her mind and Levity under her eye; but she had decided to leave them as long as possible with their particular friends and duties. It was never good in her experience to keep girls idle and anxious, amid a lingering suspense.

So they had sat through preparation with their classmates, and then gone to the dining hall as normal. After supper and prayers, Juniors were sent off to their houses to play quietly for an hour before bath and bed. Again, Charm was no exception. By Rowany's much-resented fiat, this was the time that Middles went to the gardens, to weed and hoe and water. Levity found herself on hands and knees beside Lise, grubbing out shadowroot spores under Miss Hendy's watchful eye.

"No one wants a shadowroot infestation," she told them, holding one root in her palm as an example. "They blow in on the wind, then burrow deep. If they're allowed to establish a colony, they'll leach all the goodness from the soil, and our carrots and potatoes will wither and starve."

Other girls might have giggled a little, at the thought of a hungry carrot; but not Lise the farmer's daughter, and not in fact Levity either. She had seen failed crops down on the plains, and their effect on the people. No one was allowed to starve any more—indeed, it was a matter of pride for all Martians that they grew more food than the colony needed, and had shipped great quantities to Ireland during the dreadful potato famine, more than repaying the debt owed from their own lean years, when the Empire had kept Mars fed—but it took time to organise relief, and hunger was a swift and bitter foe.

"You say they burrow, Miss Hendy," Levity said, "but they're not alive, are they? Not living creatures, I mean, like insects or worms...?"

"No-o," Miss Hendy said judiciously. "Something between animal and vegetable, I believe, although that is still the subject of debate. Certainly the spores are not static like seeds, lying where they fall. They have no consciousness, no nervous system, no instincts—but they can burrow, yes. Away from the light and the dry, into dark and damp. They can expand and contract by simple capillary action, and so shift themselves through the soil, more or less like grubs though without even so much purpose."

It did look like a grub, more or less, pale and moist against her skin; and it felt that way too, the girls knew already, leathery on the outside and pulpy within. Miss Hendy tossed hers into a bucket, dusted off her palms and straightened up.

"If you remind me, next period, I'll go into the science a little more deeply, at least as far as we understand it. Now carry on, girls. Try to clear this bed before dark, or it'll be twice as much work tomorrow."

Lise grumbled, but *sotto voce*, and not till the mistress was safely out of earshot. "Oh, my aching back! Isn't this why we have gardeners?"

"I thought you wanted to be a farmer?"

"Oh, I do. I will. It's not a matter of wanting, it's, it's *fore-ordained*. The land's there, it's ours, of course I'll be a farmer. But not on hands and knees, not with my *fingers*. I'll go to college first, and work out a better way to tackle shadow-root..."

At the end of the hour their backs indeed were aching, their hands and overalls—and, alas, their faces—filthy; but their bucket was full of spores bound for the incinerator, and the vegetable bed was as clear as they could hope to make it.

"Good work, girls," Miss Hendy said, coming to check as they helped each other up with many a theatrical groan. "*Excellent* work. You can be justifiably proud of yourselves. Now, a visit to the bathrooms seems in order. When you've washed and changed, Levity, you are excused the extra sewing for tonight. You must try to make the time up later, or your Plains frock won't be ready when all your classmates' are. As soon as you look like an English schoolgirl again and a little less like a denizen of the lower deeps, come to find

197

me in my room. You know where that is, don't you? Third floor in the east tower. Briskly, please. I'm away to fetch your sister."

And with that she was gone, brisk herself along the path.

The two girls gazed at each other. After a moment, Lise said, "Well, *I* know why you're missing the sewing—and frankly I'd rather be stitching another hem in that horrid grey stuff they gave us for our dresses. But no one else knows, and fair warning, some of them are going to be idiots about it. Obnoxious idiots."

"I know," Levity said, on a sigh. "But even so, don't tell them, Lise. I can put up with a bit of idiocy. That's nothing, compared to what I'd face if they all knew the truth."

"Oh, I won't say a word in your defence, don't worry— except maybe to point out that it's a staff who called you away, and none of us gets to argue with a staff. Though if the truth did get out, I think you might be surprised. Mostly here at the Crater School we judge people by who they are, not what their parents have done."

"You think so?" Levity felt she'd endured a lot of unwanted attention already, merely by dint of who her mother was. Let news of her father leak out, she thought there would be no end to the staring, the murmuring, the downright antagonism. Where her mother was the object of awe and almost hero-worship, her father was...something else. There would be loathing and hissing condemnation, transferred from the absent traitor lurking overhead to his daughters, very much here below. She thought discovery was inevitable now, and she dreaded it—but not quite as much as she dreaded this evening ahead.

"I think you should trust your friends, your house and your school," Lise said stoutly.

"I trust you," Levity said. "That's as much as I can manage."

"Only because you've never been in school before. You don't know what we're like when one of ours is in trouble, when the chips are down—wait, what's that funny smile for?"

"Oh, nothing," Levity said, swallowing hastily. "Only, I don't think you should use gambling metaphors. I don't think Miss Peters would approve." And then there were tears threatening behind the giggles, and Levity could do nothing but squeeze her friend's hand and hurry away.

A quarter of an hour later, hastily washed and brushed and as neat a schoolgirl as she could make herself in the time, she hurried up the turret steps, knocked at Miss Hendy's study door and heard herself called in.

Through the door, every step portentous now, another step towards inevitable destiny. Here was Miss Hendy, ready for her, and here too was her little sister, looking anything but ready for anything but bed. Charm was perched on the edge of a cushioned settee, sipping a cup of cocoa. She looked up with hope, with relief, with longing; Levity settled next to her, slipping an arm around narrow shoulders and squeezing warmly.

"Levity, thank you for being so prompt. You've just time for a cup before we go up. Yes, I know it's hard to swallow when you're nervous, but it'll be chilly up there on the tower top, and it'll do you the world of good to have something warm inside you. Set your sister a good example, even if you don't want it for yourself. Neither one of you is going up those stairs before these cups are empty, and so I warn you."

With that mix of inducement and bullying, Miss Hendy inveigled them both into gulping down the last dregs of the sweet and soothing cocoa. Then she marshalled them onto their feet and marched them out to the staircase.

Hand in hand, the two sisters climbed. Levity had been this way earlier, but it was all new to Charm. There were lamps set in niches, where the electricity hadn't reached; she should have been peering about in fascination, not staring at her feet as they mounted step after step, nor clinging so tightly to her sister.

Levity squeezed back, knowing just how Charm was feeling. Hating their unknown father just a little more for putting them through this, for stirring everything up when they should be settling down to life as carefree mischievous schoolgirls...

Still. Here they were, stepping through the open doorway, out onto the roof. With a longer wire to the aerial, no doubt they could have done all this indoors; but actually, privately, Levity was just as glad to be in the open air, under the mighty distant stars. If not for her own sake, then for her sister's. It did give Charm something to focus on, beyond the bulk of the radio equipment, the sharp glowing lights, the looming shadows of two more grown-ups.

"Nothing yet, Miss Leven. She'll have to rise above the crater rim before we can catch a signal."

"Very well, Mr Felton. Do keep trying, because it could be any minute now."

Levity gripped Charm by the shoulders and steered her to the battlements, turning their backs to their company. It might be shockingly rude, but it was very necessary.

"Look," she said, pointing westerly. "Can you find Earth? The sun's only just gone down, she should be there, or thereabouts. Our very own Evening Star. Let's wave."

It was all distraction, of course, and they both knew it. Still, it worked well enough. They fixed on the brightest point in the westering sky, declared that to be Home, and waved thoroughly. And argued about how to work out whether England was looking in their direction, whether anyone there could be waving back—and none the less were instantly alert when the radio speaker's steady static broke suddenly into a blurt of Morse code followed by a listening hiss, that moment before Mr Felton said, "Here you are, ma'am."

"Thank you, Mr Felton. Stand by, please." She took the microphone he handed to her, lifted it to her lips and spoke carefully into it. "Here is Miss Leven of the Crater School. Do I have Phobos?"

After a moment, a voice replied, smooth and insinuating and so very clear that Charm startled and gasped. Levity herself nearly looked about to find him on the tower-top.

"Actually, Miss Leven, I believe that we have Phobos, and Deimos too; but this is certainly our broadcasting-station on Phobos, yes."

"Who is speaking, please?" She must know full well who was speaking; it was the same voice that Levity had heard that afternoon, *Phobos calling...* But of course he had to declare himself, before anything else could happen.

"My name is Peregrine Murray, and you have my daughters in your care. Are they present?"

"They are."

There: it was said. Charm had both hands now wrapped about her sister's. Levity murmured in her ear, "Let me do the talking. You don't need to say anything at all, if you don't want to. Okay?"

Charm nodded abruptly.

"I should like to speak to them, please," the voice—their father!—went on. "If you would pass the microphone, Miss Leven, I should appreciate that."

"Very well. Though you should understand, Mr Murray, that I will be listening in, and I will have a finger on the switch."

"I expected nothing else. It's unfortunate, that a man may not have a private conversation with his own children; but in the circumstances, you carry on, Miss Leven. Listen in all you like. I shall say nothing subversive. I wish only to lay a proposal before them. You will have all the time and opportunities you could desire, to persuade them otherwise; allow me at least this one chance to speak with them unfiltered."

"You have your chance, Mr Murray. That is why we are here. I am passing the microphone now. Be brief; I stand *in loco parentis* here, and all other considerations set aside, I will not keep the girls out for long in this night air."

The microphone was like a rubber cup full of darkness, set on a short wooden handle. A curling wire connected it to the wireless set that Mr Felton crouched above, his fingers set lightly on knurled knobs, nudging them to and fro.

Levity took the microphone from Miss Leven, momentarily surprised how much it weighed. She lifted it hesitantly to her lips, as her headmistress had—and then was struck mute, with absolutely no idea what to say.

"Greet your father, child."

Miss Leven sounded kind, but firm. Levity took a breath, and managed, "H-hello?"

"Olivia? Is that you?"

My name's Levity, but she didn't say that. She was strangely glad that he used a name that she had abandoned long ago, that didn't mean her at all. Just as she was glad that his voice struck no chords in her memory. This man had no place in her head or in her heart. She glanced up briefly, and her eyes found Phobos, rising swiftly above the crater rim; she glared at it, and still thought it was the best place for him. Cold, barren, desolate.

"Hello," she said again, the best way to avoid saying *yes* or *no* to a question that really had no answer.

"And hello to you too, my dear, dear daughter. I know Charlotte's with you too; will she say hello to her father?"

"I've got the microphone," Levity said shortly, meaning *she really doesn't want to talk to you.* As if to make that absolutely clear, Charm buried her face in her sister's shoulder. Levity thought it was a pity the man up there couldn't see this. Then she remembered the many excellent telescopes the British had abandoned on the moons, and glanced up anxiously, wondering if perhaps he could.

"And the elder can speak for both, eh? Very well, then. I hope she's listening, at least. It is such an immeasurable pleasure for me to be speaking to you—to you both—at last, at long last."

"Mamma always said you didn't care about us, or you wouldn't have gone off the way you did." *To the enemy, to the Tsar...*

"Oh, my sweet child. Your mother is...perhaps not the most reliable judge in this. Or the most trustworthy witness. I would have stayed if I could; I would have taken you with me, if I could. But my honour prevented the first, and she herself the second. I could not have remained the Queen's loyal subject, when everything in me drew eastward to the double-eagle of the Romanovs; but I made the mistake of too much honesty, and said as much to your mother. When I returned from...making arrangements, I found that she had fled, and taken both my babies with her. I heard the police arriving at the front door to arrest me, on an information she had laid, as I slipped out at the back. I don't suppose she ever told you that, did she?"

"No. I wish she had." *I would have cheered.*

"Yes, well. Now you know. A wife should respect and honour her husband, who is head of the family. Instead she betrayed, she sought to destroy me. And then she stole my children, and it has taken me so long to track you down, so very long."

"We're her children too," Levity said stoutly, meaning *we're her children, full stop.*

"Of course," he said placatingly, "but she cut me out of your lives, and I think I deserved better than that. She changed your names and took you to another *world*, Olivia. I scoured the old Empire, before ever I thought to look here."

And now you come to us, just when Mamma has left us alone. She was too old to believe that a coincidence, whatever he might say. She thought he had tracked them down some time ago, and watched, and waited for his chance to strike. If Mamma had been here, she would never have let him even this close, even talking-close. Miss Leven couldn't refuse him so much, Levity understood that—but Mamma would have refused him, yes. And then taken them out of school, changed their names once more, moved them on in a hurry.

"But enough recriminations," he said. "You are here now, and so am I; and I have a proposal for you. You are still my daughters, and I would dearly love to see you. I...cannot come down to Mars"—*no*, she thought, *we would hang you for a traitor*—"but I can arrange for you to have safe passage up here, to see me. You could come at half-term, and not miss any schooling. I'd sooner have you for longer, and take you to see Russia, my chosen country—how I would love to show you Moscow, and my little dacha by the lake!—but one thing at a time. I am sure Miss Leven would accept my word of honour, that I will have you back at school in time and in good order; nevertheless, I am suggesting that a mistress accompany you on the journey, so that no one can have any cause for doubt. What say you, my dear child? Will you come and meet your papa?"

Levity drew a breath, and then didn't know what to do with it—but Charm did. Charm snatched the microphone from her, and yelled fiercely into it. "You're not our father, Mamma divorced you ages ago. You're a *coward* and a *traitor* and we *hate* you, and we *never* want to see you, never *ever...*!"

And then she flung the microphone over the battlements and kicked the radio speaker after it, burst into tears and plunged back into Levity's arms, sobbing wildly.

CHAPTER EIGHTEEN

The Wrong Twin

"Levity! Come here, child!"

Rankling just a little bit, because no girl of fourteen likes to be called "child" under any circumstances, Levity turned obediently and retraced her steps to where Sister Anthony loomed at the end of the corridor.

"The postmaster in town has just telephoned, to say that a delivery has arrived from Aspell's in Marsport. I spoke myself, and I am in no doubt that it contains your uniforms and your sister's, arrived at last. There is no real urgency about it, at least as far as you're concerned," and her lip twitched, the closest that austere personality had ever been seen to a smile, as she ran her eye over Levity's dress, "and certainly he could send it up by the funicular this evening; but today's post has already been and gone, of course, so that would require Jenkins to stoke up his steam-wagon and make a special trip to bring it to us. I see no need for that, when a passel of healthy girls could just as well go down to town to fetch it."

"Uh, yes, Sister." Levity almost had to work it out on her fingers, but she was fairly sure that she was being offered an immeasurable treat here. Crater School Saturdays were as ordered and organised as any weekday; there might not be formal lessons, but nevertheless every hour was accounted for with one activity or another. Prefects and senior girls— *very* senior girls—were allowed to catch the mid-morning funicular and spend the day in town, but not more than once in half a term. It wasn't an opportunity offered lightly to their juniors. *Or offered at all*, Levity's friends might have said, with years of experience behind them.

"I know that Miss Harribeth has errands of her own in town today, and I dare swear she'll be willing to shepherd you down and up again. Now, who would you like to have with you?"

"Lise, please," Levity said immediately. Even if she hadn't liked Lise so much—if she hadn't told her so much—that would still be an obligation, to share the treat with her sherpa. "And Charm, of course; and the twins and Rachel, and—"

"Steady, now. I didn't say you could take half the school. I think three will be sufficient, to carry the parcels I expect; and I don't want to burden poor Miss Harribeth with a mob, all unasked. Besides, weren't Charm and Rachel both involved in that disgraceful scene yesterday? They may have been excused punishment, but they have certainly not earned themselves an outing. Lise you may have, certainly; and one of the twins, no more. They won't suffer, for spend-ing half a day apart. Hurry along and find them. The funic-ular leaves in an hour, and you'll want to change. Craktereans abroad on licence are expected to be a credit to the school. That...garb...may be practical, but it speaks not well of you as needlewomen. I'm afraid I must insist that you turn out in proper uniform."

That made it not only a treat, but a blessing. Yesterday had been a black day indeed, when the Middles had finished, and then been obliged to start wearing, their handmade pioneer smocks. The coarse wool was prickly, the dye was patchy, the garments were shapeless sacks with inevitably crooked hems; of course the Juniors had mocked delightedly at first sight of them. And of course the hotter tempers among the Middles had reacted with fury; and of course Levity's sister and her impish pals had been one side of that row, and unhappy short-fused Rachel on the other. If Miss Whitworth hadn't been quite so quick to descend on them all like the wrath of God, it might have come to fisticuffs.

As things were—well, Levity was sorry that her sister must miss out on the day's fun, and regretful for Rachel's sake too. Still, a chance to change back into her regular uniform was an unexpected gift; and one she could offer her friends too, at least a pair of them. Running in the corridors was strictly prohibited, but no one could see her feet beneath this long flapping skirt, so she chanced a kind of quick stiff-legged jog that might almost have been very hurried walking. The last she'd heard, Tawney had been headed for the library, so she ought to be able to intercept her...

Levity all but skidded around a corner, and yes: there was a familiar figure walking away from her, long ponytail swinging gracefully in time with her steps. Shouting was as forbidden as running, anywhere in school buildings, but no one else was around, so she took another risk and called out, before the girl ahead could reach the library door and enter the *sanctum sanctorum* where a raised voice was sure to bring down doom upon her.

"Tawney, wait...!"

The figure paused, and turned; and Levity saw the mischief in her smile and the spark in her eyes, and knew immediately that she was wrong.

"Tasha! I'm sorry, I thought you were running errands for Miss Leven."

"We swapped. It was her turn." The twins had a personal and complex economy of trades and favours, that no one outside themselves could ever interpret or account for. "How did you know it was me, though, as soon as I turned around? If you were expecting her?"

"I always know. I don't know why other people can't tell. You may look alike, but you're two different people inside, and you...sort of wear your skins differently?" Levity wasn't going to mention that first moment of disappointment. They were two different people, and she liked them both—but not equally. Tawney was more comfortable to be around, her nature closer to Levity's own. Mamma would no doubt hold impulsive Tasha up as a prime example of everything a girl should be, but Levity preferred to think things through and step wary.

Tasha's face screwed into a peculiar grimace, as she thought about what Levity had said. Then she grinned and shrugged and said, "I expect we do. Not many people can see it, though. Sometimes even I only know she's her because I'm fairly sure I'm still me. What did you want Tawney for, anyway? And will I do instead? She'll be busy for half an hour. That's why I was going to look for a book."

Really, Levity had no choice. She could not say *Actually I wanted to invite your sister on an outing without you.* Instead she said, "You'll do splendidly! That's if you don't mind changing out of these smocks and spending the day in town with Lise and me. Only you, though, and we have to go now, so hurry."

Needless to say, Tasha hurried. The two of them swept Lise up from where she was laying out her mending, and bore her away. They ran to their respective houses to shed the hated pioneer outfits, and reappeared as matching schoolgirls just in time to waylay Miss Harribeth on the castle steps.

Clearly she was expecting them. She looked them up and down, and nodded briskly. "Very trig, girls. And probably a little more comfortable, yes? Very well, then," laughing at their emphatic agreement. "Now, which way shall we go to the station—sheep-paths, or lake? I think we have time for either."

"Oh, lake, please, Miss Harribeth!" Lise said, with some urgency. "We haven't been allowed, you know, since the start of term. Levity's barely seen it, except from this far away."

"It doesn't look that much different, close to. As you wish, though—if Tasha's comfortable with that? If you are Tasha," added a little doubtfully. "Either way, I think you twins had the worst of that adventure, so..."

"Tasha, yes—and I'd love to go by the lake, Miss Harribeth, if we may."

"Splendid. Best foot forward, then, and no loitering. I don't suppose nymphs will strike twice, but if we miss the funicular there's nothing to do but come home again and go on with the day as before."

That dreadful prospect once laid before them, they stood in no danger whatsoever of missing the train. The girls didn't quite *push* Miss Harribeth along when it seemed to them that she was dawdling; but they did everything they could to hurry her along, short of laying actual hands upon her person. More than one of them was reduced to dancing impatience behind her back, when she seemed inclined to stop and lecture them on some interesting point of school or Lowell Crater history.

She may have known quite well what she was doing, and what they were doing too. Levity was fairly sure she detected a wicked twinkle in her teacher's eye. Nevertheless: when they reached the station platform, they still had ten minutes in hand. The train was there already, the engine chuffing gently as it built up steam for the descent. Miss Harribeth bought return tickets for them all, and distributed those among the girls; then they found an empty compartment and climbed aboard.

"Now, how shall we pass the time? It's a slow journey, and two at least of you have taken it often enough to lose the thrill. If you were Juniors, I'd offer peppermints and puzzles; but girls your age..."

They hastened to assure her that despite their long legs and advanced years, they were yet fond of peppermints. She relented, laughing, and passed a bag around.

"You don't need to distract us with puzzles, though," quoth Tasha, spying a sudden opportunity, "if you would only tell us some of the secrets of the castle. Are there any puzzles there, built into the walls—any secret passageways, or doors that can't be opened, or...?"

Miss Harribeth eyed her shrewdly. "Would you have me do your punishment for you, Natasha Mishkin?"

Of course she knew about the twins' enforced project; all the school knew by now. Still, Tasha met her eye to eye and said, "Yes, please." Levity and Lise gasped aloud, and Miss Harribeth quirked a notorious eyebrow, but Tasha went on boldly. "At least, Rowany said we should come to you if we had any questions, and—well, the thing is, we've mapped and measured everything, we've looked everywhere, we've opened every door that isn't locked—we even chanced Mrs Bailey, and checked every cupboard in the kitchens—and we can't find anything that's not supposed to be there."

"Well, but my dear girl, what did you expect? No, don't tell me: or rather, you've told me already. Secret passageways and doors that can't be opened, yes? You have to remember, Tasha, that the castle wasn't really built by a robber baron in mediaeval times, however much it might have wanted to pretend. It was meant for a hotel, and it's not yet a hundred years old; its design may not be particularly practical, but it isn't whimsical either. At least, not consciously whimsical," she corrected herself, belatedly honest.

"No, but if it was trying that hard to pretend, *shouldn't* it have secret passages and so forth?"

"Well, perhaps it should. And perhaps it does; I don't know everything about the building even now, and if they're secret, they ought to be hard to find. If I were you, I'd ask Mr Felton."

"Would you? The janitor? Why?"

"Think about it, child. Who could possibly know the building better, who gets to pry into every corner with his mop and his polish and his rags? If there's a disguised lever that moves a hidden spring, he must have dusted it. He's had a better chance than anyone of uncovering the castle's deepest secrets, even if only by accident."

Tasha's mouth widened slowly into an O of understanding. Inevitably, her head swivelled then towards Levity. "Liv, you're friends with Mr Felton, aren't you?"

"Well, I wouldn't say friends, 'zackly." He was a grown-up; how could he be a friend? "But I do like to visit him in his cubby sometimes. He makes tea, and we do the crossword together."

"Excellent. You can ask him while it brews. '*Inarticulate*, four letters beginning with M—and by the way, Mr Felton, have you found any hidden doors or secret rooms while you janitored?'"

"While he *what*?" Miss Harribeth gasped.

"Um, janitised...?"

T he train pulled at last into its station. An authoritative voice from the platform boomed, "Terminus!" and the girls caught one another's gaze and giggled in unison.

"And the joke is?" Miss Harribeth enquired, as she opened the compartment door and herded them out.

"Oh, it's silly, really. But we had a lesson in English about puns and double meanings, and someone came up with 'zackly this. The stationmaster says that every time, but is he telling us the name of the stop, or is he saying it's the end of the line, like they do on the buses?"

"Of course, he could be doing both at once," Miss Harribeth said judiciously, "but that's not a silly question at all, Lise. It's a philosophical riddle."

"Oh. Is it?" Lise looked a little taken aback, at having perpetrated philosophy before noon on a weekend.

"Of course. What else is philosophy, but a discussion of language and meaning? Here's another one for you. We each have tickets to ride the train," showing hers to the stationmaster as he came along the platform, while the girls lined up to do the same. "But did I pay for the ticket itself, this little piece of card, possession of which then entitles me to ride? Or did I pay for the right to ride, for which this ticket is a receipt and a guarantee? Think about that, girls, argue it out between yourselves. Not too heatedly, please. By all means tell me your conclusions on the journey home. Now: who knows the way to the post office from here?"

Lise and Tasha both raised their hands emphatically.

"Good. Can I trust you to go there, collect Levity's parcels and bring them back here to the left-luggage office, to be collected when we return this afternoon?"

"Of course, Miss Harribeth," spoken in unison, with a mutual indignation.

"Excellent. You girls run along and do that, then, while I pursue my own errands; then take your time, explore the town, treat yourselves. I don't suppose any of you have any money, so here: this is a gift from me, not an advance on Bank." She dispensed a shilling to each of them, and shrugged aside their thanks. "We will meet again for lunch, at the Cadena. One o'clock, and don't be late. Afterwards I'll take you to the locks, where one canal lets down into the other. With any luck, there'll be a ship coming through. I'd like to show you that. But the architecture is monumental in itself, and all the old questions hold true, there more than anywhere I know: who built this system, and where have they gone? Because certain sure, it was not that race we call the merlins..."

If it was a long-standing Crater School tradition that senior girls were trusted to go out in public quite unsupervised, it was also a tradition—not so much flourished, but strictly observed—that Middles most emphatically were not, and with good reason. All the long history of the school spoke to the innate ability of the Middle School to find trouble even where it was not looked for. Many of the legends revolved around specific girls in their very specific wickedness, and no small number of those legends already featured Tasha's name. Lise was considered steadier, but even so: the two girls were left gaping at each other, as Miss Harribeth walked swiftly away.

Levity looked from one to the other, and giggled. "You two look like stranded fish."

"I feel like that, almost." Lise shook herself briskly. "Pinch me, Liv. Just to make sure."

Obligingly, Levity pinched her arm.

"Ow! All right, I'm not dreaming. Which means you're not either, Tash."

"I could pinch you too, to prove it," Levity offered. "In fact, I could just keep pinching both of you until you tell me what's the why of this."

"She left us alone," Tasha said. "Us! In town! Without a second thought or a backward glance, she just left us. Why, we could do anything!"

"Which is why we won't," Lise said, with a sigh of imposed virtue. "Right, Tasha? She trusted us, she didn't even put us on our honour, not in so many words; so for the honour of the Lower Fourth, we just have to be good."

"I'm afraid we do." Tasha sounded even more dismal about it. "We'd best think of ways of being extra-good, just to make sure she gets the point."

"Well, but it might pay off, further down the line. If she tells the staff what little saints we were, maybe they'll all slack off a little."

"Dream on," Tasha sighed, but she did perk up a little. "Okay: villainy is postponed, *sine die*. Which is something Dad says, and he's a lawyer, so don't argue. Virtue is triumphant. Which is the quickest way to the post office, O you virtuous maidens...?"

Virtue triumphed at least that far, seeing them to the counter in short order, with all fascinating distractions dutifully ignored. They charmed the postmaster, and remembered to tip the boy who brought out five hefty parcels from the back; they weighed them judiciously and distributed them among themselves, each according to her ability; they set off confidently, Levity leading, out onto the street and—

"Wait just a minute, Liv! Let's not go back the way we came, that's boring. There's a walk down by the canal here, it won't take five minutes longer and we've got two hours. There are always swans on the water, and this time of year they might have cygnets."

Tasha had already turned onto the gravel path leading down beside the stern stone wall of the post office. Levity glanced at Lise, who shrugged amiably. *"C'est un fait accompli, n'est-ce pas?"*

"C'est vrai."

They followed along, still practising their French, down to the towpath that bordered a narrow canal. This was man's work, not Martian. At least, they were all Martians now, but no alien hand had dug this channel. Irish navvies, rather, or coolies from China or India. The Empire had fetched in labourers from all over, from the earliest years of the colony, and Dutchmen to organise the work. The great canals they'd found waiting for them were stitched together by ever more seams like this, waterways for transport and for irrigation and for power. Even the major cities of Mars were built around their networks of canals. More Birmingham than Venice, more utilitarian than lovely, but nevertheless: from above, wherever green spilled over the red, the Charter lands were overlaid by a delicate and ever-expanding lacework of water.

As promised, this particular thread in all that lace offered swans, and cygnets too. The girls heaped their parcels on a convenient bench, lamented their lack of sandwiches, searched blazer pockets for something, anything they might offer to demanding birds—and were taken quite by surprise when a voice behind them said, "Excuse me..."

They caught each other's eyes, startled, frowning, trying to place a voice they were sure they knew; then they turned as one, and gasped as one.

The face was known, familiar, impossible; the uniform was bizarre, outrageous, unthinkable.

"Rachel?"

The girl before them shook her head. "No—but I am right, aren't I? You are from the Crater School?"

The Craterean three looked at each other one more time, with a wild surmise. When they turned back to the newcomer, it was Levity who broke their awed silence.

"Jessica?"

CHAPTER NINETEEN

One Girl too Many

R eally, things couldn't have worked out better.

So Jessica thought, at least. She'd been sitting on a bench alone, staring at swans, wondering quite how to carry on. When she heard voices, she'd scuttled back behind the shelter of some shrubs, because nothing attracts the attention of strangers so readily as a schoolgirl adrift in a strange town. Especially in the wrong uniform.

But the owners of the voices came closer, and were quite clearly girls themselves; and as far as she knew, there was only one school nearby that could account for them. She risked a peep through the leaves, saw green-and-gold, and was certain. Rachel and others had described the Crater School uniform to her, in infuriating detail.

So she took a breath, and took a chance. When the girls occupied her bench with their parcels, she stepped out from behind the shrubbery and approached them. Her heart was in her mouth, but only for a moment. They seemed to be her own age, more or less; when they hailed her with her sister's name, she knew she was among friends.

Baffled friends, but only for a moment. She could see the penny drop, in their amazed faces. Then one of them cried her own true name, and she confirmed it with a nod.

That broke Babel loose upon her. They were three, and they were suddenly all talking at once, all gripping her by the hated blazer and guiding her to the bench, pushing parcels heedlessly aside to make space, urging her to sit. *I was here first,* she thought rebelliously. But they didn't know that—as far as they were concerned she had come out of nowhere, fallen from the sky—and it didn't really matter. She was in no position to play hostess, even if she'd wanted to. They must think of this as their own territory, and of her as an uninvited guest; and as sure as wild redberries give you tummy-ache, she did need their help.

So she sat where they invited her, and all three of them crowded in around her; and their babble of questions was still too much for her. She buried her face in her hands and hunched her shoulders against them all.

They fell suddenly silent, and one crisp voice called out above her head: "All right, people. Don't overwhelm the poor girl. She must have had adventures getting here, whatever's the why of that, and she doesn't need three of us interrogating her all at once. Am I right, Jessica?"

She nodded wordlessly into her palms; then decided she was being feeble, and sat up straight and said, "I'm sorry. Of course you have questions, and I owe you answers. But—one at a time? Please? And—please, who *are* you?"

"Oh, good grief." That same voice again, and this time she had a face to put to it: a strong, sensible, sporty face, framed with neat brown hair. "Here we are, so knocked all askew by the sight of you, we're forgetting all the rules of hospitality. I'm terribly sorry, Jessica. My name's Lise, Lise Harper; and these are Levity Buchanan and Tasha Mishkin."

"You...you wrote to me. All three of you. I remember those names. That was so kind, so impossibly kind, you have no idea..." She almost lost control again, thinking how often she had read and reread those letters, how hard it had been to leave them all behind; but here was something more that needed saying, one more acknowledgement of just how far she'd come, and how alone she'd been. "And you're a twin," addressing lanky blonde Tasha, "you said it in your letters, and your twin wrote too. Though my sister had already told me about you two."

Tasha nodded matter-of-factly. "Me and Tawney, yes. We've been Rachel's sherpas all this time. We're Russians as well; I think maybe that helps too. But never mind us, we know all about us and so do you, mostly, 'cos we told you. Tell us about you. Especially, how did you get here?"

"But first," the other girl—Levity, the vivid redhead—cut in, "tell us what you're wearing. Is it fancy dress, or a costume from a school play, or—?"

"No such luck," Jessica said ruefully, though in truth she was glad of an excuse to talk about something that wasn't truly important. Just for a minute, before she had to come to the confessional. "You wouldn't believe it, but this is the uniform of the Low Bridge School. Isn't it awful? 'Rose and gold,' it said in the prospectus. Rachel and I almost fought over whether that would be better than your green-and-gold. Only then when I got to school and saw the truth—well, I suppose they do it deliberately. They'd have to, wouldn't they? It couldn't be by accident. Maybe they think it makes us easier to spot, across the dreary miles of the Plains."

Certainly it made her stand out among these girls, the loathed sugar-pink blazer fighting inexorably with the orange tunic beneath, while they seemed so trim and trig in their smart rich green with the warm gold piping. She knew what a fright she looked, no one better.

"Maybe they do think that," Tasha said judiciously. "Maybe it does. But they didn't spot you, did they?"

Here it was, then: the moment she'd been dreading. At least these were girls like herself, not adults, not mistresses—that was yet to come, and would be worse than this—but even so. The words tasted sour in her mouth as she spoke them, as she confessed.

"I left just after lessons, when I knew no one would miss me till suppertime," she said, as matter-of-fact as she could make it. "The school sits at the junction of two canals, and there's always traffic. The boatmen are used to giving girls a ride; I must've been twenty miles away before anyone thought to come down to the water and ask about me."

"You mean you ran away?" That was Lise, gaping a little.

"Of course she did, idiot!" Tasha said sharply. "Except it's more like running towards, isn't it, Jess?"

"Yes. Yes, that's it exactly. Oh, I'm so glad you understand..."

"Of course I do. We'd have done the same, Tawney and I—except we would probably both have done it at the same time, and turned up at the wrong schools and missed each other utterly. At least Rachel's still here, so you can be together again." *Until your parents descend like the Judgement of Solomon and tear you apart again.* Tasha didn't say that, but Jessica heard it none the less. She thought they all did. "But what did you tell the boatman, that would persuade him to take you away from school?"

"Nothing but the truth," Jessica said stoutly. Then, faltering a little, "Well, almost the truth. I hope it's true. I said I was coming to spend half-term with my sister, at another school. I never said I had permission, I just sort of...let them assume that..."

It sounded weak and dishonest, even to her own ears. She didn't want to look up at the other girls' faces, for fear of what she might read there; so she stared at her shoes instead, until a warm arm came around her shoulders and gave her a little shake. She looked up, startled, into the forest-green eyes of redheaded Levity.

"Well, then, let's make it true. We'll get you into school somehow. Subjudiciously. Is that a word? Possibly not, but you know what I mean. We'll smuggle you in the way you smuggled yourself out of that other awful place, and get you together with Rachel, so that the two of you can work out what's best to do now. Won't we?" She looked around at her two friends, almost glaring.

"Of course," Tasha said. "We were always going to do that. You're in with us, Lise, yes?"

Of the three of them, Lise was the one who looked doubtful; but she was outnumbered, and seemed a little bit awed by her friends' determination. "I suppose so. Yes. It's the sporting thing to do. Only, how can we...?"

"The first thing is to get Jessica out of that uniform," Levity said, "and that much we can do, here and now. I know Rachel and I take the same size, so my new things should fit you, Jess. May we call you Jess? Rachel does, I know."

"Oh, please do! I've been 'Jessica' to everyone all term, and I'm tired of it. I'm always Jess to my friends, it's just that I never made any friends there. They were truly the most awful snobs."

"Is that why you ran away?" Lise asked.

"No, not really. Not at all. There was no one there I cared about or wanted for a friend. I was there to work, and I did try, but I just couldn't bear it without Rachel. Our parents say she distracts me, and they're probably right, but—oh, when she's not there, her absence is so much worse. It's like a hole in the world, a whirlpool, sucking and sucking at me... You understand, Tasha, don't you?"

"I do, but you'll never make a grown-up see it." Tasha spoke ruefully, and from the heart. "They always think it's a good idea to separate us, so that we'll settle down to study. It doesn't ever work. Tawney and I learn best when we're together, when we can help each other along. I don't know if that'd really be true for you two, though. Rachel says you're the clever one, streets ahead of her."

"Did she? She's such a fibber! She's really bright, so she can afford to slack off while I have to put my head down and struggle to keep up. That's why we were sent to different schools, because she'll walk into Oxford when the time comes, but I need to grind to get there. But I still need her more. I'd rather skip Oxford than be without Rachel. But the parents won't listen, they're both dead set on us both having our degrees from their own alma mater, where they met. I don't know what would happen if I said I didn't want to go. But I don't honestly know what I do want—except this one thing, I don't want to be apart from Rachel. And I won't be. If they try to send me back, I'll just run away again."

No one said *How if your parents send you back to Earth, to a school in England? What will you do then?* She knew they were all thinking it, but of course it was the impossible question. She knew the answer no more than they did. All she had was hope, and the stubborn determination that had brought her this far.

And luck too, she had that, perhaps: the luck that had brought these particular girls to the towpath just when she needed them. Neat-fingered Levity was untying the string from a parcel, folding brown paper back to show a tidily folded blazer, with more clothes beneath, all in Crater School colours.

"Here you are, Jess." Levity picked up the blazer and shook it out. "And here's a gymslip, and stockings too. You won't need more than that for now. Put these on, and you'll look like a Crater School girl; no one will think twice, seeing you around town. We can't take you back up with us, we're with a mistress; but there's a path, I know. Tash, can we get her started on that?"

"Yes, of course. You can't get lost; it only goes up and never branches, and it'll bring you to the school in the end. One of us will meet you at the top, and we'll smuggle you in. We know all the secret places now. Then we'll fetch Rachel, and—"

And she stopped there, because she no more than Jessica knew where they would go from there, and she was honest enough just to shrug at it.

Practical Lise said, "Hurry up and change, Jess. You can go into the bushes there, in case anyone comes by on the canal. We need to take all this to the railway station, but that's where the path starts in any case, so we can see you on your way. And there's a booth there that sells pies and sausage rolls and lemonade. It's half a day's walk, but if we pool our money we can buy supplies to see that you don't starve."

"What about my uniform," Jessica asked, tugging at it with distasteful fingers, "what shall we do with this?"

"Wrap it up with the rest. We'll hide it somewhere when we get back to school; and if Sister Anthony sees it first, well, Aspell's just made a mistake and sent the wrong girl's clothes."

"They've got name-tapes in, though. No one could confuse Abramoff with—Buchanan, did you say, Levity?—even if they were colour-blind."

"Yes, but we've got an Abramoff of our own," Tasha said insouciantly. "Mistakes happen. Even utterly mad ones, like pink blazers. Go on, scoot—we haven't any too much time left, if we're to set you on your way and see you at the school and settled before dark."

It wasn't much of a plan, perhaps, but it was miles better than anything Jessica could have come up with by herself. And it would see her safely to the end of her journey, which was as far as her imagination could see, as far as she had ever tried to look: arriving at the Crater School and finding Rachel. After that, let come what may. She'd be with her sister, and the two of them together were indomitable. That was the best thing she'd learned all this nightmare term, the word "indomitable".

Thinking indomitable thoughts, she retreated into the shrubbery to change clothes. She supposed there must have been other girls before her who donned a uniform they weren't entitled to wear, of a school they didn't belong to— but not many, surely. And certainly none could have done so for as good a reason as her own, she was determined on that. Indomitable. Yes.

Five minutes later, four neat, excited schoolgirls in identical green-and-gold carried their burden of parcels into the left-luggage office at the railway station. And emerged empty-handed, and hustled off the platform and out into the street. There they turned towards a flight of stone steps leading down to a gravel path that ran pleasantly between the long station building on the one hand and a meandering stream on the other—

—and were promptly hailed by a short, stout, middle-aged lady much beset by parcels of her own.

"Girls! Have you only just done with your errands? I'm astonished, but not ungrateful. A little help here, please; if you take one packet each, then I can handle the last, and—oh," as she found herself unexpectedly bereft. "Wait, I know I had four parcels, so between the three of you..." She counted heads, and frowned, and peered at them more closely. "Rachel Abramoff! Where did you come from? You were most certainly not on the train. Did someone drive you down?"

Jessica stood mute, of necessity. Tasha at her side said, "Please, Miss Harribeth," and then dried up unexpectedly, finding herself with no ready story. Perhaps she had only said that much to help Jessica out, to put a name to the mistress now bristling before them; if so, that was kind of her and thoughtful too, but not particularly useful just now, when there was nothing Jess could truthfully say. Part of her worried that even standing silent was a lie of sorts—but Parson Meadows had devoted a whole sermon over Easter to the sin of being too nice in one's arguments, too overweeningly honest, too arrogantly virtuous. Very well, then: she would say nothing, and let Miss Harribeth continue to mistake her.

"What, none of you with anything to say? Very well, then: I must suppose that you made your own way down here, Rachel, and without licence. Not on the train, I know: did you walk, child? Down this path, all that way? You must have left close after breakfast if you did, to be here now. And your friends met you at the post office, perhaps? By chance, or otherwise? Ah, now we're getting somewhere. Yes, Tasha?"

"Yes, Miss Harribeth," in a mumble.

"Yes. And of course they won't give you away, but it doesn't take a great mind to guess what you were doing there. All the school knows that you've been forbidden to write to your sister. Rightly or wrongly, and I'm not about to share my own opinion with the Middle School; but doing it behind our backs and sneaking down here to mail your letters undetected is a rather shabby way of going on, don't you think, Rachel? Besides the anxiety it must have caused up at the school, when you were found to be missing. Or did you have that covered, are your classmates primed to explain that you were a last-minute addition to our party? Is this a grand conspiracy...?

"Well, never mind," as Jessica flushed fiercely, an underline to her silence. Knowing that Miss Harribeth could only misread that as an admission merely added fuel to the fire in her skin. "I'm afraid your behaviour has cost everyone their treat, for I must keep you all sternly under my eye now. It's such a shame, when girls your age can't be trusted. We'll go to lunch, and then I think to the library, and you can read quietly until it's time for the return train. I am profoundly disappointed in you, Rachel. And in all of you, if silence indicates complicity. Probably I should send your whole troop to Miss Leven, but this once I'm willing to say nothing further, so long as I have your word, Rachel, that you will never pull this trick again. Here and now, please."

Jessica took a slow breath, tried to ignore her burning cheeks, and said, "Miss Harribeth, I promise, I will never come to Terminus to post letters to my sister." There. Nothing in that was quite a lie—although it tasted in her mouth like the most dishonest thing she'd ever said.

"Very well, then. Follow me closely, please, the four of you. You'd best croc, like little girls."

They fell in obediently behind her, two by two; and as they walked, the four girls exchanged horrified glances. What in the world were they to do now...?

CHAPTER TWENTY

A Case of Taken Identity

It had been a long day for Rachel. Any day would probably seem long, of course, when you were obliged to wear a scratchy sack and know that every Junior and every Senior you met was secretly laughing at you. But more than that, when she looked about for her preferred companions, Tasha or Levity, she could find neither of them.

She did in the end find Tawney, who had been running errands for the head from house to house.

"I can't find them either," Tawney said. "Tash was supposed to be waiting for me in the library, and I thought Liv might be with her, but they're not there. Perhaps they've gone down already to join the gather for this awful walk? We'd better go anyway, or we'll be late, and Miss Hendy does *not* love to be kept waiting."

The last hour of Saturday mornings was sacred to games practice, warming up for inter-form matches in the afternoon. Or it was meant to be. It was another mean idea of Rowany's that had barred the Middles from their chief delight. "Pioneer girls worked too hard to play sports," she had explained cheerfully, "even if vigorous games had been considered a decent occupation for young females at the time, which they were not. You do need exercise, of course, besides all the gardening; and you need to learn more about the wild plants hereabouts, both native and introduced. The pioneers would have learned by trial and error, but we can do better than that. We have Miss Hendy, who has very kindly volunteered to take you about and show you what's what. Especially what you can eat and what you absolutely can't."

In ordinary circumstances, a nature ramble with Miss Hendy would have been a treat, even if it cut into their games. But nothing was ordinary now. No one wanted to be paraded about on the hillside in these wretched garments, for their friends the shepherd-boys to mock and whistle at. And who could enjoy anything when it came as part of a gruesome punishment? Really, every day was worse now than the day before; not a Middle in the school but was praying for half-term, and an end to this torture.

At least they were all suffering together, that was something. Rachel found herself bonding more closely with her classmates because of it. Odd, that something so hateful should make her feel even a little warmer towards the school, but there it was. The Crater School was an odd experience altogether, she was finding.

They hurried to the castle courtyard, where they found Miss Hendy already waiting, with the rest of the thronging Middles.

From the top of the steps, from their tiptoes, Rachel and Tawney scanned the crowd—then they looked at each other, and shook their heads. Neither friend nor twin was there. What could have happened to them? There was still a chance, of course; they'd been so nearly late themselves, it was always possible for two scatterbrained girls to be later yet.

But Miss Hendy had a list in her hand, and she'd clearly been taking call-over. Now she ticked off two last names—*Rachel Abramoff, present; Tawney Mishkin, present*—and folded the list and put it away in her pocket.

"Come along, then, girls. I won't make you croc, when we're so far from anyone who might be bothered by a gaggle of schoolgirls—but groups of no fewer than four, please, and no more than eight. Don't rush ahead, and don't dawdle; this is neither a route-march nor a picnic. Lead off, Chantry and Florimel."

Rachel and Tawney hung back as long as they could, until quite half the Middle School had marched out through the rear archway. At last, though, they had to give up any hope of a miracle. They had to approach the ominous figure of Miss Hendy, who was already eyeing them askance, because neither one was inclined to be a lagger; Rachel had to nudge Tawney into speaking first, into saying, "Please, Miss Hendy, I don't think we're all here."

"What? Nonsense, Tawney. Whom do you imagine is missing?"

"My sister, and Levity Buchanan..."

"Oh." Miss Hendy's brow cleared. "Weren't you told? Miss Harribeth's taken them down to town on the funicular. Lise Harper, too. They're on an errand for Sister Anthony: collecting the Buchanan girls' uniforms, I believe. You won't see either of them now till mid-afternoon. Join Izzy's group, would you? I can't have the two of you branching off alone. And I'd rather have all the madcaps in one place, under my eye..."

So much for suffering all together. It wasn't a trouble shared if your twin and your new best friend didn't have to share it. Rachel and Tawney found themselves in absolute agreement on that, and amused themselves—if not Miss

230

Hendy—by grumbling about it all through the walk. Especially once Brigitta said that she'd seen them leaving, and that none of the party were wearing pioneer smocks.

That was insult added to injury, Ossa heaped upon Pelion. Finally, a use for Classics lessons! They said it again and repeatedly, *Ossa upon Pelion*, and it added fuel enough to keep them glowering all through lunch, plotting myriad unlikely revenges on the class-traitors who had abandoned them this way.

There was no chance to spend the afternoon looking out for them, laying an ambush, lying in wait. Lunch was followed by half an hour of sitting quietly and being read to from improving texts. With eagle-eared and ever-alert Melanie Fitzwalter doing the reading—and clearly enjoying herself hugely, laying great emphasis on the moral lessons of a hundred years ago—no girl was about to risk so much as a whisper, never mind a glance outside.

At last Melanie put her dreadful books away, but they still had no opportunity to find out if the lucky threesome had come back to school yet. She declared, "You had a walk this morning, in lieu of practice. That's as much exercise as any pioneer child could hope for, and a good deal more than many ever saw. Miss Leven says you have to be out in the open air this afternoon too, though. With sports off the agenda, we've decided to put your willing hands to work, down at the boathouse.

"No," she went on quickly, as the buzz of murmured interest threatened to rise to a crescendo of questions, "Miss Leven hasn't lifted the ban on boating quite yet. But that could change; the merlins haven't shown themselves again all this half, not even the occasional nymph begging for scraps. So we need to be ready, for when the ukase is lifted. What's that, Bryony? You don't know that word? Look it up, and be ready to explain it to me at supper. You can't spell it? Ask your friends. If no one can help you, you may ask a prefect. Not a staff.

"Meantime, as I say, we want the boats ready for the water. Which means they all have to be scraped clean, examined for rot and worm, and coated with mariner's paint.

"This is our plan for your afternoon. You'll march down to the boathouse, carry the boats out in crews of six, lay them on the grass there and ready them for the water. We'll have three or four prefects with you all the time, watching for merlins and keeping an eye on progress. Mr Felton will inspect each hull and approve your work. You should be finished well before supper. And this is absolutely the kind of thing that pioneer girls would have faced, year in and year out. They had to learn how to preserve timber on Mars, on and off the water; we are the fortunate inheritors of their hard-won knowledge. Any questions? No? Very well. Stand! March!"

The Middle School as a whole wasn't quite sure whether to grumble at being made to work this hard when they should have been playing games, or to be excited at the prospect of getting out on the water at last. To be sure, Melanie had promised no such thing—but the school would never make them go to all this trouble if they didn't mean to lift the ban soon. Even if the prefects were mean enough to do it, the staff were not. They said that to each other over and over as they hauled the heavy boats out of winter storage, as they scraped wearily at peeling paintwork and sanded down rough patches, as they stirred the thick glutinous revolting mariner's paint with its vile slick layer of oil floating on top and its disgusting stink.

Like the nature walk, they might have enjoyed the rough physical labour for its own sake, if it hadn't felt like ongoing punishment for what was more a kindness than a sin. Even getting smeared and filthy wasn't so bad when you were all in it together and you could laugh at each other. When you weren't wearing an itchy gunny-sack that had everybody else in school laughing at you.

Rachel had never felt less like laughing in her life. She stepped back from the reeking hull of their upturned skiff, wiped her brow with the back of her hand and knew in the moment of doing it that she'd just left a streak of paint all over her forehead. Paint which would never just wash off, because of course it was waterproof and long-lasting, that was the point; and it was black, because black absorbed heat and you could never be too warm in the thin air on the high canals and the crater lakes. It wasn't true on Earth, perhaps, but here cold did more harm to timber than sunlight ever could.

They'd learned that in one of their pioneer lessons. It would almost have been interesting, if it hadn't been tied in with this humiliating, infuriating, endless charade...

Thoroughly out of sorts, Rachel glared around at her classmates. Most of them were as smeared with paint as she was herself, but even so. Let just one of them catch sight of her and giggle, or even oh-so-helpfully point out what she'd done, and oh, that girl would be so sorry she'd ever been *born*...

Perhaps they had all sensed her mood, and were sensibly avoiding her eye. That, or they were just wearily concentrated on their own work. At any rate, none of the girls near at hand so much as lifted her head. Dissatisfied, because she would so much have liked a row right now, Rachel looked further afield—and there was Tasha, waving wildly from the corner of the boathouse, then ducking out of sight before reappearing to hold her finger to her lips in exaggerated dumbshow, before beckoning broadly and ducking out of sight again.

Rachel nudged Tawney, because whatever Tasha meant or wanted, her twin was certain to be included in her plans or expectations.

"Come with me," Rachel muttered, her eyes scanning for trouble. The prefects were all standing dutifully on the towpath with their backs to their charges, watching the water; Mr Felton had looked the boats over and departed; the coast was clear.

"Why, where are we going?"

"Shh! Just come. Don't say anything." And then, to the others in their crew, because six hardworking girls can't suddenly become four without at least a hint of explanation, "Tawney and I are just going to stretch our legs, thataway," with a nod towards the boathouse. "We can do this, two by two; the prees aren't looking, and four can do what's needed here without knocking elbows all the time. Sort out between yourselves who goes next; we'll be back in a minute."

Slipping away was easy; keeping upturned hulls between themselves and the oblivious prefects was second nature; trusting the other girls they passed not to betray them was an absolute. Middles hang together, that's a primal law.

Except when they fight each other, of course. Rachel came around the corner of the boathouse with Tawney in tow, and there were Tasha and Levity, both of them looking neat and spruce and *clean* in their charming and comfortable uniforms, after their day of idle shopping, far from the griefs and hardships of the pioneer lifestyle. Rachel could cheerfully have slain the pair of them. Was halfway to doing it, indeed, and never mind whatever wrath that might draw down on her accustomed head; it would be worth it, worth any price, just for that moment's satisfaction.

But Levity clasped her arm and said, "Oh, Rachel! Such a mess, and I've no idea how we'll get out of it—but oh, Rachel, she's *here!*"

"What?" Knocked all out of her stride, Rachel could only gawp. "What are you talking about? Who's here?"

"Make sense, you goops," Tawney added, mostly aiming that at her twin, who was still miming: astonishment and awe now, while she left the actual explanation to Levity.

Who took a breath, hugged Rachel's arm even closer, and said, "Jessica," triumphantly. And then, in case there was any doubt, "Your twin, Jessica. She's run away from her school, and come here to find you."

That stole all the breath from Rachel and all the fury too, all the defiance. If a staff or a prefect had found her then, they would have had a penitent, tearful, hopeful child on their hands, asking only to be reunited with her sister.

Left alone in the company of her peers, though, she swallowed down that tendency to tears and said harshly, "Where? Where is she, then?"

It was impossible, but she wanted to believe it; but Jess was certainly not here, with them. Lise was at the other end of the boathouse, keeping *cave*, watching the prefects as intently as they watched the water, ready to duck out of sight at a moment's notice. The rumoured Jessica was nowhere to be seen.

"Ah. Well, that's the thing. Miss Harribeth is really cross with her, and she's marched her off to San to be put in isolation until she realises the enormity of her sins."

"...What? What's Miss Harribeth got to do with Jess? What sins? Oh lor', she didn't *confess*, did she?" It would be just like her, to make a clean breast of everything to the first authority figure she came across. But that would make a nonsense out of everything she'd done, because as sure as merlins laid eggs, Miss Leven would send her straight back to where she was meant to be.

"No, no," Levity reassured her. "Nothing so awful. Only, of course Miss Harribeth thinks she's you; and she thinks you sneaked down to town to post letters, and she was being very forgiving and took us all off for lunch, and of course Jessica could hardly say a word because she didn't know anyone or anything we were talking about. So Miss Harribeth decided she was being sullen at getting caught—and you have to admit, Rachel, she did have reason: you have been most frightfully sulky since you came—and she was very offended, when she was being kind enough to overlook the whole sneaking-away-from-school thing and try to sneak you back without running you into trouble. So now she's marching you—I mean Jessica—off to San to see if solitary confinement can teach you to be grateful."

"It's not uncommon," Tasha put in. "A mistress decides that an afternoon in isolation will be good for your soul; Sister Anthony is always willing to oblige. And to make the poor girl feel like half a worm," she added feelingly, as one who had been on the receiving end of this treatment more often than she quite liked to remember. "But the thing is, it's reckoned to be punishment enough. It won't be written up in the report book, and it won't be mentioned at staff table or anywhere. Really, she's doing you a favour. She's still trying to cover for you. I mean Jessica. I mean..."

No longer quite sure what she meant, she ran dry and fell silent. Rachel found herself in the unusual position of being in trouble for something she hadn't actually done—except that it was her twin in trouble on her behalf, and now she too felt the urge to confess. If she walked into Miss Harribeth's study and told the truth, then at least Jess would be released from durance vile, and they could perhaps have at least a little time together, if the authorities allowed it.

Soon enough, though, she knew Jessica would be packed off back to her hated school at the other end of the province. Which would make this whole escapade null and void, even before Rachel had had the chance to hear all about it.

236

"We'll just have to swap me back for her," she said. "You can hide her, can't you, somewhere in the school grounds?"

"Well, that was our plan," Tasha said, "in so far as we had one—but I don't think we can do that now. Jessica is not just being Rachel, she's being Rachel in trouble. Which means that every staff and every prefect will have an eye on her. The story getting out is that you—that she, I mean—cheeked Miss Harribeth, and nobody likes that. And everybody believes it of her, I mean of you, because of what you were like at the start of term. So every man's hand is against you, and you—I mean she—will be watched like a hawk, and we'll have no chance of swapping you one for the other today. None at all."

"Except that we do have to go and see her," Levity added, "because Miss Harribeth says that when we change back into our pioneer smocks, so must she. So we're going to need that," with a nod towards the hated garment Rachel was wearing. "We've an hour's grace, because it's too late for us to join in with what you're doing, but as soon as you're done here, you'll need to give us that, if we're to keep this quiet."

"Oh? And what do you propose I wear?"

The two girls looked at each other, and positively sniggered. It was Tasha who said, "Jessica's uniform, of course. We managed to separate that out, once it was clear what a mess we were all in. Miss Harribeth's a dear, but she's really not terribly observant. That's how Jessica could fool her, of course. Miss Leven wouldn't have believed it for a minute. Nor would Rowany," added with feeling, one twin to another.

"Wait a minute. Are you suggesting that while Jess is pretending to be me, I should pretend to be her?"

"No, not at all. What would be the point of that? What we're suggesting—it's the only thing, Rachel, honestly—is that while Jess has to pretend to be you, until we can swap you back again, then you should just disappear. And you'll need something to wear, but we can't take anything of yours or Sister Anthony's sure to notice that it's missing, you know how often she inspects the dormitories and goes through everything we own; so it's Jessica's things or nothing, I'm afraid."

"Well, it won't be the first time we've worn each other's clothes. Or each other's names, for that matter." They were twins; of course they'd traded identities on occasion, for convenience or for wickedness or for simple curiosity, to find what it was like to live in their sister's skin for a while. *Surprisingly different* was the answer to that one. It took them aback every time. "Lay on, MacDuff."

"*P*ink? Pink and *orange*?"

Now Rachel understood the sniggers. And remembered Jessica's descriptions of her loathsome uniform, and had some words of her own that she'd like to add. Still: what wasn't silk was good Martian wool and cotton, and oh, so much of a relief to draw on after that abomination of a smock. She shuddered at the colours, but if their plan worked no one except these few friends would actually see her in them. Indeed, anyone else's seeing her would be a definition of absolute failure and doom.

They were safe for now, the twins keeping watch while Levity helped her change, while Lise scuttled back to Sister Anthony with the forsaken smock. Even so, Rachel looked about while Levity's nimble fingers straightened blouse and tie for her, and said, "I can't stay here."

"No, of course not." They were ensconced for now in the boot-boy's den. Properly he was the boy-of-all-work, only he did see to all the staff's footwear and boot-boy was shorter to say; and he was never here on Saturday afternoons, because he went home to his parents in the village and wouldn't show his face at school again until after Sunday chapel.

His den was known to be a temporary refuge for plotters and evil-doers of every hue. There was no mirror, though, which was why Rachel endured Levity's fussing; it was pointless if nobody saw them, and it was pointless for other reasons if anybody did see them, but even so. If you were going to wear nice clothes—even *pink*!—it was as well to wear them nicely.

It was known, though, that staff on their rounds always checked the boot-boy's den before retiring, and were inclined to lock it. That meant Rachel couldn't spend the night here. Dark was already threatening outside, and they'd hatched no plan to swap herself for Jessica. No workable plan, at least. It was easy to say "If we smuggle you into a bathroom, then Jess can go in all innocence, and you can come out, and no one any the wiser," but it was impossibly difficult to manage that first smuggling, on busy corridors with prefects and staff always about and ever alert.

Tomorrow was Sunday, though, and things might be easier to manage then. "Listen," Rachel said, "how's this? If I can get out of school without being seen, I'll just scoot up to Sister Anthony's Eyrie. I've been there before, I've spent the night there before; it wasn't comfy or fun, but I know that I can do it. If you can get Jess through school tonight and the early morning tomorrow without giving herself away, then they'll let you go for a walk on the sheep-paths after chapel, if you all go together. You can come and find me, and we can swap then, out of sight of everybody," and Rachel could finally actually see her sister in the flesh, which was the most frustrating part of this whole lunatic adventure.

"Wait here till suppertime," Tasha said, "and you'll have a clean run. Everyone will be in the dining hall, staff and all, and even the windows don't overlook the lake. You can go down through the Mistresses' Garden, along the lake path and then up the way we went before. If you think you can manage the climb on your own?" she added doubtfully.

239

"Of course I can. I didn't need your help last time, did I? And this time I know where I'm going."

"Well, but be careful. I got hurt last time, remember; and if there's no one with you..."

"I'll be sure to hold on tight if I meet any sandcats," Rachel said. "You just bring Jess up in the morning, and you'll find me right there waiting for you. Grubby and cold and hungry, I expect. Smuggle me as much breakfast as you can manage, will you?"

"Yes, of course," Levity said. "Between us, we should be able to feed you. What about tonight? Look, there's a blanket right here; it smells a bit of shoe-polish, so I expect he uses it to cover that table when he's working. You can tie it around you like a shawl, and climb with your hands free. What about food, though? You'll be missing supper too."

"You sit tight with Rachel here, Liv; we don't need to abandon her yet. Tawney and I will go and see what we can scrounge. I think we've got some fudge left, haven't we? And I know Paula has a cake. Well, half a cake; she was complaining earlier that it arrived broken. I expect we can beg a bag of crumbs for you, Rachel, if we're all mysterious. She loves conspiracies and secrets. If you ask me, Miss Peters should stop her reading all those wild romances, she's starting to think they're real life..."

CHAPTER TWENTY-ONE

They Came from the Water

It was quite clear to Levity that she still had a lot to learn. Unlike Charm, who was quite clear in her turn that at thirteen she already knew it all, Levity was even prepared to admit that school might have something to teach her. Not the tedious matter of lessons, of course: declensions and dates, voltages and the Vulgate were of no possible interest to anyone except teachers, who obviously depended on them for their living. In matters closer to a girl's striving heart, though, the company and wisdom of older girls—and conceivably even mistresses, unlikely though it seemed—might well have something to offer.

On the matter of friendship, though, Levity knew already just where she stood. Neither she nor her sister had had much chance to make lasting friendships in their peripatetic life, but their mother's stories and example gave them a strong foundation: for Isobel Buchanan maintained networks of friends old and new across two worlds and the gulf between. Furthermore, Charm's favourite reading served as another kind of example. School-stories might as well be

241

called friend-stories, really, that just happened to be set in boarding schools.

Levity had never expected them to prove so true to life. She might owe Charm an apology: for here they were, and really this first term was proving to be all about the duties and rewards of friendship, with the interests of education coming in a distant second.

There had never been any doubt that they would rally around Rachel and the astonishing arrival of her twin. That was written into lore. And for Levity, that meant that there was truly no chance that she would leave Rachel to make her own way out of school and out of bounds alone.

"I can't come all the way with you," she said stoutly, "because they'd be sure to notice I was missing"—where "they" was to be read as a malign cocktail of staff and pre-fects, as Rachel immediately understood—"and besides, I'm honestly not that good a climber. I get dizzy and fall off stepladders, so. But at least I can see that you get safely up to Sister Anthony's Step. And if you fall and break something," she added gruesomely, "I can run for help."

"And leave me to be eaten by the merlins meanwhile? Thanks so very much."

"No one's seen the merlins all this half," not since that first day when they'd both seen merlins far too close. "Perhaps we should take something to fend them off with? Feed them off with," added with a giggle. "Though Mrs Bailey isn't keeping that bin of old veggies by the door the way they say she used to, now that the lake path is out of bounds; and I don't see how we could sneak anything out of the kitchen and not be noticed."

"We wouldn't need to. We could sneak a cauli from the form gardens, as soon as supper's being served. But they'll notice you're missing anyway, Liv, if you come with me."

"Let them. They'll send someone up to San in case I'm sick, and when that turns up a blank they'll send someone down to Stokes, and one or two other likely places. By the time they start worrying about the unlikely places, I'll be back. With some fabulous excuse, which you and I will think up on the way. I'm not letting you go off on your own, Rachel, so don't you think it."

The others came back then, with whatever they had gleaned. A strange supper it would be, of sweets and pastries mainly, and a bottle of lemonade to wash it all down: too sweet for Levity, but Rachel took it in her stride. As she said, she had fared worse with less, and survived it.

"Just mind you come and rescue me with breakfast in the morning," she said. "And bring Jess!"

With everything bundled up in the boot-boy's blanket, and that slung over Rachel's shoulder to test the weight, Levity couldn't resist a chuckle.

"You look like one of my mother's sculptures," she said in quick explanation, when everyone looked at her askance, "the bold pioneer girl heading off into the unknown, with only as much as she can carry." *You look like me* was what she really meant but wouldn't say, *when I was modelling for Mamma.*

The supper bell sounded, and everyone turned by instinct and training to the door. "You all go on," Levity said quickly. "I'll see Rachel out." *And further than simply out*, but she didn't say that either.

"They'll ask for you," Tawney said, "if you're not in your place, Liv. They always notice," meaning the prefects, of course. Staff came later.

"Say you saw me—oh, I don't know. Running back to the house for a clean hanky or something. Or if you don't want to lie," because the duties of friendship were sometimes in conflict with the duties of honesty, "then just say that I was horribly mysterious about where I was going," which was even more true than they realised, "but that you know I was going somewhere, on some urgent mission." That almost made it sound like she'd been sent, by someone with the authority to send her. That might mute the prefects, at least until a staff noticed her empty place setting and enquired about it.

"Well, but—"

"No, I'm serious, Lise. You go on, quick, before we're all in trouble. I can take whatever's coming, but someone needs to see Rachel off."

They went at last, anxious and uncertain. The second bell sounded, the one that said *you're late!* Latecomers had to report to the duty mistress for a scolding at best, order marks most likely unless they had a very good excuse. No one wanted that, and besides everyone was hungry by first bell, so the corridors should be empty by now. None the less they lurked together, Levity and Rachel, for another five minutes, until they were sure; then they scuttled from cover, taking the safest route they could think of out of the castle and hopefully out of sight, if not—in Levity's case at least—out of mind.

They daren't cut through the courtyard, through Mr Felton's passage and across the drawbridge. That was the obvious way and the most direct, but dining-hall windows overlooked the courtyard. Anyone might glance out and see them.

They hurried along the corridor to the library, then, only hoping that no staff had decided to absent herself from supper for the sake of some quiet time among the reference books and a tray in her study later.

Either they were lucky, or else that imagined mistress was lurking in a far alcove, and tóo absorbed in her work to hear two unlikely schoolgirls skipping their own supper in order to tiptoe swiftly from one heavy door to the other.

They weren't supposed to use the library as a shortcut, Levity remembered, almost having to choke down a giggle as the outside door creaked slowly closed behind them. They were committing so many other graver sins right now, this one seemed trivial. Besides, everyone did it. There was never enough time to get from where you were to where you were supposed to be. She suspected that the school timetable was designed that way deliberately, to keep you on your toes, always on the very edge of trouble. Shortcuts weren't just a blessing, they were a necessity.

Reminded of another equally forbidden, she glanced anxiously across the archway to the door that led into the chapel, and from there through to the dining hall. If she and Rachel could ignore a rule, so could other people; and what was forbidden to girls was often allowed to staff, or even to prefects. Anyone might slip away from the riot of supper, sidle apologetically through the stained-glass glory of the chapel and emerge without warning, right in front of them. Someone might be sent, even: going down to Stokes, say, to search for missing Levity, cutting through the chapel with special permission because the errand was so urgent...

Levity grabbed Rachel's wrist and positively hustled her around the corner and along the castle wall.

"What, did you see someone?"

"No, and I really don't want to. Let's be quick."

"Well, but we can't dash or we're certain to look suspicious, if anyone does happen to look out of a window. Besides, this bundle isn't easy to handle even at a decent walk. If I try to run, I'm going to spill everything everywhere. Let's just try to look innocent and odd, can we? We're Middles; they all think we're weird anyway."

"They all think we're wicked anyway. They're going to think the worst of us, however slow we go."

"And they're right to, aren't they?" Rachel said, grinning. "I am running away, sort of. Seriously, though, Liv, I can't run with this. I'll just have to walk away, and hope that no one's looking."

The path that ran beside the castle moat was overlooked by all the windows ever made, it seemed to Levity. On this side, though, they all belonged to classrooms and store-rooms; there really shouldn't be anyone in there, looking out. Not at supper-time.

Just as there really shouldn't be anyone—or any two—out here, walking around the moat, carrying a blanket-wrapped burden. And yet here they were. So Levity watched all the windows as they passed, anticipating a face at any moment.

None showed itself; and here was a distraction, because the moat and the castle ran one side of the path, while the other held the forms' own kitchen-gardens. These were nothing like the regimented rows and columns that Mrs Bailey harvested for her fruits and vegetables. Here the girls were given their heads, and let plant what and how they chose, with no more than guidance from wiser heads. The results were haphazard at best. This year the gardens were actually doing better than normal, because the Middles had put so much extra work into them since Rowany pronounced their doom—but still, here was a cauliflower long since run to seed, and here a brussel that had totally failed to sprout. Levity pulled them both without a second thought, and tucked them like batons beneath her arm. Then she and Rachel hurried back to the path, and pressed on.

Another corner-tower to be rounded with yet more anxious glances at blank unrevealing windows, and they came at last to the front of the castle, with its great gatehouse. That was Mr Felton's territory, and he never ate any meal with the girls. Did he eat downstairs in the kitchen, with Mrs Bailey and the maids? Or privately in his own quarters, sitting by one of his high windows, keeping a watch out for the comings and goings of wicked schoolgirls...?

They didn't know, they couldn't guess. All they could do was act unconcerned. Trying very hard to look as though they were about their lawful occasions—difficult though that was, with a blanketful of contraband slung over Rachel's shoulder and an armful of vegetables for Levity, and Rachel's vivid and peculiar pink-and-orange uniform blazing like a beacon amidst the more common glories of the Mistresses' Garden, clashing horribly with Levity's red hair—they walked down between beds of roses and hollyhocks to the lakeside path.

There, no one from the school could possibly imagine they had licence to go unsupervised. They were reminded weekly that the waterside was out of bounds without either a mistress or two prefects to watch over them. But if they'd avoided notice thus far, there was a fair chance of getting clean away—or so they told themselves, at least. So they told each other, quite firmly. Quite convincingly, Levity thought.

And they were right, seemingly, because no one came raging down to intercept them, to demand explanations, excuses, return. It seemed strange to Levity that they could simply walk out without challenge, however carefully they'd timed it. In all her life, she'd never been watched over so strictly or had her time marshalled so thoroughly as here at school; she'd begun to believe the watchers omnipotent, both staff and prefects, so that you couldn't take one step off the regimented path without being descended upon and hauled back into line. Obviously that wasn't really true, but she was surprised to learn quite how easy it was to evade scrutiny. Mamma said that any society was governed by trust; Levity was beginning to understand that it was as true of school as any other.

She didn't want to think about that, though, because that made this a breach of trust, rather than a great and spirited adventure. Instead she turned her eyes deliberately ahead.

"I don't think they can see us now, from the castle. And look, there's the cliff you climbed, that took you up to Sister Anthony's Step."

Rachel laughed. "It's hardly a cliff. What is it, fifteen feet up that first pitch? And then another ten, from the ledge to the Step. It's nothing, Liv, truly. I could do that in the dark."

"You'd better get a move on, or you'll have to." She glanced westerly, towards the lowering sun. "And then you've a long climb after, up the path to the Eyrie."

"We ended up in the dark before; and this time I know what to expect. There's just the one tricky scramble, the rest is only slog. Don't *worry* so, Levity. Watch me up if you want to, but truly, I'm fine now. I know exactly what I'm doing."

"Really? How are you going to climb with that great blanket bundle, then? Even you can't do it one-handed, however good you think you are."

Rachel grinned annoyingly. "Just watch."

She laid her bundle down on the path, and spread the blanket out flat, leaving its curious contents in a heap at the centre. Then she folded one corner over to its opposite, making a triangle; then a flip and a clever twist, and she had turned her burden into a kind of sausage that she could sling across her back and hold in place with a single knot at the front.

Levity had watched the whole thing happen, and even so, "I have no idea how you just did that."

"There's a village of Lithuanian exiles on our estate, and Jess and I spend a lot of time there in the holidays. Far too

248

much time, according to our father," she added with a scowl. "The women carry everything in their shawls, and this is how they tie them. We learned it long ago; it's second nature now. And very handy, when you want both hands free. To climb, or other reasons."

She glanced assessingly up at the rock face. To Levity it still looked daunting, but not apparently to Rachel. She tied her tumbling dark hair back into a knot, rubbed her hands together and glanced back over her shoulder.

"Here I go, then. Watch me up if you must, but don't try to catch me if I fall. I—"

"You what?" Levity asked, when Rachel seemed to have lost track of her thought altogether, staring out over the lake.

"Oh, I weigh too much, you'll only break yourself and not save me—but look. Do you know who those people are, out on the lake?"

Levity turned to see, and there indeed was a boat on the lake. It shouldn't have been such an extraordinary sight, but it absolutely was. Of course Miss Leven had passed word about the merlins, to the Sanatorium across the water and all the local villages; there hadn't been a boat out since. Until, apparently, this evening.

"Fishermen, perhaps?" Levity conjectured.

"No one fishes this lake. The nymphs need all the fish and more, to feed their naiad. It's an absolute rule, apparently; if we started taking fish, they'd start taking us. When things are normal, people row back and forth between the school and the Sanatorium, or all the way over to the little chapel on the far side. Some of the Basques keep a boat on the water too, to visit relatives or ferry sheep across. Tawney says it's really funny to see a boatload of lambs all leap ashore one after another. But that's all—and nobody's using their boats at the moment."

"Well, somebody is." She could see three men, in a small dinghy. One had the oars, though he seemed less than handy with them; the other two were sitting in the stern, and both seemed to be staring straight at her. As she watched, one took something from the pocket of his overcoat and lifted it to his head. To his face, to his eyes. Using both hands, elbows akimbo...

"He's using binoculars!"

"Maybe he's just astonished by the sight of schoolgirls adrift. Maybe they're naturalists, come to look for birds or whatnot, and our plumage caught his eye. All sorts of birds around here, I expect," Rachel said vaguely.

Levity—whose eye was trained to observation, and who had indeed seen many kinds of birds and other wildlife since they arrived—giggled, and said, "I expect that's it. They might not know, if no one thought to tell them. Well, I hope they don't get eaten. You'd better go, if you're going to get up before dark. If you meet any sandcats, try not to get eaten yourself." *Be careful,* she meant. *Don't take any foolish risks.* Now they had come to it, she didn't like to see Rachel go off alone. There was a reason that Pioneers always went about in threes, after all. Even two was better than one. If she were any kind of climber, Levity thought she'd just go with Rachel now and never mind what trouble that might cause. As things were, though, she'd probably fall off and cause trouble on her own account. With those men watching from the water, too...

"I'll see you tomorrow morning," Rachel said brusquely, as if she harboured no doubts herself. Or wanted Levity to think so. "With breakfast, don't forget—and Jess. Make sure you bring Jess."

And with that she set her hands against the rock-face and began to climb.

Levity watched her, up and up: up to a ledge, a brief pause for breath and bearings, and then up again, higher yet.

Then she vanished, stepping forward out of Levity's sight for a moment, only to reappear waving cheerfully. That must be Sister Anthony's Step. The first and worst of her solitary climb was over, then, and there was nothing more Levity could do here. She waved back, and turned towards her own solitary walk back to school.

Running excuses through her head, trying to find something she could say that wouldn't be a downright lie, it took her a little while to realise that the boat on the lake was suddenly a lot closer. Two men had taken an oar each, while the third—the one with the binoculars, though he had put them away now—was urging them to pull harder.

At least, she thought that's what he was saying, from his body's pose and motions. She could hear his words, but not actually understand them.

She was fairly sure he was speaking Russian. The twins did sometimes, all three of them, so she was developing an ear for it.

They were going to come ashore right by Levity. From all that she could see or sense, that was exactly what they wanted. What they intended.

Hesitantly, uncertainly, Levity began to run.

Behind her the voices were suddenly more urgent, the rowing splashier. That would cost them a little time—and confirmed that they were strangers to boats, or at least not practised oarsmen, so likely not Mars-natives—but even so. Could one frightened girl on foot outpace two strong men on the water?

Levity didn't know; but she put her head down and her best foot forward. Every instinct told her not to let those men catch up.

Arms pumping, she realised ridiculously that she was still clutching their booty from the kitchen garden, great long batons of brussels-stem and cauliflower. She should just drop them. Of course she needed to get rid of them, they were slowing her down; but—

Almost to her own surprise, she stopped dead on the path and turned to face the oncoming boat. And whirled one of the heavy awkward plants above her head, and threw it out as far as she could.

The man in the stern said something. One of the rowers looked over his shoulder, saw what she was doing and checked in confusion. That spoiled the other's stroke, and the boat stalled in the water.

The cauliflower fell—harmlessly, pointlessly—between herself and the boat. The man in the stern laughed harshly, and gave the order to row again.

Grimly, Levity whirled and flung the brussels sprout stem, though it was costing her time and distance.

And prayed silently, though she wasn't really the praying kind, she hadn't been raised to ask for outside help; and waited a moment longer, just long enough to see just what she'd been praying for, an answering swirl in the water, rising from deep deep down.

Even Mars natives would be taken aback, afraid, if they didn't know how the school fed the merlins here. And these men were strangers to Mars, she was sure; they likely had no fingertalk, likely had never come face to face with any merlin.

She didn't wait to see the nymph rise up. Just turned and ran again.

Head down, focused only on the path immediately ahead, she barrelled straight into someone else. Another man, who had obviously seen her coming and set himself to seize her. Even the head-first impact of a panicked girl didn't shake him. She felt his arms close around her body, and tried to fight him off, but—

"Steady, lass. Hold hard, now." The voice was somehow familiar, and the smell of old tweeds and tobacco unexpectedly comforting. Levity risked a glance upward.

"Mr Felton!"

"Aye. Will you stand, if I set you loose?"

She nodded, gasping, and he relaxed his grip.

"I saw the two of you head away," he said. "You were hard to miss, what with your head and her outfit. I thought I'd best come down and see what's what. Only one of you coming back, and you in such a pelting hurry, glad I did. What's to do?"

"Th-those men, in the boat. I think they're chasing me."

"Them? Aye. I thought that. I thought the sight of me might be enough to turn them away, but no need for that, you did it. See?"

And he took her by the shoulders and spun her around, so that she could see the boat pulling away from shore now, more frenziedly even than it had tried to close in, as a nymph stood high in the water, all claws and eyes, its antennae flourishing fruitlessly.

"That was well done, lass. Well thought of. Russians again, though," he went on meditatively. "I heard them talking; sound carries over water, and I know the lingo still, from my war days. I think Miss Leven needs to be told, don't you?"

"Oh, but—"

"But you and that Rachel are up to something, I know. Something different, yes?"

"Oh, yes. Nothing to, nothing to do with..."

"Then I needn't tell her that, need I? Nor that you were straying where you oughtn't be. Nor summoning merlins, which you really oughtn't be. Come along, now. I'll be your excuse for missing supper. You saw a boat on the water and something made you doubt them, yes? And you were looking for a mistress and you found me, and I took you out to show me, and we saw a nymph rise up and the boat took off. But we were close enough to hear that they were Russians. I think that'll do, won't it? Your sharp eyes, and my responsibility. But I want you to tell me what's truly going on, that too. What's that imp Rachel up to, why's she wearing those clothes she don't belong in, and why're you coming back without her? And her sack? I won't tell, but I might interfere..."

CHAPTER TWENTY–TWO

"Where's My Sister?"

Jessica awoke with a start to find the skies darkening through the big San windows, and Lise sitting beside the bed with a very intense stare. She was wearing—well, the most peculiar garment Jessica had ever seen on a living girl. She remembered a museum diorama, where model pioneer children had been dressed in something similar; but even the mannequins' smocks had been better made than this, and looked more comfortable.

"I—I've been asleep," she said stupidly, for want of any other words.

"Yes. Yes, that's right, *Rachel*." Lise laid heavy stress on that last, and jerked her head across the long room to where Sister Anthony was making her way methodically from one window to the next, opening the lower panes and pulling curtains as she went.

"I only took my things off and lay down because she said I had to," Jessica muttered, hopefully low enough that the sharpest adult ear wouldn't pick up her words. From the momentary hesitation in Sister Anthony's arm as it reached for the next curtain, she thought perhaps she'd underestimated the carrying power of her voice. "I never thought I'd really fall asleep."

"I expect you were tired," Lise said—*after coming so far on your own* was what she didn't say, but something of that was in her eyes, Jessica thought—"and that's why you've been so grumpy with everyone today. Sister Anthony says that you can get up now and come to supper with the rest of us, so long as you apologise properly to Miss Harribeth for being a trouble to her."

There was some other message in Lise's eyes now, and in her expressive face, but it was too complicated for Jessica to make out. It was hard enough, she found, not to burst out giggling at the bizarre twitches and fluttering eyebrows of her new friend.

"I—all right. I can do that." Indeed, the very mention of supper made her realise how very hungry she was. Even though every step were perilous between here and the dining hall, she was suddenly frantic to get there.

"Good. Here's your smock," Lise said, holding out a replica of that very peculiar thing that she was wearing. Was that sackcloth, Jessica wondered, and would there be ashes involved? And what kind of school had she come to, anyway? "Stand up," Lise went on, "and I'll help you into it. I expect you're still a bit groggy, aren't you?"

I expect you wouldn't have the first clue how to get into it was what she clearly meant, and she was absolutely right. Jessica would have fumbled around in a bewildered manner, and probably given them all away. She already had a wary respect for the gimlet-eyed Sister Anthony, and was keen to escape her vigilance as swiftly as might be.

Lise dropped the smock neatly over Jessica's head, and had it tugged down into place in two shakes of a lamb's tail. At least, she seemed satisfied, and Jessica supposed that it might be meant to hang this loosely. *It fits where it touches,*

256

as Mum would say, she thought gloomily. *But surely it can't be meant to itch like this?*

She glowered suspiciously at Lise. The other girl was wearing something much the same, but she might have dosed this one with itching-powder or some such. Jessica was already frantic to scratch, but Lise had hold of both her wrists and was shaking her head imploringly, even while she tugged her towards the door, even while she said, "Come on, we'll have to hurry, Rachel; there's barely time to wash before the supper bell."

Like Lise, Jessica was urgent to be away from here, where they could talk in safety, not watched or overheard. Nevertheless: she pulled her hands free on an impulse, and went— heart in mouth!—to confront her greatest fear.

Who watched her come with an interested quirk of her eyebrow, and waited in patience while Jessica stood as straight as she could in this appalling costume, folded her hands neatly behind her back and said, "Please, Sister Anthony? I'd like to apologise to you, too. I know I've been a nuisance this afternoon, and I'm truly sorry that happened." Whatever else came of this madcap adventure, she meant to smooth the waters for Rachel if she could.

"Very well...dear. That was nicely said. Run along now with Lise, and we'll hope to hear no more about it."

This time it was Jessica who snatched Lise's hand and all but towed her out of the San. As soon as the high doors were safely closed behind them, she hissed, "Did you hear?"

"Hear what? I heard you doing the decent thing, which I don't care if you did have a, an interior motive, that was absolutely nice of you, and absolutely the right thing to make Sister Anthony think better of you. Of your sister. I mean..."

"I know what you mean. But didn't you hear how she hesitated, then didn't say my name?"

"She doesn't know your name."

"She knows Rachel's. And I swear she was going to use it, and then she didn't."

"Oh, half the staff are always forgetting our names," said blithe Lise. "That's why they call us 'dear' all the time, to cover up."

Jessica might have believed it of Miss Harribeth. Said of Sister Anthony, though, it was pure slander. Jessica considered again those dark solemn bird-bright eyes, dipped equally from the wells of wisdom and sorrow, as it seemed to her; and she shuddered and said no more, for want of her twin to say it to. Lise was practical and pleasant and sporty, which Jessica could warm to far more than Rachel ever would, but not one to share deep thoughts with.

Levity was another matter. Jessica thought she could talk about anything with Levity, if they could only find the space and the time and the privacy. All those things seemed to be at a premium here at the Crater School, as though staff and prefects were engaged in a conspiracy to keep the girls too busy to conspire on their own account. So Rachel had suggested, at least, in one of her many letters—and that sudden rush of letters from other girls here had only confirmed it. It sounded nothing like the leisurely, not to say dull, life at Low Bridge School. There was almost nothing to do there but conspire. And no one worth conspiring with, and nothing to conspire to do. Except run away, of course, and she'd managed that on her own, thank you very much.

Jessica was more grateful than ever now for all those letters, as Lise led her down a fine sweeping staircase into the grandiose hallway of this peculiar school-in-a-castle. It obviously wasn't a proper castle; was it even a proper school? Certainly it was nothing like Low Bridge. But at least she had half a notion what to expect, thanks to all those letters.

Across the hall with barely a pause to gawp up at the high timbered ceiling with its ironwork chandelier, barely a jump when the deep resonant note of the school bell rolled out, seemingly right behind her.

Actually it was right behind her, or behind and above. She remembered someone saying that the duty prefect went into an alcove off the hall to ring it. Miss Pinkett had a gong that she struck herself. A bell was more impressive, some-how; that low note seemed to go straight through her. Jessica gazed about, just in time to see an older girl emerge from behind a curtain.

"Hurry along, you two, or you'll be late."

"Yes, Melanie..."

Lise managed—just—not to catch Jessica by the hand again, to hurry her along. Rachel would have hated that. Besides, Rachel was nobody's follower. And by all reports she'd made a point of resenting authority here, in whatever form it came.

Accordingly, Jessica glared back over her shoulder with her best imitation of a Rachel-scowl. "We've been with Sister Anthony," she said sullenly. Or as sullenly as she could with her heart suddenly in her mouth. She felt like she was run-ning with the bulls, or baiting lions in their own den—but Rachel certainly would have done it, and so she must.

"I know that. And now you get to be with us again, if you can only behave. Honestly, Rachel, I thought you were get-ting better, but you can't go about cheeking the mistresses. Not at the Crater School."

"No. I—I am sorry, Melanie." *Melanie Fitzwalter*, she remembered, *games prefect, head of Stokes House*. Not her own house—or rather, not Rachel's; she was in Jopling—but Lise's, yes. Lise thought sports first, last and always; her letters to Jessica had been all about games. And the games prefect, who was apparently something akin to a goddess. "And I will try to do better. I am trying. But it's so *hard...*" Yes, that struck the right note. Rachel was infuriating, and could carry a grudge for ever; but only persuade her that she was in the wrong and she could be penitent, even confessional, and full of good intentions.

"School can be, when you're new," Melanie said, much more sympathetically. "Don't I know it? I was a rebel too, when the parents first sent me here."

"You, Melanie?" Now it was Lise's turn to gawp, without even trying to hide it. "I don't believe it!"

"Oh, trust me. I missed my home, I missed my brothers; I did *not* want to be stuck out here at the back end of nowhere. We're from Marsport, you know; Daddy's a doctor there. I'm a city girl through and through. I thought this was the dreariest place God made, and I was determined to enliven it so much—so *badly*—that Miss Leven would be forced to send me home. I may not be the only girl who came here determined to be expelled, but I may fairly claim to be the worst. No, no tales now"—as both younger girls clamoured for them—"that was the supper bell, remember? We're all going to be late, if we don't scoot. Washed your hands and faces? Good. Come along, then. Best foot forward, Rachel..."

And the goddess of the sports field flung a friendly arm across Jessica's shoulders as she hustled them through the quad, and the girl suddenly felt nothing but mean to be lying to her this way.

S till, there was no help for it. If they were to preserve her secret—and keep Rachel out of more trouble than she deserved, for something that her twin had landed on her willy-nilly—then Jessica simply had to go on lying, to Melanie and the whole school. At least until tomorrow, when they hoped to swap back again, and try to think of some good way out of this terrible muddle.

Jessica had been rather dreading supper, feeling that under the scrutiny of a tableful of interested girls, she was certain to give herself away. No sooner had they sat down, though, than the prefect at the head of the table said, "We seem to have an empty seat. Where's—let's see, Levity, isn't it? There's no missing that red head. Except that I don't see it, here or anywhere. Anyone know where Levity is?"

No answer was forthcoming. Messengers were despatched first to the San, and then to Stokes House. With still no sign of the absent Levity, the prefect—*Mary Holmes, library pree, perfectly friendly but seemingly nobody's particular friend*—was obliged to make her reluctant way up to the staff table, to report to Miss Leven.

A degree of discreet fuss followed, with staff themselves running messages now, or else going off to search for the absentee. Mary was sent back to her tableful of agog Middles, absolved of responsibility, much to her visible relief; and now a dozen schoolgirls could speculate wildly over what might have happened to their missing classmate, and not care at all about the one who'd simply spent the afternoon in San. That worked to Jessica's relief, at least until Miss Leven herself came frowningly over to their table.

"Girls, I will be asking the whole school if I need to, before you are dismissed to your houses—but it seems only sensible to come to you first, as she is your classmate and companion. Does anyone at this table know of Levity Buchanan's whereabouts, or of any reason why she might not be here with us at supper tonight?"

Her question met with a terrible silence, which only grew worse when—wise in the ways of Middles—she began to ask them individually, working her way steadily around the table. Jessica guessed that her new friends enjoyed lying no more than she did; what would they do, then, stand mute, with all the guilt that that implied?

Possibly. Probably. All that she was sure of, already, was that not one of them would betray Rachel. It might fall to her, then, to betray herself, sooner than watch these girls squirm on the hook of their loyalty.

Miss Leven came all too quickly to Tawney, who certainly knew all that her twin knew and was certainly determined not to spill it. Jessica drew a breath, ready to confess all—and then came abruptly to her feet, and said, "Please, Miss Leven?"

"Yes? What is it, what do you have to tell me?"

"Levity just walked in, Miss Leven. With,"—*brown overall, janitor, Levity's friend the janitor, what was his name again...?*—"with Mr Felton."

The whole table gasped, but no one was quicker than Miss Leven to turn and look, to confirm it.

"Very well. Thank you. As you were, girls. Mary, Mrs Bailey's excellent trifle is doing no good sitting in its bowl there. Hurry up and serve it out."

Not even the qualities of the trifle could prevent the girls from watching sideways as Miss Leven met janitor and errant pupil in the doorway of the dining hall. Not that there was much to see, or not for long: the headmistress listened briefly, then swept them both out again. To her own room, to the Sanatorium, to some grisly and unimaginable punishment...? There was no telling, but an awful lot of guessing, which Mary tried and tried to crush, to no avail.

After supper, the girls were dismissed to their separate houses: which meant no more news for Jessica, as she—or rather Rachel—and the twins belonged in Jopling, while Levity would go back to Stokes if she was allowed to.

"She insisted on going with Rachel, at least as far as the cliff," Tawney murmured, "so she was always going to be late—but she should never have been that late, and I've no idea why she came back with Mr Felton. I mean, I know she likes him, for whatever weird reason, and he seems to like her too which is even weirder, so perhaps she asked him for an alibi, but even so..."

Even so: they could speculate wildly, but not with any conviction. And no one came to offer them satisfaction, so they had to go to bed still ignorant. For Jessica that meant Rachel's bed, of course, with all Rachel's things about her. The twins guided her subtly through all the rituals beforehand, so that she didn't use the wrong bathroom or do something foolish with her clothes, but in the end she had to pull the curtains shut around her cubicle and be on her own. And peep out of the window at the rising crater wall, and think of her sister somewhere out there in the dark and the cold, more truly alone than this; and feel guilty and anxious, and wonder once again if she shouldn't just seek authority and confess all to bring Rachel safe back tonight.

And picture her twin's fury if she did, and decide one more time to play the hand she'd been dealt, and just cross her fingers and hope for all to turn out well in the morning.

And go to bed, and never expect to sleep, and...

And wake to bright early sunlight beating in at that same window, and the sounds of a dormitory rousing—girls grunting, murmuring, shrieking according to their nature, bare feet and slippered feet pattering back and forth, the dormitory prefect urging all and sundry to make less noise and to hurry, hurry, hurry—and the sudden vision of Tawney resplendent in lurid pink pyjamas and a purple velvet dressing gown, appearing through the cubicle curtains and beckoning hastily.

"Get up, get up! We never have time in the mornings, and you're next after me for the bathroom..."

Based on Jessica's limited experience thus far, they never had time at any time of the day, but she had no time to say so. Tawney was gone already, vanishing as quickly as she'd come.

By nature, Jessica was slow to wake and slow to rise. It was already clear that those habits would never do at the Crater School. By the time she was out of bed, slippered and robed and starting to think about running a brush through her hair, Tawney was back, a little pink of skin and damp about the edges, almost pulling her out of her cubicle and propelling her down the corridor. Before she was anywhere near finished with the hastiest bath of her life, the next girl in line was already hammering on the door. By the time she got back to the dormitory, the twins between them had stripped her bed and tossed the cubicle curtains up over the rail in the only way approved of by Sister Anthony, "and she's certain to check," Tasha grumbled, "and she thinks nothing of hauling you out of class to put things right if there's anything wrong. You have to leave your hairbrush just so, too, and everything tidy in your drawers as well as on the dresser, and—"

"Rachel, don't you know the rules *yet*?" cried Harmony the dormitory prefect, with some justification, this far into the term. The three girls looked at each other, a little aghast; it was Jessica who found to wit to mutter, "Yes, of course I do. They're just being busybodies, that's all," for all the world like a sullen Rachel being told off.

"Just saving you from an order mark and an irate mistress too, and Harmony and all of us from a scolding for not training you better," Tasha offered in rejoinder. "Now come on, or we'll be late for brekker and then we'll all get order marks and it'll be your fault, Rachel."

"Don't forget your prayer books and collection money," Harmony said sweetly, sailing out ahead of them. "Chapel's straight after breakfast today, for reasons known only to the mighty, and you won't have time to come back up for them."

This intelligence was met with squawks by the twins, although they must certainly have been warned more than once before. Concerted dives into their cubicles produced prayer-books and sixpences; but Jessica of course had no idea where to look, so Tawney had to guide her to the right drawer for her prayer-book, and wherever Rachel kept her money, it wasn't there. A hasty search produced nothing. In the end, Tasha shrugged and offered six carefully hoarded pennies of her own.

"We're not allowed to loan," Tawney said doubtfully.

"No, but we're breaking so many other rules, this is hardly going to matter," said insouciant Tasha. "In the greater scheme of things," a favourite phrase of their father's. "Now come *on*, or we really will be late!"

They came in to breakfast on time, if only just; and took their seats under the frowns and glares of the duty prefects, just moments before Miss Willoughby said grace and thus unleashed the wild babble of two hundred schoolgirls who had been preternaturally silent until now.

This at least was something Jessica recognised. She supposed all schools must be the same in this, that mealtimes would be a rushing river of noise. Or perhaps a weir said it better, because all their talk had been artificially held back until now.

At least nobody expected her to speak. Not this morning. She still couldn't put a name to half the girls at the table, despite the twins' helpfully saying everyone's name at every possible opportunity, however strange it sounded; but it didn't matter, because no one wanted to hear from Rachel. Levity was back in her seat, and her extraordinary story was all that anyone cared about. She stumbled in the telling of it, and saved herself only by mumbling that Miss Leven had told her not to talk too much about it. Several of her listeners understood that she'd tripped between the public version and the private truth, so they hastened to help by offering wild speculations about what Russians might be doing on the lake. Which of course was exactly what Miss Leven did not want discussed, and truly neither did Levity, to judge by her reluctance to chime in.

Still, it kept any attention off Jessica, which was simply and uncomplicatedly welcome. She contented herself with making a good meal and keeping a low profile, or trying to. Mrs Bailey's Sunday marmalade buns were legendary, or so Tasha airily informed her, drawing more than one puzzled glance from elsewhere at the table, because of course Rachel must have discovered that by now. Today's more honest discovery was that deceiving everyone was difficult, and having partners in crime only made it harder.

Still, they survived to the end of breakfast with no accusations being flung at her guilty head. When Miss Leven struck the little bell on the staff table and rose to her feet, Jessica and all the school looked to her for release, for dismissal first to chapel and then to their own affairs.

Instead, Miss Leven said, "Girls, I know how much you look forward to your Sunday rambles after you've written letters home, and I know how much you've missed walking down by the water. I had hoped to lift that ban, or at least to ameliorate it; but circumstances have changed, unexpectedly." If she didn't look at Levity then, she must have been almost alone; the redhead's pale cheeks burned, under the collective glare of the entire school. Russians might not be her fault, nor even strictly her responsibility, but even so: rumour was rife and intelligence limited—very limited, to judge by some of the whispers making their way from table to table—and it was clear that Levity lay at the heart of whatever had actually happened, so Levity must be to blame.

"Not only must you keep away from the lake a little longer," Miss Leven went on, "but I'm afraid I must add more restrictions to your walks. I don't propose to put the sheep-pastures entirely out of bounds, but there will be no more hikes around the coach road to the Sanatorium. Furthermore, no girls may leave school grounds at all except in parties of six or more. No Juniors may go anywhere without a prefect to supervise their group, and no Middles without at least one Senior. Heed me, please, girls. I hope this will not be for long, but until I have received certain reassurances from other quarters, we will be enforcing these rules strictly. Any girl caught in defiance will be gated for the rest of term, and severely punished besides."

No punishment known to schoolgirls anywhere on Mars could be worse than gating, as she well knew. What value could life hold, if you were not free to wander this red beloved land, beneath its tawny sky? Even these new restrictions were a bane, that brought down many an unspoken malediction—for Crater School girls were nicely trained, but also generally accustomed to easy bounds and wide licence—upon poor Levity's innocent head.

We might hope that she was unaware, so new to school as she was; but her vivid flush abided, long after Miss Leven had finished speaking. Jessica was implausibly new herself, but she knew school in general, if not this school in particular. Out of sympathy and solidarity, she attached herself to Levity after chapel was over, just in case any girl was not quite so nice after all. And where Jessica went, necessarily the twins went with her, and Lise too.

Besides, the Crater School girls had an errand, and Jessica was it. She had to be delivered to her sister, up on the height. Which was not exactly out of bounds now, but suddenly harder to achieve. They were debating softly between themselves just which Senior they might ask to go with them, which they might hope to deceive, when they fell abruptly and mutually silent, as another girl joined them unexpectedly. A smaller girl, with hair as fiercely red as Levity's: who

267

slipped her hand into what was obviously her sister's, and murmured, "Liv, would you come with us? Please?"

"Charm, darling, I can't. You're a Junior; you heard Miss Leven, you have to have a prefect with you. I'm not even a Senior, we need someone older ourselves if we're to go anywhere," *and we have a mission, and we can't drag a Junior along*.

"Yes, I know—but we've already got our prefect. And it's Rowany, and she's wonderful and everything, but—oh, would you please just come? Just to have someone who can, you know, *talk* to her?"

Several Middles earned their place in heaven at that moment, by managing somehow not to laugh aloud. They all knew, though, exactly how Charm was feeling. Rowany was admired throughout the school, adored by many; but she was Head Girl, and impossibly important, and no Junior could conceivably think of her as someone they might have a comfortable chat with.

Most Middles, to be honest, still felt exactly the same way. Jessica could see it in their faces. Even so, before Levity could reply, Tasha answered for her. "Of course she will, kid," she said gruffly. "We'll all come. You run along and tell Rowany, and we'll be there in a minute."

Charm skipped away, and the rest of their group turned on Tasha as one, demanding to know if she'd taken leave of her senses.

"Oh, don't you see? If we had a Senior with us, she'd be watching us all the way, and suspicious as anything, because they're not used to that level of responsibility and they all think Middles are the worst because they were so recently Middles themselves. That's exactly why Miss Leven said we had to have a Senior. But nobody's more senior than Rowany, she counts double in anybody's book; and if we have a bunch of Juniors along for cover, she's going to be taken up with them, and she won't give half as much thought to what we're up to. And there are enough of us that a couple should be able to slip up to the Eyrie and swap Jessica for Rachel, with nobody any the wiser; and then Rowany stands as our guarantee, like a, what's the word, a stamp of approval...?"

"Imprimatur," Levity said. "And—well, it's worth the risk. Isn't it?"

Tawney was not so sure. "Rowany sees everything," she murmured. "All the time. But I don't see that we have a choice, now. Tasha's committed us, so all we can do is give it our best shot and hope."

"It'll be fine," Tasha said, ever cavalier. "You'll see. It'll all work out for the best."

If this was the best they could hope for, Jessica thought perhaps they should be worried. The tall cool blonde Head Girl eyed this sudden party of volunteer Middles with a detachment that was not so much suspicious as experienced, and disturbingly all-seeing.

Still: she didn't exactly express any objections, and disingenuous Tasha was happy to explain that this way they didn't need to trouble anyone else, so it worked to the overall good if the most senior of all Seniors did double duty, didn't it?

"So you're not seeking me out for the pleasure of my company, but only my convenience?" Rowany laughed. "Tasha, I'm hurt!"

No one was quite ready to tell her that they'd actually been sought out themselves, for the reassurance of the younger girls who stood in too much awe to be comfortable. Perhaps Rowany knew already. At any rate, she was happy to let them sort themselves out, so that Levity and Lise attached themselves to her, while the others ranged further along the sheep-paths as they wandered the back slopes of the crater.

It was a plan so clear that no one need spell it out, that Jessica and the twins should range further and further until they were comfortably out of sight, at which point they'd make a dash for the Eyrie and the essential swap. It was the only card they had to play; it must necessarily be a winner.

Except that they never got to play it, because while they were still testing their range, moving ever further ahead without yet straying out of Rowany's sight, they heard Levity's voice rise in sudden alarm: "Charm? Charm!" And then, a dreadful silence later: "Where's my sister...?"

CHAPTER TWENTY–THREE

Too Many Twins

Rachel had passed the strangest, most unexpected, not exactly solitary night of her life. She hadn't slept. Stiff in every joint, deeply scratched and starving hungry, she crept out of Sister Anthony's Eyrie at first light and perched herself on a high rock that overlooked the crater slopes. She could see halfway to the school from here, and miles down the valley to the far glint of early sun on arrow-straight lines that marked out the two canals. Squinting, she thought perhaps she could make out a rising thread of smoke, which might pinpoint either the railway proper or else where the funicular sat working up steam for its first climb of the day.

Her plan was so simple and satisfactory, it hardly qualified as a plan at all. She meant just to sit here on this comfortable rock and watch the world wake up. Sooner or later—sooner she hoped, later she expected—she would see little trickles of green-and-gold issue forth along the sheep-trails that twisted and tangled all across the slopes below. From up here they'd be little more than dots, more shadow than substance; but she would see them and know them for what they were, the Crater School girls released. And she would watch, and among them would be some in drab smocks rather than school colours, her own kind, the Middles; and one small group of those would filter off upslope, drawing ever closer, coming more in her direction every time the paths divided, making all the choices that would bring them up to her. And eventually she would be able to identify individual girls, by the way they moved even if she still couldn't see their faces; and one of them would be her twin, and she was still hoping she would be able to sit calmly here on her rock until Jess came up to join her.

She didn't think it likely. She thought that as soon as she was sure, she would shriek loud enough to wake the neighbourhood and go charging down the slope pell-mell, while Jess was hurtling upslope much the same. And they'd meet halfway, and their encounter would jar two hemispheres. And she'd like to say that to Miss Peters, just to make the point that she really did listen in poetry lessons, except that of course she couldn't because nobody was supposed to know that Jess was here. Such a shame, a literary witticism wasted.

Still: Jess would come, they would meet, everything would suddenly be better. And meantime she could sit and look out over the world, and see the boys leading their flocks of sheep out from the caves where they'd sheltered overnight, and ponder her own night just gone, with all its uncertainty and wonder, and try to guess how that too might change her life in days to come...

A sudden movement snared her eye. Still too soon for anyone from school, and nowhere near the sheep-caves. Curious, she wondered who else might be awander on the crater this early in the morning. She couldn't guess, and so of course she watched them, two dark specks with long morning shadows, that her mind translated easily into big burly men in heavy coats.

Big burly men behaving strangely, lurking behind a rocky outcrop and taking turns to peer down towards the school. They were trying very hard to stay unseen, little guessing that there might be another watcher above them on the height.

Rachel couldn't imagine why grown men might want to spy on schoolgirls, but that was the only explanation she could find. Certainly they were trying to spy on someone, and there was no reason to suppose anyone other than schoolgirls might come up from that direction.

Rachel had time on her hands, and curiosity enough for a regiment. Besides, her sister was down there, and would be headed up here soon; and her new friends too. And besides again, she was starting to feel an unexpected and reluctant attachment to the school itself, at least in comparison to all other schools she'd ever come into contact with. Her loyalty was always hard-won, but diamond-hard thereafter. If those men were spying on the Crater School, then by definition they meant no good. And she was the only one who knew, which made it her task to discover more.

Accordingly, she slithered down from her rock of vantage and began to make her way cautiously towards the men. They were so focused on the view downslope, schoolwards, she thought they were unlikely to look up and back behind them. So long as she stayed as high as she could for as long as she could, she should be able to creep close enough to spy on them in her turn. And as the men themselves had discovered, there were plenty of outcroppings to hide behind.

She and Jess had both been enthusiastic Pioneers from the day they were allowed to don the scarlet uniform and take their vows as solemn eight-year-olds. Tracking and scouting were skills they had practised assiduously, if generally with evil intent. It was easy, Rachel found, to tread silently on the thick coarse sheep-cropped turf, and finding cover comes naturally to a fourteen-year-old girl out where she doesn't belong. She made ground carefully and steadily, and was soon close enough to see the men clearly, close enough to overhear their conversation. Thinking themselves alone but for the occasional distant shepherd-boy, they didn't trouble to keep their voices low.

And perhaps there was another reason why they wouldn't worry about being overheard, because they were speaking neither the Queen's English nor the shepherd-boys' Basque. They must have thought themselves quite safe from eavesdroppers.

Alas for them: they simply hadn't budgeted for Rachel. Who had been listening with interest for some moments before the penny dropped and she suddenly thought, "Oh! They're speaking *Russian!*"

It made no difference to her. She and Jess had been raised in a noisy polyglot household, speaking English to their parents and Urdu to their ayah, Cantonese to the houseboys and Hindi to the syce, an entirely private gobbledegook to each other—and Russian to their beloved grandparents, who struggled gamely with any language else. They were entirely and glibly accustomed to swapping languages mid-thought, let alone mid-sentence. It was no surprise to her that she took some time to notice what these men were speaking, when it only really mattered what they said.

It was genuinely a surprise, though, to learn where the men had come from. Something in their manner made it clear that these were authentic Russians, subjects of the Tsar. Nothing like her refugee grandparents, who—like the Mishkin twins' family and so many, so very many others—had fled pogroms and oppression in their native land. Theirs had been a strange journey with a stranger conclusion, here where they were literally as far from Russia as it was possible to be, on a whole world where everyone was a subject of the British crown and the Empress Eternal.

Well, almost everyone. And almost no one was Russian, which almost mattered more. Even before the Great War, the Tsar could never hide his envy of the British, who had beautiful and fertile—if admittedly unpredictable, and of course inhabited—Mars to colonise, where all he had was the living hell that was Venus. His people were rarely glimpsed and never welcomed beyond the spaceport at Elysium Fields; there wasn't even a Russian consulate anywhere in the province. The reliably neutral Swiss hosted Russian diplomats in their own legation, the very few permitted.

Fewer than ever, since that terrible war. But Russians had expressed a profound interest in the Crater School recently, or in particular pupils here who weren't Russian at all, except that their father had gone over to the Tsar. He was a terrible traitor—and his daughter Levity was a friend of Rachel's and had been a friend in need to Jess, and there was no doubt in Rachel's mind. When one of the men said, "We almost had her at the lake last night," and the other one replied, "If that creature hadn't risen up between us," she knew instantly who and what they meant. She had seen the merlin rise, from her perch up on Sister Anthony's Step. Now she understood, at least a little.

These must be the same Russians who had come before, as emissaries of Levity's father. Everyone in school had heard that story by now, despite the staff's best efforts to suppress it. Actual Russians driving to the castle and walking its corridors, sitting in Miss Leven's study, in her very chairs? There had never been any hope of keeping that quiet. And then the Buchanan sisters' late-night radio conversation from the tower-top—with an actual condemned traitor, on actual occupied Phobos!—which again could not be kept under wraps. Charm was something of a popular heroine among her set and wider too, for the way she'd brought that conversation to an abrupt close.

But apparently the sisters' father had not yet given up, or else his Tsarist masters were determined to deliver his daughters to him, willy-nilly. Like many a child of Mars, Rachel had sneaked into her parents' sitting-room one afternoon in their absence, her sister at her side, and illicitly tuned their wireless set to the infamous frequency when Phobos was riding high in the sky. *Phobos calling, this is Phobos calling...* That smooth, insinuating voice had settled itself into her bones, as it seemed. The twins had sworn eternal hatred that day to Peregrine Murray and all his kind, even while they listened in rapt horror to his lies and maledictions. Of course they had still been crouched there, appalled and fascinated both, when their parents came home and caught them. There had been stern talkings-to, and promises extracted, but no actual punishment, because apparently even parents could understand the awful draw of the utterly malign. But now the traitor's daughters were Rachel's compatriots at school, and one was a friend and classmate. A fierce and patriotic hatred of the man had suddenly become personal and profound. These men were here at his behest or on his behalf, one or the other, and they were an absolute threat to Levity and her sister.

It was very clear, from their conversation. They had been reconnoitring from the lake last evening, when they'd seen Levity out on her own—easily recognisable from distance, thanks to her vivid red hair—and made an attempt to snatch her there and then. A merlin had driven them off, rising unexpectedly from the dark waters of the lake. Listening between the lines, Rachel guessed that Levity had raised it, and gave silent thanks for cabbages and sprouts.

Now the men had abandoned the water, and turned to the slopes behind the crater's crags. Whether they knew it or not, that was a bright move. Rachel didn't see how they could have learned that Levity would indeed be heading up this way. Perhaps they only knew that half the school would spill out across the sheep-pastures after chapel; perhaps they were only chancing their arm, or still reconnoitring.

That last seemed actually most likely. Rachel snorted softly to herself: if they were hoping to hide out here behind their rock all morning, watching how the school conducted itself abroad, they were due for a startling disappointment. Some feral pack of Juniors was safe to discover them within half an hour of release. She had learned this much at least in half a term, that Middles had their favourite places and would head straight for them, while Juniors were still learning the lie of the land and would simply go everywhere. And then no doubt apologise nicely to the men they had so abruptly disturbed, and then talk about them all the rest of the day, so that everyone would know that there were Russians about on the hill.

That might not be such a bad outcome, actually. Juniors could never keep a secret, so someone in authority was bound to hear. Then they could put two and two together and decide what was best to do, and Rachel need not say a word to anyone. That way she wouldn't have either to lie or to confess, which would sit a little easier on her conscience, and she could be sure that the right people knew what was happening. Yes. She should just leave it to the Juniors.

Even so: she settled down behind her own chosen rock, and spied on the men as they spied on the slope. She would watch and listen and keep safely out of sight, and that would be that. Surely she could rely on some stray gang of Juniors scaring the men away long before her own cohort decided it was safe to peel off from the main pathways and seek her out. Surely so...

If she had learned anything in the course of a tempestuous life, it should surely have been not to tempt fate, not to give hostages to fortune. It was a difficult lesson, though, and one she'd always resisted. So she sat and watched the watchers, *custodying the custodes* as she termed it to herself with a private grin, and felt cheerfully confident and only impatient for everything to happen as she had decreed it should.

The men grumbled through their long wait, and shrugged off their heavy black woollen coats as the day warmed up, and smoked Russian cigarettes whose smell was long familiar to Rachel and made her nostalgic for the days of long ago, sitting on her grandfather's knee while he showed her photographs and told tales of the old country. If she were closer, she could have heard more of their conversation, but she didn't really need to. She knew enough, and could guess the rest. And warn Levity, the first chance she had; and find some way to make sure that Miss Leven knew too, if the Juniors didn't see to that for her...

And right on cue, here came the Juniors. Only two of them, which was surprising, given how they tended to go everywhere mob-handed, but two should be enough— except that one of these two had vividly red hair, the first thing Rachel glimpsed as the girls came over the rise.

Fate was taking a hand, in the most malign way imaginable. That was Levity's kid sister Charm and her friend Marigold, heads together and nattering away, oblivious to the world around. For a moment the two Russians couldn't believe their luck, just as Rachel couldn't believe the cruelties of misfortune. Then they simply reached out and snatched up both little girls, smothering their startled cries behind big strong hands.

How they might have hoped to get two kidnapped girls off the crater wall, Rachel couldn't conceive. Nor what they would do with the spare, for they surely didn't want Marigold. Perhaps they'd try to swap her for Levity? Miss Leven would never allow that—but it didn't matter anyway, because Rachel was already on her feet, out from cover and yelling wildly.

"School, help! Crater School! Mayday, mayday! SOS! Pioneers, close on me! Help, help...!"

She made all the noise that she could, with the aid of two exceptionally healthy lungs and a frantic anxiety. The two men stared in bewilderment at this screaming hoyden seemingly sprung from nowhere. Neither of them could react otherwise, because each had a struggling kicking double armful of girl to wrestle already.

Rachel's voice was high and clear, rolling over the hillside. No Pioneer girl could mistake that ululating call for aid. Nor would any girl of Mars use it without reason; they knew too well how often it had saved a life. A false alarm would be anathema, unthinkable.

Rachel heard half a dozen answering cries, from further down the hill. Still, she didn't dare to wait for help to arrive. The men were on the back foot now, startled and uncertain; she mustn't give them time to recover, or to plan.

Instead she simply hurled herself at them, a dervish, all fists and feet and fury. Charm was the girl she knew they wanted, so Charm's captor bore the full brunt of her assault. He was in difficulties already, trying to subdue a lanky, frenzied creature composed of whipcord and willow. Now suddenly here was a second girl, older and stronger and better trained, just as vicious. He had to let go of the first, to defend his eyes against a pair of driving determined thumbs; and even then the redhead, the child they had come for didn't try to run away. She came back at him with knees and elbows and teeth too, biting his wrist to the bone just as he thought he'd finally got a grip on the other girl.

He cried aloud, and tore himself free of both; and called to his colleague to join him in despair, and frankly began to run just as a stream of further girls—demons from hell, every one of them!—appeared, led by an impossibly tall blonde vision, like an avenging angel...

Rachel held tight to Charm, now that she had her safe; and gathered the abandoned Marigold in too, as they stood gasping for air and watching the two Russians flee. For a moment it seemed as though the hunt was up, with Rowany leading the chase; but after a few yards the Head Girl threw her hand high and slowed to a halt, calling in her hounds.

"No, come back, everyone. Lise, you too. I mean it. Let them run. They can't go far—and we can't exactly arrest them. Anyone got handcuffs and a truncheon? No? Well, then. Back, all! Close on me!"

There wasn't a Crater School girl yet born who would disobey Rowany in that mood, with that tone of voice. Rachel saw her rescuers gather around their leader, and for a moment felt nothing but overwhelming relief. Then she saw two girls separate themselves from the throng, and turn back towards her.

One was Levity, of course, under her blazing crown of red, her hat long lost, coming to take her sister from Rachel's temporary care. The other was equally bareheaded, exposing dark tumbling locks as wayward as Rachel's own, exactly as wayward; and a spirit to match, just as everything else matched between the two of them. And oh, this was going to get complicated any moment now, just as soon as anyone registered that there were two of them irredeemably alike— but at least they could have this moment first, this brief perfect moment where arms and heads could lock together and they could shut out everyone else and just be together, the two of them as they were made to be, Rachel and Jessica Abramoff, sufficient to each other and the rest of the world go hang.

It couldn't last, of course. In the end and all too soon, they had to peel themselves apart and turn to face authority, hand in hand and each with the same stubborn devil-may-care expression on their identical faces, if they had only known it.

Authority in this case meant Rowany de Vere. Who stood gazing down at them with an air of cool comprehension that was somehow much harder to confront than the perplexity they were used to. She looked from one to the other, then unerringly turned to Jess.

"You must be Jessica, I suppose. Much is made clear to me, that was murky before. I know you don't have any kind of permission to be here, but that's for Miss Leven to deal with; all I need do is deliver you unto her. And you too, Rachel, yes, I won't split you apart now. Though you will need to change out of that...uniform. Yours, presumably, Jessica? Yes. You had probably better swap back, as you're certainly not entitled to wear the Crater School colours. We're rather fussy about that, and we don't like impostors."

Jessica flushed scarlet suddenly, under that swift condemnation. Rachel wanted to leap to her sister's defence, but could find no safe grounds; and besides, Rowany had already turned away dismissively.

"Charm, Marigold—is either of you hurt? No? Good. Just shaken up, I know. Don't worry: we'll march you back to Sister Anthony now, and she'll tuck you both up with a glass of hot milk and a story-book and you'll be right as rain once you've had a nap. I don't think any more black-clad kidnappers are going to leap out of the shadows, but just in case, we'll have you in the centre of the throng—yes, Levity, you too. Take an arm of each, if you will; this is a Buchanan adventure, and Marigold must be an honorary redhead for the day. Abramoffs, you're a sideshow, but let's have you under my eye too, shall we? Come on now, quick march. The sooner everyone's home and under Miss Leven's watchful eye, the happier I'll be."

It was hard to resist that clarion summons, but Rachel managed it somehow. Strengthened by her twin's presence at her side, and by the urgency of her message. "Please, Rowany, we can't."

"Oh?" One supercilious eyebrow, rising perfectly towards that perfect hair, quite unnecessarily. Rachel was not often intimidated, but apparently Rowany could achieve it with a word. No, not so much as a word: a mere syllable.

Nevertheless, she stuck to her guns. "Not yet, I mean. We, we need to go up to the Eyrie first."

"Whatever for? I take it that's where you passed the night, while your sister pretended to be you"—and it was Rachel's turn to flush, that dull fiery red that she hated so much—"but if you've left baggage up there, you can retrieve it later. I think getting Levity and Charm to safety might just be more important."

"It's not that. And yes, of course we need to see them safe." *How do you think I got all these bruises?* She didn't actually say it, but she fiercely wanted to. "But, but there's a pair of sandcat kittens sheltering there. I think their mother must be dead, she didn't come all night and I know the shepherds here lay traps for sandcats, but they're starving hungry and we can't just leave them." She had done what she could, giving them everything that she thought kits might be able to eat, even though that left her with little more than chocolate to see her through the night; but the only thing she knew for sure was that it hadn't been enough.

"*Sandkits?*" For a wonder, even Rowany seemed briefly taken aback. She recovered herself swiftly and went on, "I'll say this for you, Rachel, life is rarely boring when you take a hand. All right, but not you two. Tasha and Tawney, will you take this on? Go up to the Eyrie and salvage Rachel's sandkits? Lord alone knows what we shall do with them, but no doubt someone will think of something, and we can't leave

282

the poor things to starve. Tell you what, take those coats our recently-departed friends have left behind them; kittens like to be swaddled, and you may like some defence against teeth and claws if they feel you're a poor substitute for their mother. Go on, gather them up and take them down to the stables. Find an empty stall to stow them in, don't spook the poor ponies. You can stay with them if you want to, help to settle them down. Rachel, no, you two may not go with the twins—excuse me, the other twins. They know the way perfectly well. And you may not visit the sandkits either, until Miss Leven says you may. I suppose the kits count as twins too, don't they? That's all we need. But I don't care how closely you've bonded with them overnight, I want you where I can see you. Both of you, so that I don't trip over which is which," as if she ever would. "Everybody clear? Good, then. March!"

CHAPTER TWENTY–FOUR

Consequences

L evity had kept her sister tucked close against her side ever since that frantic encounter on the hillside. Literally so at first, on the march back to school. Both Charm and Marigold had been shaking with reaction; they had seemed glad to have her arms around their shoulders, their own friends and hers crowded around them, Rowany looming watchfully at their backs. Rowany above all: if those Russians had dared come back for another try, Levity thought they would have received short shrift. And more than they had bargained for. Was that a paradox, or could both of those actually be true? She pondered the question briefly, and decided that they could, with Rowany in the case. All her classmates stood in dreadful awe of the Head Girl. It had taken Levity less than half a term to understand that, and start to feel the same way.

Mamma might not approve—she had cautioned both her daughters not to idolise either senior girls or staff—but Mamma hadn't met Rowany. Besides, Mamma was mysteriously away. Leaving Levity and Charm to fend for themselves, alone against Russians and their father and all...

No. Not alone. That might be the chief lesson of all their schooldays, however long those lasted: that so long as they were Crater School girls, Levity and her sister need never feel themselves alone again. She felt the press of her cohort about her, and was almost overwhelmed. Gratitude, relief, community: the feelings were complex and confusing, but she thought they all came down to a sense of belonging. For the first time, she felt as though she belonged to something broader than her family. It had been Mamma and Charm and herself for so long, for all the life she remembered; and now that tight little circle had been torn asunder. Mamma was gone, who knew where, and in her stead there were so many new people, classmates and housemates and prefects and staff, all dependable in their own way, all reaching out to encompass herself and her sister, and all a part of this great strange institution called a school...

Levity had plenty of time to mull things over. As promised, Rowany had steered Charm and Marigold directly to the San. One look at their wan little faces, and Sister Anthony had tucked them briskly into two adjoining beds with a cup of hot milk and strict orders not to talk. Then she'd peered judiciously at Levity, clearly considering whether she needed a dose of the same medicine.

Levity shook her head determinedly. "I'm fine, Sister Anthony. Truly. But I'd like to stay with my sister, please."

"Yes, of course. Very well. Here's a chair between the beds; you find yourself a book from the shelf and sit here beside them. It'll be a comfort for all of you, no doubt. You'll take a cup of milk yourself, though. It's been a shock for you too, even if you're not feeling it so deeply. Your face is all eyes and freckles."

Levity wondered if perhaps Sister Anthony had slipped something extra into the milk, because both Juniors were asleep within five minutes. She regarded her own cup with a wary suspicion. But Sister Anthony said, "Drink up!" and so she did; and she had found a history-book about the early pioneers on the San's library shelf, which she thought sounded really interesting, so she settled down happily enough.

Perhaps it was just the somnolent atmosphere in that long sunny silent room; Sister Anthony would have had no good reason to dose her, after all. Perhaps her book was less interesting than she'd thought, and her chair more comfortable than it looked. Perhaps it was the company she kept, two dozing girls and no patient else to keep her alert or amused. Perhaps sleep was merely infectious. That might be why no girl, not even Rowany, had a bedroom to herself, so that they could all infect each other every night...

Levity drifted away in mid-speculation, feeling the warm welcome blanket of sleep fall upon her and finding no strength to toss it off again. She woke, rather startled, at the sound of the luncheon bell. Charm and Marigold were sitting up in bed, looking tousled but rested and far less anxious than they were before. Sister Anthony was just coming down the ward with a trolley.

"Yes, that's better," she said, inspecting all three of them with a judicious eye, as though even Levity was a patient under her care. "Nothing beats sleep, for knitting a ravelled soul together again. I expect you're hungry now. Marigold, you can skip off and join your friends in the dining hall; have a wash-and-brush-up first, and don't worry if you're a minute or two late. You'll be excused, this once. Buchanans, you're to eat here, and see Miss Leven immediately afterwards. Run to the bathroom now and tidy yourselves up, while I set your trays out ready. Look sharp, now. Time's a-wasting while you dawdle."

Those trays held cold meats and salad and lemonade, with a slice of ginger cake to follow. Everything was delicious, and both girls did full justice to their meal—and nevertheless the contents of their trays could barely hold a fraction of their attention, under the threat of what was to follow.

"Are we, you know, in trouble?" It was the obvious, the only question. Charm voiced it at last, her green eyes wide and fretful.

"I don't think so, lovely. I don't see how we can be. We haven't done anything wrong. Well, you haven't," Levity went on, inveterately honest. "You didn't even know about Jess Abramoff and the swap. You were just unlucky," twice unlucky, being manipulated by a scheming sister and then—or therefore—walking into an ambush. Levity's conscience was working overtime by now, and she was entirely sure that she deserved to be in trouble, whether she was or not.

She wouldn't say any of that, though, not to alarm her sister further. "I expect Miss Leven just wants to hear what happened, from the horse's mouth. That's you. I'm just there to make up the numbers," *because she knows I wouldn't let you go in there alone,* something else that really didn't need saying.

"Marigold's a horse too. In that case." Charm's mouth twisted at the description, but she couldn't manage a proper smile. "Why did she get sent away?"

"Because those men weren't interested in Marigold, I suppose. They were there for us, and everybody knows it."

Charm shuddered. "What were they going to do with us, though?"

Levity remembered her close encounter on the lake shore, just last night, and felt a sympathetic shudder of her own. "Take us to, to our father, I suppose. Whichever one of us they had, if they couldn't manage both." Last night they'd have found it easier, bearing her away across the lake. Quite what they'd had in mind this morning, if they'd thought it out at all, she couldn't conceive. More and more she thought it had all been happenstance, Charm just chancing upon them, an opportunity they couldn't resist.

"They might have got away with it, with me," Charm muttered, "if Rachel hadn't been there."

"Oh, I don't think so, sweetheart. I'd missed you already, and we were starting to search even before Rachel yelled. It was very brave of her, and we both have cause to be grateful, but those men had nowhere to go, you know. They could never have got you off the hill unseen."

Charm didn't look convinced, and Levity couldn't blame her. Despite her words, she was bound to wonder: could they have managed it after all? Upslope, away from the searching girls, to Sister Anthony's Eyrie, and then down the cliffside path to her Step. A rope from there to the water, and then their boat, and Charm would seemingly have vanished from human ken. Until another message from their father, *The girl is safe with me; and if Levity wants to see her sister again, she must come too*, and who could doubt Levity's answer? No one would choose to leave Charm alone among her country's enemies, even at the cost of another Buchanan's freedom.

Still, it hadn't happened. "Buck up, old thing," Levity murmured. "Here comes Sister Anthony now, to take us down. Finish your cake and wipe your chin and remember Daniel in the lions' den. Nobody's going to eat us either. We're the Buchanan girls; look on our works, ye mighty, and despair..."

It was the family motto and their war-cry at need, instituted by their mother long ago. Even so, it rang a little hollow now, as Levity and Charm sat on a bench in the alcove opposite Miss Leven's study door, awaiting their summons. Levity had her arm once again around her sister's slender shoulders, and it didn't seem enough.

At last, at long last—it might have been five minutes, but it seemed so very much longer—the study door opened, and the Abramoff twins emerged. Even used as she was to Tasha and Tawney, even having known all along that Rachel had a twin, Levity still found it hard not to gape. They were so utterly alike, as though the same girl had been replicated somehow. Despite their wildly different uniforms, she gazed from one to the other now and truly struggled to know which was which. They even both looked equally pale and strained. Which anyone might, to be fair, after a difficult interview with the Head.

"You're to go in now." That was Rachel, to be sure—but Levity only really knew it from the Crater School colours, and the bruises that marked where she'd fought off the kidnappers this morning. Shouldn't she be rewarded for that? Nothing in her face or manner suggested that any kind of praise or acknowledgement had been offered her behind the study door.

Well, if Levity's eternal friendship meant anything, at least Rachel should have that. And should know it. It was hard to say anything meaningful, without sounding trite or sentimental, which any girl of Mars would shy away from a thousand times. If they'd been boys, a simple silent hand-shake would have done the trick. As it was—well, all she could offer here and now in the corridor was a touch and a glance, no better than a lick and a promise when you were too late for a proper wash.

No better, but no worse either. Rachel understood, she thought; at any rate, dark brows lifted in response and lips quirked with the touch of a smile. There was no time for anything more. Levity drew Charm up beside her, tucked her once again against her side, and carried them both over Miss Leven's threshold by sheer force of will, for certainly nothing less would have sufficed.

"Yes, come in, girls. Close the door, Levity dear, then come and sit down." Her hand directed them towards the window-seat, and Levity felt a rush of relief; her informants—long-experienced, and hopefully reliable—had assured her that a seat in the window was like a promise, that this interview would not be difficult. Malefactors toed the line, directly in front of her desk. If you got as far as the window, you were safe.

No such assurance could ever quite be enough, of course. Charm's fingers were ice-cold where they interlocked with hers. Levity was almost afraid to squeeze, in case they shattered.

Still, Miss Leven had a smile on her face, albeit a small one. She said, "Now, first let me tell you what's occurring as a result of this morning's incident. The police have been informed, of course. There's no one at the Terminus station of sufficient rank to address the problems thrown up by this, so a team is being sent out all the way from New Victoria. There'll be a senior police officer, and also a gentleman from the Colonial Service. They'll both want to speak with you, but don't worry. I'll be there too, as a stand-in for your mother. *In loco parentis*, if you know what that means—yes? Both of you? Good. Of course we have sent messages to your mother, but we're not quite sure of her whereabouts just now. 'Towards your mother' might be a more accurate way to say that.

"Meanwhile, every available policeman is engaged in the hunt for these two Russians. They'll not get far. There's a watch on the canals and the railway, and patrols searching all the local country. No one hereabouts is likely to give them shelter, and if they try to make it on foot across the desert—well. They wouldn't survive that. Even then, though, likely we'd find them before the worst happened. Our police inspector has a small airship of his own, and sharp-eyed observers already aloft.

"So there's that," she said, as final as closing a book. "Now. Levity: nobody has said so, but I suspect that you were as guilty as anyone, in the matter of the Abramoff twins. Yes?"

"Er, yes, Miss Leven. Not Charm," added hastily, looking up from where her fingers seemed suddenly to be tying themselves into knots, "she didn't know anything—"

"I am quite sure that is true, or you would be in a great deal more trouble than you are. Middles are sufficient unto themselves, but I take a very dim view of girls involving their juniors in any manner of mischief. And this was more than mere mischief. You encountered Jessica on this ridiculous escapade of hers, running away from her own school; you disguised her as one of us, and took insolent advantage of Miss Harribeth's good nature to smuggle her into school; and then you heaped Ossa upon Pelion by smuggling Rachel *out* of school, and letting her spend the night alone on the crags. You even inveigled Mr Felton into supporting you in your subterfuge. Great heavens, girl, didn't it occur to you how dangerous that exploit was? When you knew from your own experience that there were merlins and sandcats abroad, aye, and Russians too?"

"Please, Miss Leven"—Levity was very conscious of Charm gaping in wide-eyed wonder at this catalogue of sins, and thought that any mitigation would be better than none at all—"I didn't know about the Russians until after I'd seen Rachel on her way. I couldn't have called her back then."

"No, but you might have reconsidered an act of folly, and told us where she was. That's the worst of this, Levity, that a girl under my authority was absent my care when she might have needed it most. How should I have explained that to her parents, if so be the Russians had decided to overnight in Sister Anthony's Eyrie, as they very well might have done?"

Her parents should never have tried to split her from her twin, that's how all this started—but new as she was to school, Levity wasn't fool enough to blurt out that particular truth. She only sat mum, and waited for doom to be pronounced.

"It's half-term at the end of this week," Miss Leven went on slowly, "and as you know, those girls not going home have been promised an expedition to Laramie Canyon and the settlement at Twin Rapids. It's an exciting trip, and I'm sorry to have to do it, but I've already told Rachel that she may not go. Nor Jessica, of course. Pending word from their parents, I don't believe I can trust either one of them off school premises just now; I want staff or a prefect with clear sight of them at all times. And I'm afraid the same has to apply to you, to both of you. So long as those men are loose in the area, you're still at risk; and even once they're taken, I see no way to be confident. There might be others. And you have not shown yourself to be exactly reliable, Levity, on a loose rein. No: until I have a chance to talk matters over with your mother, I believe I've no alternative but to keep you close. There's a lot of fun you'll be missing, I'm afraid, but perhaps you'll learn from that. Run along now; find your own kind, join in their activities, and do your best to forget this morning. Yes?"

"Yes, Miss Leven. Thank you..."

Her sister's nudging elbow at the door reminded her to turn and bob the little curtsey that custom demanded. Then they were out in the corridor, the door was safely closed, and she felt that she could breathe again.

"Liv, did you truly do all that?"

"Yes, I'm afraid that I did. Well, we did. But—listen, Charm, don't go shouting it abroad, will you? I'm not exactly proud of it, and we're supposed to be trying to fit in, remember? Mamma told us to sing small and not draw attention to ourselves."

"Yes, but—well, I'll have to tell Marigold, obviously," as though being incidentally kidnapped qualified her friend to know all their family secrets. Perhaps it did. Levity felt too confused to be sure of anything any more.

"Well, all right." If one thing was certain, it was that Charm would need to spill it all to someone. "So long as you swear her to secrecy."

"I'll do my best," Charm said, a little dubiously. Which meant, Levity guessed, that some swollen version of the tale would be all over the Junior School by close of day. Oh, well. There was probably nothing she could do to prevent it; and if it started with Charm, at least it shouldn't end up too wildly far from the truth. *Perhaps,* she added to herself, remembering games of Martian Whispers where the exact opposite proved to be the case.

"It's half past two," she said, changing the subject rigorously. "Do you know where Marigold and the rest of your crew will be right now?"

Charm nodded. "Confirmation class, with Father Mungo."

"You'd better scoot, then. If he's cross, say you were with Miss Leven."

"Father Mungo's never cross. He's a great sweet bear of a man." Nevertheless, Charm scooted, at a rate that was safe to call down a reprimand from any authority she ran into. All too literally, all too likely. Levity considered calling after her, but held her tongue; was she her sister's keeper? *Only when it matters.*

Instead, she wanted to seek out Lise and the twins—the Mishkin twins, at least—and knew just where to look for them, in the stables with the sandkits. But there was something else she must face first, a necessary duty; she had to find Miss Harribeth, and apologise for misleading her that day in town and all the journey home. Miss Leven hadn't said so, but it was an absolute essential for clearing the air between them. She was tolerably sure that the others would have done so already, all together or else one by one as they thought of it.

Even before that, though, she had something more on her mind and her conscience both. She had to find Mr Felton, and make sure that her co-conspirator was not in trouble himself for his part in the affair.

He wasn't in his cubby, though, where she'd ordinarily look to find him on a Sunday. He wasn't anywhere that she could find, though she searched all through the corridors; and when she gave up and went for Miss Harribeth instead, the mistress was equally and frustratingly missing. Not in her study, neither in her classroom, neither wandering the castle in any place that Levity was allowed to look.

At last she gave up virtue, then, and went in search of her friends—and there she found Mr Felton and Miss Harribeth and half the school besides. Of course she should have thought of that. Who wouldn't want sight of sandkits? The prefects were policing the crowd, as best they could with their own heads constantly twisting on their shoulders for a better view. Miss Harribeth was gathered in a little huddle with other staff, while Mr Felton was constructing a run of timber and wire netting, leading out from the end stall of the stables to a patch of grass beyond.

"Hi, Levity Buchanan! Where do you think you're going? You keep back with the others."

Of course Melanie Fitzwalter was alert to the very moment that Levity stepped across the invisible line the prefects had imposed. The common theory was that she had eyes in the back of her head: useful for lacrosse or hockey, no doubt, but a wretched nuisance to that generation of Juniors and Middles unfortunate enough to live beneath her governance.

In a moment, Levity recovered all her abandoned virtue, just when she needed it most. "Please, Melanie, I need to speak with Mr Felton. And with Miss Harribeth too," she added, catching herself in a virtuous cycle that should probably lead to sainthood before term's end if there were any kind of justice in the world. "I've just come from Miss Leven." There. Not a word of a lie. And if Miss Leven hadn't actually *told* her to apologise, it had surely been implicit. And if not *exactly* implicit, it was undoubtedly a good thing, and Miss Leven would approve, so flourishing her name wasn't really cheating at all, was it...?

Cheating or not, it worked. Melanie waved her through with a nod. Levity thanked her politely, then skipped across to Mr Felton.

"Please, did I get you into trouble with Miss Leven? Because I'm terribly sorry if I did, that wasn't what I meant at all."

He laughed shortly. "People almost never mean trouble, lass. And it almost always happens anyway. But don't you worry about me. Miss Leven and I understand each other very well. Now, you hold this end of the wire while I unroll it, and we'll get on twice as fast."

"Um, in just a minute, Mr Felton. I have to go and apologise to Miss Harribeth first," and Miss Harribeth was standing just by the door to the stall; and the top half of that door was open, and Levity could see Tawney standing there with something bundled in her arms, and a stray beam of sunlight was striking a reflection from two vivid, curious, bright green eyes...

CHAPTER TWENTY–FIVE

Out of the Gondola—

"No, don't attack this end, you idiot, this is the end I'm holding! See, copy your brother, go after the end that's free..."

"Actually, I think this one's the boy and that's his sister."

"How can you tell? They both look alike to me."

"She's the smart one. Knows which end of a rope is which."

"Good point. All right, call this one the boy—but could you pick him up and plonk him over there? Before I bleed to death?"

It was the second day of the half-term holiday. Yesterday had been hectic, with half the school departing. The corridors had been crowded with girls saying goodbye and parents arriving to ferry them away, the roadway behind the castle a chaos of cars and steam-wagons, until Rowany and the prefects took a hand to introduce some sense of order. It didn't matter if you were a station porter or a bishop, or an army sergeant three times her age; if Rowany ordered you off the road to let a motor-coach come by, then off the road you went.

And if you were a Middle in the middle of a throng, and Melanie Fitzwalter told you to fetch up the luggage piled in the hallway of Stokes House, then piled luggage was what you fetched. It was almost a game to play at porter half the day, hauling bags and running messages—"Oh, please, Miss Leven, has anyone told you about Colonel Anderson yet? He thought you were in your study and he's been waiting outside for half an hour, and I'm afraid he's getting a little stewy"—and it was certainly good to be kept busy, so that you barely noticed how everyone else was going to have such fun and you weren't.

This morning had been harder, when the charabancs arrived to take the rest of the school away on their trip. The small handful of sinners left behind had to wave them all off with bright smiles, not to spoil things for their friends; and then they had to turn to face the resonantly empty school, and the empty days ahead...

Except that the school at least was not entirely empty, for there was Rowany, gazing down at them from her own great height and the top of the library steps to boot, which seemed like taking unfair advantage. Puzzled, they gathered below; it was Rachel—of course!—who found her voice first.

"Aren't you going on the expedition with everyone else, Rowany?"

"Evidently not," said the Head Girl, with a kind of weary acceptance of the inevitable. "Someone had to stay to keep an eye on you four, because it may have escaped your infantile minds but the staff deserve a holiday too. Lord knows they've earned it, this half. And I've seen the canyon before—more than seen it, we canoed it end to end, Canadian-style—and the other prefects hadn't, so I stepped forward before I was pushed. Miss Leven was half minded to keep back everyone who was involved in your little impersonation project, but I pleaded for mercy and she relented in the end. Two sets of twins is quite enough, I say."

"*Two* sets?" Jessica echoed, frowning.

"Certainly. Have you forgotten the sandkits already? Or simply not realised that you four are the only ones left to look after them for the next week? You can't expect the staff to do it, neither the servants. They're all off on their own holidays anyway, except for Mrs Bailey herself. No, it's down to you crew, I'm afraid. All the ponies to feed and groom, too. Sorry, Charm, I know how very much you'll hate that, playing stable-boy all week long." Charm was already beaming, wide enough almost to split her face in two. Rowany carried on relentlessly. "In fact, you'd better start now. One of you cut down to the kitchens and beg Mrs Bailey for a bowl of meat scraps, and anything else she thinks sandkits ought to eat; I know Miss Hendy drew up a list and left it with her. The rest get along to the stables—oh, but come to think of it, you'd better all change into work-clothes first. There are half a dozen stalls to muck out, before you even come to the kittens. I'm sure Charm can show you how. Chop-chop, now. Time and tide wait for no girl. And we may not have tides as such, but sandkits' appetites are just as regular and just as reliable."

Was this meant to be a punishment? None of them was quite sure, except for Charm, who knew absolutely that it was a treat. Little by little, the older girls felt dismay give way to delight. Even shovelling manure could be fun, with friends around you and joy to come; and once the dirty work was done they could spend an hour rollicking with the kittens, letting them out of their run and chasing after them with shrieks of horror when they ventured out beyond the stable-yard, encouraging them to chase the trailing end of a rope, trying—vainly, thus far—to train them to play with soft paws, not to claw skin and sleeves and stockings indiscriminately.

Like any young predators, they would play-attack anything that moved, including each other. Anything that kept still, they would climb onto and explore thoroughly. Keep still long enough, and they would curl up separately or together, emit the strange rumbling rasp that the girls took to be purring, and fall asleep right there in your lap or across your shoulders. It was hard to keep still that long, though, when you were young yourself and not at all sleepy. Mostly, then, the kits were played with, to their point of exhaustion; and then suddenly there was Rowany again, as though she knew just exactly when enough was enough.

"I know those two creatures are overtired and overfed," she said, "but what about the rest of you?" And then, in the face of their blank bewildered looks, "Have you forgotten entirely about lunch?"

Of course they had; and they gazed at each other in shock, realising suddenly how desperately hungry they were, and then turned as one back to Rowany. Levity spoke for them all: "Oh, we're terribly sorry! We didn't hear the bell at all! Is, is there anything left, is Miss Leven terribly cross...?"

"Ah, that's showing proper priorities, Levity." Astonishingly, Rowany seemed to be laughing at them. "Oh, you goops—do you imagine you'd be let miss lunch? There was no bell, and no one is eating in hall this glorious day. The staff have borne Mrs Bailey off for their own amusement; you lot are condemned to picnic on the lake with me. As soon as you're cleaned up and looking decent, that is to say. Give those poor kits a rest, and hurry off to change. Everything you want is in the San, or should be; no need to go back to your houses. Meet me on the drawbridge in ten minutes, or I'm leaving without you."

None of them believed her, of course, and nevertheless: inside their time they were all assembled as bidden, though Levity had had to help Charm with her hair and even now it was more of a thatch than a plait, all ends sticking out all over. Rowany regarded it with a jaundiced eye, and visibly decided not to say anything, just this once.

"Take a handle each," she instructed instead, waving towards two stacked and satisfactorily heavy wicker baskets, "and follow me."

"Are we really to be allowed on the lake?" Charm asked boldly, when it seemed that no one else was going to. "We haven't been, all term. And, and Miss Leven said we weren't to leave school grounds, Liv and me..."

"You should say 'Liv and I,'" Rowany corrected. "But for the purposes of the act, the lake has been decreed to be school grounds. So long as you're prepared to pull an oar, that is. I'm hanged if I'm rowing the four of you all over."

The Martian girl is not born, of course, who cannot pull an oar at need, or will not on request. Or at any opportunity, largely. Charm indicated as much, volubly; and could only be interrupted by her sister, and only then by a hand firmly placed over her mouth.

"What about the merlins, though, Rowany? We haven't been let out on the water all this time..."

"And the merlins haven't shown themselves all this time, apart from your cabbage-stalk adventure, which is normal behaviour for them although your poor Russian kidnappers didn't know it. Honestly, I have it in me to pity those men, coming up against the Crater School Middles in their wrath. The Tsar himself and all his hordes would never have stood a chance. Anyway, Miss Leven and Miss Hendy between them have decided that the naiad must have fallen back into somnolence. It might only last another week, another day; but it might be months or years before she emerges again.

300

We really don't know. And summer is coming, and it seems a shame to deny everybody the water just in case. We're to be the sacrificial victims. If we don't get eaten today, or for the rest of the week—because one test run is never enough, so I'm afraid we'll have to be out on the water as often as we can manage it, these coming days—then all the school can row out once they return. Apparently Miss Leven feels that we're expendable, we five. So out we go—and you remember that I said the staff would be off on their own occasions? Those happen to mean a second boat, and a separate picnic, not terribly far at all from ours. I think they're hoping that we'll be slower than them, and if the naiad rises it'll be us that she eats while they row hard for shore. So let's show them otherwise, eh...?"

Of course she meant no such thing, but it was a delightful conceit, and they fell on it with glee. The Abramoff twins in particular were determined to show what they could do. They had spent a very uncomfortable time in Miss Leven's study, and had felt the burden of the staff's watchfulness since very keenly. No one, after all, likes to be told they aren't trustworthy. Besides which, they had been on tenterhooks for days now, only waiting to learn their fate. Miss Leven had written to their parents demanding a decision about both their futures, here or elsewhere, together or apart. Doom might befall them any day now, with any post. Nothing about this seemed quite fair to them, and most of the possibilities were appalling. Work was a useful distraction, and nothing is more work than rowing. They were very much on their mettle, determined to show that they could at least do one thing well.

Along with the other Middles, Rachel had been released from the hated smock and allowed to don her Crater School uniform again. For want of anything else, Jessica too had been dressed temporarily in green-and-gold. If both girls felt that this might be an opportunity to show that they were both deserving of that uniform, neither one had voiced it, even to herself.

Rowany brought them to the school's landing-stage, where a skiff lay waiting in the water. A small dot out towards the centre of the lake drew sharp-eyed Levity's attention. "There's a boat out already. That must be the staff, I suppose, Rowany?"

"Yes, indeed. And they have not been eaten, I am pleased to see. They're safe to be watching us now; let's show them a clean stroke, please. No splashing inboard, or our sandwiches will get wet, and so will I. There's only one thing worse than soggy bread, and that's a soggy Head Girl."

With those awful warnings in mind, all four younger girls settled to their oars determined to pull well and not to splash at all. At Rowany's suggestion, Charm took stroke; that way she could set the pace, and the older stronger girls wouldn't exhaust her unduly. She looked a little awed at the responsibility, but took her seat and set her oar—and her jaw—determinedly.

Levity sat beside her in the number three spot, while Rachel and Jessica took bow and two respectively. Rowany would sit in the stern sheets, steer and cox.

"One more thing, Charm—don't overcook yourself," she said quietly, unhitching the painter from the landing-stage and stepping aboard. "If you need a spell, just say so and I'll take over."

"I won't need a spell," Charm growled through gritted teeth. "Levity and I have always rowed together. I can keep up with her."

"Of course you can. Just remember you don't have to. It does the crew no good for one member to exhaust herself. Now: everyone ready? Let's be off, then. Starboard, shove off! Port, one stroke—pull! And one more—pull! Starboard oars

302

out! Take your time from stroke, remember; and don't pull your arms out of your sockets, Abramoffs. It's not genteel. Ready? Row!"

It was tolerably clear tolerably early on that Rowany was under firm instructions to keep her boat within hail of the staff's, and to be prepared for orders.

It was equally clear, equally early on, that her crew was determined to display a proper independence, and keep as far from staff supervision as they might be allowed. Didn't they have Rowany, and in what sense could she possibly not be enough? *Rowany*, it had been rightly said, *is the big battalions.*

Compromise doesn't come easily to a general's daughter, but her loyalties were torn. On the one hand, she had been raised obedient to authority, and there were clear dangers here, with clear help just across the way. On the other hand, she was the epitome of a Crater School girl, with all the fierce self-reliant spirit that phrase could imply. She brought her boat within call, then, as she'd been instructed—and had the girls ship oars the very moment she judged that a loud hail might just carry. Close enough for obedience, far enough for pride: that would do nicely. Certainly it was far enough to suppress any incipient mutiny in her crew. They looked, and judged, and smiled contentedly upon her.

"Is it time for lunch yet?" asked insouciant Charm. "I don't know why, but being on the water always makes me ravenous."

"That's because you've been working your little heart out," her big sister said tenderly. "Don't pretend you weren't overreaching to match us, because I know you were. You'd best give her a sandwich at least, Rowany, if she's to be any use for the next stretch."

"I think we could all use a sandwich," Rowany said equably. She was very well aware that Charm needed a rest and a boost before she could row again. "And while we eat, we can consider what to do for the next stretch. You all rowed very neatly this far. Twins, would you feel up to sculling for a while? This skiff's not too heavy, even with the three of us as dead weight, and I'd like to see your form when you work together. One wide lap around the staff boat, say, keeping this distance all the way?"

The twins, needless to say, would be delighted. But there was the question of that sandwich first; and a sandwich led to calls for lemonade, and perhaps another sandwich, and then there was that delicious-looking slab cake, and...

"Luckily for you lot," Rowany said at last, "the staff is just as greedy. I've been keeping an eye, and there's no more left of their picnic than there is of ours. They wouldn't have a leg to stand on if they chose to decry your gluttony." She made no mention of her own, though she had participated with a will in the general demolition, and she still had half a mind to broach the last greaseproof-wrapped packet of sandwiches, in the hope that they might prove to be another round of ham. That packet had been left by unspoken consent as a kind of token offering, because no one aboard was fool enough to suggest an actual offering to the merlins. It was school custom, deep ingrained, but they all knew that the first sign of disturbance in the water would see them rowing pell-mell for shore, with the staff boat herding them all the way.

Rowany was fairly sure that an extra ham sandwich—if they were ham—would trump even the most passionately meant of gestures; but her juniors might well feel that they needed to earn it first.

"Are you twins fit for that sculling, then?"

Being doubly assured that indeed they were, she reorganised the boat, calling both Buchanans to the stern with her while the Abramoffs took a thwart and two oars each.

Everyone was ready and she was just on the point of giving the off when a sound impinged on her consciousness. Or rather, she noticed Charm's alertness and her twisting head; a second later, she realised that she had been subconsciously aware for a while that there was a curious drone in the air. Now that she was deliberately listening, she could identify it quickly. "That's an airship," she said. "We don't often see them out this way. I wonder—?"

The boat rocked dangerously beneath her, beneath them all. Everyone yelled, and Rowany and Levity both took action, each reaching out an arm to seize Charm and pull her back onto the bench again.

"My dear child, do you want to have us all in the water? You can't just stand up in a skiff this light, without due notice given."

"Sorry, but I wanted to see," quoth heedless Charm. "There it is, just coming over the Devil's Teeth..."

And there it was indeed: a speck that grew to a dot that grew swiftly to a definite shape, the unmistakable bulbous silhouette of a zeppelin coming in.

"I believe it's going to land here," Rowany said, struggling a little to sound cool and matter-of-fact. In a landscape and a society where civilisation still clung largely to the canals and waterways, it was not truly so remarkable; many, even perhaps most airships were adapted to land on water. Even so: it had seldom happened during Rowany's time at school that any had come down here, on their own lake. Of those few that she did remember, most had been emergencies for the great Sanatorium across the water. Young Pat Cadigan, of course, had been one of those in reverse: evacuated by air from the Sanatorium. One or two girls from wealthy families had been delivered or collected by airship, once or twice. Never more than twice. It was frowned on by the school at large, as a rather nasty kind of exhibitionism, and the girls in question had swiftly persuaded their parents not to do that again.

This certainly wasn't the official emergency airship, though, with its white balloon and the vivid red cross on both sides. It might still be a private vessel bringing in a patient—but Rowany had a feeling otherwise, even before the Abramoff twins looked at each other with a mutual, painful surmise.

"It might be Daddy," Rachel said.

"Worse," said Jessica. "It might be Mummy."

"Well," Rowany said briskly, "whoever it is, no doubt we'll find out soon enough; and meantime it behooves us to give them clear water. See, the staff are already headed this way, to shepherd us off. Best that we pre-empt them, yes? Twins, back to your single oars; Charm, come here, take the tiller and cox for us, yes? I'll sit stroke, in case we need to pull like fury if they misjudge their splashdown. Careful not to upset us, now, this would be the worst possible time..."

Under her watchful management, they changed seats again without incident. By the time they were settled, though, the staff boat was nearly upon them, with Miss Peters making imperative signals from the bow: *head straight to the landing-stage, don't loiter, we will herd you in.*

She was actually close enough to have called her orders across quite clearly, but there was no need. Rowany was of the same mind, seeing the airship circling above the lake, lower and lower with every turn. She did *not* want herself or any of her charges anywhere near that contraption when it came down to the water.

She bent her back to the oar and drove her crew hard, perhaps to the limits of their strength. Not past those limits, though; her bones remembered being fourteen, and how much they could manage then, and how much more they might try for.

The staff boat kept pace without crowding, which contented her. Behind that she had a perfect view of the airship on its last run now, seeming to chase them down the lake. Its floats stuck out sharply on either side of the gondola, like duck feet splayed for landing; the note and rhythm of its steam-engine changed, beating across the water low and slow, infuriatingly out of sync with her own steady rhythm.

"Charm! Eyes forward!" she called sharply, seeing the youngster twist around to stare.

Guiltily, Charm recalled herself to her duty, watching the landing-stage approach and issuing self-conscious guidance to the Head Girl herself: "Steady. Twenty yards... Ten yards... One more stroke. Ship oars, both."

A moment later the boat bumped lightly against the stage, and Rowany saw as much as heard Charm's huge sigh of relief.

"Well done, young 'un," she said cheerfully. "Do that a few times more, and we'll give you a run as cox for the senior eight. You're light enough, and you've got a good eye and a clear call. Everyone out now, and make room for the staff."

What she meant, of course, was *Everyone cram to the end of the landing-stage, so that we can all watch the airship come in.*

So that's what they all did: Levity keeping a firm grip on her sister's shoulders, just to be sure, for there was no rail to stop anyone going over the edge and into the water. After her last lakeside experience, she had not forgotten that there were hungry merlins down there, accustomed to rise and harvest whatever splashed.

The twins were on one side of her, trying to look nonchalant to hide their nervousness; they had completely convinced each other that their parents were aboard that 'ship, come to split them up once more. Rowany was the other side, not too grown-up yet to let her excitement show.

Briefly, Levity was aware of more figures crowding in behind, the four oarswomen from the staff boat, and Miss Leven, and Mrs Bailey too. This arrival must be unusual indeed, to hold everyone's attention this way. Unless they all just liked to watch a splashdown...

Splashdown duly came, with a bright dense spray of water flung high to either side, enough to swamp any unlucky boat caught beneath it. One reason to be glad, perhaps, that the merlins had stalled any water-traffic until today.

Safely down, the airship chugged slowly in towards the landing-stage. Definitely it was coming to the school, then, not to the Sanatorium. It seemed somehow smaller on the water than it had been in mid-air; there'd be room enough for it to tie up on the other side of the stage here. Though its great envelope of gas was going to look mighty strange, looming above the boathouse.

A boy appeared suddenly on a narrow walkway between that envelope above and the wooden gondola beneath. No, Levity corrected herself a moment later: not a boy. The hair was chopped short, the overalls were mannish and there was soot and muck everywhere, but that was surely a girl under-neath it all.

She waved an arm that was deeply tanned beneath its layer of grease, and called out, "Ahoy below! Stand by for mooring-ropes, will you?"

The twins ran off to the other end of the stage; Levity and Charm stayed with Rowany. Soon enough a long rope came snaking down. Levity and Charm both jumped, but Rowany only had to extend one absurdly long arm to snare it in mid-air.

"You two know how to tie a mooring hitch?"

"Yes, of course!" That was Charm, offended by the very question. "It was the first thing they wanted to teach us in Pioneers, but we both knew already."

"Splendid. Carry on, then." Rowany passed the rope's end conspicuously to Charm rather than Levity, and then conspicuously didn't stay to check her knot, but moved off to join the staff where they had forgathered further down, amidships, waiting for a gangplank and presumably a guest.

Their own duties done at the vessel's bow, Rachel and Jessica came squeezing back past that group of grown-ups to join the Buchanans where they stood and watched, interested but not involved.

"It'll be Mummy or Daddy, you'll see," Jessica lamented.

"What if it's both?" Charm asked, inevitably.

The twins shuddered, as one. No further answer was offered, or indeed required.

"What if it's neither?" suggested Levity, trying to lift their mood a little. "Just because you're in trouble doesn't mean that every unexpected thing has to be about that trouble. This could be a, a millionaire bringing a new pupil, unannounced..."

"Not it," Rachel declared. "It'll be a millionaire coming to take a pupil away, you'll see."

"I shan't go," Jessica said helplessly.

"You won't have the choice. But maybe if I behave really badly, Miss Leven won't want to keep me, and they'll have to take us both..."

Here came the gangplank now, run out by that same oil-stained girl. She came trotting down to secure the foot by some arcane ropework, then looked about her, spotted her natural allies, and walked briskly down to join them.

"Hi. My name's Pete." She thrust out a grubby hand, then looked at it a little dubiously, drew it back, pulled out a handkerchief that was grubbier still, and finally shrugged and put both hands behind her back. "Sorry. We had a little trouble with the valves, and I had to take the engine apart mid-voyage. All the perfumes of Arabia could not sweeten this little hand. Consider yourselves shaken."

"We'll do that." *Pete?* She was—just—too polite to challenge a stranger, but it really didn't seem likely. "I'm Levity, and this is my sister Charm. These are the Abramoff twins, Rachel and Jessica."

"Ah, right." Pete looked at them alertly. "One of our passengers came on a mission to you two."

The twins groaned in unison. "We knew it. Which is it, who've you brought, Mummy or Daddy?"

"No, it's—"

She broke off, as an elderly figure appeared at the head of the gangplank.

"Why, it's old Mr Murchison!" Jessica exclaimed, *sotto voce*.

"Who's he?" Charm asked, when clearly no one else was going to.

"Our family solicitor. What on earth...? Oh, lord: don't tell me someone's died?" Rachel was suddenly unnaturally pale, and clinging to her sister.

"Not that," Pete hurried to reassure her. "I'd better not say more, it's not my place, but the old fellow told us all about it on the trip up here, and—well, at least I can say it's not that. No one's dead."

Both twins sagged with relief. Rowany reached a friendly arm around the shoulders of each, and gave them a little shake. "Of course it's not that, why should it be?" she asked, blithely ignoring all she knew of the whole history of humans on Mars. "Bear up, you two, and don't be such mooks. No doubt you'll find out soon enough."

Sooner than that, perhaps. After a swift word with Miss Leven, the newcomer had turned and was coming along the landing-stage towards them. He looked the very image of the family solicitor, in his old-fashioned suit with his eyeglasses and malacca cane; but his eyes twinkled unexpectedly, and when he held out his free arm both twins rushed to him.

"Now, you two. Up to sin and mischief as usual, I hear. Especially you, Jessica." He knew her unerringly, despite their matching dress.

"Guilty as charged, Uncle Murch. And I'm truly sorry, but, but they shouldn't have tried to separate us. If they'd only asked you, you could have told them..."

"Indeed; but they didn't ask me. Also, if they'd wanted that ruling to hold, they shouldn't have gone jaunting off to England and left me in charge of the pair of you."

"They—I'm sorry, what?"

"They left on last month's aethership," he said gently. "Thinking you both settled in your separate schools, they left me *in loco parentis* and departed. Perhaps for six months, perhaps a year: you know how uncertain those voyages can be."

"But—oh, Uncle Murch, if you're in charge of us, do you think you could persuade Miss Leven to let me stay here with Rachel?"

"I don't know, Jess," Rachel said quickly. "It'd take an awful lot of wheedling. If you ask me, she'd sooner be rid of us both than lumbered with us both. Poor Uncle Murch would really have to beg. Consider his dignity..."

Mr Murchison gazed benevolently from one to the other, and said, "You don't fool me in the least, you know. I've known you all your lives."

"Yes, but we're serious about this," Jessica said, kicking her twin rather hard on the shin. "Never mind her, she's gaming with you—but please, we do have to be together. And, and we would both like to be here, if Miss Leven will have us."

"Well. I'll talk to her. That's why I came here, after all. I'd meant to come by train, of course; the ways of flight are not for us humble country lawyers. But I had to change trains and overnight at Marsport, and I happened to meet someone at dinner in the hotel who turned out to be coming here herself. As soon as we discovered that, she insisted that I join her in her chartered 'ship, and my goodness, I wasn't about to say no. Now, you two, I am about to speak to you like a Dutch uncle, so perhaps we should be alone this little while, hmm?"

He had turned the girls as he spoke, and started to steer them away. That left the fascinated Buchanan sisters to turn their scattered attention back to the gangplank, where another figure had suddenly appeared.

Tall and slender, with a head of flaming red, woven through these days with hanks of pure white...

"Mamma!"

Two girls abruptly running, tumbling over their own legs and each other's, pushing heedlessly past those in authority to hurl themselves upon the newcomer as she stepped ashore.

"Steady the Buffs!" she cried, laughing. "You'll have me in the water, you two monstrous creatures. When did you get so leggy? You can't have grown in half a term, surely! And yet I'd swear that you have, both of you—"

"Mamma, look round. Look, Liv!" That was Charm, unexpectedly urgent, breaking free of her mother's arm and pointing out across the lake.

Looking is infectious. Soon enough everyone was staring; no need for Charm to keep pointing, although she did. Out on the water—no, *in* the water, rather—was a violent disturbance. It showed itself with a churning maelstrom, as though the very lake itself were being sucked downward. As well that their little boats were clear, and all safe ashore!

Almost all. Pete shrilled a warning, and a man appeared on the gangplank.

"Is that your father?" Rowany asked, manifesting suddenly beside them.

"Uncle," Pete muttered.

"Uncle, then: well done, for calling him forth. Now do you think you could hustle him along? It behooves us all to move a little further away. Mrs Buchanan, if you would? Miss Leven is rather keen to see us off the landing-stage before those merlins get this far."

Pete seemed to bristle a little at Rowany's assumed authority, but the danger they'd both seen was very real. There were indeed merlins showing at the surface now, one so much larger than its attendants, that was certainly the naiad. And she was certainly headed in this direction.

There was no need for Rowany's chivvying. The Buchanan girls turned their mother and hurtled her to shore, shepherding Pete and her uncle along with them. The other adults had gone ahead to set an example, onto the lakeside path and then further yet, up to where the land rose behind the boathouse. From there they'd have a view, some degree of protection and a way of retreat, all the way back to the castle if need be. Miss Leven was beckoning briskly, to make sure the girls came to join them. Rowany was last off the landing-stage, ready to act as whipper-in if necessary, but it really wasn't. No Crater School girl nor any girl of Mars was likely to hang around staring with a squadron of merlins making a beeline in her direction.

"It can't be us, though. Can it? They're not really coming for us." Even in full retreat, Levity found time and breath to ask the question.

"If you ask me," Rowany said, urging them all into a trot in response to Miss Leven's increasing urgency—for she might be Head Girl with all duties and responsibilities pertaining thereto, but she was still herself a girl of Mars, and so born to question—"that airship's landing disturbed the naiad, and so she rose, and so the nymphs came after. I'm sorry, Pete, but if I'm right, I don't give your 'ship much of a future."

"Oh, but—"

Pete halted mid-stride and made to turn back, as though there were some way that she might save the vessel.

She wasn't given the chance. Rowany seized her shoulders and propelled her forward by main force.

"Don't be a fool. What could you do, alone? In seconds, which is all you'd have by the time you got back there? Apart from going down with the 'ship, that is, which no one here is likely to applaud."

It was hard to tell beneath all the smears of smoke and oil, but Levity thought she could see a flush rise to Pete's face. At any rate, the girl made no more demur, but hurried along in step with everyone else.

When they reached the grown-ups in their place of supposed safety, Pete ran straight to the man who had been last ashore and hugged him hard. Seeing him clearly for the first time, Levity thought he looked world-weary and careworn. Perhaps being in sole apparent charge of a girl like Pete would do that to a man—but she guessed that the truth ran deeper, that his life had been a hard one even before he had to stand on a hillside and see his airship menaced by merlins.

If he could watch it—and Pete too, lifting her head from his jacket and turning determinedly—then so could Levity.

And so she did: standing within the circle of her mother's arm, reaching around to find Charm's hand and hold that too, she stood straight and still, to watch while the naiad and her attendant nymphs tore that little airship to pieces, wrenching beam from beam, severing cables, piercing the great bulbous envelope above and then ripping it to shreds as it collapsed atop them in a welter of galvanised rubber and bamboo struts.

They made a churning, terrible ruin of her, and then—just when Levity thought they would go on to destroy the landing-stage and the boats moored to it, and the boathouse too—the naiad turned away and sank beneath the flotsam without warning. Her nymphs followed, dutiful as pages or ladies-in-waiting.

In the stillness after, Levity became aware that someone was moaning softly, helplessly under their breath. She just wasn't quite sure if it was the airship's captain, or his niece Pete, or even possibly herself.

CHAPTER TWENTY-SIX

—And into the Steam-Barge

Sinners they might be, and under careful watch, but at least some rules were in abeyance—they had been assured—during the week of half-term, for those girls left in school.

Perhaps that was to make life easier for the remaining staff, as much as to be kind to wayward pupils. Perhaps it was simply a recognition of the inevitable, that some rules would be victims of changed circumstance, not so much broken as entirely disregarded.

Here they all were, for example, not bedding down in their separate dormitories in their separate houses, but gathered all together in the San, though none of them was sick. Clustered together, indeed, at one end of this long high open room. There were no cubicle-curtains to separate each bed from its neighbours, for Sister Anthony held that light and air and company trumped privacy every time. During the term, her own austere presence kept whispers to a minimum after lights-out, but in this interim lively girls were sure to talk, legally or otherwise.

Accordingly, it had been decreed that they might do so—"quietly, mind"—from the time they went to bed until Rowany came up to join them, an hour later.

Tonight, they had not only the day's excitements to talk over one more time. They had a guest too. Where else would the school house an unexpected fourteen-year-old, but with her own kind?

Pete—*Pete!*—had been scrubbed once today already, by Sister Anthony's own hand, with curious chemicals guaranteed to dissolve all the grease and grime with which she had so generously slathered herself. Tonight she had bathed again, as school custom and practice demanded; and now she stood scowling in the doorway to the San, wrapped in a borrowed dressing gown several times her size, with her chopped-short hair sticking out damply all about her head.

Guessing that the scowl was meant to disguise a sudden rush of shyness, Jessica waved wildly.

"Come and take this bed next to me, Pete! We totally new girls have to stick together."

"I'm not any kind of new girl," Pete growled—but she came none the less, if only to argue further. "Don't you want to have your twin in the next bed to you?"

"Can't," Jessica said. "Rowany's forbidden it. No sisters side by side, she says it's a school rule and not in abeyance. Hence Rachel on that side, in between the Buchanans; and me all on my lonesome own on this side, unless you join me. Oh, and Rowany of course, in the end bed, but she's not up yet so she doesn't count."

"Rowany's that big girl, isn't she? I thought she was a teacher."

"Worse," Rachel put in, arriving from her own bath, sponge bag swinging from one heedless hand. "She's Head Girl. But we call them mistresses here, not teachers. Where do you go to school?"

"I don't," Pete said shortly.

"Goodness, not at all?"

"No. I was supposed to, but my parents died; and there wasn't any money, and Uncle Raymond only barely earns enough to put food on the table and keep the *Spiderfly* in the air, so there was no question of school after I came to live with him. He needs me aft in the engine-room and up in the rigging, not stuck in some classroom somewhere writing essays and learning to be dainty. I'm the best engineer-deck-hand he's ever had, he said so himself. And besides, I'm family. The *Spiderfly* knows, she's always answered best to, to—"

Her voice broke and her face twisted sharply, as she recalled too late the fate of her beloved airship.

Her listeners understood. Levity and Charm had come in while she was speaking, and settled themselves as quietly as they could manage, not to interrupt her flow. Now, from her thoroughly illegal perch on the foot of her sister's bed, where she was using Levity's upraised knees as a back-rest, Charm said, "What will you do, though, now that your 'ship is sunk?"

It might have been cruel; it was certainly tactless; but Charm was not named in vain. Her question had all the honest innocence of the curious young, and its simple practicality was something for Pete to hold on to, to keep her from submerging altogether in grief. She shook her head sharply, and perhaps some of her audience knew that she was shaking tears away. "I don't know," she said. "I can't think. We kept *Spiderfly* going on a breath and a prayer, Uncle Ray used to say. We couldn't possibly afford to buy another airship. One thing I do know, though, he's going to need me more than ever. I don't know why your headmistress wouldn't let me sit up with him tonight. That's really mean of her, when he and I are all the family we have and we really need to be planning."

"It's just as bad for us," Levity said. "We haven't seen Mamma for months, and there's been all this craziness happening, and we don't even know where she's *been*..."

"And for us," Rachel said, not to be left out. "Uncle Murch absolutely refused to say what he's planning to do with us. It's the outside of enough, is what I say—"

"Is it, indeed? Well, what *I* say is that you should be careful not to say that in term-time, or you'll be fined for slang every time we catch you."

That was Rowany, of course: appearing from nowhere, as her legend was, and strolling calmly down between the beds like Fate personified, like the very embodiment of authority, as of course she was.

"And you can all stop feeling hard done by," she went on, settling gracefully on her bed in the corner, "because of course the grown-ups want to talk things over between themselves before they discuss these matters with you. Abramoffs, Mr Murchison couldn't possibly decide what to do with you two before he'd discussed it with Miss Leven, who remains deeply unimpressed with your various behaviours so far. Buchanans, your mother has only just flown in, from, as you say, who knows where; she didn't know until this hour just what threat you two have been under, and of course she wants to hear all the details from a reliable source before she can think to settle down with you two for a good coze. And—Pete, isn't it?—as *you* say, your Uncle Raymond has just lost his livelihood and your own. He'll be needing advice and reassurance before he wants oaths of family loyalty, however passionate and well-meaning. They do you credit—here especially, where we know the value of a woman's work—but you don't need to earn credit with him, he knows already what you're worth and what you have to offer. Right now he needs to be with his own kind, and so do you. So, now that I've dispensed with everybody's grumbles," and she smiled blandly around the group of them, as though

319

daring anyone to disagree, "why don't you get into your own bed, Charm, where you belong, and I'll introduce you all to a game that's so exclusive, you're only allowed to play it here in San. Sister Anthony disapproves of it so thoroughly, we're fairly sure she must have invented it herself and regretted it ever after. It's called 'Sick Bogle Singalong', and this is how you play..."

If the gales of laughter from the Sanatorium reached downstairs to the staff and their unexpected guests, no one ever told. Decisions were made none the less, that would impact the lives of each of those girls above. Under Rowany's knowing guidance and her game's ridiculous strictures they were heedless, almost forgetful of what weighty matters concerned them, each and every one. They flung themselves hectically into round after round, until at last the role of Bogle had passed all the way around the room, up one side and down the other, from Jessica to Charm. They sang one last chorus of "Hop-Down Harlequin", and pulled the most gruesome faces they could manage as they chanted the final line, "And now you feel—*sick*!" Levity outdid them all by toppling half out of bed to hang upside down with pale arms asprawl and her long red hair puddling on the floor about her head. This rather alarmed her sister, but Rowany was right there—in her role as Butler to the Bogle—to haul her back into bed again, laughing.

"You look like a Pre-Raphaelite heroine, coming to her traditionally tragic end," she said bracingly. "Save that for when it's your turn to pose in Miss Calomy's art class. Everyone else will hate you for making things hard, but she'll love it. Until the blood all rushes to your head and you come over all giddy and faint. Then she'll have to fetch Sister Anthony, and she'll hate that, and everyone else in the class will love you for it. Fuss always goes down well, especially when it's an excuse to put down paintbrushes and gossip.

"Meanwhile," she went on, tucking Levity in, "it's high time you were all getting settled. I know, you're far too wound up to sleep just now, and that's my fault; so lie down properly—yes, Pete, that means you too, even if you aren't a Crater School girl within the meaning of the act; a good guest always follows house rules, haven't you heard that?—and I'll switch off all these lights but one, and read to you for a while. I take it no one here objects to a chapter or two of Penelope?"

"I don't know," Pete said, a little sullenly. "I've never read it. It's a schoolgirl story, isn't it? I don't read those."

No more did Levity, for preference, but even she had read *Penelope of Mars* and at least some of her many sequels. Charm had devoured the whole series end to end and more than once. She sat up, gaping across the aisle at impervious Pete, until Rowany pushed her down again, then tucked her in with such a firm hand that she couldn't have stirred if she'd wanted to.

"A school story it is, yes—but it's also a classic. It's one of the great tales of Mars, Pete. You can borrow this copy, and finish it while you're here. Lie quiet now, and I'll get you started. It begins—well, we'll let Penelope herself tell you how it begins..."

So she began to read in the darkened room, and soon enough even reluctant Pete was caught up in the great adventure. When Rowany made to close the book, hers was among the voices begging for just one more chapter. Rowany laughed, and conceded, on condition that she was subjected to no more entreaties. She left the Sanatorium silent and thoughful in her wake, and returned after her own bath to find all its occupants asleep, perhaps dreaming of the great red desert where they had left Penelope, confronting the first of her many challenges...

Next morning there was no early-morning bell to rouse the sleepers. Instead they were woken by a peal of gay laughter, and light footsteps tripping down the linoleum flooring towards their shadowed corner.

"Up you get, sleepyheads!" The window-curtains were flung back vigorously, letting in a flood of light. "Do you want no breakfast, and are we to have no adventures today?"

"M-Mamma?" Charm voiced it, but the same befuddlement was in both Buchanans' minds. Not that it was really a question. Called back from dreams, still they knew that step, that voice, that vigour. Bone-deep they knew it, though it took a moment for bedazzled minds to catch up with the wisdom of their bones, to remember yesterday and their mother's coming, wafting in unlooked-for on wings of air.

Levity could hear a general chorus of denials, assertions— of course they wanted breakfast, and adventures!—and good-mornings. For herself, she waited until her mother came from Charm's bedside to her own. Then she flung her arms around the well-beloved neck and hugged hard.

"Well!" her mother exclaimed. "What's the why of that?"

"I just wanted to be sure you're really real." Yesterday had been short of explanations, in all the excitements; Levity was a little reluctant yet to allow herself to believe it.

"Oh, trust me, child, I'm real enough. As you will discover shortly. Rowany and I have been hatching plans for your day. None of which will happen, if you don't stir your lazy bones out of bed and get yourself bathed and dressed in short order. Or shall I ask Sister Anthony to keep you here all day, on bread-and-milk and a nerve tonic?"

The threat came with a smile, but was potent none the less. Levity tumbled out of bed, grabbed dressing gown and sponge bag and hurled herself with a will into the scrum of too many bodies fighting over too few bathrooms.

Breakfast was a help-yourself meal for once, with Mrs Bailey off-duty, all her staff away on holiday and only half a dozen girls in residence. There was a tureen of porridge on a side-table in one corner of the dining hall, with sugar and cream (and salt, for those of the true Scottish blood), and bowls to serve it into. Beside that was a pile of crisp brown toast, with butter and honey and a dish of Mrs Bailey's famous Oxford marmalade.

Everyone eyed the porridge dubiously, and murmured that presumably that was an option, not an obligation—until Charm peered under the lid of the tureen and turned to her watching mother and cried, "Mamma! You made Persian Porridge!"

"I did. And if you ever want me to do it again, you'd better make sure that you eat every last scraping."

"Oh, we will, we will!" Briefly, it seemed as though she were taking that instruction to herself, heaping her own bowl dangerously high; but she turned to the others and said, "You have to try this, it's the best breakfast ever! It has apricots and raisins and sultanas and dates in, and almonds and saffron and all sorts, it's like the best rice pudding only porridge..."

"Well, leave some for the rest of us, then," Rachel said good-naturedly. "Take some toast, Charm, and sit down, do."

"I made the toast," Rowany put in pointedly, from where she was standing watch. "I nearly scorched my eyebrows for you, so show some gratitude."

If empty plates and contented sighs show gratitude, they did as they'd been bidden. When everything had been tidied up and cleared away, Mrs Buchanan called them all back to the table and said, "Now, then. I have consulted with the Powers That Be, and the net result is that you all belong to me for the day. Your mistresses will welcome the break, I am sure. Rowany has agreed to play prison guard and bloodhound, should that prove necessary, but we hope that it won't. What I propose is that we go down on the next funicular, and spend the day in town. You can be tour guides, and show me everything. In return I'll treat you to elevenses and lunch and a cream tea. If that meets with your approval...?"

She might have been deafened by the cry of acclamation, but luckily she retained enough hearing to pick up Pete's edgy little question, "What about me?"

"Oh, my dear child—did I not make that clear? You have been declared a Crater School girl, pro tem, with all duties and responsibilities pertaining. Heavens, you're even wearing the uniform," as all Pete's own clothes of course had been lost with the airship, and the school had rallied round with as much as it could muster. "You and Jessica both, you belong to us as much as any of these ruffians," with a particular glower at her own beaming daughters, "at least until the school proper returns or other arrangements appear. On your feet now, and quick march if we're to make the train. I'm told we have to go by the sheep-paths, as once again no one is willing to risk the lake. Rowany, lead on..."

They trooped to the train, where Rowany pointed out that seven was an improper number for one compartment, so they should divide in two. Pete said they could surely squash up, as she and Charm were slender creatures. Rowany resisted a sudden urge to twist the girl's ear, and merely insisted that she, the twins and Pete would make a fine foursome, if the other three wanted to take the next compartment...

Thus Levity and Charm had their mother all to themselves for the ride down to town, as Rowany had intended. For the most part it is little of our business, what they may have said to each other; but let the record show that the first thing Mrs Buchanan did was to apologise.

"I am very sorry, my darlings," she said carefully. "I was deceived. We knew of course that your father was on Phobos, making those dreadful broadcasts; but we thought that was happenstance. We truly believed that he did not know we were on Mars. We'd done everything possible to keep the lie alive that we were living under another, a different name, somewhere in the colonies on Earth. Australia or Canada, maybe, where an Englishwoman and her two girls could disappear handily. Perhaps we were naïve—but I had help from the highest levels of government, and it's hard to suppose that such men could be naïve. Maybe the Russians just have more or better spies than we knew. Such questions are sure to be asked now, at any rate. Some good may come of this, if we can track them down. Now that we know to look.

"But as I said, I was deceived. A trap was laid, and I'm afraid I walked straight into it. Word reached me, through a channel I thought I could trust, that your father's relatives had begun a lawsuit back on Earth, to give them custody and control over you. On the grounds that I was an unfit mother, if you please, and no girl could thrive living a nomad life in hiding under an assumed name. There was just enough truth in that, that I believed it; and I had to go back to England to defend my reputation and to fight for you. So I parked you here, and took passage in the very next aethership to Earth.

"As soon as we landed on the Isle of Man, I telephoned people in Whitehall, senior people, to learn just where we stood. Of course a simple case of child custody doesn't concern the mandarins, but it always seemed likely that you girls were just a pretext here. Ramifications would reach far and far, if your father's family could act effectively as his voice within the Empire.

"But the men who spoke to me knew nothing about it, and neither did my own solicitor. I don't suppose you remember Mr Eames, do you, either of you? He did come out to Mars to see me once, over a matter of papers and inheritance, but you were both still rather little. Anyway, he said he had heard of no such legal action, and he would be sure to know.

"By then it was clear to me that this whole story had been nothing but a ruse—and what else would such a ruse be for, but to draw me away from you? So I came back as soon as I could, on the very same ship that had taken me that far. I suppose I was lucky, because I know you've heard how travelling in the aether can distort the passage of time. Sometimes people lose months and months, with no accounting. Coming and going I was lucky, but particularly on the return. I was landing at Elysium Field barely two weeks after I left Earth; that's almost the fastest time we have on record. Even so, it obviously wasn't fast enough.

"I suppose he knew where you were, even before I left. Perhaps he's always known, and he's just been biding his time, laying plans, setting things in motion. At any rate: I was lured away, and then he sent his people in. First they tried to win you by deception, but Miss Leven would never allow that. Nor would your true hearts yield to his blandishments. I couldn't be prouder of you both, the way you stood up to him on that lonely tower in the dark. Yes, I know all about that. Of course Miss Leven told me it had happened, and I talked to Mr Felton too, for a first-hand account, after you two were in bed last night. I do know just how alluring your father can be, and you stood fast where many another girl would have weakened. Many an adult, too. There's a reason the Tsar is using him for propaganda.

"So then they tried out-and-out kidnapping, when it was clear that you could be won neither by seduction nor by appeal to authority. We owe your schoolfriends an enormous debt, girls; they stood up and fought for you, hand to hand, against two grown men. It's the Martian way, we don't cosset our womenfolk here, but none the less. We must none of us ever forget that day, however frightening it may have been.

Charm at least would have been lost, without their intervention."

"I would have gone after her, Mamma," Levity said stoutly.

"I know it, girlie—but then you would have been lost too, more than likely, and I'd have been left alone." Just for a moment, a shadow touched her face, a mix of melancholy and fear; but she shook her head hard against the phantom, and spoke more brightly. "But never mind that; it didn't happen, and he shan't have another chance. We're alert to the dangers now, and I shall keep a sharp eye on you, come what may. Where shall we go next? You choose. Anywhere in the Red Raj, this whole world is your oyster."

Levity and Charm looked at each other, significantly. Charm made gestures that her sister could interpret perfectly, *you're the elder, you say*—and so at last it was Levity who found words for what was in both their minds. "Mamma... Would you mind terribly much if we stayed here? We *like* school, and we've made so many friends, and we're learning so much," and not just in the classroom. "It seems such a shame to leave it all behind and move again, so soon. And, and nobody could accuse you of making us live like nomads, if we were settled here and studying hard..."

Their mother laughed briefly. "Oh, you don't need to worry about that, my darlings. The truth is, your father's relatives are thoroughly cowed and keeping a very low profile, for fear of being tainted with the same brush. I can't speak to what they believe in their heart of hearts, no one can, but their public face—in so far as they have one—is very meek and entirely loyal to the Queen Empress. As it turns out, they are watched very closely and they wouldn't dare make any move against me—or you—for fear of how that would be interpreted in Whitehall. Don't give that another thought, you're entirely safe from them. But do you really want to stay here at school?"

"Really truly," Charm said emphatically. "We really do, Mamma."

"Well, I suppose I could take a house nearby, and settle for a while myself. It would mean I had the school authorities primed to watch over you too, and twice guarded means twice safe. And it would probably do me no harm to sit still for a little. Learn this particular patch of land, catch my breath. Make friends myself, perhaps. If we do this, mind, it means staying put until you're both done with school. It'll be no good changing your mind after six months or a year, when you realise how much you miss our old life. All or nothing, girls. I mean it."

"That's what we want, Mamma. It's how our friends live, and we want the same. We've talked it over, and we're both agreed. We'd like to stay at the Crater School."

"If they'll have you. Miss Leven does have a voice in this too; she only took you for the year, you know, and I had to press for that. The school's very popular, and already oversubscribed. But—well, I wonder if you two will ever cease to surprise me...?"

The funicular steamed into its little station at Terminus, and the passengers debouched. The Crater School party assembled on the platform, the younger girls turning as by nature to their elders for guidance. Mrs Buchanan cried, "It's no good looking at me, people; I'm putting myself in your hands entirely. And you don't get to appoint poor Rowany as tour leader, either. She has enough to do, keeping you from dashing off in all directions willy-nilly. It's up to you, what you decide to show me."

That hardly seemed fair when they were all so new themselves, and had had so little chance to explore on their own account. Rachel said, "There's the railhead, I suppose; that's quite a sight, for people who like steam trains."

"No, the Pool first," her twin disputed. "Where the two canals meet. I mean, it's not like Grand Junction, or any of the other great crossing-places, but it's impressive enough. And the weir between the two levels is phenomenal."

"And?" Rachel said knowingly.

"And the railhead is something we built ourselves, but the Pool is ancient, and we hardly know anything about the race that must have built it. That has to be more interesting, surely."

"And?"

Jessica glowered at her sister, then shrugged sourly. "And the nice Dutch people who brought me on this last leg might still be here, and I'd like to catch them if I can, just to say thank you one more time."

"There. Why didn't you say that first off? I knew there had to be something, if you didn't want to go and stare at steam engines."

"I'd like to stare at steam engines," Pete said, a little wistfully.

"I know you would. You and Jess are sisters under the skin, that's why I suggested the railhead. After lunch we'll go there, and you two can indulge your mysterious passion to your hearts' content. Contents, I suppose, if you're both contented. Or is content a virtue, like grace, all one however many share it? Never mind. All right, Mrs Buchanan, we've decided: the Pool first, and then the railhead. I expect that seems quite feeble to you, but this is only a small town; we've nothing to show you really, except the ways of getting in and out."

"What could be more important," she challenged, "here on the edge of everything? All right, Rachel, lead on. Pete and Jess, you stick with her; I'll come along with my two," who were still firmly glued, one to either arm, "and Rowany in the rear to sweep up stragglers, if any. Off we go!"

329

As an order of march, it served as a beginning. Soon enough, though, without their quite understanding how it had happened, the Buchanan sisters found themselves walking in the rear with Rowany. Meanwhile, their mother had somehow detached Pete from the Abramoffs and was having a quiet conversation with her, head to head.

"...So you see, my dear, your Uncle Raymond will be obliged to look for some kind of work, now that he's lost his airship. He might find something locally, but the odds are against that, I'm afraid. He may have to travel quite some distance before he can find a place."

"Yes, I understand that. I thought it through in the night. He's going to need me more than ever."

"Well, that's the thing, you see. I know you're used to being his deckhand, his engineer, his helpmeet—but until he's settled, having a young girl in tow will be frankly more a drawback than an asset. And here you are in the perfect situation, at a school where you can be looked after, and welcome so. It'll be a stretch, but Miss Leven assures me that you can be squeezed in."

"No! No, he wouldn't just leave me here...!"

"I'm afraid he must, Pete. It may only be for half a term, but—"

"But he can't possibly afford it. We haven't any money, and I know places like this cost a lot, so..."

"They do, ordinarily; but there are funds the school can draw on for emergency situations like this, and scholarships for the longer term if he should decide that would be best for you. Don't worry about that aspect, or any; you can help him best by settling your mind to this quickly, that for the rest of this term at least you'll be a Crater School girl."

Pete scowled, and shook her cropped head hard. "No. I'll never settle to that. I want to talk to Uncle Ray."

"Of course you do, and so you shall—but that's why he asked me to break this to you, so that you'd understand that it was fixed and final before you speak with him. He knows your stubbornness, and his own partiality; he feared he could never insist, if it came down to a question of wills between you. Whereas I'm a stranger, but I understand both of you absolutely. I'm afraid you will just have to give way in this, Pete. He would never have chosen this if there were any other choice to be made, he values your company that highly; but for these next weeks he has to go door-to-door and ask for work, which is a blow to any man's pride. He'd find it only that much harder, don't you see, if he had you at his heels, seeing him brought so low, where he used to be independent and free. For his own pride's sake, do him this courtesy, and accept the situation, can you? Give it just half a term, and see how you like school then. Is that really too much to ask...?"

And again that mysterious, almost magical shuffling, and Pete found herself mooching along beside Levity, while Charm kept Rowany company and Mrs Buchanan was suddenly in front with the Abramoffs, arm in arm in arm; and if she had essentially the same news for them, at least it was more brightly received.

"Oh frabjous day! You mean I really can stay?"

"Well, you're only guaranteed half a term here, Jess. Half a term for now. It depends on your parents, ultimately," and what Mrs Buchanan thought of those two worthies was far better left unuttered, at least in the presence of their daughters, "but for so long as Mr Murchison stands *in loco parentis*, he thinks it best to leave you both here. So I suppose you can go down in the annals as the first girl who ever ran away *to* the Crater School. I wouldn't build too much on that, though," she went on warningly. "It's no great recommendation, especially in the eyes of the staff. You'd be better to do your work and keep your head down and hope people forget how you came here, and only remember the impression you make as a Crater School girl."

"Yes, Mrs Buchanan." No doubt Jessica was doing her best to seem humble and contrite and grateful; but she couldn't keep her feet from skipping or her dark eyes from flashing delight at her twin, even after Mrs Buchanan had gone on, "And the first thing you should do when we get back to school is write a letter of apology to your previous headmistress. Even before you write another to your parents. Remember it'll be their decision in the end, whether either of you gets to stay here. That decision will likely depend on your behaviour hereafter. You should both write, and try to sound contrite."

Terminus might be little more than a settlement at the very edge of the colony's reach, but even so: ancient Martian building-work was never less than impressive. There were broader canals, to be sure, and more complex engineering; there were extraordinary sights elsewhere in the province, and Mrs Buchanan might have seen them all. Nevertheless: here at Terminus, two canals met at a hairpin angle, and it was a sight worth travelling to see.

They met, but didn't exactly join. One stood thirty feet higher than the other. The first ended in a great circular pool, a perfect harbour for all its human traffic—and a perfect headwater also for the lower canal. A broad section of its circumference—*sixty degrees of arc*, said the mathematically minded—had no containing wall, only a railing erected latterly by the army's engineers as a safety measure. The pool's water cascaded constantly over that rim and down a steep stone channel to find and feed the other branch. A mile away, the other side of town, a great system of ancient locks connected one to the other, moving traffic up and down now as it must have done in the unimaginable past; here, all they shared was their water.

"There's Mrs van der Haaf!" Jessica shrilled, waving wildly as they came in view of the Pool. Three, four dozen vessels were tied up around the long curve of the red stone harbour wall. Sailboats and steamboats, fishing smacks and tugs, barges loading and unloading behind mountains of bales and barrels and crates. Their crews were as mixed as the vessels, Indians and Egyptians and Scottish and Chinese—all Martians now.

Even amid that riot of colours and cultures and design, one vessel stood out. Others were as clean, perhaps, and as orderly abovedecks; others were as brightly painted; none could echo the same sense of calm preparedness. Also, none had a stout middle-aged woman set firmly in the prow, crocheting something neat and lacy. Perhaps that sense of calm emanated from her, rather than from the boat she sat on.

At Jessica's cry she looked up, smiled broadly, then called down into the vessel's well. By the time the school party had reached the boat, a burly man with a thick curling moustache had come up from below, wearing oil-stained overalls and wiping his hands fastidiously on a cloth.

"Ah, Jessica!" he called down. "Welcome! It is good to see you again. Come aboard, all, and make yourselves known..."

A gangplank was in place already, leading up to the foredeck. The girls clattered up delightedly, needing no further invitation. Rowany and Mrs Buchanan were a little more watchful, aware just how much of a nuisance so many youngsters could be, arriving without warning.

"Mynheer, Mevrouw van der Haaf: this is my sister Rachel, my twin, obviously. I told you all about her. These are Levity and Charm, they're sisters too; this is their mother, Mrs Buchanan. The short one's Pete and the tall one's Rowany. She's our Head Girl," which was the first time

Jessica had laid legitimate claim to any aspect of the Crater School. She seemed to feel it, standing straighter for a moment, wearing this uniform like a declaration.

"Welcome, all." Mr van der Haaf inspected his hand briefly, decided that it passed muster, and shook hands all around the party. "Agnes will make tea, and perhaps find some of those koekjes that Jessica liked so well. I must go down to the engine again, to finish my work there; but in ten minutes she will be running sweetly, and I can wash and change my dress and join you."

"Oh—please, may I come with you?" Nothing, perhaps, could have drawn Pete out of a fit of the sullens so swiftly as news of an engine in pieces.

"No, no," he said, laughing, "an engine-room is no place for a young lady. See me all oil and grease..."

"Oh, that doesn't bother me. And, and—"

And she broke into a stream of fluent Dutch that none of the others could follow except presumably Rowany who could do anything, and perhaps Mrs Buchanan. She was still something of an unknown quantity, despite everything her daughters had thought to say of her or felt it proper to repeat.

Mynheer van der Haaf listened with an expression of startled wonder, answered briefly in the same language, and then checked himself. "But it is not polite to speak in a tongue your friends do not understand, little one."

"No, but they don't understand engines either, or why I love them so much. Oh, *please* may I come down and help you? Or just watch? I could promise not to touch anything, if you like."

"Even touching nothing, I cannot promise that you will not get muck and oil on your clean uniform."

"I don't care about that."

"Perhaps, but others may." He looked to Mrs Buchanan, as the adult of the party. She laughed, and said, "Oh, take the child if you're willing, mynheer. She knows airship engines inside out, I can tell you that much, for I've seen her with the pieces spread about all over and herself in the middle, as happy and busy as a bee in clover. Whatever you can show her, she'll soak it up faster than her clothes could soak up paraffin—and those are only old cast-offs, they're of no concern. If we have to, we can tub her and scrub her again when we get back to school. Don't worry about that."

He needed no more encouragement; indeed, he seemed quite charmed by the thought of a girl so eager to join him down below. So down they went; and meantime Jessica was helping Mrs van der Haaf pass around the tea and a plate of little butter-cakes and biscuits.

"This uniform sits better on the eye than that other," their hostess said. "That pink, ugh! So you have changed schools, from that to this, yes?"

"Yes, mevrouw," Jessica said, hoping not to be interrogated further.

"That is good. Sisters should be together. And we will hope to see you more, when we are in the Pool. We take girls often, this way and that," she went on to Mrs Buchanan, "but this one was a special pleasure. Quiet and helpful, not too proud to scrub; I had an idea to keep her, if it would only be allowed."

By this point Jessica was blushing furiously, while her cohort gazed at her with interest. Rowany laughed, and said, "I wish we might send all our Middles with you for a week or two, if you can teach them to be quiet and helpful. And to scrub."

That raised voluble protests, as it was meant to. Mrs Buchanan raised her voice above the hubbub: "Yes, well, I think you only prove Rowany's point, girls. And I do feel that six of you is too many to impose on Mevrouw van der Haaf without warning. I know Jessica would like to stay a while, and it would be an unkindness to tear Pete away just when she's got her hands sunk deep into an engine—though what I'm to say when I have to hand her back to Sister Anthony, I don't know—but if my two will drink up and hurry up, yes, and Rachel too, they can take me off and show me what else this town can offer, and that'll leave the van der Haafs at least a little room to breathe on their own boat. If you wouldn't mind staying to keep an eye on things here, Rowany? We'll come back to collect you all at lunch-time."

Rowany didn't mind in the slightest, and said so. Even for the Head Girl, opportunities to sit and stare were passing few at school. She'd be glad simply to watch the boats in the harbour and the people on the shore, try another of those charming biscuits and chat a little, test out her nascent Dutch, if Jessica ever let her get a word in edgewise.

Jessica glowered at that, but didn't noticeably stop talking. It was Rachel who protested: "Oh, but Mrs Buchanan, wouldn't you rather just take your own daughters? I can stay with Jess, I'd be glad to…"

"Oh, no," Mrs Buchanan said, laughing. "What kind of a locum would I make, if I took every opportunity to be alone with my girls and left all the rest of you on Rowany's hands? And you twins particularly: we know what kind of mischief you get up to on your own, and I can only imagine what you might achieve together. I'm sure Rowany would prove sufficient unto the day, but nevertheless. You come along with us, my child, and see if you can behave like a civilised being. Nothing dreadful is going to happen to your sister in the next hour, without your being here to prevent it."

Rachel made a face at Jessica, which for once went entirely unseen and so unanswered, the oblivious Jess being entirely focused on some pretty needlework that Mevrouw van der Haaf was showing her.

Mrs Buchanan's firm hand on her shoulder steered Rachel towards the gangplank, where Levity and Charm were waiting. Rachel remembered suddenly what she'd forgotten all this time, that she and Jess were after all different people, with sometimes very different interests. It was being forced apart for so long that had made them both desperate to be together; when they were together, on top of each other day and night, it was often good and occasionally vital to spend some time apart.

Let Jess coo over the mevrouw's embroidery, then. Rachel would far sooner pass an hour with the legendary Isobel Buchanan. So far she was nothing like anybody's expectation, the fey and unpredictable artist. She seemed unexpectedly down-to-earth, for all that she had arrived in an airship; she seemed not exactly strict but certainly watchful of her charges and their manners, though that didn't stop her from also being fun. Rachel wanted to call her homely, but not in the sense that mean people used it, because certainly Mrs Buchanan was still striking to look at despite her advanced years, with her daughters' vivid hair already trimmed about with white. When Rachel used the word, in the privacy of her own mind, it meant something entirely other. It meant what she and Jess had never really known, the comfort and security of a peaceful happy home. She thought Mrs Buchanan could wrap that about you like a blanket, and leave you feeling warm and welcome and at rest. According to Levity they'd never really had an actual physical home, always on the move from the big cities to the remote farming outposts to the mining communities to the great floating canal-markets, wherever their mother had found work or inspiration—but nevertheless. Rachel had nothing to go on but instinct, and yet she believed profoundly that wherever Mrs Buchanan chose to hang her hat, she'd make it feel like a home.

Just as, whatever company she kept, she'd make them feel welcome and at ease. Sooner than let Rachel walk alone, she set her daughters in the lead and took the lone twin's arm herself. "Now—having just had tea and those delicious little biscuits, I don't at all suppose you're in the mood for coffee and cream cakes, so—"

She was instantly drowned out, as she must have known she would be, in a chorus of denials and entreaties. She clapped her hands high to silence them, laughing at their greed; "Honestly, anyone would imagine that school never fed you at all! You beware, or I shall tell Mrs Bailey, and she'll send you all to Sister Anthony for a bread-and-water diet for the rest of the holiday. Now! At the very least, I insist on a short walk before we even look for a coffee-house. Say to the end of the harbour wall, there where the canal comes in; then we can cut through towards the centre of town, and see what we may find..."

As they walked, she talked of boats she had known and sailed on, with or without her daughters: Earth-boats and Mars-boats, small yachts and great liners and everything in between. Rachel thought she could listen to her forever, that sweet strong voice with such endlessly interesting tales. It wasn't only that Mrs Buchanan had led a fascinating life, since she brought her small family to Mars; she had the storyteller's knack of enthralling her audience with those little details that bring grand settings down to a human scale, the butler's bad feet in the Viceroy's mansion, or the prospector at the foot of Mount Olympus who had the marsles and couldn't stop sneezing...

Rachel was still giggling over that as they swung around a corner away from the quay and here was a most unexpected find, a small shop selling books and prints; and there in the window was a framed etching that made Mrs Buchanan blush and half turn away, half reach to hurry the girls along, even as arty Rachel said, "Oh, wait—isn't that one of your sketches, Mrs Buchanan? It is, it is! See, it says, one of the *Pioneer Girls* series. We have half a dozen of those, climbing up the staircase at home..."

And maybe it was just in the way the Buchanan daughters reacted, blushing as brightly as their mother and turning in just the same way; or maybe it was because she was still caught up in Mrs Buchanan's way of seeing the world, but Rachel looked again at the etching and immediately said, "Oh, but that's you two, isn't it? When you were younger? Much younger, but surely you must have looked just that way."

And the sisters' scowls confirmed it, as did their mother's approval of her perspicacity; and Levity was just in the middle of explaining fiercely to Rachel how she must never, *never* say that to a single soul at school, no, not even to her own twin, when a man came hurrying around the corner behind them with his head bent and a sou'wester pulled down low over his face, as though a storm were blowing.

And he couldn't see at all where he was going, so that he walked right into Rachel where she stood in the middle of the pavement.

His head jerked up in startlement, and they gazed directly at each other, from barely a foot's separation. Rachel saw a heavy face, dark brows, marked with livid scratches around both his eyes...

The man swore explosively, spun on his heel and ran back the way he had come.

"After him!" Rachel cried, even as she plunged forward in pursuit. "That's the man who tried to kidnap Charm! Don't let him get away again!"

Later, it was agreed by all concerned that there might have been a better way. To have both Buchanan girls give chase to the very man sent to kidnap them was perhaps not the brightest move. What if the Russians had laid another ambush, for which this man was the bait and the lure?

At the time, though, nobody thought about that. Not even Mrs Buchanan tried to call her girls back. This was hot pursuit, and the two sisters pounded after Rachel while their mother followed after as fast as she could.

Meanwhile, Pete had emerged from belowdecks with Mr van der Haaf, both of them contentedly streaked with redcoal dust and smudged with oil. Behind them, the steady beat of a healthy engine pulsed through the air.

"Sister Anthony will have kittens at the sight of you," Jessica said, giggling. "And never let you off school grounds again, most likely."

That reminder that she had to be a schoolgirl for the next half-term at least almost soured Pete's mood—but she could never be truly downcast when she had grease under her fingernails and the smell of a hot engine in her nose. She just pulled the worst face she could manage on the spur of the moment, and turned to the man beside her. "Mynheer, I still think we need to strip her down completely, to find what's causing that tick. I know she's running sweetly now, but—"

A yell came from shore, a *view-halloo!* in a voice that Jessica had known from birth. She swivelled around to stare, and saw first a man pelting along the harbourside, and second her twin in chase, with the Buchanan girls after her and their mother gallantly bringing up the rear.

"Jessica! What is happening?"

That was Mr van der Haaf, coming to stand beside her. Feeling suddenly grateful for grown-ups, she peered at the running man as he raced by. "I—I think that's one of the Russians we fought on the hillside—oh, but you don't know about that, mynheer. They tried to kidnap Charm. The police are looking for them."

The good boatman needed to hear no more. He vaulted the rail to land neatly between the fugitive and his pursuit and held up one massive hand to stop the schoolgirls in their headlong chase. "Leave this to me. You wait here, with the mother, yes?"

And then he took off after the fleeing Russian—but too late. That brief delay had allowed the fugitive to race up the gangplank of another boat. A second man snatched up the plank, while the first frenziedly cast off the stern line.

"They're getting away!" Jessica shrieked.

"Not they," Pete said at her side. "We can still stop them, can't we, mevrouw?"

"If we go now. Jessica, the sternrope; Rowany, the bow."

The Dutchwoman stepped to the tiller, firm and authoritative. One glance at Pete, and "We need steam, little one, and maximum revolutions," sent her ducking back down to the engine-room. Mrs van der Haaf looked fore and aft, engaged the engine and flung the tiller over. Her husband and half the eager schoolgirl crew were still ashore, but never mind. The chase was on!

E xcept that really it was no chase at all. The two Russians had pushed their boat away from the quay with boathooks, by main force, leaving the mynheer frustrated; but now they were simply wallowing in the middle of the Pool.

"They've got no steam!" Pete crowed, bobbing her head up from below to see what was afoot. "By the look of it, they don't even have a fire in the box; see, there's no smoke from the stack. It'll take them half an hour to work up a head of steam, starting from scratch."

"We're not going to leave them bobbing about out there for half an hour," Jessica said, all too aware that other boats might cast off at any moment.

"We are not going to leave them at all," Mevrouw van der Haaf said firmly, with a glance back that said she was no more keen than the girls to let her husband or any other men have all the glory. Or the fun.

She hefted a great boathook with one hand, and steered towards the Russian craft. What she meant to do once they'd hooked on, how she thought she and a skeleton crew of girls might subdue two burly men, was unclear to Jessica.

In the event, though, they didn't get that far. As soon as she began probing for the vessel's rail, one of the Russians seized the brass business end of her boathook and heaved. Mrs van der Haaf hung on determinedly—and was pulled clean across the stern rail, plunging with a squawk into the turbid waters of the Pool!

"That's torn it!" cried Rowany from the bows. "Jessica, can you turn around?"

"No need!" By this time Pete had abandoned her post altogether, scrambling up to join Jessica at the tiller. "She's waterfolk through and through, and there'll be a fleet of other boats headed this way any minute, if the mynheer has anything to do with it. She'll do fine."

Indeed, one glance astern showed the mevrouw head-up and treading water. Perhaps she expected them to come back for her—but no, she was waving them on, *do your work, girls, never mind me.*

At least, that was how Jessica chose to interpret her gestures. If Rowany had been on the tiller, perhaps they would have gone back; but Rowany was up in the bows, and for the moment at least the younger girls had control.

Jessica said, "What can we do, though? We can't board them, they'd just throw us overboard too—and look, see how they're drifting towards the overflow, where all the water runs down the sluice to the other canal? I don't fancy getting caught in that, the currents must be fierce over there."

"That gives me an idea," Pete said. "Let me have the tiller, quick, before Rowany decides to come back here and be all grown-up and in charge..."

Nothing loth, Jessica handed over the tiller. The shorter girl eased the boat forward, until her bow just nudged the other. Nudged and pushed, leaning in hard, as Pete spun the regulator-wheel that quickened the beat of the engine and sent more power to the screws.

The Russians tried to push her away with boathooks, but only made their own position worse, pushing themselves further into the sluice-stream. When they realised their danger, they tried to do the opposite, reaching to hook on and pull themselves close to the boat that threatened them, close enough to board and take her; but Pete flung the tiller over and backed water hard, and the men couldn't hold her.

And then they could do nothing but hold on, as their boat was sucked irresistibly into the current and dragged to the very edge of the spillway. There it came up against the army's guard-rail, which kept it from being swept over the edge; but the current was strong enough to hold it there, and to keep the men from escaping, until such time as they could be rescued and arrested.

"They'll try to get their fire going and hope that steam will save them," quoth Pete, hugging herself with delight at what she'd done, "but it won't, oh, it won't! There they are and there they'll stay, till our side goes to save them. Which I hope won't be for hours yet," she added vindictively.

By this time, Rowany had made her way back to the stern. "Yes," she said, taking firm control of the tiller, "I'm sure you're pleased with yourselves, the pair of you. Now let's get back and see if we can rescue poor Mrs van der Haaf, shall we? Before her skirts waterlog and drag her down to a watery tomb?"

Too late: she had been rescued already, by her husband aboard a commandeered fishing-smack. She was glad enough to board her own boat, though, and retire below in search of a warm towel and a change of clothes.

The mynheer let Rowany take the boat back to her moorings, where a bevy of Buchanans waited impatiently, alongside Jessica's twin. Grown-ups and schoolgirls alike seemed uncertain whether to praise or scold, and in the end they seemed to come to an unspoken compact to do neither.

"Miss Leven may have more to say," warned Rowany. "She's seldom very taken with her girls' dashing off on mad adventures. Or with the prefects who let it happen on their watch," she added, a little mournfully. "If you lot find yourselves in trouble, so shall I. But we'll face that day together, shall we?" she went on, looking from one face to the next, along the line. "You're all five of you new girls, and some newer than others," she added, with a grin for Jessica and Pete, "but if you've proved one thing today, it is that you're all true Crater School girls at heart. Now, who's hungry...?"

THE END

Acknowledgements

The first order of the day is to thank all my Patreon subscribers, anyone who's ever dropped a dollar in the jar. Without them, this book would very literally never have come to exist. They have been enduringly and endearingly patient, as well as remarkably generous, and I am deeply and abidingly grateful for their supporting what was something of a peculiar project from the start.

And then there's m'wife, Karen. It was she who brought me to California, aye, and all my books together. Without her, similarly, none of this could ever have happened. It's been a strange and challenging nine years thus far, and I wouldn't have missed a day of it.

The Crater School is greatly indebted also to Cliff Winnig, who not only read this book to his twins but was instrumental in its earliest formation, taking me to many a SETI symposium at a time when Curiosity had just landed and Mars was on everybody's tongue. The whole Mars Imperial project was born as a result of those conversations, and has consumed most of my writing-time since.

Cheryl Morgan is a long-time friend of mine, and I was thrilled when she offered to publish these books. She's been a delight to work with: creative, punctilious, just what I needed. She it was who inveigled Ben Baldwin into creating this magnificent cover for us, after I had previously inveigled Elizabeth Leggett into designing the school badge and the uniform.

John Jarrold was my editor once, and almost twice; he's been my agent for a long time now, and I remain profoundly grateful for his work on my behalf (and also ongoingly awed at the depth and breadth of his knowledge of the field).

Coffee Club and Thursdays have been the fixed points of my social life here in Silicon Valley; I love and miss you all, in these pandemic times.

I am grateful to all my friends and fellow authors who took the time to read this book and comment kindly upon it. With corrections. I do love writers, they're so ... particular.

Also, I'd like to note here that I stole one line of this book directly from m'friend and fellow author Ken Scholes, and I'm not giving it back.

About the Author

Chaz Brenchley spent his childhood in Oxford, one of four children. It was a rule of the household that he read everybody else's books as well as his own; from his elder brother he acquired a love of science fiction, and from his sisters a devotion to the Chalet School books by Elinor M Brent-Dyer.

In his adolescence, he was sent to boarding school. Unhappily, it was almost exactly nothing at all like the Chalet School, nor the Crater School neither.

He sold his first stories at the age of eighteen, and has been a professional writer ever since. His work ranges from science fiction to epic and urban fantasy, from mysteries and thrillers to romance and horror. He's published upwards of forty books, and many hundreds of short stories.

Nine years ago he moved from bachelordom to marriage, from Newcastle to California, along with 120 boxes (115 of which were books), two squabbling cats and a famous teddy bear.

http://www.chazbrenchley.co.uk/

@ChazBrenchley

THREE TWINS AT THE CRATER SCHOOL

Lightning Source UK Ltd.
Milton Keynes UK
UKHW012039160421
382126UK00001B/70